Money to Burn

ALSO BY JAMES GRIPPANDO

Intent to Kill

Born to Run★

Last Call★

Lying with Strangers

When Darkness Falls★

Got the Look★

Hear No Evil★

Last to Die★

Beyond Suspicion★

A King's Ransom

Under Cover of Darkness†

Found Money

The Abduction

The Informant

The Pardon★

And for Young Adults
Leapholes

★A Jack Swyteck Novel
†FBI Agent Andie Henning's Debut

Money to Burn

A Novel of Suspense

James Grippando

An Imprint of HarperCollinsPublishers

HarperCollins books may be purchased for educational, business, or sales promotional use. For information please write: Special Markets Department, HarperCollins Publishers, 10 East 53rd Street, New York, NY 10022.

FIRST HARPERLUXE EDITION

HarperLuxe™ is a trademark of HarperCollins Publishers

Library of Congress Cataloging-in-Publication Data is available upon request.

ISBN: 978-0-06-194622-6

10 11 12 13 14   ID/RRD   10 9 8 7 6 5 4 3 2 1

In memory of James V. Grippando . . . Papa.

"It's another beautiful day in paradise."

Wall Street got drunk.

—GEORGE W. BUSH, JULY 2008

Money to Burn

November 20, 2003

1

The warning signs were there. I just couldn't see them. My nose was in my BlackBerry—"crackberry"—except when I was talking into it.

"Can you get me the numbers on Argentine debt denominated in Japanese yen?" I said. I was on with my Asia investment team leader.

The cabdriver glanced at me in the rearview mirror as if I were speaking Martian.

"Michael, give it a rest," said Ivy. "We're supposed to be on vacation."

Ivy and I were stuck in traffic on the busy Dolphin Expressway, having just flown in from New York. We were headed to the port of Miami for a Caribbean cruise that was luxurious by anyone's standards, all expenses paid—one of the perks of being a top young producer at Saxton Silvers, one of Wall Street's premier investment banking firms.

"This is the last phone call, I promise."

She knew I was lying, and I knew she really didn't mind. More than any woman I'd ever dated, Ivy Layton understood my world.

We'd met when she was a trader at Ploutus Investments, a multibillion-dollar hedge fund with offices in Manhattan and—where else?—Greenwich. It was also Saxton Silvers' biggest prime brokerage client. Ivy's boss managed the fund and steered all that business my way because he was incredibly intuitive and completely understood that on the day that I was born the angels got together and decided to create a—*puh-LEEZ*. Chalk it up to the fact that I was one of the lucky bastards who had correctly timed the burst of the IT bubble, making me a financial genius in a field of idiots. Idiots who apparently believed that overpaid CEOs of dot-com darlings didn't have to do anything but pick out flashy corporate logos for negative earnings reports and watch the NASDAQ rise like a helium balloon on steroids. I gave Ploutus a reality check on a barfing—yes, barfing—dog that looked like a sock puppet but turned out to be the proverbial pin in the bursting bubble. Ploutus made me the go-to guy on Wall Street, which would never change so long as those aforementioned angels continued to sprinkle moon dust in my hair and starlight in my . . . whatever.

"Whoa," Ivy said. "I haven't seen this many fifty-story cranes since Shanghai."

I glanced up from my BlackBerry. She was right. Downtown Miami had more empty towers under construction than South Beach had palm trees. I tried to imagine the skyline without the works in progress—what it must have looked like just three or four years earlier. Maybe a handful of skyscrapers over fifty stories.

"Condo crazies," said the cabbie. "I bought one pre-construction in dat building over there."

Our driver was a Bahamian immigrant, which was cool. It was as if we were already in the islands.

"Congrats," said Ivy.

"And one in dat really tall one, too," he said, pointing upward.

"Two condos in downtown Miami?"

"Plus three more in Fort Lauderdale."

I was going back to my BlackBerry, but Donald Trump with the island accent had snagged my full attention. "You own *five* condos?"

"Yeah, mon."

"No offense, but—"

"I know, mon. I drive a cab. But my mortgage broker says no problem."

"Who's your mortgage broker?"

"A friend who live in Little Haiti. He used to drive a taxi like me. Dresses really smart now. We call him the Haitian Sensation. Got me a NINA loan for one-point-six mill."

NINA—no income, no assets, no problem. Just find a property appraiser to certify that the real estate was worth more than the amount of the loan and $1.6 million was yours. All you needed was a credit score and a pulse. Actually, that pulse thing was optional, too. Reports of dead people getting loans were proliferating. To me, the whole subprime market was beginning to stink like an old fishing boat, and I was glad to have absolutely nothing to do with mortgage-backed securities—even if they were making a few guys at each of the major investment banks filthy rich.

"They tell me so long as the property value keep going up, I'm safe, mon. I just flip dis condo, make a nice flippin' profit, pay off dat flippin' mortgage, buy another flippin' condo. Just keep on flippin' and flippin'."

"That's the flippin' theory," I said.

He changed lanes abruptly, blasting his horn at a speeding motorcyclist who apparently thought he owned the expressway. Our driver was suddenly agitated, but it wasn't the traffic. He looked genuinely worried. I could see it in his eyes in the rearview mirror.

"So," he said in a shaky voice, "you think it keep going up, mon?"

Sure, if the law of gravity somehow changed. "We can only hope," I said.

I went back to my BlackBerry. Ivy was now listening to her iPod, moving to the music. Salsa. I didn't know she was a fan, but apparently a visit to Miami made her feel more connected to her half-Latin roots.

We exited the expressway and were headed into downtown Miami. The port was all the way east, near a waterfront mall that Saxton Silvers had financed.

"What the hell is that?" Ivy said.

I looked up. Flagler Street was Miami's east-west version of main street, and we were a block or so north of it. If your principal needs in life were YO ♥ MIAMI T-shirts, sugarcane juice, and any kind of electronic device imaginable, this was your little slice of paradise. For me, it was an area I couldn't get through fast enough—especially today. It was only two o'clock in the afternoon, but the shops had already closed, the doors and windows protected by burglar bars and steel roll-down doors. Something was up.

"Looks like Biscayne Boulevard is closed," the driver said, stopping at the traffic light.

Biscayne was Miami's signature north-south boulevard, four lanes in each direction that were divided by an elevated tram and rows of royal palm trees down the middle. Office towers lined the west side of the street, and to the east beautiful Bayfront Park stretched to the waterfront. Over the years it had served as everything from the famous hairpin turn in Miami's first Grand Prix road race to the televised portion of the Orange Bowl Parade route. These days, the Grand Prix had moved elsewhere, the parade was no more, and Biscayne Boulevard had been swept up in the high-rise construction craze. We had to get east of it to reach the port. But on this sunny Thursday afternoon, all cross streets were a virtual parking lot.

"We're not moving, mon."

We sat through a complete light change and still didn't budge. I got out of the cab to see what was going on. Up ahead, traffic had ground to a halt as far as I could see. I stepped up onto the doorsill for a better view. The one-way street was like a shadowy canyon cutting through tall office buildings. Peering over the endless row of stopped cars in front of us, I got a cross-section view of the intersection at Biscayne and spotted the problem. Barricades appeared to be blocking all vehicular access to the boulevard. Mobs of people were marching down all eight lanes.

I climbed back inside the car and said, "Some kind of protest rally."

"Oh, yeah," said Ivy. "FTAA is in Miami this year."

The Free Trade Area of the Americas was an effort to unite all the economies of the Western Hemisphere, except Cuba, into a single free-trade area that reached from Canada to Chile. Each year since 1994, the leaders of thirty-four democracies met to work toward eliminating barriers to trade and investment. Opposition was passionate, critics fearing the concentration of corporate power and the worst of everything that came with it: layoffs and unemployment, sweatshop labor, loss of family farms, environmental destruction. Thousands of those critics had descended on downtown Miami today to decry the FTAA's eighth ministerial meeting.

"Not sure where to go," said our driver.

"Obviously not this way," said Ivy.

He somehow maneuvered around stopped cars and headed north on Miami Avenue, the plan being to cut east to Biscayne on a higher cross street. It was worse. Not only were the cars immobilized, but pedestrian traffic was also jammed. We saw a sea of young people, most of them wearing bandannas over their noses and mouths, many wearing protective goggles or helmets. A few wore gas masks. Two men had climbed atop lampposts to wave red flags, one with the image of Che Guevara and the other with Mao Tse Tung. Banners and posters dotted the crowd, the messages ranging from GIVE PEACE A CHANCE to SUPPORT THE POLICE: BEAT YOURSELF UP.

"This looks bad," said Ivy.

I got out of the car and again climbed to my perch on the doorsill, peering out over the roof.

"Michael, get back in the car!"

I heard Ivy's warning, but I had to look. Never had I seen such a showing of police muscle. Rows of fully armored and helmeted police moved in formation, meeting the crowd of demonstrators with a line of riot shields and control batons. As police advanced, the anti-FTAA chanting intensified.

Greed kills.
Die, Asses of Evil.
Fuck the Aristocratic Assholes.
Anarchy Today, Anarchy Tomorrow, Anarchy Forever!

Demonstrators either yielded to the oncoming wave of police or were pushed back into the throbbing crowds behind them.

"There's nowhere to go!" people shouted. "Nowhere for us to go!"

Squeezed between the surge of police and the barricades behind them, the crowd had run out of room and was growing angrier by the second. A small group at the front fell to the ground, their actions seen as resistance by club-wielding officers.

"Michael, get in here!"

It was crazy, but I was mesmerized. I saw about a dozen canisters launch in volleys from somewhere behind police lines. Tear gas. They landed in the crowd, unleashing panic. One hit a demonstrator in the head and knocked him to the sidewalk. People were soon stepping over other people, coughing and wheezing as they ran. A few held damp rags to their mouths, which eased their breathing but did nothing for the skin and eye irritation. A woman in agony ran past screaming "Pepper spray, pepper spray!" A crack of gunfire erupted, and people on the front line writhed in pain from rubber bullets, beanbags, and chemical-filled pellets. It was impossible to count the number of rounds fired, but it had to be in the hundreds. Angry youths cursed as they picked up the smoking canisters of tear gas and hurled them back at the oncoming police.

"Michael, get back inside!"

Someone grabbed me and threw me against the car. It was a man—incredibly strong—dressed all in black, a helmet protecting his head. A bandanna covered his nose and mouth, but his eyes were still visible and they were downright threatening. His knee came up and hit me in the groin, and my face was suddenly on fire with pepper spray.

"It's only gonna get worse," he said in a voice that chilled me, and then he was gone.

Ivy pulled me back into the car and yanked the door shut. The driver switched on the locks. I couldn't see, and the sting was almost unbearable. Ivy had bottled water in her purse, which she poured on my face to wash away the spray.

"Are you okay?" she asked.

I blinked hard, but it would take a while to find relief.

Ivy glanced out the car window. "There's a medic tent over there," she said, pointing toward the courthouse on the corner.

"They actually set up medic tents?" I managed to say. Apparently Miami learned from former host cities to expect protests and injuries.

"I see people getting treated for pepper spray," she said. "Come on, let's go."

She paid the cabdriver and told him to keep the change. He thanked her and handed her a business card.

"My cell number is on there," he said. "Call me if you know anyone. Maybe it's you, your housekeeper, your doorman. Whoever."

"Anyone who what?" asked Ivy.

"What we were talking about," he said. "Anyone who wants to buy a condo. I get you a killer deal on a very good pay-option, negative-amortization loan, mon."

The expression on Ivy's face was one of complete incredulity. "Let's go," she told me.

I pushed open the door. We grabbed our bags, and together we zigzagged through the crowd and confusion, stopping only when we reached the Wellness Center beneath the giant flag of Che Guevara flapping in a breeze tinged with tear gas.

2

Ivy Layton was about to blow her brains out. Not literally—but sudden and certain death did seem preferable to the conversation that surrounded her. Ivy stepped away from a circle of women she didn't care to get to know and grabbed a frozen rum runner topped with a floater of 150-proof Trinidadian spirits.

"Careful," said the waiter holding the silver tray of cocktails. "Those be strong, love."

Ivy smiled and thanked him. Since stepping foot on the Saxton Silvers yacht, she'd been "darlin'," "honey," and "love," all of them as harmless in the islands as "mon."

"Strong is good," she said. And after a day like today, she really meant it. "Mon."

Ivy and Michael had ended up returning to Miami International Airport, flying to Nassau, and catching up with the private cruise there. As far as Ivy was concerned, though, one less day with the top young producers at Saxton Silvers was a blessing. There was only one she cared to be with: Michael Cantella, a veritable rock star among the firm's fiercely competitive under-thirty-five-year-olds. Michael had an uncanny knack for making the rich richer, which earned him seven-figure performance bonuses and plenty of free trips—South African safaris, New Zealand wine and adventure tours, and other five-star destinations around the globe, none of which he could fit into his relentless schedule. But this time was different. He had made a point of planning their first trip out of New York together after dating for three months. Ivy had been excited about it—until tonight. Michael didn't know it, but if she had to spend one more cocktail hour on deck with the spouses and significant others while the Wall Street wonders smoked Cohiba cigars with the captain on the bridge, either she or Michael was going over the ship's rail.

She hoped he wasn't too drunk to swim.

"Did you hear about Dwight Holden?" asked Shannon Ware, one of the wives.

Here we go again, thought Ivy. Shannon was married to a high roller in the L.A. office who, according to Michael, owned more sports cars, more jewelry, more high-end toys than any human being should ever own—in short, the worst damn case of "affluenza" on record. Ivy had known Mr. Affluenza's better half for only twenty minutes, and Shannon had already earned the title "World's Biggest Gossip/World's Smallest Brain." The five other wives in the circle were riveted.

"Do tell," said the tall blonde.

"Totally blew up," said Shannon.

"No!"

"Yup," said Shannon, snapping her fingers. "Just like that."

"I thought Dwight was set for life and on track to retire before his fortieth birthday."

"*Was*," said Shannon. "Apparently the boy wonder wasn't quite ready to cut the cord with the mother ship and manage his own hedge fund. Their house went on the market last week. Total fire sale. Only listing on the water under ten million."

"Poor Gwen. Where are they moving to?"

Shannon lowered her voice, as if this part were particularly delicious. "I hear they're moving in with her *parents*."

"*NO!*" said blondie.

Ivy rolled her eyes. Somehow she knew it wasn't true—worse, Ivy would have bet that even *Shannon* knew it was just a vicious rumor.

"Where is it?" asked another.

"It's some little town..." Shannon cringed, as if it pained her not to have every juicy detail at her command. "Oh, hell, I know this. It's—shit, how's a left-coast girl supposed to know? It's like ... Gonorrheaville. But not Gonorrheaville."

"Gonorrheaville?" said Ivy, coughing on her rum runner.

"You know what I'm trying to say," said Shannon. "It's that town in Connecticut with the same name as the disease."

"You mean Lyme?" said Ivy.

"Yes, that's it!"

The other women laughed, and Shannon was clearly embarrassed that she'd drawn a blank on Lyme. Ivy hated to be mean, even if Shannon did deserve it, but she was feeling the effects of her rum runner and couldn't help singing to the tune of the old Jimmy Buffett song: "Wastin' away again in Gonorrheaville."

"Very funny," said Shannon.

"Searching for my lost blood test results."

The laughter continued, but Shannon was getting pissed.

"Some people say that there's a pool boy to blame."

"Okay, enough. Who died and made you sorority president?"

Shannon was glaring. The other women fell silent, unable to believe what they'd just heard. The tropical breeze blowing across the deck suddenly felt ice cold.

Ivy could have stood her ground—hell, she could have shattered Shannon's jaw with a 540-hook kick worthy of Bruce Lee—but the mean girl wasn't worth the effort.

"No one died," said Ivy, leaving her final thought unsaid: *Yet.*

She turned and walked away, absolutely certain that Shannon and her troop of character assassins would spend the rest of the cocktail hour gossiping about the bitch Michael Cantella had brought along this year.

Ivy went to the portside rail and gazed toward the magenta-orange afterglow on the horizon. With her back to the gossip, and as she soaked in the last vestiges of a spectacular Caribbean sunset, it was hard to argue that this wasn't paradise. The three-hundred-foot private yacht—one of three "boats" owned by Saxton Silvers' CEO—was totally pimped out with a wave pool, a seventy-five-foot dining table custom made by Viscount Linley, and a Sikorsky S–76B helicopter with a landing pad that doubled as a basketball court. Ivy had yet to see all the toys, but the vessel was supposedly equipped with a retractable beach resort, which slid out over the sea from just below the starboard side deck, complete with sand, palm trees, and deck chairs. A crew of fifty served the passengers' every need. Their first stop would be the Exumas, followed by Harbor Island, and then an undisclosed destination that catered to British royalty, Grammy-winning rappers, and every multimillionaire in between. Wall Street certainly knew how to reward its winners. Despite the pampering, however, the thought of so much structure to her week with Michael left Ivy wanting. Five days in the islands could have been perfect—without the Saxton Silvers crowd.

Her frozen rum runner was melting in the warm night air and losing its kick. Ivy poured the remaining half overboard, watching the wind catch the potent slush and turn it into cherry-red vapor before it could fall into the sea. Then she smiled to herself, a brilliant idea coming to mind. She turned quickly, her flats squeaking on the polished teak stairway as she climbed up to the promenade deck, that tune still stuck in her head.

Wastin' away again in . . .

She found Michael with six other guys, each of them exhibiting the kind of athletic good looks that were almost a cliché at Saxton Silvers. The entire investment banking world was in many ways a cliché: elite firm No. 1 dominated by humorless grinds, No. 2 by strait-laced rich kids, No. 3 by backslapping Irishmen, and so on. Even before meeting Michael, Ivy had regarded Saxton Silvers as the Duke lacrosse team of Wall Street frat houses. She loved Michael anyway, this grandson of a blue-collar Italian immigrant made good—even if he was plainly playing the game tonight, pretending to care as one of the boys waxed on about an exceedingly rare Super Tuscan that he'd scored in Hong Kong last week.

"Michael?" she said.

The men kept talking, but a woman in a nearby cluster of superstars threw her a not-so-subtle look, as if to say, *Please go back to your place downstairs with the other spouses.* Amazing, thought Ivy, the way women were always tougher on other women. Michael excused himself, and Ivy led him away.

"Hey, having fun yet?" he asked.

She gave him a half smile, trying to be a sport. "Honestly?"

"This is the only event like this," said Michael. "Some genius in New York thought the spouses might enjoy one cocktail party where they could get to know each other without us at your hip."

"It's not that."

"What's wrong?"

She turned her head slowly, drawing Michael's gaze toward the lower deck. He caught on quickly.

"Ahh," said Michael. "I see you met Shannon and her gosse."

"Gosse?" said Ivy.

"Gossip posse."

"Good one. That's exactly what those women are."

Ivy stepped closer, arms at her side as she laced her fingers with his. Their bodies weren't quite touching, but she flashed an expression that would have tempted any man with an ounce of imagination.

"Can we get out of here?" she said.

"You mean go back to our cabin?"

She shook her head. "I mean ditch this cruise and lose these losers."

"But . . . we just got here."

She glanced across the glistening sea, toward the moon rising over the island's silhouette in the distance. "This is such a beautiful place. Let's hire a captain and charter our own sailboat. Just you and me."

"Are you serious?"

"Does a Shannon Bear shit on her friends?"

Michael smiled. "You really want out of here?"

She draped her arms atop his shoulders and looked into his eyes. "I'm very possessive of my playthings."

"All right," he said. "I've had enough of these blowhards myself. We're in port tomorrow morning. Consider it done."

She rose up on her toes, hugged him around the neck, and whispered, "This is one move you will never regret, Michael Cantella. I promise."

3

I couldn't wait to get off the Saxton Silvers party boat the next morning, and by noon the sails were full on our private charter. It was a fifty-foot Jeanneau International, which was probably more boat than we needed. But Ivy kept her promise—*"This is one move you will never regret, Michael Cantella"*—and we spent each of the first three nights breaking in a different stateroom. "A promise is a promise," she told me, and by now I knew everything about her was as advertised. She hadn't become the love of my life by pumping me full of candy-coated popcorn and then skunking me on the prize.

The past three months had been picture perfect. My relationship with Ploutus Investments had been well established by the time Ivy started working there, and she was just a month into her new job when I invited her to lunch. She turned me down—repeatedly. Ivy was serious about her career, and dating a guy like me could have created a conflict of interest. Or maybe she thought I was just another Wall Street jerk. Whatever the reason, we worked it out on the condition that I say nothing to her boss, agreeing to keep our first date "just between us." By the second date, sparks were flying. Ten weeks later, we were sailing the Bahamas together.

"Michael, can you help with the anchor?"

"Got it," I said.

This was our fourth day away from Saxton Silvers and the MS *Excess*. Just Ivy, me, and a Bahamian captain named Rumsey who lived in a T-shirt that read RELAX: IT'S *MON*-DAY, MON. Ivy had raced J/24s in college and was a skilled sailor in her own right. Our captain knew the waters and was also a fairly talented chef. I did all the important stuff, like phoning ahead to the marinas to restock the liquor cabinet—and helping with the anchor.

"Try not to fall overboard this time, okay, honey?"

"I didn't *fall*. I just picked a not-so-convenient time to go for a swim."

The fact that I couldn't even stand on the bow of a sailboat and operate a motorized anchor reel was doubly embarrassing because my father lived for deep-sea fishing. People expected me to have boating in my blood, but in reality I hardly knew my dad, who had never married my mother. Mom died when I was six, and I was raised by my maternal grandparents, "Nana" and "Papa," a couple of Depression-era immigrants who had grown up on the south side of Chicago and who regarded recreational boating as the sport of kings and millionaire tycoons. When I finished high school, Papa retired and we moved to south Florida, just a few miles from the ocean, but by then the die was cast. I had spent my formative years in a two-bedroom house that was across the street from an endless cornfield on the Illinois-Wisconsin border. Bowling, not boating, was what we were about. I could also kick anybody's ass in Ping-Pong or bumper pool, but only if the match was held in an unfinished basement.

The electric motor whined and the heavy metal chain rattled as the anchor rose through water so clean and clear it seemed I could have reached in and touched bottom. There were no mishaps this time, and with the anchor aboard and the sails trimmed, we were on our way. Our plan was to sail from port to port as we wished—swimming, relaxing, snorkeling, relaxing some more. At the end of each day, if there was no slip available at the marina, or if we felt like a night away from civilization, we would find protected water off a deserted beach and simply drop anchor. Sometimes I called ahead to a local restaurant to arrange for a team to motor out to the sailboat at sunset and pamper us with fine wine, a local feast, and first-class service. On other nights we would "rough it," take the rubber dinghy to shore, and sample the local brews as we explored the town.

I relaxed on the bow, watching Ivy at the helm. Right about then it occurred to me that the string bikini had been an excellent invention.

"What are you looking at?" said Ivy.

"Perfection," I said.

"Thanks, mon," said Rumsey. "You pretty cute you-self."

We laughed, but Rumsey roared. Most Bahamians I've met have a great sense of humor and a joy for life. Yesterday, we'd sailed into a marina that was little more than a wooden shack where you could catch a rum buzz and dance to reggae. It was called "Happy People"—and everyone there really *was*. When I asked Rumsey about that now, he just shrugged.

"Some people happy. Some people not happy. You choose, mon. Not all Bahamians choose happy."

"Like our cabdriver in Miami," said Ivy.

I was sorry she'd brought that up. I'd been trying to put the FTAA riots out of my mind, but Ivy did have a point: Our driver definitely didn't own any condos at the Happy People Marina. His life had probably been pretty simple back in Nassau, I thought. Now—driving a cab in Miami—the poor guy was stressed out enough to work the residential mortgage desk at Saxton Silvers.

"So, choose happy, mon," said Rumsey.

I smiled and climbed into the boat's hammock with my BlackBerry. I loved people for whom life was so simple. I hated people for whom life was so simple.

I woke to the sound of steel drums.

I had no idea how long my nap on the bow had lasted, but the boat was anchored, the sails were down, and we were twenty yards from shore floating in a bay of sun-sparkled turquoise. The beach stretched for miles in either direction, a seemingly endless pinkish-white ribbon of sand. It was deserted, save for a tiki bar we'd stumbled upon, where a half-dozen recreational boaters like us relaxed to calypso music. The choice between light or dark rum would be our only concern.

"Hey, Rip Van Winkle is up."

It was Ivy's voice, but she was nowhere to be seen. I walked toward the cockpit and spotted her floating on an inflated air mattress near the boat.

"How long was I asleep?"

28 · JAMES GRIPPANDO

"Forty years," said Ivy. "The market crashed, we lost the house, the kids hate us, and a pack of IRS bloodhounds turned us into a couple of island-hopping fugitives. Welcome to paradise."

I removed my figurative bachelor's hat to process that one. With the exception of the kids hating us, Ivy's look into the future had its allure. It was arguably better than forty years in a capitalist-eats-capitalist world where there was an open trading market—a place to scratch, claw, and make money—every minute of every single day.

My BlackBerry rang. It was in the hammock thirty feet away, but I could hear it loud and clear, even over the steel drums. New mothers who instinctively knew the sound of their crying infant had absolutely nothing on guys like me and the sound of a ringing BlackBerry. I ignored it, jumped overboard, and took a leisurely swim toward Ivy. Three days in the sun had bronzed her Pilates-toned body, and it would have been easy to think only of taking her back to the boat and checking out the tan lines.

"I had a strange dream," I said, resting my forearms on the edge of her air mattress.

Ivy lay on her stomach, looking straight into my eyes. "Tell me."

"The sun is just coming up, and I'm alone on my bicycle, pedaling hard down the highway. A black SUV

with dark tinted windows is approaching in the opposite lane, faster and faster. All of sudden it swerves into
my lane and, before I can react, the bumper clips my
front tire and sends me flying into the ditch."

Her eyes clouded with concern. "Don't let that jerk
with the pepper spray in Miami get to you," she said.

"He did creep me out," I said. "The way he looked
at me and said, 'It's only gonna get worse.' It was like
a threat."

"That's what the whole FTAA protest was about.
Corporate greed: It's only getting worse."

"You're probably right, it's just . . ."

"Just what?"

I pulled myself closer up on the raft. "The thing is
that the dream I just told you about—the car running
me off the road—actually happened to me."

"What? When?"

"About ten days before our trip."

"Were you hurt?"

"A few bruises. My elbow still kind of hurts. Worst
part is that the jackass in the SUV kept on going, as if
he couldn't have cared less if I was alive or dead."

"Why didn't you tell me about this?"

"Because you would have told me to stop riding my
bicycle on the highway at sunrise."

"And now you're having nightmares about it?"

"I don't know if you'd call this a nightmare. It was kind of goofy."

"How do you mean?"

"In my dream the SUV stops," I said. "The driver gets out, runs around to the back of the car, throws open the doors, and grabs a dog."

"A dog?"

"Not just any dog. It's Tippy, a black Lab my grandparents gave me for my sixth birthday, right after I moved in with them. She has him in her arms and runs toward me, yelling, 'Hurry, let's go, Tippy's gonna die if we don't get him to the DQ!'"

"You mean the ER?"

"No, she's definitely taking him to Dairy Queen."

"That's too weird. But back up a second. You said the driver's a 'she'?"

"That's the even weirder part," I said. "It's you."

"*I* ran you off the road?"

"Not on purpose."

"No, of course not. I was just in too much of a hurry to get Tippy over to the DQ for a hot fudge sundae and save his life."

"Crazy, I know."

"Nah. Any skilled psychiatrist would give you a very simple interpretation of the underlying meaning."

"And that would be . . ."

"Don't have piña coladas for breakfast."

I pushed up from below and flipped her air mattress. Ivy screamed and went under, then popped right back up and grabbed me in a scissor hold, my face somehow buried between her breasts, her thighs squeezing the air from my lungs. If ever a man was going to drown, I figured this was probably the way to go.

Damn, she's strong.

"Had enough?" she said.

"Uh-uh," I said, her bikini-top string in my teeth.

We started laughing so hard, the hedge fund in total control as Wall Street hung on by a thread, so to speak. I cried uncle, and we were still laughing and coughing up water as we swam back to the air mattress.

"I'm so glad we ditched Saxton Silvers," I said as I laid my head next to hers.

"Me, too."

"I really like being with you."

"Me, too."

"I love you."

"I love you, too."

"We should get married."

Instantly I started thinking of ways to retract my words, to explain them away—I didn't mean *now*, I meant ten years from now; or I didn't really mean it at all, it was just a follow-up joke to the crack she'd made earlier about losing the house and the kids hating us. But I'd found success by trusting my instincts, and even though we'd dated only three months, something about my slip felt oddly right.

"Okay," she said.

I was suddenly having trouble understanding. "Okay what?"

"Let's get married," she said.

Her response was so casual that I thought she was kidding. "Are you serious?"

"Michael, read my lips: Yes."

My mouth fell open, but no words came. I was about to grab her and give her a kiss, but she sat up quickly, her legs straddling the air mattress.

"We should do it here."

I looked around. "Like a destination wedding where we invite—"

"No invitations. I mean do it *today*."

She looked so beautiful sitting there, and every fiber of my body was singing.

"Rumsey!" I called out.

Our dreadlocked captain rose up from the sailboat. "Yeah, mon?"

"Find us a preacher."

4

My wife was unemployed. I found out ten minutes after saying "I do."

Surprise!

Our afternoon nuptials had played out exactly as you might expect, assuming you'd smoked way too much ganja. Ivy found a suitable dress in a boutique next door to a combination doughnut/sushi shop. I rented a moped and rode to the other side of town to check out the old wooden church. The whitewashed doors were locked, but the sign said, IN CASE OF EMER-GENCY, CALL BIG NED'S BAIT SHOP. Ned—five feet tall, but "big" in the sense that he was four feet wide—hooked me up with a priest who wore a madras shirt with a Roman collar and who looked like Bob Marley. The tavern down the street emptied out at precisely five P.M., and a dozen drunks showed up at the church to witness the ceremony. Our maid of honor was a two-hundred-pound cocktail waitress known locally as Valerie Bang-Bang. Rumsey declined my invitation to be the best man, confessing that he "ain't never brought nuttin' but bad luck to marriage, mon." Valerie Bang-Bang's brother stood in for him. His name—no lie—was Chitty. I didn't ask him about the other brother Chitty.

"You're angry, aren't you?" said Ivy.

We were returning to the sailboat as husband and wife, riding down a bumpy dirt road in a battered golf cart with monster-truck tires. Ivy looked amazing in a sleeveless white dress that would have worked either for cocktails on the beach or a spur-of-the-moment wedding. We sat side by side in the jump seat, our backs to Rumsey as he drove. The tin-roofed spire of the little white church seemed to rise up out of the cloud of dust we were leaving behind.

"I would never be mad at you for walking away from a grind like Ploutus Investments," I said.

"But I should have told you I was done with the hedge-fund world."

Two weeks earlier, Ivy had asked me to manage a chunk of money for her. It would have been nice to know her career plans before investing for her—not to mention *marrying* her—but I didn't want to spoil the moment. "Let's not talk about this now," I said.

"I'm really sorry," she said as she leaned closer. "Do you think wild honeymoon sex would make it all better?"

I smiled. "Let me go way out on a limb on that one and say yes."

We gave Rumsey the night off, spread out a blanket on the beach, and cooked dinner on a little hibachi. Given enough butter and lemon, even I could grill lobster. It was a perfect evening until an hour before sunset, when the townies showed up. Nothing against local partiers, but a bunch of drunks and the smell of ganja in the air wasn't our idea of a wedding night. We took the dinghy back to the sailboat and motored out another half mile to more secluded waters. The hammock on deck was the perfect place for watching a sunset. We finished off another bottle of wine while rocking back and forth in each other's arms. The sky went from pink to purple to midnight blue, and when the last of the clouds vanished on the horizon, the first star of the night appeared directly overhead.

"We're married," I said.

"To each other," she said in equal amazement.

The hammock rocked gently in the breeze.

"You want to make a baby?" I asked.

"Nope."

"You want to practice?"

She raised her head and smiled.

The waters were calm even this far offshore, but still I struggled out of the hammock and staggered across the deck. Apparently I had outpaced Ivy on the wine, and she was helping me more than I was helping her as we climbed down into the cabin. We were kissing and undressing each other as we fell onto the mattress.

"Wait," she said, her smile turning mischievous.

"What's wrong?"

"You are going to be one happy boy when I show you Valerie Bang-Bang's wedding gift to us."

Events beyond that were hazy at best. There was more kissing and definitely naked flesh, and I seem to recall a joke about wedding-night performance anxiety. My next clear memory was that of waking in total darkness and checking the alarm clock beside the bed. It was 5:05 A.M. I reached across the mattress for Ivy, but she wasn't there. I propped myself up on one elbow, then dropped back down to the pillow. My head was throbbing—way too much to drink. If someone had suggested amputation as a remedy, I might actually have considered it. I called for Ivy but got no reply. I rolled over and reached all the way across the bed.

I was alone. Maybe she was in the bathroom. I was in desperate need of water.

"I-veee."

I waited but there was only silence, save for the waves brushing against the hull. I forced myself to sit up, then pushed away from the mattress and let my feet hit the floor. When the world finally stopped spinning, I switched on the light, which was about as easy on my eyes as staring into a blast furnace. Squinting and still feeling a little drunk, I climbed halfway up the ladder. The breeze on my face felt refreshing. Sunrise was two hours away, and the deck was shrouded in darkness.

"Ivy?"

Too much wine could make me snore, so I was sure she was asleep in the hammock, away from the noise. I climbed up on deck and stepped toward the bow.

The hammock was empty.

I walked portside from bow to stern, then back again on the starboard side. No sign of Ivy. I knelt down, poked my head through the open hatchway, and called her name again. No reply. I checked the dinghy, which was floating behind the boat. It, too, was empty. Concern washed over me as I gazed out toward the sea. The setting moon was behind clouds, and there was no discerning the black water from the night sky.

"Ivy!"

I grabbed a handheld VectorLite from the cockpit and switched it on, the powerful beam sweeping across the gentle waves. I called her name again and again, louder and louder, but I heard only the sound of halyards tinkling against the barren mast in the wind.

"*Ivy!*"

May 2007, New York

5

There was a time when people all but worshipped guys like me, but not anymore. We were the ones with the seven-, eight-, nine-figure investment portfolios, the private corporate jets, the yacht that had to be a Riva and not merely a Hatteras, the penthouses and vacation homes, and all the female companionship we wanted. Before Lehman went under and the billionaires came knocking for government bailouts, the major banks, hedge funds, and brokerage firms were swimming along in a sea of sludge so heavy with bad debt and corruption that we barely noticed we were all sinking together. The media have covered the fallout from every angle. Almost. When it comes to financial crimes, secrets, violence, and even murder, my Wall Street tale proves that sometimes you can clean up toxic waste, and other times it goes up in flames.

Intense, hot, uncontrollable flames.

It started on a fairly typical weekday, and I was on my way to yet another black-tie dinner—yes, that was "fairly typical." This one, in the Grand Ballroom of the Pierre Hotel in Midtown Manhattan, was the annual *Securities Industry News* awards ceremony. A colleague at Saxton Silvers was up for Collateralized Debt Obligation of the Year. The CDO—a financial tool that repackaged debts supported by collateral (like mortgages) for sale to investors—had once been the twenty-first-century darling of Wall Street. The subprime crisis in late 2006 had changed all that, eerily enough right around Halloween. I nearly skipped this year's award ceremony, embarrassed for my firm, unable to fathom how anyone could walk on stage to accept an award for an investment instrument that had nearly destroyed the global financial system. For Saxton Silvers, however, a win was a win, and you were nothing if not a team player. So there I was, answering the call of duty.

Work had been my solace after Ivy's disappearance—years ago. No one knew for certain what had happened to her that night in the Bahamas. Suspicion surrounded me at first—the husband was always the first suspect—but I passed a polygraph exam with flying colors. My undying hope was that Ivy would somehow return unharmed—a high-powered career woman who had jumped into marriage while on vacation, freaked out, and escaped to some far corner of the earth to sort out what the hell she'd just done. But there was never the slightest indication that she was alive. No sightings of her anywhere in the world. No cell phone calls. No record of any travel or credit card purchases in her name. Her newly opened, half-million-dollar account at Saxton Silvers—the money she had entrusted me to manage—went untouched. Eventually, the Bahamian investigators likened Ivy's disappearance to the accidental death of Natalie Wood in the early 1980s. The only difference was that we had anchored our sailboat near "the wall," as it is known to scuba divers—part of the continental shelf where shallow turquoise seas less than a mile from shore suddenly turned into a dark, shark-infested ocean. For two weeks search parties combed the beaches. But on day fifteen the official mourning period began. A fisherman reeled in a thirteen-foot tiger shark. The contents of its belly looked suspiciously human, and authorities determined that it was part of a woman's shoulder and upper arm. A hair follicle taken from Ivy's hairbrush provided a DNA match. Since shark attacks are rare,

I took solace in believing that Ivy had drowned before meeting up with nature's most efficient predator.

The alternative still gave me nightmares.

"Excuse me, Mr. Cantella. You want the Fifth Avenue entrance?"

"Cruise the block, Nick. Drop me off on Sixty-first."

The limo and driver were a bit ostentatious, but I had passed the point in my career when I could spend a third or more of my eighteen-hour day working from the backseat of a cab. Maybe I'd lost a little of my drive. After Ivy was gone, the relentless pursuit of money had seemed a little pointless—not a good mind-set for Saxton Silvers' youngest-ever investment advisor of the year. I was looking for real purpose, and I was about to ditch Wall Street altogether to join the Make-A-Wish Foundation.

Well, not exactly.

But I had given more than just passing thought to getting out, which told me that I probably needed a change. So I called in a few favors and went to the Assessment Center, which sounded like something out of an old Woody Allen movie, but it was actually a boot camp for Saxton Silvers' managerial prospects. You go in like a West Point plebe, and if you survive the stress, lack of sleep, and psychological games, you come out feeling like the newest member of an elite Wall Street fraternity—or like a made man in the mob. At the end of my three weeks, I was given the investment-banking equivalent of the secret handshake and Sicilian oath: I was invited to join management. But then came the kicker, straight from the lips of the assessment team leader: "And of course, we will assist in reassigning your book of business." At Saxton Silvers, you were either a producer or a manager, not both. Investment advisors were expected to give up their clients in order to join management, which as far as I was concerned meant that management was more like the *crock* at the end of the rainbow—though my change of heart was not at all driven by money.

Well, not exactly.

But it had been one of those times in my life when the pot of gold was a distant second—to power. Or perhaps efficacy was a better word. *Give up my clients?* It seemed like a page out of the psychological playbook of Jim Jones, the doomsday cult leader who'd told his followers to hand over their wallets and follow him to Guyana, making it physically and financially impossible for them to say "See ya" when it came time to drink the Kool-Aid. So I told management to stick it where the sun doesn't shine.

Well . . . not exactly.

Luckily, my mentor had stepped in. A deal was struck. I was allowed to keep my best clients—I was still a producer—and the firm created a management position that I could hold until I agreed to drink the Kool-Aid, so to speak, and assume a more traditional post. Keeping one hand on the production side while transitioning into management wasn't really a breach of company policy, we rationalized, because my newly minted position had no history, no precedent.

My new charge was to position Saxton Silvers as the leader on Wall Street for investment in environmentally friendly and socially responsible companies. This, of course, was an instant source of sidesplitting laughs around the watercooler. Someone even taped the name MIKE QUIXOTE to my office door. It was a tough assignment, made even tougher by the difficulty in defining a "green" investment. One of the Harvard environmental fellows on my team calculated that each second of time spent on the Internet contributed 20 milligrams of CO_2 to the environment, which is to say that if Al Gore invented the information superhighway, the inconvenient truth is that the carbon footprint of the IT industry is equal to that of the aviation industry. I let the academics argue over that one, and instead focused on turning the "windmill division" into a serious profit center for the firm.

"Here we are, sir," said Nick.

The limo stopped. Nick jumped out to get my door, but I beat him to it. No matter how many times I told him that I could open my own door, he was too programmed to stop himself.

"Don't go too far," I told him. "I won't be staying long."

"Yes, sir."

It was after seven o'clock, and I was already late. I knew Mallory wasn't going to be happy with me. After nearly two years of marriage she was beyond tired of these black-tie events, especially on crazy days like this one when I had to have my tux delivered to the office and Mallory had to ride alone and meet me there.

My phone rang as I entered the lobby. This time it was my Asia team leader calling about the surprising surge at the morning bell for the Tokyo Financial Exchange.

"Mr. Cantella?" I heard a man say as I rounded the corner.

I quickly finished the call and tucked away my cell. In front of me were two men, each wearing a trench coat and an exceedingly serious expression.

"Who wants to know?" I said.

The older man flashed a badge. "Agent Fairchild," he said. "FBI."

My heart skipped a beat. Nothing prepared you for a moment like this, especially in an era when finding a federal regulator on Wall Street was like finding a Walmart on Rodeo Drive.

"What's this about?" I asked.

The agent put away his badge, but he didn't seem inclined to answer my question. He grabbed my right arm, and the other agent took my left.

"Come with us, sir," he said, and they escorted me from the lobby.

6

Mallory Cantella checked her watch. She would have bet her Jimmy Choos that Michael was going to be late, as usual, so there was no point getting upset about it. But with nearly a hundred of his closest friends and colleagues waiting, she couldn't stop the stress from turning the back of her neck into one huge knot.

Where the heck are you, Michael?

By Saxton Silvers' standards, Michael's surprise thirty-fifth birthday party was hardly an exercise in keeping up with the Joneses. That would have meant five hundred guests at a society-page event—perhaps a re-creation of Havana's famous Tropicana nightclub in its 1940s heyday, complete with a salsa orchestra, casino tables, showgirls in feather headdresses, and dinner catered by Bobby Flay. Mallory hadn't even considered it. Michael wasn't cheap, but a blowout to end all blowouts in celebration of an accomplishment as meaningless as reaching the age of thirty-five? Never. Not Michael. She had to keep it simple. The Pierre Hotel didn't really fit that bill, but it was needed for the ruse—a venue she'd chosen to make Michael think that he was on his way to another dull black-tie business event. All would be well when he unwrapped the case of Montepulciano that she had been able to cajole from an obscure Tuscan vineyard by learning to pronounce it *with feeling*—"Mon-tah-pool-chah-no."

Assuming he ever gets here.

Mallory downed a Cosmopolitan and was headed toward the bar for another when her best friend came over and grabbed her.

"He's in the building!" Andrea told her.

Since marrying Michael, Mallory had struggled for acceptance by the Saxton Silvers "It girls," and Andrea was the first real connection she'd made. It was probably because Andrea wasn't in the club either. Andrea's fiancé was new to the firm, the couple having moved from Seattle just eleven weeks earlier.

"Are you sure?" asked Mallory.

"Has my intelligence ever failed you?"

It was true: Andrea's information was consistently reliable, unlike the usual Saxton Silvers gossip that wound its way from the Pilates studio, to the coffee-house, to the Madonna-inspired Power Plate workout, to the white-wine-and-salmon-tartare lunch at Barneys.

Mallory hurried up onto the stage and grabbed the microphone. The band stopped, and the event coordinator flashed the lights to get the crowd's attention.

Exactly on cue, the main doors to the ballroom opened, and Michael entered in the company of two men wearing trench coats. The band immediately started playing "Happy Birthday," and from the stage Mallory caught Michael's eye as she led the crowd in singing to him. It had been Andrea's idea to hire the actors to pose as G-men and haul Michael into the ballroom—a gag that Mallory loved. He looked genuinely stunned.

"Happy birthday, Michael," she said when the song ended. "I love you."

A long round of applause followed. A waiter handed Michael a glass of champagne, which he raised in a toast to his wife as he mouthed the words back to her, *I love you, too.*

It probably would have been too much to expect Michael to climb on stage and say those words into a microphone so that everyone could hear. It would have made Mallory's night if he had, but it was enough that the weight around her neck was finally lifted.

Mission accomplished.

7

At one thirty A.M. I was standing at the window in the penthouse suite of the Pierre Hotel with a glass of champagne in my hand. If a sea of lights was a sign of life, then the city that never sleeps was living up to its name.

I wasn't from New York, hadn't grown up wanting to live here, and fifteen years ago would have laughed in the face of anyone who told me that I would spend my thirty-fifth birthday looking down at Fifth Avenue and Central Park from the forty-second floor of a five-star hotel. Why on earth Mallory and I needed a two-bedroom suite for twenty minutes of birthday sex and a few hours of sleep wasn't entirely clear, but that was the thing about having money and living in Manhattan. Cummerbunds were stupid, but I owned at least a dozen of them. Champagne gave me a headache, but some well-trained staffer had placed a glass in my hand as I entered the room, the hotel put it on my bill, and I said thank you. I suppose I also should have thanked the guy who had guaranteed me a clear view of my wet, naked wife by designing a shower stall with warm water running between double panes of glass to prevent fogging. I couldn't explain this life—not to myself, and definitely not to Papa, who of course had been the first to call earlier in the day and wish me happy birthday. The call had ended the way our phone conversations always ended. "Tell your beautiful wife hello for me," he said. "And love each other. That's the main thing." Coming from anyone else, it would have sounded like Pollyanna. But Papa was the real deal. To him, Wall Street was one big "Fonzie scheme," no matter how many times I told him that Ponzi had nothing to do with *Happy Days* and Arthur Fonzarelli. Anyway, I took his meaning, and on some level he was right. But tonight I let myself feel the accomplishment of conquering the most amazing city the world had ever known, and like the song goes, "If I can make it there . . ."

"I can't wait for your fortieth," said Mallory as she came up from behind and put her arms around me.

Papa's favorite crooner was still on my brain, and it suddenly occurred to me that Sinatra's most depressing song—the one about getting old—skips straight from "when I was thirty-five" to "the autumn of the years."

"Let's not think about forty," I said, still staring out the window.

Mallory rose up on her tiptoes and bit my earlobe. She was still dressed in her evening gown, still wearing her makeup.

"Turn down the bed," she said. "I'll be ready in ten minutes."

We mimicked one of those black-and-white-movie moments where the couple slowly slides apart until their fingertips finally separate as the woman heads off to the dressing room to "slip into something more comfortable." Mallory was fun that way. Last week, she'd sent me a sexy video by e-mail as an "early birthday present." It was a parody of Marilyn Monroe singing "Happy birthday, Mr. President" to JFK. (Mallory was certain that I would someday replace my mentor as president of Saxton Silvers.) It was hilarious, but it was also racy enough to warrant an e-mail subject line that read "Just Between Us." That unique ability to make me laugh and turn me on—sometimes at the same time—was one of the reasons I finally was able to let go of Ivy and remarry.

Ivy.

I was trying not to think of her tonight—it wasn't fair to Mallory—but Ivy was inevitably a part of my reflective mood. She just filled a different place in my heart, though I could never admit this to Mallory. Mallory and I had been good friends in high school but had never dated—and the entire student body wondered, Why not? She was the salutatorian of our senior class and went on to Juilliard to study dance. I went to the University of Florida, the best school that in-state tuition could buy. We lost touch until Mallory read about Ivy's disappearance in the *Times*. She was divorced and living in an efficiency apartment in the Village, an intermediate-level instructor at a modern dance studio, when she called me to lend the support of an old friend. That was exactly how it remained for almost two years until suddenly we asked each other the same question: Why not? We married six months later.

Funny, for all the talking we did about Ivy, I couldn't help but feel that Mallory's true impression of her was based on tidbits of information that she had picked up at firm events—and from rumors started by Shannon and her "gosse" of Saxton Silvers wives who had met Ivy that one time. Even though I counted my blessings for reconnecting with Mallory, I sometimes wondered how my life would have turned out if Ivy and I had just stayed on the cruise as planned. On our last night together, Ivy had made it clear that she was burned out and fed up with Wall Street. Without question, being married to Ivy would have meant leaving New York. Would my life have been better? I couldn't say. All I knew for certain was that with a beautiful wife in the next room, one who had picked up a microphone and said "I love you" in front of a roomful of invited guests, thoughts like that made me feel guilty as hell.

"Can you pour us some wine, honey?" she called from the next room.

"You got it."

I went to the wet bar and dumped my overpriced glass of champagne down the sink. I had a conference call with the German Aerospace Center in Stuttgart at nine A.M.—solar power was a hot green investment, and the Germans were years ahead of anyone in the United States—and I couldn't risk a headache in the morning. Champagne was the only wine that affected me that way, which was one reason I never fully understood the horrific hangover I'd woken up with on the morning of Ivy's disappearance. And there I was thinking of Ivy again, even as I was opening a bottle of pinot grigio for a woman who was determined to make my thirty-fifth birthday a night I would never forget. Papa's husky old voice was suddenly inside my head, uttering what had become one of his favorite words since moving to Florida.

Schmuck.

I poured the wine and then checked the label. It was the same Italian wine that Mallory and I had shared on our honeymoon on the Amalfi Coast. Somewhere in my DNA was a male chromosome that wanted to give myself points for at least noticing her sentimentality, but it was Mallory who deserved all the credit tonight. I was thirty-five years old, this was my life, and it was time for me to be more like Papa and focus on what I had, not on what I'd lost. Mallory was not a woman I had settled for. I was lucky to have her. My career was soaring beyond my wildest dreams. Eleven years ago, fresh out of business school, I'd set rather realistic goals to have a net worth of such and such by age thirty, by age thirty-five, and so on. I was *way* ahead of those numbers.

I took the wine and knocked on the bathroom door. The shower was running, and I knew what that meant. Mallory always showered before marathon sex. Tonight would be no quickie.

"Your wine, *madame*," I said as I opened the door.

That double-paned shower really *didn't* fog, just as the bellboy who'd showed us to our room had promised. As I stole a glimpse of my fitness-crazed wife, I went ahead and silently thanked that voyeuristic genius, whoever he was, for having invented it.

"Thanks, honey. Leave it on the counter."

The deluxe suite came with satellite everything, so I found a jazz station on digital radio and then swapped out my tuxedo for a bathrobe. It had been at least seven hours since I'd been online—a world record for me—so I opened my laptop and kicked up my feet. Hoping to fall deeper into a "be thankful for what you have" mind-set, I went to the Saxton Silvers Web page, entered my ID and password, and logged onto my personal investment account. I'd stopped managing my own portfolio years ago, and my buddy out in San Francisco, James Dunn, had agreed to do it only if I promised not to second-guess him on a daily basis. I checked it every few days, and today was a milestone. My liquid assets alone—excluding real estate and other things that couldn't be quickly converted to cash—were almost ten times the "age thirty-five" goal for my *entire net worth* that I had set for myself not so many years ago, and I was feeling pretty smug with the anticipation of seeing the numbers on my LCD. I clicked the Account Overview button on the menu, and my heart nearly stopped.

"Ready or not, here I come," said Mallory.

The bathroom door opened, and she stepped out with the glass of wine in her hand. She was wearing a red teddy, but I was almost too stunned by the on-screen numbers to notice. The look on my face immediately threw her.

"What's wrong?" she said.

I was still processing things, and it took me a moment to answer. "Were those phony FBI agents at my party the end of the birthday jokes?"

"What do you mean?"

"Did you put someone up to messing with my personal account? As part of a joke, I mean."

"No," she said as she slid onto the bed and sat beside me. "Why do you ask? And why are you checking investment accounts now?"

I showed her the screen, and her jaw dropped.

"How can that be?" she said.

"Mallory, please tell me if this is a joke."

"No, I swear. That's not even close to being funny. I would never do anything like that."

The stunned expression on her face didn't lie—and neither did the account summary.

Zero balance.

I clicked the Refresh button on the tool bar. Same result: zero balance. I clicked Refresh twice more, then completely logged out of the Saxton Silvers Web site and logged back in. Each time, I got the same result. Zero. Nothing. *Nada.*

"It's a mistake, obviously some kind of mistake." I was mumbling to myself, repeating that word— *mistake*—over and over again, as I clicked around and reviewed my account trading history. Then I froze.

"Michael?" she said with trepidation.

"This is crazy," I said.

"What?"

"It's all been liquidated. My entire account—everything was unloaded."

"Did you sell it?"

"No. That's the point. Timing is everything in the market. I got killed on most of these transactions." I kept scrolling down through the history.

"Then why would James have pushed through all these orders?"

"He wouldn't," I said. "And from the looks of this summary, he didn't. Look at this stock here, for example. It was an after-hours trade through an ECN."

"A what?"

"An electronic communications network. Some are regulated, some aren't. This one looks like it's unregulated—which has me even more freaked out. The only seller identified in the transaction reports is me."

"But you just said you didn't sell."

"I didn't. And some of these transactions are more complicated to unwind than a simple sell order, but it's the same result. I'm shown as the one who authorized the transaction."

"How can that be?"

"Don't you get it? It must have been somebody posing as me."

"You mean like an identity thief?"

I was suddenly dizzy. My mind didn't want to go there. "That's why I was hoping you were going to tell me that this was somebody's idea of a joke."

"Michael," she said, her voice quaking, "did someone take our money?"

The answer was also on the screen. It had all been moved to a low-risk account that I hadn't touched in years. "It's okay. It's there. It wasn't a good time to liquidate most of these holdings, but it looks like the cash is still with Saxton Silvers."

"You have to do something. Reverse the transactions, right?"

I grabbed my cell and dialed James in San Francisco. He was asleep—a West Coaster who lived on Wall Street time—but the problem I laid out for him forced him out of bed and over to his computer.

"Holy shit," he said over the phone. I presumed he was looking at the same screen I had in front of me—the long list of premature sales and other poorly timed transactions.

"Tell me about it," I said. "I look like the moron who bought high and sold everything low."

"I'm not talking about the individual transactions," he said. "I'm looking at where all the money went. Your custodial account."

"No worries," I said, "the funds in that account just sit there earning interest. It's at zero risk."

"I hate to tell you, but right now there's *no* money in it."

"*What?*"

"Everything in your portfolio was liquidated—most of it at a loss. The cash generated from those transactions was transferred out of your personal account and into the custodial account—which now shows a zero balance. There was a lump-sum transfer."

"To where?"

He paused, then said, "Michael, I'm starting to get a little concerned here."

"*You're* concerned? Where the hell is my money?"

I could hear him clicking frantically on his keyboard.

"Let me ask you this," he said. "I'm looking at it here on the screen. Do you have a numbered account in the Cayman Islands that I don't know about?"

I froze, unable to speak. Mallory was close enough to hear what James was saying, and she squeezed my wrist so tightly that her nails left marks in my skin.

"Michael, honey: Where is our money?"

"*I don't know*, damn it." My tone was harsh, but Mallory seemed to understand that it wasn't directed at her. "Everything was liquidated and then wire-

MONEY TO BURN • 63

transferred to some offshore account that I've never heard of."

James said, "Don't panic yet. Let me investigate this."

"No," I said. "We need the entire damn army moving on this tonight. Get the head of IT and the head of security on the phone and call me back pronto."

"Will do."

Mallory was still digging her nails into me as I hung up with James.

"My God, what is going on?" she said.

I drew a breath and let it out slowly. "Either this is some kind of mistake," I said as I speed-dialed the firm's general counsel, "or I am totally screwed."

8

Mallory watched from the bed as I rifled through the garment bag in the closet for something to wear. She'd fully intended to pack a business suit for me, knowing that I would have to go to work in the morning. Somehow my clothes hadn't made it, though Mallory had managed to pack three outfits for herself to choose from. Unless I wanted to squeeze into a size 2 Chanel sundress with a scoop neck and a flirty, loose bodice, I was stuck in my wrinkled tuxedo for my emergency meeting with Saxton Silvers' general counsel.

"I'm so scared," she said.

So was I. When I was thirty-four, it was a very good year. I had a personal investment portfolio valued at eight figures. Then I turned thirty-five, and suddenly I didn't have two nickels to rub together. I had been gypped, big time. Even by the measure of Sinatra's depressing old song, I was entitled to one more year of riding in limousines with my blue-blooded wife of not-so-independent means. Violins, please.

"I'm sure the firm can get this straightened out," I said as I pulled my tuxedo shirt back on.

"What if they don't?" she asked. "It's all insured, right? Through that—Sip and See—or whatever it's called."

She meant the Securities Investor Protection Corporation. "SIPC doesn't cover identity theft. It protects you from a firm that goes belly up. Our loss is way above their coverage limit anyway."

"I don't understand any of this," she said. "What was this account they moved all our money into?"

"It's a numbered account. Offshore. Obviously someone trying to take advantage of bank secrecy."

"No, I mean the one before that. You said these identity thieves moved the money from our joint account into some other kind of account with Saxton Silvers. Then they moved it to the offshore account."

I was suddenly fumbling with my cuff link. I had a major problem on my hands, and tracking down our stolen money was only the half of it.

"It was opened a while ago, before we were married."

"So it's an account for my benefit?" she asked.

"No. This is something that existed long before we got together."

Her voice was getting increasingly tense. "Then who is it for?"

"Honey, the general counsel is on her way into the office as we speak. This is really not the time."

"Who is it for, Michael?"

I'd never heard that tone from Mallory. It was as if she were telling me that if I wanted to stay married, I had better finish this conversation—*now.*

I sat on the edge of the mattress and pulled on my shoes.

"It's not what you're thinking," I said. "That account was not our money."

"Oh, so now we have *our* money and *your* money, is that it?" She was sitting up straight, arms folded in a defensive posture.

"No, that's not what I'm saying. I haven't been stashing money away from you. When I say that the money in that account was not ours, I mean it's not yours or mine. It doesn't belong to either one of us."

"Then whose is it?"

I hesitated, knowing that my response was sure to hit a raw nerve. "It was Ivy's."

Mallory took a deep breath. She'd never come out and said it, but I knew that she had heard through the

MONEY TO BURN • 67

gosse that my first wife had been smart and beautiful, and that she was my true love. Sometimes a Wall Street investment bank could be like high school.

"Michael," she said in an even tone, obviously trying to remain calm. "Why do you have an account for your dead wife?"

I wanted to hold her and reassure her that I did indeed have a good explanation, but her body language was telling me that there was no such thing. I gave it a shot anyway.

"Ivy had no will at the time of her death," I said, "so everything she owned went to me—her husband. But I never touched the money."

"Even though it's yours," she said.

"No, it's not mine."

"You just said that everything Ivy owned went to you."

"That was the problem," I said. "It didn't feel right to keep it. Ivy and I had been married only a few hours. I wanted Ivy's mother to have it, but when I offered it to her, she refused to take it. So I kept the account separate and just let it earn interest. I figured Ivy's mother would change her mind when she got older and really needed it."

I studied Mallory's expression. She wasn't exactly famous for her poker face, and the emotions flashing in her eyes were decidedly negative. She moved to the other side of the bed, showing me her back.

"Please try to understand," I said.

"This really hurts," she said.

"It shouldn't," I said. "When Ivy died, that money should have gone to her mother. I didn't need it then. I don't need it now. We have plenty," I said.

As of two hours ago we did, that is.

"It's not about the money," she said. Her voice was trembling, and I heard a sniffle. I walked around the foot of the bed and sat beside her. I tried to take her hand, but she pulled away.

"I'm sorry I didn't tell you," I said.

"No, I'm the one who should have said something."

"What do you mean?"

"I've kept this bottled up inside me for a long time. I know I've had a lot to drink and you have to go . . . but I have to say it."

"Say what?"

"It's so clear: You have never stopped loving her. I can't compete with that. You still love Ivy, and you are incapable of ever loving me."

"That's not true," I said.

"I'm pretty, I'm nice, I try to make you happy. And I think you really like being with me—just the way you liked being with me in high school. But if it was a career woman you wanted, then you should have found yourself another Ivy. You don't love me."

"How can you say such a thing?"

"Because it's *true*."

She rose quickly and went for the box of tissues on the bureau.

"Mallory, I—"

"Stop," she said, cutting me off before I could say it. Then she took a breath to compose herself. "Let's just forget it, okay? I shouldn't have said anything. Go see your lawyer."

It was an awkward moment. I hated to leave like this, but I really did have to meet with the general counsel.

"We'll talk more when I get back," I said.

"No," she said. "I don't want to. Don't worry. It's off my chest."

She seemed to be trying to convince herself, not me.

"Are you sure?" I asked.

"You just go and take care of what you need to take care of."

I rose and started toward her, but my phone rang. It was the general counsel wanting to know where the hell I was.

"I'm on my way," I said before quickly hanging up.

I tried to find parting words that might reassure Mallory. Before I could speak, my laptop sounded from across the bed. I had a new e-mail in my in-box. Mallory and I exchanged glances, as if we both sensed that I needed to check it before leaving. I crossed the room to do just that.

The sender's address was unrecognizable, a random mix of numbers and letters. But the subject line told me that it wasn't spam.

It read, *Zero balance.*

I glanced across the room at Mallory, telling her without words that it was indeed important. I opened the e-mail and read the message aloud.

"Just as planned. xo xo."

It wasn't enough for the thief to take my money. Now he had to taunt me with "hugs and kisses"—as if it were personal. Things were getting creepier by the minute.

"What does that mean?" Mallory asked.

"It means I've got one hell of a mess to sort out," I said.

9

I was in the backseat of a yellow taxi, about two blocks away from Saxton Silvers' offices on Seventh Avenue, when Sonya Jackson, my firm's general counsel, phoned me with a change in plans.

"Go directly to the FBI's field office at 26 Federal Plaza and look for my car on Duane Street. I'll have Stanley Brewer, our outside counsel, with me. He's a former federal prosecutor who specializes in identity theft issues, and he's excellent. You're in good hands."

I was glad to see the firm treating the matter so seriously. On the other hand, a former prosecutor taking the matter straight to the FBI didn't exactly send a message that there was nothing to worry about. I thanked Sonya and redirected the driver toward downtown.

I found Sonya's black Mercedes parked a block away from the security barriers that protected the FBI Field Office. Sonya was behind the steering wheel and Brewer was on the passenger side. I climbed into the rear seat behind Sonya, and the three of us spoke in the privacy of a virtually soundproof sedan before going inside the building.

Before becoming one of the most respected corporate officers at Saxton Silvers, Sonya had worked with Stanley Brewer at Coolidge Harding & Cash, and she was the first African American woman to make partner at the prestigious firm with a presence on Wall Street that predated the transformation of the *Customers' Afternoon Letter* into the *Wall Street Journal.* The unofficial motto of CH&C was "You get what you pay for," which explained why it was simply known as "Cool Cash." I assumed the meter was running as I told Brewer everything, from the separate account for Ivy, to the most recent e-mail I'd received before leaving the hotel suite.

Sonya spoke first. "Sounds like a well-organized identity theft."

"The e-mail confirms as much," I said. "Why else would they say 'Just as planned'?"

"Yes," said Brewer. "But I find the way the thief signed off—'xo xo'—far more interesting. That tag at the end was designed to add insult. It's as if the thief takes more satisfaction in the way the scheme hurts you than in how it benefits him."

"That was my reaction," I said. "It almost looks to be more about revenge than outright theft. Or at least equal parts theft and revenge."

"I'm theorizing at this point," said Brewer. "But the very nature of your business puts you in a position to hurt people financially, even if it's not your intention to harm anyone."

"Transactions have ripple effects," said Sonya, "and when you're talking about the kind of transactions that Saxton Silvers is involved in, these ripples can reach all the way across the globe."

"That makes it even more unsettling," I said.

"It does," said Brewer. "Because when the motive is revenge, you never really know when—if ever—they are going to call it even."

Everyone on Wall Street had rivals, even enemies, but my stomach knotted at the thought of someone out to completely destroy me.

The clock on the dash said 2:55 A.M. I knew how quickly money could move across the globe. With every tick of the clock, I could feel my fortune slipping through the cracks of bank secrecy, untraceable.

"Shouldn't we get the FBI moving on this?" I said.

"They're already going strong," said Sonya. "I sent the account details to the Computer Crime Division right after I called Stanley."

"I'd still like to get face-to-face with them," I said.

The two lawyers exchanged glances. Brewer then looked at me and said, "Sonya and I talked while you were cabbing it over here. We agreed that it would be best if you weren't part of this initial meeting with the bureau."

"But it's my money."

"I understand," he said.

"My entire personal portfolio has been cleaned out."

"I'm not minimizing that."

"I'm the victim."

"It would appear so," he said.

"So I have to be there when you talk to the FBI."

Brewer took a breath, letting it go as he spoke. "Michael, I can't begin to tell you how many times I have seen law enforcement treat the victim as a suspect."

I suddenly thought of the way the Bahamian authorities had treated me after I reported Ivy's disappearance. Not even a clean polygraph exam had convinced some of them of my innocence.

"I understand where you're coming from," I said. "But I didn't do anything here but check my account balance."

"I know how these agents think," said Brewer. "If you set foot inside that building, they will shift into fact-gathering mode and will want to know everything about every transaction you have ever structured that involves an offshore bank. That's sensitive information that you and your clients don't want to hand over freely, and just as soon as you put up any resistance to their inquiry—*bam.* You go from victim to suspect in their mind."

The man was making sense, but I kept coming back to the bottom line. "This is my life savings."

Sonya chimed in. "Let Stanley and me deal with the FBI. I've called in our head of security. The best thing you can do right now is go to the office and use the firm's internal resources to find out what happened."

Another good point. When money went missing, private security was often more effective than law enforcement, especially in international matters.

"All right," I said. "That sounds like a reasonable plan."

I handed Brewer my business card and told him to call me day or night. Then I stepped out of the car. The lights were burning brightly at the old fire station on Duane Street. Even so, everything else was quiet in this city that never sleeps; there wasn't a cab in sight. The night air wasn't quite cool enough for me to see my breath, but I was feeling the chill. I buried my hands in my pants pockets and walked up Broadway, where, for fifty bucks—maybe my *last* fifty—I convinced a taxi driver with a Ukrainian accent to switch off his off-duty light.

I started to give him the firm's cross streets—"Seventh and . . ." but stopped myself. It was time to lose the tuxedo. We headed up Broadway to Fifty-seventh and then east to my apartment at Sutton Place. The driver waited with the meter running—he should have worked for Cool Cash—as I hurried into the building.

"Mr. Cantella!" the doorman called.

"Gotta hurry," I said as I punched the call button for the elevator again and again.

"Delivery here for you, sir. Courier brought it by an hour ago."

"I'll get it later, Juan."

" 'Urgent' marked all over it," he said, walking over and handing it to me.

I grabbed it as the bell chimed and the elevator doors parted. I swiped my security card and punched twenty-six. The doors closed, and I inspected what Juan had given me. It was the size of a FedEx envelope, but it was from a local courier service—probably delivered by one of those maniacs on bicycles who pedaled as if they got paid extra for bumping off pedestrians in crosswalks. I had one eye on the numbers over the elevator doors blinking with each passing floor—fourteen, fifteen, sixteen—as I found the zip tab on the package and pulled it.

There was a sudden flash of red and yellow, and I wasn't sure if the package flew from my hands or if I had thrown it to the floor. The elevator stopped immediately, and the alarm sounded. I was stunned for a moment, then smelled smoke. My sleeve was on fire, and flames were at my feet. I ripped off my jacket and stomped on it and the package in a frantic effort to extinguish the flames. I was winning, but barely. The package seemed to contain some kind of substance that burned with resilience. I smothered it with my jacket until the flames died, but the smoke continued to thicken even after the fire was finally out. It had a chemical odor, and my hands were stinging from the burn. Breathing was nearly impossible in the smoke-filled elevator.

"Are you okay in there?" the voice on the intercom asked.

The car wasn't moving, and I felt on the verge of succumbing to the smoke. I grabbed the seam between the doors and pulled as hard as I could. At first the doors didn't budge, but on the second try, they separated—not enough for me to climb out of the car to safety, but at least I could stick my nose and mouth out into the shaft and breathe.

"I need help!" I yelled.

"We're on our way!" the response came.

I stood there with my face in the crack between the metal doors. I was light-headed but refused to let myself pass out. My focus was purely on survival, but as I caught my breath, Stanley Brewer's words came back to me.

"When the motive is revenge, you never really know when—if ever—they are going to call it even."

I cast my eyes downward, peering into the dark elevator shaft below.

"Not good," I told myself. "This is definitely not good."

10

I could have been killed.

The thought was sinking in as I stood outside the closed door to Eric Volke's office. The president had the largest corner office on a highly secured floor that was reserved for nine of Saxton Silvers' most senior executives. Visitors knew they were in the right place as soon as the elevator doors opened: They could smell the flowers. Roses, calla lilies, crepe myrtle, and other assortments were abundant and fresh every day, a two-hundred-thousand-dollar line item in the firm's annual operating budget. An extravagance, to be sure, particularly since no more than two or three executives were actually in the office on a typical day. Today obviously wasn't typical. It wasn't even nine o'clock and the place was buzzing.

"He's on the phone," said Nancy, Eric's assistant.

Of course he was. Eric Volke off the phone was like Tiger Woods off the golf course. "I'll wait," I said.

I took a seat on the leather sofa, and suddenly I had to catch my breath.

Damn, I really could have been killed.

Things were moving so fast. I hadn't really processed how close I'd come to burning alive inside an elevator. My hand was still stinging and red. I had decided not to go to the emergency room, even though that flaming package had probably given me a second-degree burn. I had bigger problems.

As I waited, I wondered how much more harm the anonymous sender had intended.

My cell rang, reminding me that the wheels of commerce were still turning. I had to cancel today's trip to Chicago, where I was supposed to consult with a group of real estate lawyers, bankers, and architects to make sure their multiuse building qualified as green. It was a nine-figure deal put together by our Investment Banking Division, and by missing a key meeting I ran the risk of some engineer making a decision that would throw the whole thing out of LEED compliance—no more green stamp of approval for the socially responsible class of investors I was trying to make richer. One successful green project had a way of blossoming into more, so it would hurt to lose this one, but not nearly as much as losing my entire personal portfolio.

I checked the call, let it go to voice mail, and peered through the beveled glass door. Eric was pacing from one end of his silk Sarouk rug to the other, speaking into the headset of his hands-free phone. The signs of stress were all over his face.

Eric was my mentor, the man who had hired me out of business school. Two years ago, when ditching Wall Street and changing careers had seemed like a good idea, it was Eric who'd convinced the firm to let me split my time between production and management. It sounded like two jobs, but it was more like twenty. In theory, putting Saxton Silvers' Green Division on the map meant training investment advisors across the country to "think green," but all the training in the world wasn't going to convince them to make *less* money for the pension funds, retirees, and other investors who counted on the brilliant minds at Saxton Silvers to maximize their returns. Expanding "green" beyond charitable trusts and other special investor groups that were either required or predisposed to go green meant assembling and supervising an investment strategy team like no other, and then traveling across the globe to identify and nail down socially responsible opportunities that would actually make money—*lots* of money. "*Show them*—don't tell them—that green belongs in their portfolio," was Eric's charge to me. His own career had soared since then, and for the past thirteen months he'd served as president of Saxton Silvers. Subprime fallout had made the last three hell.

"Does he know I'm here?" I asked his assistant.

"Yes. It'll be just a few minutes more. Mr. Volke wants to see you as soon as he hangs up."

I returned to my seat, and my phone buzzed again. It was Mallory, who was still at the Pierre Hotel. This was the third time she'd speed-dialed me since I'd called to tell her about "a little mishap" in the elevator.

"Why is there a security guard outside my door?" she asked.

I could hear the strain in her voice, and I tried to reassure her. "Honey, it's like I explained earlier: The lawyer thinks somebody might be trying to even an old score with me. It's better to be safe than sorry, so I asked the firm to arrange for a bodyguard."

"Michael, you're not telling me everything. Juan called over here from the front desk to see if I needed a ride home. According to him, everyone in our building is talking about the package that burst into flames and almost burned you alive in the elevator. The FBI was even there."

It had been a mistake not to tell Mallory the whole story, but my intentions had been good. "I'm sorry. I didn't want to freak you out. I've already talked with the FBI, and the security guard outside your door is just a precaution. This is going to be okay."

"How can you say that? Somebody tried to kill you!"

"Nobody was trying to kill me. Even the FBI said so."

"What?"

"It was just a stunt. The only reason it was dangerous was because I happened to open the package inside the elevator, where the smoke got to me. There was no way the sender knew where I was going to open it."

"Well, I suppose that's true. But it could have killed you. And whatever it was, it sure wasn't a love note."

"You're right. Someone is definitely trying to scare us."

"And doing a damn fine job of it. This is all too crazy. Why is this happening?"

"We don't know yet. But we have the best of the best working on it. I'm meeting with Eric as soon as— wait. He just got off the phone. I have to go, okay?"

"Call me just as soon as you know anything more."

I promised I would and hung up.

Nancy opened the glass doors and escorted me into the president's office. Eric was a handsome man with a touch of gray hair at the temples, the strong handshake of a former Olympic rower (Munich '72), and impeccable taste in custom-tailored suits from Hong Kong. Decorating the walls of his spacious office were a dozen large underwater photographs that he had taken while scuba diving the most spectacular reefs in the world. He was the one senior manager who consistently took the time to talk one-on-one with up-and-comers like me to make sure we weren't getting too wound up and heading toward burnout—which was amazing, given the constant pressure he worked under. He was president of an institution that derived 40 percent of its annual revenue and 70 percent of its profit from its most risky and volatile line of business: trading and investing. Even in bull markets, the firm's trading desk spent forty days a year operating in the red. In other words, Saxton Silvers' Investment Banking Division could arrange the biggest deals in town, its Asset Management Division could manage client portfolios with precision, and one boneheaded call by a single group of traders could still land the entire firm in the toilet.

This morning, the stress had tightened its grip on Eric's facial muscles beyond normal. Before he could even try to flash a semblance of a smile and greet me, he was on another phone call and speaking into the headset. He motioned for me to sit on the couch by the window. Listening to Eric, I quickly realized that he was talking to our CEO, who, as usual for this time of year, was in Palm Beach. It was the first time I'd witnessed Eric in what appeared to be the financial equivalent of code blue. He spoke clipped, rapid-fire sentences into his headset.

"As of this morning cash reserves were at twenty-nine billion," Eric said. "I've checked with the finance desk, the repo desk, the treasurer and asked each of them point-blank—has anyone heard of any margin calls from our major lenders? No. A trade gone bad? No. Anything out of the normal course? Across the board the answer was absolutely not. No problems."

The call lasted another two or three minutes, and it was abundantly clear that my identity theft and personal financial problems were not on the president's radar. Eric ended the call by ripping off his headset and throwing it on the floor. He was seething, apparently in desperate need of a punching bag. But he was the ultimate multi-tasker, never missing anything out of the ordinary.

"What the hell happened to your hand?"

I looked down and saw it was turning lobster red. I told him quickly about the package.

"Shit like that happens when people lose money. We've had nuts walk into branch offices and start shooting. Be careful. Did you call the police?"

"Sonya's got the FBI on it," I said. "But this is just the latest in a much larger problem."

"No shit," he said, and suddenly we were no longer talking about me. "Biggest financial crisis Saxton Silvers has faced in its hundred-fifty-seven-year history, and I can't get our CEO to cancel his tee time and deal with it."

I said nothing. I knew by now when to shut up and let him process his anger. Finally he looked at me and said, "It's going to hit the fan today—huge."

"What's wrong?"

Eric went to the window and looked off into the distance. The morning sun gave a warm glow to the new leaves and blossoms in Central Park, confirming that April showers really do bring May flowers. Eric seemed oblivious to the spectacular view, still stuck in the icy grip of winter.

He said, "The plan had been to hold the bad news until after the close of trading today. But it leaked. Nothing we can do now but watch the big board and hold on to our asses."

"How bad is it?" I asked.

He shook his head and said, "Another subprime write down."

I swallowed hard. At the start of the housing slump last autumn, Eric had been forced to confirm a leak to the media that Saxton Silvers would burn $1.6 billion of its cash reserves to bail out two of its wholly owned hedge funds that were on the brink of bankruptcy from subprime losses. The firm still managed to report a profit of $9.3 billion for the year, even after payment of $16.5 billion in compensation and benefits.

"How big is this one?" I asked.

Eric turned and looked at me. "Twenty-two."

The number hit me like a five iron to the forehead. "I assume you don't mean million."

"If only," he said with a mirthless chuckle.

It was a staggering sum, but it was what happened when mortgage originators linked up with an unregulated Wall Street—two wires you really don't want to cross. The irony was that since 9/11, most of the federal dollars that had gone toward regulation of financial institutions had been redirected to Homeland Security. Now, in the absence of that regulation, Saxton Silvers was writing down another $22 billion in losses—nearly half the entire annual budget for Homeland Security.

"Is it all subprime?" I asked.

"Every penny."

Eric turned away again and looked out the window. His gaze swept across Midtown from Madison to

Seventh Avenue, where in turn he could literally see the shining world headquarters of Bear Stearns and then Lehman Brothers. Sandwiched between the two, painted on the side of a building, was a big blue-and-white ad for AIG.

"And who the hell knows where it really ends?" he said.

11

Chuck Bell got to work early—eight hours before he usually checked in for his talk-and-analysis program, *Bell Ringer*, the top-rated television show on Financial News Network.

"Morning, Chrissie," he said on his way through the FNN lobby.

Bell called the receptionist Chrissie only because everyone knew that he hated to be called anything but Christopher. Bell continued through the lobby, slowing only to rub the hoof on a miniature replica of the famous seven-thousand-pound bronze sculpture of a charging bull that sits in the Financial District two blocks from the New York Stock Exchange. Bulls are good on Wall Street. Bears are bad. The financial world is big on animal references, most of which come from the nineteenth-century London Stock Exchange, including "lame duck," which originally meant a debtor who couldn't pay his debts.

This morning, Bell was poised to break a story that would turn plenty of bull riders into lame ducks in the classic sense.

Bell had made his mark as a hugely successful hedge-fund manager, and then he retired at the age of thirty-seven to pursue a second career in journalism. His first show on FNN—a serious attempt at market analysis—was a total flop. His research was suspect, his predictions were usually wrong, and the "nice-guy" demeanor the network foisted upon him just didn't fit. Bell had been notorious for his temper in the business world, and finally the geniuses at FNN realized that he came across as someone who knew what he was talking about only when shouting angrily at the top of his lungs. They renamed the show *Bell Ringer*, created a set that looked more like a boxing ring than the stock exchange, and let Bell just be himself. The show was an instant hit. "Suze Orman meets Jerry Springer," critics called it. Viewers especially loved his stunts— like the time Bell rolled up his shirtsleeves, pulled on a pair of boxing gloves, and beat the living crap out of two guys dressed up as Smokey and Yogi the last time the market went from bull to bear. Whenever something good happened—a stock catching fire, or a bear hitting the canvas—it drew the same reaction from the host:

"That's a Bell Ringer!" he would shout.

Normally Bell's show didn't air until five P.M., but today's big news was happening before breakfast. Bell wanted a piece of the story in real time.

"Go home, Chuck."

Bell turned to find Rosario Reynolds standing two feet away from him. Rosario was the female half of FNN's popular morning duo—the young, energetic, and gorgeous counterpart to the stodgy old Wall Street fat cat who, bloggers said, couldn't keep his dirty-old-man eyes off her breasts.

"Rrrrrosario," Bell said, trilling the *R* for added annoyance. "How's my international superstar this morning?"

"Back off, Bell. If you think you're going on the air this morning to scoop the Saxton Silvers news, dream on. Roger and I are live in ten minutes."

"Rosario, Rosario," he said with a condescending shake of the head. "Don't you know that at FNN the Money Honey is always the last to know?"

"This Money Honey has a bigger set of balls than you do. So like I said: Back off. This story is mine."

"You don't have a story."

"I broke it this morning. Another twenty-two billion in subprime write-downs."

"That's not the story," he said, smiling thinly. "That's the tip of the iceberg."

Her eyes narrowed. "What do you know?"

He laughed way too hard, then snagged an assistant producer as she was trying to sneak past the two clashing stars in the hallway.

"Sandra," said Bell, "how are we coming on the Palm Beach connection?"

Sandra checked her clip board. "Shooting for nine forty, maybe nine forty-five at the latest."

"That's during my show!" said Rosario

The assistant producer hurried away without a word. Rosario shoved Bell so hard that his shoulder blades bumped against the wall.

"What are you trying to pull?" she said sharply.

"I'm not *trying* to do anything. It's done. FNN is bumping you for a special edition of *Bell Ringer.*"

"That's not fair! I worked hard on this story."

"Aww," he said, patting her head. "Poor Money Honey."

She knocked his hand away. "You're such an asshole."

"Thank you."

"I am *not* going to let this happen," she said.

"You don't have a choice," said Bell. "If these sub-prime write downs create the kind of liquidity problems that people are talking about, this could be the beginning of the end for one of the oldest investment banks on Wall Street. But all you've got are rumors. I've got a source."

She gave him an assessing look. "You're lying."

"Maybe I am. Maybe I'm not."

"I'll have your ass if you bump my show and don't have someone on the inside."

He smiled thinly. "Under normal circumstances, I might be worried. But you're overlooking one crucial fact, Rosario."

"What?"

He leaned closer, as if to share a secret. "There really is no adult supervision at FNN."

12

The thumb and index finger on my left hand were starting to blister. I didn't think I needed a doctor, but it hurt enough to make me reconsider the sender's agenda. Maybe the FBI was wrong. Maybe it wasn't just a warning.

Maybe he did want to see me dead.

I was still in Eric's office waiting for a chance to fill him in on my situation, and he was still on the phone talking through his headset. He suddenly stopped pacing long enough to grab the remote control from his desk and switch on the flat screen that was mounted on the wall above the wet bar. Like everyone else on Wall Street, Eric's television was pre-set to FNN. The only thing worse than a business news network spreading rumors was being the only financial player in New

York who hadn't heard them. Chuck Bell was on the air, which caused me to do a double take. I'd been awake all night and my internal clock was off, but I was pretty sure it was just coming up on nine-thirty A.M., not Bell's regular time slot.

"Good morning, all you mavericks and moneymakers," he said, his usual greeting. "And welcome to the second half hour of this special edition of *Bell Ringer*."

The familiar *ding-ding-ding-ding* of the NYSE opening and closing bell pulsated over the television, followed by a streaming banner at the bottom of the screen that proclaimed the reason for the special edition of Bell's show:

LIQUIDITY PROBLEMS AT SAXTON SILVERS?

It was classic FNN: report something outrageous and potentially libelous to grab the viewers' attention, and then put a question mark after it to keep from being sued.

Eric was red faced with anger. "Bell, you son of a bitch."

Bell continued on the air. "Rumors, rumors, rumors. Such a vicious thing on Wall Street."

"Then why do you start them?" Eric shouted at the screen.

Bell said, "We here at FNN are dedicated to bringing you only the facts. Unfortunately, the facts have investors, lenders, and players at every corner of the financial world nervous about one of the most prestigious institutions on Wall Street: the investment banking firm Saxton Silvers."

Eric took a seat, glancing nervously back and forth from the television to the NYSE ticker that streamed across the wall behind his desk. As always, trading had started at nine-thirty A.M., and we were keeping an eye on the price of Saxton Silvers' stock.

"Here is what we know as trading begins this morning," said Bell.

"God help us," said Eric.

"Fact: Saxton Silvers reported last fall that a write-down of one-point-six billion in subprime losses would stop the bleeding. Fact: FNN has confirmed that Saxton Silvers will announce another twenty-two billion in subprime losses later today."

Bell paused, and Eric looked at me, as if to will Bell to stop right there. It was merely a pregnant pause, however, and Bell proceeded to do what he did best, throw gasoline on smoldering embers.

"The question becomes: Can Saxton Silvers take a hit of this magnitude to its capital reserves? Is this latest write-down of twenty-two billion dollars really the end of the downward spiral? Why should investors think so when management told us six months ago that one-point-six billion was the real number? Could Saxton Silvers face charges from regulatory authorities for misleading investors about the full extent of its worthless mortgage-backed securities? Rightly or wrongly, can multibillion-dollar class actions alleging fraud and mismanagement be far behind?"

Bell kept talking, but I was watching Eric, who truly looked to be on the verge of an aneurysm.

"Somebody needs to shut that lunatic up," said Eric.

Bell said, "Joining me now from Palm Beach is Saxton Silvers chief executive officer Stuart Wyle. What better person is there to address these issues? Sir, thank you very much for joining us on *Bell Ringer*."

"Uh, you're very welcome."

I couldn't help but cringe. Bell had just laid out a case of financial Armageddon for Saxton Silvers, and pictured on television screens everywhere was our fearless leader speaking from the golf course at the Breakers Hotel, his nose shiny with sunscreen and a plaid golf cap atop his head. He must have looked ridiculous to anyone who wasn't within three blocks of tony Worth Avenue.

"Mr. Wyle, let me begin by asking you this: Why are traders dumping their shares in Saxton Silvers?"

"No one's dumping anything," said Wyle.

"Sir, it is now nine forty-six A.M. Eastern time, and in just sixteen minutes of trading your stock has dropped from one hundred ninety per share to one hundred thirty."

"Because of you!" Eric said to the screen.

Our CEO, fortunately, kept his cool. "The firm's capital reserves are more than sufficient to cover the write downs that we will announce later today. The market will correct itself, and the price will come back just as soon as these silly rumors stop."

"If that's the case, sir, then why are Saxton Silvers' most talented people dumping their stock in the firm?"

"That's ridiculous. I don't have any idea what you're talking about."

"Well, let me give you an example. Michael Cantella has twice been named Saxton Silvers' investment advisor of the year, correct?"

"I believe that's true."

Eric and I looked at each other, equally confused.

"He also holds the title of vice president, as head of your Green Division?"

"He's certainly one of our most outstanding young talents."

"No argument there," said Bell. "He's appeared a half dozen times on FNN, including twice on my own show—which, by the way, normally appears Monday through Friday at five P.M., so viewers, please set your TiVo."

"And your point is?" said Wyle.

"Simple," said Bell—and he seemed to be struggling not to smile. "My sources tell me that just yesterday, Mr. Cantella liquidated his entire personal holdings in Saxton Silvers—nearly two million dollars' worth of stock and options."

On screen, our CEO looked stunned. Across the room, Eric looked even more stunned. I stared at the screen with my mouth hanging open.

Bell said, "Sir, what about that?"

"I—I can't comment, except to say that it sounds like more silly rumors."

"It's no rumor," said Bell, holding up a document. "I have here—"

My cell rang, and I recognized the incoming number: It was Sonya, the general counsel.

"Be in my office in two minutes," Sonya said, without even a hello.

"Michael, what the hell is going on?" said Eric.

"I can explain," I told him, then went back to the phone. "Sonya, I'm with Eric."

"I'll be right there," she said, and hung up.

"I'm listening," said Eric.

"This is not what it looks like," I said, taking a deep breath to start my story.

But Eric was now staring past me in disbelief. On FNN, Bell was going to a commercial—but not before the network flashed a new BREAKING NEWS banner on the screen: SAXTON SILVERS "ADVISOR OF THE YEAR" DUMPS ALL S&S HOLDINGS.

My burned hand was stinging worse by the minute, and echoing in my ear once again was Stanley Brewer's warning about the type of work I did, the enemies I'd surely made—enemies I didn't even know I had.

"That's the thing about revenge," I said, watching the screen.

"Revenge?" said Eric. "Who said anything about revenge?"

"No one, forget it," I said, but the lawyer's words were still ringing.

You never know when—if ever—they are going to call it even.

13

Eric didn't often make me sweat, but he wasn't wearing his mentor hat this morning. It was hard to believe that twelve hours earlier I had been celebrating my birthday with scores of guests—including Eric—who probably thought I was one of the luckiest guys on the planet. Not one of them would have traded places with me now.

"Stuart is going to call me as soon as he putts out on the next hole," said Eric, only slightly facetious about our CEO's priorities, "so I need some straight talk: Is there any truth to what Chuck Bell just said about selling your stock?"

Eric had only a rough idea of my identity theft problems, so I laid out the details as quickly as I could. Sonya arrived just as I was getting to the FNN report:

"In typical FNN style," I said, "the report is technically accurate, but it's grossly misleading. True, all of my stock in Saxton Silvers was liquidated, but it was liquidated along with all of my other holdings—not by me, but by an identity thief who has taken everything I own and moved the cash into a secret offshore account."

I expected Sonya to jump in and second my explanation, but she was silent. Not merely silent. She seemed skeptical.

Eric said, "Is there something you'd like to add, Sonya?"

"I'm concerned," she said.

My stomach churned. I didn't know where this was headed, but I suddenly recalled that it was within Saxton Silvers' protocol to fire someone so long as there were more than two people in the room. At least I still had clients to go with me.

Thank God I didn't drink the Kool-Aid.

"Concerned about what?" I asked.

She came to the edge of her chair and leaned toward Eric, hands folded atop her knees. It was her I'm-talking-to-the-president-and-only-to-the-president posture.

"Here's the thing," said Sonya. "Michael's in management—an officer of the company—with access to inside information. He sold his shares the day before the firm publicly announced another twenty-two billion dollars in subprime write-downs. That could trigger an SEC investigation for insider trading."

"But *I* didn't sell anything. An identity thief liquidated my account and moved the money offshore."

"But if I'm the SEC, your explanation raises an obvious question: Who controls the secret Cayman Islands account? In other words, are you operating behind a cleverly crafted financial and corporate shell game to avoid going to jail for illegal insider trading?"

"I hear what you're saying," said Eric, shaking his head. "But that's a very cynical view."

Sonya said, "I'm not making any accusations, but from a regulator's standpoint, the timing of the sale and resultant profit seem a little too convenient."

I checked the TV on the wall. The audio was muted, but Bell was still on the air and the breaking-news banner proclaimed that Saxton Silvers' stock was down another thirty dollars per share—about ninety dollars for the day.

"Do the math," said Sonya. "How many shares did you hold, Michael?"

"About ten thousand and change."

"So the difference between selling yesterday and selling today . . . about a million dollars, right?"

Her theory couldn't have been further from the truth, but the implication still gave me chills.

"Look, I didn't do anything wrong," I said. "I have no idea who accessed my account, and I have no clue where that money is headed. Why would I use the firm's outside counsel to enlist the help of the FBI if I was the one behind the scheme?"

"As I recall," said Sonya, "hiring Cool Cash and going to the FBI was my idea."

Her remark made me bristle. "What are you trying to say?"

"The fact that the firm called the FBI won't stop the regulators from being highly suspicious about the timing of your 'identity theft.'"

I showed her my hand. "What about the package I got this morning? You and Brewer told me not to talk to the FBI, and I talked to them anyway when they came to check out the elevator. Is that what a crook does when he's hiding something?"

She didn't answer.

"The fact is," I said, "I didn't know about the additional subprime write-down that was going to be announced today. Eric just told me about it ten minutes ago." I glanced at my mentor. He looked ashen. "Isn't that right, Eric?"

He breathed in and out, staring at the television.

"Eric?"

"I just did the math for myself," he said. "I lost two-hundred-forty million in the last forty-five minutes."

I ran a hand through my hair. "This is insane."

"It also changes things," said Sonya. "It no longer seems appropriate for the firm to have its outside counsel dealing with the FBI on your behalf."

"Why not?"

"Conflict of interest. Saxton Silvers shouldn't use its lawyers to represent someone who might be accused of illegally trading its stock."

"My life savings are disappearing deeper and deeper into the international banking system with every passing minute and you want me to change lawyers now?"

"The FBI has already been alerted. Agents are on the case. There's really nothing more for you to do on that front. It's only a question of follow-up."

"Now you're pissing me off, Sonya."

"Calm down, Michael," said Eric.

"No," I said. "I've done nothing wrong, and without the proper follow-up, I could lose everything!"

"We all could," said Sonya, "if we don't get our hands around the bigger crisis."

Eric's gaze drifted back toward the television screen. "Three hundred million," he said, muttering in disbelief. "Now I'm down three hundred million dollars."

There was a knock on the door frame that rattled the glass. Before Eric could ask who it was, the door flew open. Kent Frost burst into the room. Eric's assistant had him by the arm, having failed to keep him from entering unannounced.

"Eric, I need you right now," Kent said.

Kent Frost was a few years older than me, but we'd started at the firm around the same time and had competed for Eric's praise for almost ten years. Each year in December, without fail, Kent made it known throughout the firm that his annual bonus dwarfed mine. Frost ran the Structured Products Division, and his specialty was collaterized debt obligations made with subprime mortgages. He was the shameless recipient of the award given at the banquet I had gladly missed for my surprise birthday party.

"What is it?" asked Eric.

"A new wrinkle," said Frost.

"Don't tell me," I said, trying not to scoff. "You left off a zero in the twenty-two billion?"

Kent glared. Up until six months ago, he had at least tried to hide his contempt for me and anyone else who disagreed with him. That all changed in October, when I aired my view that with one out of every five mortgages in America being "subprime," the whole market was a ticking time bomb—another one of those "Fonzie schemes," as Papa called them. Admittedly, criticizing the business activities of a sister division was overstepping my authority, but if the subprime guys refused to rein themselves in, someone had to blow the whistle.

"Eric," said Frost, "this is private." He meant it was not for my ears. Eric nodded.

"Holy shit," said Sonya. She was looking at her BlackBerry.

"What now?" asked Eric.

"Our stock was at ten times normal volume in the first hour of trading. At this pace, we could be looking at seventy million shares by the end of the day."

Eric massaged the bridge of his nose, as if staving off a migraine. "One thing at a time. Kent, take a seat. Michael, we'll talk later."

Frost entered. I started toward the door, then stopped. The firm's subprime crisis had to be the president's priority, but I needed someone to focus on a problem we could actually fix—mine.

"One more thing," I said.

The three of them waited, but I paused. That blowhard Chuck Bell had told the world that the Saxton Silvers' investment advisor of the year violated every securities regulation imaginable to cash out before our stock went into free fall. The market was now tanking, and, when the dust cleared, it was entirely possible that none of us would have anything left but our reputations. I had the right to clear mine—to tell the truth that my identity was stolen. End of story.

"What is it, Michael?"

Eric was definitely feeling the stress. Now was not the time to ask for permission. Later, I'd ask for forgiveness.

"Nothing," I said. "We'll stay in touch on this."

14

I came to my senses in the elevator. Of course I wanted to take my case to the airwaves and give *everybody* hell, not just Chuck Bell. But I also still wanted to have a job at the end of the day.

Keep your cool, Cantella.

It was the Kent Frost effect. The guy just had a way of setting me off.

Fortunately, our paths didn't often cross. The subprime alchemists worked in their own building, three modified apartments on Manhattan's Upper East Side. The official name was the Structured Products Division, but everyone called it the CDO factory— collateralized debt obligations. I'd gone there only once, last October, just to check things out. Luckily, Frost had been out when I arrived. I got thirty minutes alone with his financial engineer—a Twinkie-eating, twentysomething geek named Wayne who spent every waking hour staring at trading screens. It positively thrilled Wayne to find someone willing to listen to him talk about what he did all day long. We went straight to the latest data, and Wayne gave me a primer on the sixteen million subprime mortgages in Frost's CDO factory.

Frost had his suppliers all over the country: banks and mortgage companies that loaned money to people like that Bahamian taxi driver Ivy and I had met in Miami—borrowers with credit scores under 500 and no money for a down payment, no income to make their mortgage payment, and no business having a credit card, let alone a half-million dollars or more in subprime mortgages. The lenders didn't worry about it because they immediately sold those toxic mortgages to Frost and others who pooled all of them together into mortgage-backed securities. Frost didn't worry about it because the theory was that not *all* the mortgages would fail, and Frost spread the risk even wider, taking little slices from lots of different mortgage-backed securities to create CDOs, which he sold to really smart investors like insurance companies and pension-fund managers. The smart investors didn't worry about it because they controlled the global pool of money—

about seventy trillion dollars—and they were earning 10 percent returns instead of the measly 1 percent that the Fed was offering on T-bills and other safe investments. If the really smart investors wouldn't buy them, Frost still didn't worry, because little towns in places like Norway or Iceland would. They were always looking for "safe" investments, and Frost had no trouble getting the Triple-A stamp of approval from the rating agencies, who based their ratings on mathematical formulas that assumed home values would continue to rise 8 percent annually in perpetuity. That was like an insurance company writing life insurance policies based on actuarial tables that assumed the insured would never get sick, never get old, never die. All I could figure was that those rating geniuses had been under the influence of triple shots of tequila.

"I'm getting a little nervous," Wayne had told me, "because we're starting to see something we've never seen before. Borrowers defaulting on their very first payment. It's weird."

It wasn't weird. It was the burst of the housing bubble. Taxi drivers in Miami who counted on flippin' one flippin' condo to pay the flippin' mortgage on their next flippin' condo suddenly couldn't flip a flippin' thing. I started to explain this to Wayne, but that was the moment Frost returned to the CDO factory, physically pushed me aside, and chewed out Wayne for showing me the data.

"Get the fuck out of here!" Frost had told me.

The "conversation" had gotten much uglier than that, ending with me charging out of the factory and swearing on my mother's grave that I was "not going to stand by and watch one greedy son of a bitch fly the plane into the side of a mountain."

It may not have been the perfect metaphor, but with Saxton Silvers stock in the tank this morning on the heels of yet another subprime write-down, it just about summed things up.

"Forty . . . two," said the mechanical voice in the elevator.

That was my floor, but I decided to stay in the car and pushed nineteen. Sonya had pulled Cool Cash off the trail of my stolen money, but she'd put no restriction on my using the firm's internal security force. This was a sensible application of the "Better to ask for forgiveness" rule.

"Going . . . down," the elevator voice said.

As the doors were closing, I spotted a familiar old man in the reception area. I couldn't believe my eyes, but I hit the Open button too late, and the elevator started downward. A flurry of button punching brought the car to a stop. I got off on forty and ran up two flights of stairs, but the reception area was now empty. I hurried down the hall to my office and found him standing at the window, taking in the view of Midtown.

"Papa?"

He turned. "Surprise!"

I went and gave him a hug. "What are you doing here?"

"We've come to celebrate your happy birthday, of course."

Papa never celebrated just birthdays; it was always "happy birthdays," as if the two words were a single, inseparable noun.

"Got here for free, too," he said. "Remember those frequent-flier passes you gave us?"

"You were supposed to use those for a trip to Europe."

"Been there once before. Ended up having a pretty miserable time at a beach called Omaha."

I heard the toilet flush in my private bathroom, and Nana stepped out. It was her first stop wherever she went: big heart, small bladder.

I gave her a kiss, and the three of us shared a group hug. It had been three months since I'd last visited them in Florida, the longest stretch in years. They never seemed to change, which was what I loved about them. The bruise on Papa's forehead, however, was definitely new.

"What happened there?"

"Ah, nothin'."

Nana busted him. "Your grandfather isn't seeing so well at night lately. Refuses to get his eyes checked. Walked straight into a lamppost."

"Ouch. That had to hurt."

He leaned closer, as if to let me in on a secret. "It's all about attitude, dummy."

We shared a smile. He truly lived by that creed. When throat cancer left him with just one-quarter of a single vocal cord, he had to train himself to speak in a voice that no longer sounded like his own. Naturally, Papa had been the first to joke about sounding like Marlon Brando in *The Godfather*.

"So cancel your noon appointments," he said. "It's your happy birthday, and we're taking you to dinner."

"You mean lunch?"

"No, I mean dinner. When you get to be my age, dinner is at noon."

My heart sank. For the first time in my life they had pulled off a surprise like this—and they couldn't have picked a worse day.

"Papa, I'm really sorry, but—"

"No excuses. Your grandmother and I are taking you to the finest Italian restaurant in New York City."

In my book, that meant Il Molino, but Papa was the kind of guy who could win the lottery and still agonize over buying a new pair of shoes every two years. On a day like today, it made me realize why they called his the greatest generation.

"We're doing Sal's Place," he said. "Marie, give Michael his happy birthday gift."

Nana pulled a teddy bear from the shopping bag on her arm. SAL'S PAL was stitched on its big belly, and when Papa poked it, the bear sang out like a mechanical Dean Martin: *"When the moon hits your eye like a big pizza pie—"*

"That's amore!" sang Papa.

It was suddenly impossible to breathe a word to him about my identity theft. "Papa, I promise we'll do lunch together, even if we have to order in from Sal's and eat here in the office. But the next two hours are crazy for me."

"You do what you gotta do," he said—one of those expressions that really did make him sound like the Godfather.

My phone chimed with an e-mail from one of my analysts. "Check out FNN," it read. A sense of dread came over me as I switched on the television in my office.

"Wonderful," said Nana, "I can watch my soaps."

"Uh . . . exactly," I said, handing her the remote. I promised to return as soon as possible, then bolted down the hall to the nearest conference room. FNN was playing for a handful of staff who looked seriously worried.

"Is that Chuck Bell on the trading floor?" one of the secretaries asked.

It was. Chuck Bell had taken his show from the studio and was broadcasting live from the floor in the New York Stock Exchange. The commotion behind him naturally lent an air of excitement to "this special edition of *Bell Ringer*."

Another signature FNN banner scrolled across the bottom of the screen, the knife-to-the-heart update once again punctuated with the cover-your-ass question mark: "REPO LENDERS NOT RENEWING OVERNIGHT LOANS TO SAXTON SILVERS?"

"As I first reported in October," said Bell, "the internal crisis at Saxton Silvers is personified by two of the president's protégés, Michael Cantella and Kent Frost. It seems Cantella was talking in Volke's right ear while Frost had his left ear. It all came to a head early in November when a blast e-mail went out from the residential mortgage desk to the banking industry, announcing that Saxton Silvers was getting out of the subprime business. Sources tell me that Michael

Cantella was a major force behind that announcement, even though he had no direct role in the subprime business."

Bell was dead-on accurate—and I was beginning to get a little nervous about his "sources."

My cell rang. It was Eric from his office. He had me on speaker.

"You watching FNN?" he asked.

"Yes."

"I need you there."

"What?"

"That bastard Bell will try to corner one of our traders and get him to say something live and on the air that'll make this worse than it already is. I need somebody I can trust to make sure that doesn't happen."

I needed to meet with Saxton Silvers' director of security and—now that I didn't have a lawyer—do my own follow-up with the FBI.

"Bell's not allowed to interfere with the floor traders," I said, knowing immediately how lame that sounded.

"Well then, he'll fucking follow them to lunch. Damn it, Michael. All I need is someone I can count on to go downtown and stop Bell from pulling off an ambush."

"I'll do it," I heard Kent Frost say over the speaker. I didn't even know he was still there.

"No, *I'll* do it," I said.

"Good, keep me posted," said Eric.

He hung up, and as I hurried to the elevator, my cell rang again. It was Papa.

"Michael, you know I never pressure you, but Nana just noticed that these ten-percent-off coupons I got for Sal's are good for in-restaurant dining only."

"Papa, something's come up. I can't do lunch."

"Oh. Well, all right," said the Godfather. "You do what you gotta do."

The disappointment in his voice was far worse than my financial worries. "How about dinner?" I said.

"Sure. Sal's Place?"

The elevator doors opened, and as I entered the car I knew I was about to lose my signal. "No, not Sal's," I said.

"But—"

"Let me pick. It's my birthday, right?"

"Your *happy* birthday," he said. "Sure, you pick."

The elevator doors closed, and I lost the call. As I rode down, I probably should have been thinking about identity theft, burning envelopes, the firm in crisis, and Chuck Bell. Instead, I was thinking about Sal's Place.

Sal's had once been one of my favorite restaurants—mainly because of Papa. After my last visit, however, I had vowed never to return. I blamed my bad experience at the time on an unsettling exchange with a stranger. Now, given today's events, I was starting to wonder if anything was random.

It was the first week of November—coincidentally, two days after Saxton Silvers announced the end of its subprime business, the controversial blast e-mail that Chuck Bell had just resurrected on FNN. I was seated alone at a small table for two, waiting on an order of linguine with clam sauce, when the stranger sat down in the wooden chair across from me. I was pretty sure I had never seen him before, but I was certain of this:

I would never forget him.

"Another beautiful day in paradise," the man said.

It was a warm day for early November, and I was seated near the open French doors at the front of the restaurant. I looked up from the newspaper I'd been reading. A quick glance around the restaurant confirmed that there were plenty of open booths and tables—no apparent need to share with a stranger. That was strange enough, but it was his words that had taken me aback. *Another beautiful day in paradise.* That was what Papa always said as he headed out of the house for his morning walk.

"Do I know you?"

"You tell me," he said.

I looked at him carefully. He had piercing ebony eyes, and the dark complexion fit the hint of an accent I detected. It sounded Indian, though I knew from my business travels that it was difficult to generalize about a country that had twenty-nine different languages that counted more than a million native speakers. In any event, it was his appearance more than his voice that defined him. His build was that of a weight-lifting fanatic—someone who worked out not for the health benefits, but because he liked to intimidate. His hair was hidden beneath a black knit beanie, but the sideburn on the left side of his face was longer and thicker than the one on the right. A broad scar or some other deformity started at the right earlobe, continued under his jawbone, and disappeared somewhere beneath his black turtleneck sweater.

"I've never seen you before," I said.

He reached inside his coat pocket, pulled out his wallet, and removed a hundred-dollar bill. He flattened it out on the table, rather ceremoniously removing every last wrinkle. Then he held it over the glass votive on the table, not actually putting it in the candle's flame, but it was dangerously close.

"Watch," he said.

My gaze fixed on the crisp bill resting atop the glowing votive. A black circle emerged beside the image of Benjamin Franklin as the candle scorched the underside. A wisp of smoke appeared, and suddenly the yellow flame poked through the watermark. In another second, the bill was burning like dry tinder.

"It's a crime to burn money," he said, holding the flaming bill.

"Excuse me?"

"I just committed a crime," he said. "Burning money is a federal offense."

I watched him, not sure what to do, wondering if this guy was playing with a full deck.

"Are you going to turn me in?" he asked.

"I think you should leave."

"But I need to know," he said. "Are you going to turn me in?"

"Just beat it. I'm not going to turn you in."

"That's good," he said, rising. Then he tossed the remnants of the burned hundred-dollar bill on the table and said, "That makes you part of the cover-up."

I watched with curiosity as he turned and walked away, leaving me alone with the ashes.

15

Wall Street.

Midtown had been a comfortable home for Saxton Silvers since the destruction of its offices on 9/11, but actually standing before the New York Stock Exchange building and seeing the huge American flag draped over its massive stone columns never failed to get my pulse pounding. I was in a hurry, but I stopped for a moment to take it all in. History oozing from a concrete jungle of tall towers on narrow streets. Floor traders hustling back from lunch or the gym for the end-of-day frenzy. People everywhere, rushing with purpose.

And a seven-foot bear in a boxing ring.

"What the *hell?*" I said to myself.

The Exchange was actually on Broad Street, which was closed to cars. FNN had re-created the *Bell Ringer* set outside the building, complete with the signature boxing ring. Waiting "in the other corner" was a man dressed up like that lovable bear from *Jungle Book* who made "The Bare Necessities" one of Disney's most hummable tunes. Bell was still inside the building, but his plan clearly was to don his boxing gloves and beat the snot out of that poor sloth in the road-show version of *Bell Ringer*.

"You got a cigarette?" the bear asked as I passed.

Immediately I suspected a setup—a test question planted by FNN to see if the founder of Saxton Silvers' Green Division and chief proponent of investment in socially responsible companies supported Big Tobacco with his own nasty personal habit. I was officially paranoid.

"Sorry, dude," I said.

Security at the NYSE was tight, but I had clearance. I was emptying my pockets at the metal detector when my cell rang. I stepped out of line to take the call. It was Eric.

"Change of plans," he said. "We cut a deal with Bell."

"A deal?"

"He's been killing us for refusing to address the rumors, but if senior management responds, it only legitimizes them. Bell agreed to back off if we just give him someone to talk to."

"Like who?"

"You."

"*Me?*"

A minute ago I wanted to take it to Bell. But now I was afraid of what I might say to him.

"Listen carefully," said Eric. "You are not the firm's spokesperson on the subprime write-downs. But this nonsense about our former investment advisor of the year dumping his stock has to be stopped. Here's the plan: You go on the air with Bell, you tell him about the identity theft, and you make it clear that you're still bullish on Saxton Silvers. That's it. You got it?"

"Yeah."

"Michael, I need you to knock this out of the park. Understand?"

"Totally," I said.

"Good. Just keep it short. I'll be watching."

I made it through security as quickly as I could, and fifteen minutes later I walked onto the trading floor. The "Big Board" is a truly grand space, and even folks who know nothing about the market are impressed by the marble walls rising up seventy-two feet to an ornate gilt ceiling, two more dramatic walls of windows, and the famous skylight through which many a devastated trader has looked up to the heavens and asked, "Why me?" Most trading was done away from the floor these days, but the NYSE still did some of it the old-fashioned way, with traders gathering around posts to buy or sell in an open outcry auction. Even with the rise of electronic trading, it remains an icon of American capitalism, the source of countless images of despondent traders, palms to forehead, personifying the pain and tumult of Wall Street's slides.

I walked through a section of the floor known as "Jurassic Park," a place where older traders, many of whom started out as runners, rested and reminisced about that one golden year—they all claimed to have had one—in which they raked in a million bucks in commissions. I was headed for "Rodeo Drive," the corridor of elite trading posts for firms like Saxton Silvers leading up to the famed NYSE bell.

"Mr. Cantella?" a woman said, catching up to me.

I stopped, turned, and saw her FNN credentials hanging around her neck.

"You're on in five minutes," she said. "Mr. Bell told me to do your makeup."

I considered it, then reminded myself that my grandparents were in town. Papa had grown up on the south side of Chicago, stood in bread lines at age nine, and fought with the fair-haired kids in the neighborhood who had a problem with the fact that little Vincenzo's first and last name ended in a vowel. He just wouldn't understand makeup on his grandson.

"I'll pass this time," I said.

"Suit your shiny self."

Say that three times fast, Papa would have said. I just didn't have his gift for small talk—though no one could compete with the man who had managed to be on a first-name basis with every checkout girl at Publix a week after moving to Florida.

"Chuck's waiting," said Little Miss Anti-Shine. "I'll take you to him."

I followed her through the maze of trading posts, passing dozens of frenzied floor traders dressed in their mesh-backed jackets. I probably could have spotted a few friends, but I was busy gathering my thoughts on how to match wits with the one-and-only Chuck Bell, bear-slayer extraordinaire. Since Saxton Silver's first announcement of subprime losses in the fall, Bell had been on a rampage against the firm, predicting its demise. I knew it wouldn't be easy to confine our discussion to the sale of my own shares of Saxton Silvers stock. But I had to restrain myself. Eric had made it clear that I was not the firm's spokesman on subprime.

I need you to knock this out of the park, Michael.

News stations were once unheard of near the floor, but now they routinely did live broadcasts there during trading hours. Bell was more of a studio guy, though he seemed pretty comfortable seated on his stool in front of the busy Saxton Silvers trading post. It was a high-energy backdrop for his show, and I noted that the sellers outnumbered—and were outshouting—the buyers. On the stool beside Bell was Rosario Reynolds. I was glad to see her there. Both times I'd appeared on her show I was treated fairly. Maybe it was because I was the only guy on Wall Street who didn't call her Money Honey.

"All right, let's bring on our first guest," said Bell, speaking to the camera. "We've been talking about Saxton Silvers all morning, and here with us now in another *Bell Ringer* exclusive is Saxton Silvers' two-time investment advisor of the year, Michael Cantella."

I walked in front of the camera. There was no audience, no applause. But Bell did have his portable sound-effects machine. He held his microphone to it, and with the push of a button there was a loud *plop*—the sound of a rock dropping into a bucket of water.

Bell glanced over his shoulder at the trading screens and said, "That was the sound of Saxton Silvers stock dropping like a stone this morning."

I took a seat on the bar stool next to Reynolds. Bell punched another button. It was the sound of a toilet flushing. I almost checked to see if Nana and her peanut-size bladder had crashed the Exchange.

"Will that be the sound of Saxton Silvers stock in this afternoon's trading?" said Bell.

He hit the toilet-flushing button a second time. I tried to keep my composure, but it was quickly becoming apparent that, on the dignity scale, I had nothing on that poor slob in the bear suit out on Broad Street.

"Michael, thank you for coming. Now, let's look first at some numbers."

Bell launched right into a chart that showed my holdings of Saxton Silvers stock as of yesterday, the timing of the sale, the timing of Saxton Silvers' announced subprime write-downs—and the money I allegedly pocketed by selling my stock.

"Quite a nifty job of timing the market there, my friend."

"Well, you're leaving out one key fact," I said.

"Yes, yes, yes," he said dismissively. "The most convenient case of identity theft in the history of Wall Street. You claim that someone stole your identity and unloaded all of your stock in Saxton Silvers on the night before the stock went into free fall."

"Not just Saxton Silvers stock. All my holdings."

"And why would someone target you in that way?" he asked.

"Why do thieves target anyone? Because they can, I guess."

"Well, let's look at the broader context here. Just a couple of hours ago the CEO of Saxton Silvers was on my show—"

"*My* show," said Reynolds.

"Good one, Money Honey!" he said as he pressed the effects button to unleash a mock clanging of the NYSE bell. "That's a Bell Ringer!"

"Whatever," she said.

At that moment, I would have sworn that the "F" in FNN stood for freak show.

"Back to my point," said Bell. "Stuart Wyle was on the air this morning telling *me* that everything we have reported from our sources about Saxton Silvers—the liquidity problems, repo lenders cutting off overnight lending, novation problems, and on and on—those are all just vicious rumors."

Eric's admonition—*you're not the spokesman*—was buzzing in my ear. "I'm not here to talk about any of that," I said.

"I understand. But stay with me. Let's assume that people in the market are lying about the financial condition of Saxton Silvers. Let's assume that in the same twenty-four-hour period, Michael Cantella—the firm's two-time investment advisor of the year—is wiped out by an identity thief. Is there something afoot here?"

"I don't understand your question."

"Are you prepared to say here on this show today that there is some kind of financial assault on Saxton Silvers?"

"I'm not saying that."

"I think you are."

"You're saying it, not me."

"Is it possible?"

"Is what possible?"

"That there is some connection between the rumors about Saxton Silvers and your alleged identity theft."

"I can't speculate on that."

"Are you saying it's *not* possible?"

"Well, anything's possible but—"

"Aha!" said Bell, slapping his thigh. "Folks, you just heard it here on *Bell Ringer*—right from the floor of the New York Stock Exchange. Michael Cantella says there may be some financial conspiracy against Saxton Silvers. That's a Bell Ringer!"

"What? No, I didn't—" I started to say, but I was cut off by the sound of that damn pretend bell.

Ding, ding, ding, ding.

Bell checked the board again. "Perhaps someone out there has a serious interest in driving the value of the stock down fast—in 'murdering' Saxton Silvers virtually overnight. With the stock price already down as much as ninety dollars per share today, this supposed financial assassin is well on his way."

"I'm not the one who said—"

Bell cut me off with another slap of the effects button. This time it was the sound of a telephone ringing.

"It's for you, Michael," said Bell, pretending to talk on his cell. "It's Chicken Little. He wants his sky back."

I needed this to end—quickly.

"Chuck, I'm here to talk about identity theft."

"Yes, yes, of course. Let's put this Oliver Stone conspiracy stuff aside. And for the moment, let's just assume your claim is true. Here's the question I have for my viewers," he said, staring straight into the camera. "Why would any investor trust his money with a Wall Street investment bank whose fastest-rising star can't even come up with a hack-proof password for his own account?"

Reynolds grumbled. "Oh, come on."

"I'm serious," said Bell.

"Hackers can be very sophisticated," I said.

Bell said, "Investment banks are also supposed to be sophisticated."

"I'm working with the FBI and the firm's security director now to find out exactly what happened."

"Was your account password protected?"

"Chuck, now you're being silly," said Reynolds. "Of course it was protected. And I would bet my last dollar that Michael Cantella is not the kind of dummy who would use his phone number or his wife's birthday as a password."

I hesitated. It was nice to have Reynolds' support, but I didn't want to start talking about passwords on the air. "Let me just assure our clients that their investment portfolios are intact."

"Well, I hope so."

Bell hit another button. This one was the sound of screeching tires and a car wreck.

"That's enough crashing for one day," he said. "Michael, thank you for joining us. I'm not saying that we believe you, but we do thank you."

Had he offered his hand, I wouldn't have shaken it. But he simply moved on.

"And now, ladies and gentlemen, are you ready for the *Bell Ringer* main event?"

As I walked away, I could feel the stares of surrounding floor traders who'd seen the interview—and then they ran off with their sell orders. I was trying to think of what to say to Eric, but I could still hear Bell building up the Wall Street battle of the century.

"It's time for me to step outside and put another bear on the canvas!"

Cell phones weren't allowed on the trading floor, but mine was ringing just as soon as I exited through the revolving door and stepped outside to Broad Street. It was Eric.

"What the hell just happened to you?" he said.

"He was putting words in my mouth."

"It's *Chuck Bell.* You should have cut it off. That whole exchange was supposed to last two minutes, tops."

Two minutes? I didn't know he'd wanted it *that* short. "I'm sure I would have done better if I'd actually gotten to sleep last night."

"That's not going to cut it. We're in a financial crisis. There are people in this firm who are looking to point the finger at someone other than themselves."

He meant the structured-products people like Kent Frost. "I know."

"Now they'll say our stock dropped because Eric Volke let his fair-haired boy go on FNN, not because of a twenty-two-billion-dollar subprime nightmare."

"Which is ridiculous."

"They'll say it anyway. Michael, you've always had your own mind. When we invited you to join management, you bucked company policy and refused to give up your book of business. When subprime started to look ugly, you stepped over division lines and wrote me a damned convincing memo about it. I actually respect all that. But I'm one of the few who does. To some people, you're just trouble. And now I have to tell those same people that it was *my* idea to put you on the air."

I drew a breath. "I'm sorry."

"Me, too. Because I need to know who I can count on."

My hand was shaking as I gripped the phone. I'd let him down, but I could make it up to him. I was far less sure about redeeming myself on national television, about ever seeing my money again—or about surviving a second attack in an elevator.

Stop it. Don't freak.

"You can definitely count on me," I said.

He paused—and the silence killed me.

The call ended, and I was back on Broad Street. A crowd had gathered around the FNN boxing ring, and the TV cameras were in position. Bell had already rolled up his shirtsleeves and tied on his boxing gloves. A seven-foot bear waited in the center of the ring.

"*All righty,*" Bell shouted as he climbed through the ropes. "Let's see about those *bare* necessities!"

16

Rumsey Coolidge hadn't seen Michael Cantella in years. The man towering over Rumsey didn't believe him.

"I swear," said Rumsey, his bloodied face pressed to the floor. "I'm telling you the truth, mon."

Rumsey had returned to Harbor Island in a rainstorm. A five-day sail in the northern Bahamas had left him exhausted and annoyed at the way customers just didn't seem to tip their captain the way they used to—as if the weather was *his* fault. He'd climbed the front steps to his rented town house slowly, thinking only of a good night's sleep before heading out on another charter in the morning. The sprawling tropical canopy in the front yard shielded him from the falling rain, and even though sunset was almost two hours away, the storm made it feel like night. The door was unlocked, just as he'd left it. Crime wasn't exactly unheard of in the Bahamas, but something about island living seemed to encourage unlocked doors and open windows, as if to deny, or at least defy, the existence of evil in paradise. Rumsey entered his living room and tried the wall switch. The lights didn't come on. No great surprise. Power outages were a way of life in his neighborhood, especially during thunderstorms. The hallway was dark, but he could have found the bedroom blindfolded. He dropped his duffel bag on the bed, and as he pulled off his shirt, a blur emerged from the closet. Before he could react, a huge hulk of a man hit him like a freight train and took him down.

The man was now sitting on Rumsey's kidneys, the cold metal barrel of a pistol pressing against the back of Rumsey's skull.

"I'll ask you just one more time," he said. "When was the last time you talked to Michael Cantella?"

Rumsey coughed nervously, and a little blood came up. At least one rib was broken, he was sure of it. His smashed-in nose was a mess after a face-first collision with the floor.

"The trip," he said, grunting. Talk was difficult with the man's considerable weight pressing down on his internal organs. "It was that trip with him and his girlfriend—wife—who disappeared. We ain't never talked since then, mon."

The gunman rose, and Rumsey could breathe again.

"Stay right there," the man said.

Rumsey lay perfectly still, breathing in and out, tasting the salty blood that trickled from his nose into his mouth. He had yet to get a good look at the man in the darkness, but the tumble to the floor had told him something about the man's size and strength. He listened carefully, following the intruder's footfalls across the room. For a brief moment, Rumsey's heart raced with excitement.

Is he leaving?

"You disappoint me," the man said. He pulled the blinds shut, making the room even darker, then walked back over.

Any optimism vanished. Rumsey waited for him to say more, but there was only a long, uncomfortable silence. Several strands of speculation raced through his mind, none of which led to a happy ending. The inescapable conclusion was that his attacker was simply debating whether to shoot him here, in Rumsey's own living room, or to take him somewhere else to do the job.

"Please," said Rumsey. "What you want with me, mon?"

The man's chuckle was laden with insincerity. "Good question."

He took a few more steps, as if circling his prey. Out of the corner of his eye, Rumsey caught an up-close glimpse of the man's steel-toed boots. That explained the pain in his ribs.

"I know you're lying," the man said.

"No, no! I tell the truth, mon."

The man was silent.

Rumsey swallowed hard. He wanted to speak, but he was too afraid of saying the wrong thing. He heard a faint scratching sound, and then there was a flicker of light. The man had struck a match. Rumsey gritted his teeth as the man came toward him, and he instinctively closed his eyes as the flame neared his face.

"Open your eyes," the man said.

Rumsey did as he was told, his cheek still pressed to the cold terra-cotta tile. Oddly, there was money on the floor, right in front of his nose. American money, which was no surprise. The man's accent was definitely not Bahamian. It was a hundred-dollar bill.

The man dropped the match onto the bill.

"What are you doing?" Rumsey asked nervously.

The man was silent. The lit match scorched the bill, and it was quickly aflame. The small fire threw some heat onto Rumsey's face, but not enough to hurt him.

In a minute or two, the fire burned out, and the room returned to darkness.

"I need you to help me," the man said.

He was suddenly moving quickly, and Rumsey got another dose of his attacker's overpowering strength. He grabbed Rumsey's wrists and, in what seemed like a split second, bound them together with plastic cuffs. He grabbed Rumsey's ankles and bound them in the same way. Somewhere in the back of Rumsey's mind a voice cried out, begging him to resist. But it happened too quickly. Rumsey was hog-tied.

The man stood upright, and Rumsey could almost feel him towering over his body. He imagined that the gun was pointed directly at the back of his head, and he wondered how many days it would take for the postman or a neighbor to notice the telltale odor and find him dead on the floor, shot execution style.

"Please, don't—"

"Shut up. I need your help."

"Okay, mon. You got it. Anything."

The man paused, seeming to enjoy the way silence tormented his victim. Finally, he said, "Here's the problem."

There was another pause, and fear coursed again through Rumsey's veins. He prayed that it was a problem he could actually solve.

"It's a crime to burn money," the man said.

"What?"

"You can't just burn money. It's a federal offense. They'll throw me in jail."

Rumsey could hear himself breathing. He had no idea how to respond, so he fumbled for anything.

"But—but that's American money. You in the Bahamas now. No worries, mon."

"Makes no difference. It's a crime to burn money no matter where you do it." The man leaned closer, now speaking in a low, threatening voice: "We need to cover up our crime."

Before Rumsey could say anything, he felt a cold wetness on his shirt and trousers, and then another glob of gel all over his face. It stung his eyes terribly, and the odor told him it was gasoline—goopy gasoline.

"No, please don't burn me, mon!"

His plea went unanswered, except for that dread scratch of sound again—the striking of the match, a sudden burst of light, the roar of the flames, the intense heat that consumed him.

What followed was the piercing sound of his own screams.

17

I didn't get home until six-thirty. Saxton Silvers stock ended the day down almost a hundred bucks a share, so if there was a financial assassin, as Bell had put it, he was halfway there. In between phone conversations with panicked clients, I spent most of the afternoon with our director of security trying to track down my money.

Nana and Papa were trying to track down theirs, too. They were watching *Wheel of Fortune* in the TV room, dressed and ready to take me to dinner for my belated birthday (read: happy birthday) dinner.

"Will you buy a vowel already?" Nana said to the contestant on television. The sound of her voice startled Papa, and his sleepy eyes popped open. If we didn't get going in the next forty-five minutes, dinner was going to be the gastronomical equivalent of a midnight snack for them.

I went to the bedroom and gently nudged Mallory to move it along. She was brushing her hair in front of the framed oval mirror on the bureau.

"I'm going as fast as I can," she said. "I don't see why they're so damn set on taking you out. Especially with everything that's going on. And you just had a party last night."

"Which they weren't invited to. Raising the question: Why not?"

She was still checking herself in the mirror, speaking without looking at me, her tone icy. "The party was a surprise. You have to be careful about who you let in on a surprise, or it won't be a surprise anymore."

I sat behind her on the bed, watching her in the mirror as she got progressively angrier at her hair.

"Who were they going to tell," I asked, "their neighbors in Century Village?"

"*You*, Michael. Papa would have slipped up in one of your daily phone conversations and told you he was coming to the surprise party. Then no more surprise."

"He kept today's visit a surprise."

"He probably *forgot* to tell you he was coming. Can't you see his Alzheimer's is getting worse?"

"Papa doesn't have Alzheimer's. That's just the way you are when you're eighty-three years old."

"My God, you are so clueless."

She tossed her brush aside, giving up the struggle against her hair. This was usually the moment at which I had to beg her not to make an appointment with some scissor-happy "artiste" named Francois or Diego and cut it all off in the morning.

"You look great, Mallory."

She rolled her eyes at me as she headed for the walk-in closet. I sensed another wardrobe change coming.

"Don't patronize me."

The atmosphere had officially moved from icy to frozen solid. I followed her into the closet.

"What's wrong?"

She was flipping through the rack furiously, still not looking at me as she spoke.

"What's *wrong*? Our entire life savings has just been wiped out, and this morning Saxton Silvers suddenly moved from the top of the mountain on Wall Street to somewhere deep inside the San Andreas Fault. Nothing is wrong. Life is wonderful. Another beautiful day in paradise. Just ask Papa."

"Things are going to be okay."

Her forage through the hanging clothes came to an abrupt halt, and finally she looked at me—though it felt more like she was looking right through me.

"It is *not* going to be okay. You ruined it, Michael. You ruined everything."

I stepped closer to give her a hug, but she pulled away and hurried out of the closet. I followed her back into the bedroom.

"Mallory, I need you to stand with me on this."

"You don't need me. You don't even want me. I honestly don't know why you ever asked me to marry you."

"How can you say that?"

She sat on the bed, tears about to flow. She sucked them back and said, "I saw you on TV."

"Was I that bad?"

She brought her hands to her head, exasperated. "Papa's the blind one in the family, not me."

I was getting annoyed by the way she kept dragging my grandfather into this, but I knew it wasn't anything she had against him. She was lashing out, and Papa was the nearest handle in our version of Wilma grabbing a pot to clobber Fred.

"What are you talking about?" I said.

"It's not the money. It's not Saxton Silvers. It's you—what's in your heart—that's wrong."

"You decided this while watching me on *Bell Ringer?*"

"Yes. When the Money Honey said you were too smart to use your wife's birthday as your password, I could see the guilty expression all over your face."

I took a breath, uneasy with where this was headed.

Mallory looked at me coldly and said, "Tell me what the password was."

"There were several different accounts," I said.

"Tell me the passwords."

Again I hesitated, but there was no legitimate reason not to tell her at this point. "The last three numbers of each password were different, and I changed those numbers every ninety days."

"What about the rest of it?"

"They all pretty much shared the same root password."

"What was it?"

I hesitated.

"What was it, Michael?" she said sternly.

"Orene52."

A Sudoku whiz, Mallory had a mind for codes and numbers, but she deciphered this one even faster than I'd expected.

"You son of a bitch," she said.

"It's not a big deal."

"It's 25 *enero* backward. January 25 in Spanish— your wife's birthday. Your half Hispanic, *dead* wife."

"It's just a password."

"Don't try to minimize it. She's been dead for over four years, and you still have a bank account open in her name. You never touched the money, never told me about it. And now I find out that the password for every single one of *our* accounts is *her* birthday. How is that supposed to make me feel?"

"It's nothing."

"Stop saying it's nothing! Your heart is not in this marriage."

"That's crazy. I love you."

"That's the point. You *don't.* It's not just that you're emotionally frozen and living in the past. It's worse than that. Even though the DNA tests proved that the human remains found inside that shark were hers, you have never given up hope that somehow, some way, Ivy Layton is going to come walking through that door."

"That's not true."

"It *is* true."

I took another step toward her.

"Stay away from me!"

I stopped in my tracks. I'd never seen her so upset, so inconsolable.

"This has been building inside me for a long time," she said. "It's not a knee-jerk reaction to what's been happening today. I've been unhappy far longer than you can imagine."

"Mallory, please."

"I mean it, Michael. I mean this more than anything I've ever said to you. I never thought I'd have to say these words again, but once you've been in a bad marriage, you know better than to stay too long the next time."

"Don't say it," I said, but I was talking to the walls.

"I want a divorce."

18

Mallory was alone in the bedroom when she heard the doorbell ring. She hoped it wasn't her husband.

Michael had kept his promise and taken his grandparents to dinner. Mallory had made it clear that he was to find somewhere else to sleep tonight, but she'd spared everyone the drama and told Nana and Papa that she wasn't feeling well—which triggered a most uncomfortable remark from Michael's grandmother.

"Morning sickness in the evening, maybe?" she'd said, ever hopeful for a great-grandchild.

Clueless. The entire Cantella clan is clueless.

Not that she didn't want children. She used to love working with the little girls at the dance studio before she married Michael. Sometimes she just wished that someone in the world would hear her cries for help.

Mallory went to the door, saw her best friend through the peephole, and let her inside.

"Did you tell him?" asked Andrea.

"It's done," she said as she led the way to the kitchen. There was an open bottle of chardonnay in the refrigerator. Mallory poured two glasses, and the women sat opposite each other on bar stools at the kitchen counter.

Andrea reached across and patted the back of Mallory's hand. "How are you doing?"

She drew a breath. "I guess I'm okay. It's all so confusing. Michael's not a monster. He didn't abuse me. We didn't fight over money. He doesn't hang out late with the guys."

"He didn't cheat on you," said Andrea.

Mallory hesitated. "That's the weird thing."

"He didn't—did he?"

Mallory drank her wine, and her thoughts made her wince. "With my first husband, I know of two other women. There were probably more. With Michael, it wasn't cheating in that sense."

"Cybersex?"

"No, no. Not that."

"Then *what*?"

She trusted Andrea, but Mallory was going to need a lot more wine before painting the whole picture. "Just forget it. Michael's nothing like my first husband."

"Are you having second thoughts?"

"Absolutely not. I know what you're thinking: There are plenty of women who would want my life. And maybe I would, too, if I hadn't married Michael with such high expectations. My mother wasted forty-one years of her life with a man who didn't love her. I crammed forty-one years of unhappiness into my first marriage. I don't need more of it from Michael. I deserve better."

Mallory was tearing up, but she stopped herself. There had been enough of that.

Andrea raised her wineglass, as if to help avert the waterworks.

"Well, I hope you find Mr. Right."

They drank to the toast. "Tomorrow is what I'm really dreading," said Mallory. "I'm sure the gossip wire will be at high voltage."

"Rest assured, they won't hear a thing from me."

"It will get out. Everything always does. The Saxton Silvers wives club knows all."

"You give them too much credit."

"Honey, even your little secret was out three days after you moved to New York."

Andrea coughed on her wine. "My secret?"

"Sorry, but it's pretty juicy when a woman moves to New York with her fiancé and the two of them don't sleep in the same bedroom. Housekeepers are great sources. You should be careful who you share yours with."

Andrea went white, confirming it. "He snores, and so sometimes I have to go in the other room."

"It's okay," Mallory said. "It happens to a lot of my friends, though usually not until *after* the wedding."

Andrea shifted nervously, clearly uncomfortable with the way Mallory had steered the conversation. It made Mallory feel a little guilty. Andrea had been a good friend and an amazing listener. The conversation was never about her—and true to form, she turned it back around to Mallory.

"So tell me," said Andrea. "How did Michael handle the news?"

"How do you think?"

Andrea tasted her wine. "Better than he handled Chuck Bell, I hope."

Mallory just shook her head.

Andrea said, "Do you think there's anything to that?"

"To what?"

"The things Chuck Bell was saying—that Michael wasn't really the victim here."

"Why do you ask that?"

"Maybe he's not shocked that you asked for a divorce. Maybe he even anticipated it. Rich men have been known to do some pretty outrageous things to keep the wife from getting her hands on the money in a divorce."

"What are you saying?" asked Mallory. "That Michael knew our marriage was going south so he orchestrated the liquidation of our portfolio and made it look like it was some identity thief?"

Andrea gave her a sobering look.

Mallory's jaw dropped. "Holy shit."

"Sorry, Mal. Didn't mean to drop a dead fly in your chardonnay."

Mallory froze, then shook her head. "I'm such an idiot. I was feeling like a total bitch over the way I jumped all over him and dropped the news. I've been trying to think of ways to throw him an olive branch so we can do this divorce without war."

She climbed down from her stool, went to her purse, and grabbed her cell phone.

"Who you calling?"

"Who else?" said Mallory, dialing. "My lawyer."

19

The red sauce smelled amazing, but I had no interest in the mostaccioli and meatballs in the big pasta bowl before me.

"I know nobody makes it like I do," said Papa. "But try it. You'll like it."

It turned out that the ten-percent-off coupons were good only for lunch, so we went to Carmine's in the Theater District. It was every bit as lively as Sal's Place but huge by comparison, with hardwood chairs on creaky oak floors, glass chandeliers hanging from twenty-foot ceilings, and all the trappings of a touristy Manhattan restaurant, right down to the "Old Country" photographs on the walls. It was another of Papa's favorites, even if it did only *look* as if it had been around since the 1920s. In truth, it was a vintage

1990s success story that had hit on a timeless formula: great southern Italian food at reasonable prices. *Lots* of food. Papa said it reminded him of an Italian wedding, the way they served everything on oversize platters intended for sharing. Ironic, on the night my wife asked for a divorce.

"Sorry, I'm just not myself tonight."

"Is everything okay with you and Mallory?" asked Nana.

"Fine," I lied. "It's all this stuff going on at work."

The waiter grated Parmesan cheese onto my pasta. Papa sent him back for a block of Romano.

"Don't worry about that TV show," said Papa. "The treasurer of our condo association tells me that nobody takes Chuck Bell seriously."

I wished he were right, but in reality a huge chunk of the Wall Street world—everyone from day traders to hedge-fund managers—truly believed that watching FNN all day was "market research."

My cell chimed. I had my entire team assigned to the Saxton Silvers rumor patrol, with strict instructions to e-mail or text me immediately with any updates. This one was about Chuck Bell. He'd bumped one of FNN's evening shows to air yet another special edition of *Bell Ringer*.

Give it a rest, Chuck.

Papa poured me a glass of Chianti Classico. "I haven't asked about this identity theft, but your grandmother and I are concerned."

"It's going to be okay," I said.

"Maybe it will. And you know I don't pry into your finances."

That was true. In my ten-plus years with Saxton Silvers, not once had Papa asked me how much money I was making. But he spent countless hours on the phone talking me through heartbreaks and setbacks—including the loss of Ivy. For Papa, only one thing mattered: whether I was happy or not.

"I'm only going to say this one time," he said, "so listen to me. If you're in trouble, if you need anything. I mean *anything*. Your grandmother and I—. . . we have savings. So we can . . . well, you know what I'm saying."

My eyes welled. Papa's entire life savings couldn't have covered my club dues, car payment, and annual debt service, but never had he and Nana asked *me* for anything—in fact, they'd refused my offers many times. He couldn't possibly understand the mix of emotions he had unleashed inside me. The love made my heart swell, but the knife in my belly was the shame I felt for working with guys like Kent Frost, who could run up $22 billion in subprime losses—fly the plane into the mountain—and then bang on the president's door to make damn sure he was going to keep his year-end bonus of $22 million. I suddenly realized that the entire financial world could collapse and there would be nothing to worry about—if only we could still count on the generation for whom the American dream was not just buying a home but actually paying off the mortgage.

"Michael?" I heard a woman say.

It was terrible timing, but Mallory's friend Andrea was suddenly upon us and apologizing for the intrusion. She introduced herself to my grandparents as "Mallory's best friend," then quickly shot me a more serious expression and said, "I really need to talk with you in private."

"Please," said Papa, "join us for a glass of wine first."

"That's kind of you, but—"

"But what? Life's *not* too short? Come on, I danced on these grapes myself."

I knew Papa's angle. He smelled trouble in my marriage, and just a minute or two with Mallory's best friend could surely change the course of history. This was a man who would lock his lotto ticket away in the safe deposit box *before* they announced the winning numbers. He was that optimistic.

Andrea smiled, unable to refuse Italian hospitality, and pulled up a chair. Papa poured a generous glass of chianti for her, and of course he made her a plate of mostaccioli and meatballs. He had no way of knowing that, as a general rule, Mallory's friends didn't eat.

"Thank you so much," she said. "I'm actually starved."

This shocked me—a Saxton Silvers wife-to-be feasting on pasta and meatballs. She even asked for extra cheese. Since moving to New York in the winter, Andrea had quickly earned Mallory's trust, but admittedly, I didn't know her well. All I could say for certain was the obvious: She was pretty, like most of Mallory's friends. I had a hunch, however, more substance was there.

"Did you see my grandson on television today?" Papa asked her.

"Yes," she said, averting her eyes. She seemed embarrassed for me. "I did."

"People are saying some really mean things about Saxton Silvers, don't you think?"

"Papa, let's not go there."

Andrea said, "My fiancé says it's the short sellers."

"Short?" said Papa. "You mean *paisans*?"

I chuckled. "No, not short in stature, Papa. They're going short on the stock."

"What does that mean?" asked Nana.

"You don't really want to know," I said.

She grumbled in Italian. Sadly, I'd forgotten most of her dialect since leaving home for college, but she said something to the effect that I was treating my grandparents like a couple of dummies.

"All right," I said, "here's Michael Cantella's crash course in Short Selling 101. Most people go long on stock. That means you buy it, you wait for it to go up in value, and you sell it at a profit. Short selling is the opposite."

"You sell it at a loss?" asked Nana, confused.

"No. Instead of 'buy low and sell high,' you sell high and then buy low."

"Explain this to me," said Papa, putting down his fork. "How do you sell something before you own it?"

"Good question," I said. "You borrow it. And you sell it immediately at the high price with the understanding that at some point in the future you have to give back an equal number of shares to the broker who loaned them to you. If all goes as planned, the stock price goes down, the short seller buys at the low price, and he gives back those cheap shares to his lender. He pockets the difference in price as profit."

"What happens if the price doesn't go down?"

"The short gets screwed. He has to cover the price difference in order to return the shares to his lender."

Papa shook his head, wagging a marinara-soaked breadstick like a professorial finger. "I don't believe in all this borrowing. You make what you earn, and you spend what you make. Not a penny more."

"And then there are the naked short sellers," I said, "who don't even borrow the stock before they sell it—but we'll save that lesson for Short Selling 201. Suffice it to say that a lot of smart folks think it was naked shorts that brought down Krispy Kreme."

"That *is* a crime," said Papa.

"Actually, there's nothing illegal about it, unless you manipulate things by flooding the market with sell orders. Even then, I just read in the *Journal* that the SEC brought a grand total of zero enforcement actions in response to the last five thousand complaints it got about short sellers, so you do the math on getting caught."

Papa said, "That's all just a fancy way of saying a short seller is like some guy in Atlantic City betting that the price of Saxton Silvers stock will go down."

"That's pretty much it," I said. "The farther it goes down, the more money the short seller makes. Which means they laugh all the way to the bank if they can get guys like Chuck Bell to blabber nasty rumors on television."

Andrea said, "But the question is, who are '*they*'?"

"I wish I knew," I said.

"You must have a guess," said Andrea.

"I don't like to guess."

"Oh, come on. Who do you think it is?"

"I really don't know."

"You must have thought about it," said Andrea. "Who would be able to borrow enough shares of Saxton Silvers stock to make it worthwhile to spread these rumors? And who would be that devious?"

Andrea's fixation started to feel a little awkward. "I honestly don't know," I told her.

She finished her wine and smiled politely at Papa as she pushed away from the table. "It's been lovely visiting with you. Thank you so much for the delicious food and wine. But I really do need a moment in private with Michael. It's kind of personal."

I looked at Papa, who of course said, "You do what you gotta do."

Andrea said good night, I excused myself, and the two of us went to the bar, where bottles of Campari and Amaretto Disaronno had prime shelf space on the mirrored backsplash behind a long mahogany bar. We found a couple of chrome stools at the end, away from the crowd. Just then I got another rumor alert from one of my analysts; this one was serious. I asked the bartender to tune the flat screen to FNN while Andrea and I talked. The audio was on mute, but Chuck Bell somehow still managed to be obnoxious even in closed captioning.

Andrea said, "Let me first say that Mallory didn't ask me to come here."

"Then why did you come?"

"I'm not the type to stick my nose where it doesn't belong, but I hate to see a marriage between two good people not work out."

I paused to get a read on her. I'd met many of Mallory's friends, and something about this one didn't add up. It wasn't just the way she took an interest in short sellers. It was the little things—like her pigging out on pasta, or her monochrome dye job, which completely lacked the array of highlights that cost Mallory the monthly equivalent of a subprime mortgage payment after a rate adjustment. I was getting the sense that Andrea didn't belong in the club—and that she didn't really want to belong.

"I appreciate your saying that," I said.

My cell rang again. This time it was a red alert: *TURN ON FNN!!!*

My gaze shifted to the television. I started reading the closed captioning, the several-second delay from the audio giving me some time to catch up.

"More devastating news," said Bell. "My source tells me that, earlier today, the credit department of a major

162 • JAMES GRIPPANDO

trader held up a trade with Saxton Silvers because of concerns about the firm's financial health. My source also tells me that perhaps as soon as tomorrow Saxton Silvers could be on a no-trade status that will continue until the firm solves its liquidity problems. All I can say, folks, is that compared to tomorrow, today could look like a good day for Saxton Silvers and its shareholders."

"Mallory is very serious about a divorce," said Andrea.

I heard her, but I was still numb from Bell's words.

"She already has a lawyer," said Andrea.

That got my attention, but my phone rang. It was Eric Volke. I apologized to Andrea and stepped away from the bar to take the call.

"We're sunk," said Eric.

"I heard. Wasn't Bell supposed to stop spreading rumors after you let him interview me?"

"He says they're not rumors. He stands by his source."

"Maybe Stuart should go back on the air."

"It doesn't matter what the CEO or anyone else says at this point. Once a statement like that is out there— that Saxton Silvers can't follow through on a trade— the firm is dead. Chuck Bell killed us."

"Bell and his source," I said.

"Fucking shorts," said Eric.

"What's going to happen?"

"I'm meeting with Treasury and the Fed tonight. The vibe I'm getting is that they're going to give us until Sunday to find a merger partner."

"Sunday?" I said, incredulous. "That's crazy."

"We either get it done, or we'll be in bankruptcy court on Monday."

Things were moving too fast, and Eric's use of the B-word really had my head spinning. Just two days earlier, it would have shocked me less if Bill Gates had called me to debug his computer.

"It's all hands on deck tonight," said Eric. "Your Green Division is one of the few that is completely untouched by subprime. I'll need your most current numbers and six-month pro formas. How soon can you be here?"

I checked my watch. "I'll see you in twenty minutes."

"Sooner," he said, and the call ended.

Andrea approached. "Is everything okay?"

"Something's come up. I have to go into the office."

"I'm sure it's important. But let me leave you with this thought: Use me. I think I can help with Mallory."

"Thank you."

"I mean it."

I was having my doubts. I was still hoping that Mallory would cool down and change her mind, but it struck me as odd that Andrea—someone I hardly knew—would track me down and come to my aid, especially if it was true that Mallory had already hired a divorce lawyer.

"Is there anything you want me to tell her?" asked Andrea.

Alarms were ringing in my head. Something told me not to trust Andrea, and I always went with my instinct.

"Yeah," I said, "there is."

"What?"

"Tell her it's another beautiful day in paradise."

20

I knew something was wrong the minute I smelled today's assortment of executive-suite flowers. A pair of Saxton Silvers security guards met me as soon as I stepped out of the elevator, and their expressions could have taken the bloom right off the Sexy Rexy Floribunda roses.

"I can take it from here, guys," I said. "I know my way to Mr. Volke's office."

"Sorry, Mr. Cantella. We have our orders."

"Oooh-kay."

Security knocked on the closed door and Eric let me inside. He was not alone. I recognized Sonya, of course, but not the two men standing beside her. Eric made the introductions, but I noted that he didn't look me in the eye as he spoke.

"This is FBI Agent Malcolm Spear and Agent Carl O'Neil," said Eric. "Mr. Spear is a supervisory special agent, and Mr. O'Neil works in the Computer Fraud Division of the bureau's Manhattan field office."

These were not the same agents who'd come by my building that morning to check out the fire in the elevator. O'Neil was by far the younger man, but Spear had the look of an ex-Marine, and as we shook hands I decided I would rather face O'Neil in a bar fight.

"I assume this is about my identity theft."

"Have a seat, Michael," said Eric.

"Is the news not good?"

"Please. Have a seat."

I took the leather armchair facing the agents, who seated themselves on the couch. Eric went behind his desk, and I found Sonya's positioning very interesting. She took the chair that was on the opposite side of the coffee table from me, closer to the FBI.

"At the outset," said Sonya, "let me make it clear that I'm here strictly as general counsel to Saxton Silvers. I don't represent anyone in his individual capacity."

"You mean me?" I said, trying not to sound too facetious.

She nodded.

I glanced at the FBI. "I'm guessing you don't represent me either."

"That's correct," said Agent Spear.

It wasn't intentional, but a nervous chuckle escaped as my gaze shifted in Eric's direction. "Should I have a lawyer?"

"That's certainly your right," said Agent Spear.

"Am I being accused of something?"

"No," said the agent.

Sonya started to speak but hesitated. Then, without words, Eric seemed to give her the green light.

"I would suggest that you merely listen," she said. "Eric and I wanted you to know what the FBI investigation has uncovered, but we thought it would be best for you to hear it straight from Agent Spear."

My throat tightened, which was probably a good thing. I was getting the distinct impression that I shouldn't even try to talk.

"Okay, I'm all ears."

Spear spoke in a patented FBI monotone that made things sound even more serious. "There has been a major development in our tracking of the funds from your Saxton Silvers personal investment accounts to the Cayman Islands and beyond."

"Congratulations. I guess it's true that the post-nine-eleven world of bank secrecy is not as secret as it once was."

Eric caught my eye. I was talking too much.

Spear continued. "This is what the FBI knows. Your investments were liquidated and the cash in your accounts was then immediately transferred into a custodial account in the name of your late wife, Ivy Layton. Your funds were commingled with hers, and the entire amount—about thirteen million—was wire-transferred from the custodial account to a numbered account in the Cayman Islands."

He paused, and I sure hoped there was more. "No offense," I said, "but my tech guy told me everything you just said about ten minutes after I discovered my account balances were at zero."

"Understood," said Spear. "Here's where it gets interesting. The minute your thirteen million hit the Cayman account, it was used as collateral for twenty-six million in short positions on Saxton Silvers stock obtained through various sources."

It was as if someone had kicked the chair out from under me. "Excuse me?"

"With the dramatic decline in Saxton Silvers stock this morning, you can in essence pay back your twenty-six-million dollar loan with thirteen million dollars' worth of stock. If the rumors continue and force Saxton Silvers into bankruptcy—reducing its stock value to zero—you borrowed twenty-six million and can pay it off for nothing. That's a pretty hefty profit in a couple of days."

I couldn't even speak.

"So," he said, "the question is this: Who controls the Cayman account?"

"You're asking me?"

"There are several layers of transactions involved, a number of different special-purpose vehicles," he said. That was Wall Street–speak for offshore shell corporations.

"Then you need to find out who's behind the shell game," I said.

Glances were exchanged around the room, but no one was making eye contact with me.

"Eric?" I said. "You don't think I control it, do you?"

Eric was again massaging that sore spot between his eyes, migraine central.

"Well, it sure as hell *isn't* me," I said.

Spear cleared his throat, and I braced myself. "Your general counsel tells us that you went on FNN today."

"At Eric's request."

"How do you think that went?" asked Spear.

Part of me wanted to tell him to call the treasurer at Papa's condo association and ask *him*. "Not so well," I said.

"That depends on your perspective, doesn't it?" he said.

"Meaning what?" I asked.

"I would imagine that the short sellers in control of your money in that secret Cayman Islands account were quite pleased with the way your interview went with Mr. Bell. Wouldn't you agree?"

I had to take a breath, control my anger. "I didn't bet against my own firm and then go on television to fan the flames, if that's what you're suggesting."

Spear copped a laserlike stare. "Would you be willing to take a polygraph exam on that?"

I should have taken a moment to consider the question. Instead, I looked right at Eric and said, "If that's what it takes to get the people in this room to believe me, then yes, I would."

Spear was about to say something, but Eric interrupted.

"Michael, you should talk to a lawyer."

"I've done nothing wrong."

Eric leaned forward, his hands atop his desk. "It's like Sonya said. She doesn't represent you. Her only client is this institution. Go talk to a lawyer."

I didn't know what to say, but soon enough I realized that I had best not say anything.

"All right," I said, rising. "I will talk to my lawyer."

And then I walked out—and realized I didn't have one.

The security guards escorted me back to the elevator, rode down with me, and walked me out to the street. This was getting annoying. I spotted a taxi and speared my hand into the night air. My iPhone chirped, and of course I immediately stopped in my tracks to check it. They should have called this thing "iPavlov." Was there anything more powerful?

It was a text message. I didn't recognize the sender, but the words cut to my core: *It's a crime to burn money.*

I collected myself and texted back in rapid fire: *Who are you?*

He'd sent the next text before getting my reply: *That makes you Wall Street fucks serial offenders.*

I knew it was the guy from Sal's Place last fall, but I needed more. *Who are you, and what do you want?*

The cab I'd hailed pulled away. The driver was ticked, but I wasn't about to risk losing this connection in a moving vehicle.

His reply read, *You promised not to turn me in.*

I had to think for a moment, then I recalled the strange conversation with this guy at Sal's Place. I had indeed made that promise after watching him burn the hundred-dollar bill. I kept my reply short: *So?*

His reply came so quickly I could almost feel the anger: *Stay away from the FBI. STAY AWAY!!!*

I would have bet serious money that the conversation was over, but to my surprise, one last message popped up.

That's the thing about revenge, the text read, *you never know when they're going to call it even.*

An ambulance flew by me on Seventh Avenue, siren blaring. I was oblivious to it, numbed by the words I was reading.

I pulled myself together and speed-dialed Eric Volke.

21

I spoke to Eric from the backseat of a taxi. Going back inside Saxton Silvers headquarters seemed like a bad idea. If the warning not to talk to the FBI meant anything, it was clear that someone was watching me pretty closely.

"Eric," I said, "I think Sonya's car must be bugged."

That was the only conclusion I could reach; it was the one way that guy could have known what the lawyer from Cool Cash had told me about revenge. I laid it all out for Eric, telling him about that morning's conversation in the seeming privacy of Sonya's car, about the strange guy who'd burned money in front of me at Sal's Place last fall, about the latest text. And then I put it all together.

"That firebomb in the elevator came after I met Sonya and Stanley Brewer outside the FBI field office.

I think it was intended to convey the same message that was made explicit in the text: Don't go to the FBI. I want to set up another meeting with Agent Spear, but obviously it has to be secret."

"No," said Eric.

"What?"

"The guy warned you not to go to the FBI. We don't know what kind of nut job we're dealing with. Send me the text message. I'll take care of it. You stick with your plan. Get a lawyer. I'll deal with the FBI."

"Thanks," I said. Nothing more I could say.

The cab let me off on Eighth Avenue. Two minutes later I was in Papa's room at the Days Inn. He and Nana had an "Internet special" that was barely big enough for the king-size bed I was sitting on.

"Hey, check this out," he said, grinning as he emerged from the bathroom. "Little bottles of shampoo and conditioner. And they're *free*. I love this place."

It was a tongue-in-cheek remark, Papa's way of saying, *Don't even think of pulling out your wallet and trying to move us over to the Ritz.*

Nana took her turn in the bathroom. When we were alone, Papa sat beside me on the edge of the mattress. He put his arm around my shoulder and said, "You look really stressed. Tell me what's on your mind."

I was suddenly twelve years old again, back in my little bedroom in rural Illinois with the best listener on earth. He couldn't possibly relate to the whole story, but merely sharing the gist of it made me feel better. Some things never changed.

Papa considered my words, then asked, "What is the one thing that would help you the most right now?"

"A lawyer, I guess. Sort of a legal jack-of-all-trades. I definitely need someone who can deal with the FBI, and if Mallory is serious, it looks like I'll need a divorce lawyer, too."

"How much does someone like that cost?"

I drew a breath. "A decent criminal defense lawyer in a white-collar criminal investigation like this is probably going to ask for a hundred grand up front."

Papa's jaw dropped, but he seemed to put the figure aside.

"Have you thought about calling your brother?"

He meant my half brother. At the time of my birth, Papa's only daughter had been an unmarried junior at DePaul University. Two years later she married a man who was not my biological father. My half brother and half sister came along in rapid succession. I was six when our mother lost control of her car on the Kennedy Expressway in an ice storm. She was killed instantly. My stepfather—funny, but he was just "Daddy" to me before Mom died—got engaged to a woman who promptly announced that three kids in their instant family was one too many. It was then that I moved to a small town north of Chicago to live with Nana and Papa.

"I haven't spoken to Kevin in years," I said.

It had been four years, to be exact—since Ivy's disappearance, when Kevin turned into an asshole.

"Maybe that should change," said Papa. "He *is* family. And he practices right here in the city."

"Please don't push this. I don't need another complication—especially family."

"You're right. Let's you and I talk this out for a minute. It sounds to me like someone is setting you up to look like the bad guy."

"The financial assassin of my own firm," I said.

"So let's think logically. Any successful man naturally has enemies. Who are yours?"

I shook my head slowly, thinking. "I am head of the firm's Green Division. That doesn't make Big Oil too happy."

"Yeah, right. And come June I'm going to muscle out a bunch of twenty-year-old stars and become a starting pitcher for the Chicago Cubs. Come on, *think*. There has to be someone you stepped on or maybe even squashed—not on purpose, of course—on your way to the top."

The bathroom door opened. Nana stepped out, clad in the same bathrobe she'd owned when I was in college. A silk cap preserved last Saturday's trip to the beauty parlor. She'd gone every week, worn the same hairstyle, for as long as I could remember.

"Bedtime, boys," she said.

I rose and gave her a kiss. Papa walked me to the door. Nana had her hearing aid out, so we didn't have to worry about her overhearing.

"Where you sleeping tonight?" he asked.

"I thought I would check at the desk and see if they had any vacancies."

He gave me a hug and whispered in my ear: "Call Mallory."

I wasn't sure if that was the right thing to do, but I told him I would, said good night, and rode the elevator down to the front desk. The hotel was completely booked—it must have been the little bottles of free shampoo—so it was on to plan B for sleeping arrangements. Some of Papa's optimism must have rubbed off on me. I called Mallory, and when she didn't pick up, I hesitated before leaving a message on the answering machine. Then I found myself sounding more like my grandfather than myself, saying the things I probably should have said more often in my marriage to Mallory.

"I just wanted to let you know that I love you," I said. "Please, let's talk in the morning."

Five minutes later I was in the backseat of another taxi headed up Eighth Avenue. There were two hotels on the West Side that got so much business from Saxton Silvers that they almost *had* to accommodate me, even if I did show up without a reservation. The cab was one of thousands in the city that had gone high-tech. A touch-screen monitor embedded into the bulkhead bombarded me with ads for credit cards and refinancing opportunities. Strapped into my seat, I felt like Alex undergoing aversion therapy in *A Clockwork Orange.* The ads stopped, and Taxi TV switched to actual television programming. I was hoping for the Food Network or maybe Lucy and Ricky. Naturally, I got a five-minute snippet from *Bell Ringer.* I suddenly had a change of plans.

"Make that Fifty-seventh and First," I told the driver.

Chuck Bell had been featured two months earlier in *New York* magazine, with several pictures of him in his penthouse apartment. It turned out that we were practically neighbors. The cab dropped me in front of the building, and I asked the front desk attendant to ring Bell's apartment for me.

"Tell him it's Michael Cantella."

Three minutes later, Chuck Bell and I were alone in the cavernous lobby, seated facing each other on matching chrome and strap-leather chairs. He seemed energized—hopeful that another Saxton Silvers insider was about to spill his guts.

"Can we talk off the record?"

"No," he said. "But I'll make you the same promise I made to my other source: I won't reveal your identity."

"That's actually what I've come here to talk about: your source."

He was suddenly cautious. "What about my source?"

"I'm asking you to go on the air and state in no uncertain terms that Michael Cantella is *not* your source."

"Why would I do that?"

"Because you know who your source is, and you know it's not me."

He chuckled and shook his head. "I'm a journalist. I'm never going to reveal a source, not even under a court order."

"I'm simply asking you to reveal that I am *not* the source. Even Woodward and Bernstein were willing to do that much when they confirmed that Al Haig and others were *not* Deep Throat."

"And they were lucky it didn't blow up in their faces. I'm not interested in playing a public process of elimination that will inevitably lead to the disclosure of my source. Besides," he said with a wry smile, "how do I know you're not a source for my source?"

I watched him closely, wondering if he was merely taunting me or trying to tell me something. Bell rose, and so did I. He took a business card from his pocket and wrote a number on the back of it.

"This is my cell," he said. "Call me if you decide we should talk."

I didn't take it. He placed it on the glass-topped table between us and left it there.

"Be sure to watch me again tonight at eleven-thirty," he said. "This story is getting so much bigger than FNN. I'm hosting a round-table discussion about Wall Street on network television."

He turned and headed to the elevator.

When he was gone, I took the card with his cell number and tucked it into my wallet. I didn't want to take it, but he'd managed to make me feel as though I'd need it—a feeling that triggered a sinking realization as I left his building. Chuck Bell was poison. Rat poison.

And I was the little mouse running blindly through the maze.

22

Andrea was dressed in her pajamas, standing before the bathroom mirror and confirming her suspicions: too much of her dark roots were showing. Michael Cantella had seemed fixated on them at the restaurant.

All her life Andrea had been an "exotic beauty," turning heads with the high cheekbones and raven-black hair of her Native American mother and the striking green eyes of her Anglo father. The idea of going blond for the first time in her life had been kind of fun. The maintenance, however, was a pain in the ass. And a cheap-looking blond dye job wasn't in keeping with her assumed image.

There was a knock at the door. She pulled on her robe and let in her "fiancé."

"How did it go today?" he asked.

Phil Shores was a smooth-talking James Bond wan-nabe who had managed to convince someone in a posi-tion of power that he could pull off playing an internal compliance officer at Saxton Silvers. He certainly wasn't unattractive, but he was nowhere near the eye candy he thought he was—not at all Andrea's type.

"Not great," she said. "It seems the word is out that we don't sleep together."

"According to whom?"

"Mallory Cantella told me."

"The ditz is smarter than we thought."

"She's no ditz, and she's not the only one who knows. Our maid let it slip."

"The maid? She came only once before we were told a housekeeper wasn't in the budget."

"Apparently once was enough."

He leaned against the bathroom door frame, arms folded across his broad chest. "Well, we could always put the rumors to rest—and have a good time doing it."

"In your dreams."

Andrea switched off the light, breezed past him, and went to her bedroom. She knew Phil had been kidding, but not completely kidding.

The jerk would nail anything blond.

Andrea climbed into bed and grabbed the remote. She was tired of listening to Chuck Bell, but her last assignment of this very long day was to watch his round-table discussion at eleven thirty P.M. The guy was to Saxton Silvers what the *National Enquirer* was to celebrity breakups.

Andrea watched as the show opened from Times Square with a shot of the famous high-tech display that wrapped around the cylindrical NASDAQ building. Saxton Silvers was a NYSE-listed company, but as if to underscore the pervasive impact of the story, the firm's name was all over the NASDAQ marquee that lit up Broadway with up-to-the-minute financial news-flashes. The image switched abruptly to an interior shot of the NASDAQ MarketSite. Electronic screens inside the digital broadcast studio carried live updates from markets that were open for trading on the other side of the world. Finally, the introductory credits and voice-over stopped, and Chuck Bell took over from his seat behind the news desk.

"Good evening, and welcome," he said.

The host of FNN's hit show *Bell Ringer*—he mentioned it twice in thirty seconds—was grinning widely as he introduced his panel of experts: a hedge-fund manager, a retired member of the Board of Governors of the Federal Reserve System, a reporter from the *Wall Street Journal*, and two other "experts" for whom Andrea had missed the introductions while struggling with a too-short strand of dental floss. This wasn't FNN—not the usual shouting on the set—so she increased the volume and listened to Bell "get the ball rolling" with the latest revelation from his source.

"It seems that Michael Cantella didn't just unload his holdings in Saxton Silvers the night before the stock dropped through the floor," said Bell. "My source tells me that Cantella was actually betting against his company with short sales that could net him eight figures— literally overnight. And the number just keeps getting bigger as the stock continues to drop.

"It's a short-selling frenzy," said the hedge-fund hotshot. "All it takes is one or two multibillion-dollar hedge funds to jump on the short-selling bandwagon of a failing investment bank worth seventy-five billion, and Cantella's personal profit is going to look like peanuts."

Bell said, "That's precisely the reason I have been so careful with my reporting. I trust my source."

The print journalist jumped in. "There are those who would say that Michael Cantella *is* your source."

Bell smiled and shrugged coyly, saying nothing.

Another chimed in. "Come on, Chuck. Give us a clue."

Andrea kept watching as she reached for the telephone.

Bell continued, "All I have to say on this subject is maybe it is, and maybe it isn't Michael Cantella. This journalist will never reveal his source."

Andrea smiled flatly and said, "We'll see about that."

She dialed from memory the number she could never write down anywhere, then bounced an idea off someone much smarter than Phil the phony fiancé.

23

I could have thrown the television set out the window.
Except my tiny hotel room didn't have a window.
And it smelled like mildew. Still, the accommodations
were the least of my worries. This time Bell had pushed
it too far:

Maybe it is, and maybe it isn't Michael Cantella.

I found his business card in my wallet and dialed his
cell. The call went straight to his voice mail. If the last
twenty-four hours had not been the nightmare from
hell, I probably would have stopped myself from leaving
such an angry message. But at this point I didn't care.

"Bell, this is Michael Cantella. I saw your show. I
want a retraction, and I want it tonight. If I don't get
it, you had better hope that you hear from my lawyers.
Because you won't want to hear from me."

The instant I hit End, the phone rang on the night-stand. It was the front desk telling me that there was no other room I could switch to. The Saxton Silvers go-to hotels on the West Side had been no help, and the dozen other hotels I'd tried in Midtown were also fully booked. Apparently the entire world had followed up April in Paris with May in New York.

"One other thing," said the night manager. "Your credit card was declined."

I was sure it had something to do with the fraud alert sent out today on my credit report. I offered up another card, but after hearing the words "fraud alert," the manager insisted on cash in advance.

"Do you have an ATM in the hotel?"

"It's broken."

He agreed to hold the room for thirty minutes while I went out and searched for an ATM—provided that I leave him the last two hundred dollars in my wallet as a nonrefundable cash deposit. *What a guy.* I was crossing Third Avenue, walking through a cloud of steam rising up from a manhole cover, when Eric Volke rang my cell. He'd watched Bell's round-table discussion.

"Michael, I want a straight answer: Are you Chuck Bell's source?"

"No way, no how."

"The FBI found a bug in Sonya's car."

"I told you they would."

"Which has the FBI wondering how you knew it was there."

That one had me reeling. "What? Did you show the FBI the text message? *That's* how I knew."

"That may be. But I'm telling you there's a black cloud over you right now, and you just keep making it darker."

"Eric, for the last time: I am *not* Bell's source."

"Are you denying that you met with him tonight in the lobby of his building?"

"Are you having me followed?"

"Are you going to answer my question?"

Shit. I should have realized that a face-to-face meeting with Bell might look bad. One crisis piling up after another was clearly clouding my judgment.

"I was trying to get him to admit on the air that I wasn't his source. And then he pulled this stunt. The guy's a sleazebag, and one way or another, I'm going to get a retraction out of that son of a bitch."

"You're playing with fire, Michael."

"You can say that again," I said, thinking of yesterday's flaming package.

"And I can't stand by and watch this whole thing blow up in your face and mine. You have confidentiality obligations to this firm. If you breach them, you

will be fired, and you *will* be sued. Do you understand?"

Never before had Eric used that tone with me.
He was obviously still steaming over my *Bell Ringer*
debacle. "I would never betray you or the firm."

"Then don't make me have another conversation
with you about this. Because there are people here who
want you gone. Saxton Silvers *will* go down if I have to
waste another minute going to bat for you. I've always
been your biggest supporter, and I hate having to talk
to you like this. But we're in crisis mode. I can't defend
people who fan the flames."

He hung up after a clipped "good night."

I tucked away my phone and took a deep breath. It
was after midnight, and the night was turning cooler,
downright cold. My sport coat wasn't enough to keep
me warm, but the only clothes I had were those I'd
worn to dinner with Papa. I didn't even have a tooth-
brush, and the last two drugstores I'd passed were
closed. I spotted a bank marquee on the next corner:
Forty-two degrees. Chilly for early May, but not unheard of at this hour. I buried my hands in my pockets
and walked into the wind until I reached the bank's
ATM. I looked around quickly to make sure I wasn't
going to be mugged; that would have been all I needed.
With the two-hundred-dollar deposit I'd given the

hotel manager, I needed another three hundred to pay for that ridiculously overpriced room. The machine churned and clattered, then spit out a receipt.

Non-sufficient Funds, it read.

I tried two hundred, one hundred, and then twenty fucking dollars.

Non-sufficient funds.

This was my joint account with Mallory at a bank wholly unrelated to Saxton Silvers. Even though we had taken steps to protect it this morning, I had the sinking feeling that Mallory might be at risk, too. I dialed her cell. No answer. I dialed the landline, and it kept ringing.

"Come on, pick up."

I knew the message I'd left earlier—"I just wanted to let you know that I love you"—had been too much and was probably keeping her from picking up now. I had originally resolved to leave her alone until the morning, but now I needed to get past the answering machine.

"Mallory, I'm standing on the street at the bank trying to get cash. If you can hear this message, please pick up. It's an emergency."

She picked up, startling me.

"What is it, Michael?"

It was the same cold tone she'd used when telling me to find somewhere else to sleep tonight. I quickly told her about the nonsufficient funds notice from our checking account.

"I withdrew everything this afternoon," she said.

My response caught in my throat. "You what?"

"It's what my lawyer told me to do, Michael."

Her friend Andrea hadn't lied: Mallory had a lawyer, and her lawyer already had a plan.

"Can we slow down a little?" I said. "This isn't necessary."

"If you didn't see it coming, I'm sorry, but you should have. I'll e-mail you my lawyer's phone number. Please don't call here again."

She hung up, and I was standing alone on the sidewalk. But not for long.

"Hey, pal."

I turned and saw a man wearing a camouflage jacket, torn blue jeans, and old tennis shoes. The thing on his head threw me, but finally I realized it was a metal colander that he'd strapped on like a helmet and fastened beneath his chin with a pink-and-purple bungee cord. He held out his hand.

"Dude, you got a dollar?"

I looked at him and a pathetic smile creased my lips. I couldn't help laughing as I answered.

"No," I said. "I really don't."

24

C huck Bell signed off the air at midnight. Tonight's round-table discussion was his first appearance on one of the big four networks, and he was riding high.

"Great show, Chuck," said the producer.

"I know," he said. "And this is only the beginning."

Ratings for *Bell Ringer* were off the charts, and Bell was clobbering every other financial show on television. Going on a much bigger network only confirmed that his broadcast persona was growing. Everyone wanted to know what his confidential source was going to reveal next about the impending demise of one of Wall Street's premiere investment banks.

Bell didn't want to go home. He was too excited, and too many ideas were percolating in his head as he walked out of the NASDAQ building. The glow of a billion colored lights had him soaring. The north face of One Times Square was behind him, the building famous for the dropping of the New Year's Eve ball, and Bell glanced over his shoulder to see nine hundred square feet of Bill O'Reilly on the Fox News Astrovision Screen. Charlie Gibson and Diane Sawyer were on the even larger ABC SuperSign at Forty-fourth Street. Chuck Bell was on his way.

His cell rang as he passed a guitar-pickin' cowboy wearing only a Stetson, snakeskin boots, and Calvin Klein underwear. Bell pulled the spent chewing gum from his mouth and dropped it into the singing cowboy's open guitar case on the sidewalk.

"Chuck Bell," he said into his phone.

"I want to meet," the man on the line said.

Bell stopped and pressed a finger to his left ear to drown out the sounds of the city. "What?"

"Listen to me," the man said. "I'm telling you that I want to meet."

The strange voice was distorted by an electronic device, sounding like one of those anonymous informants on TV who talked from behind screens that concealed their identity.

Bell's pulse quickened. "Who is this?"

"Someone who knows the real Saxton Silvers story. Meet me outside the FNN Studio. I'll tell you what I know as soon as you get there."

The call ended.

Bell looked at his phone in disbelief, hardly able to comprehend his good fortune. He thrust a fist into the air, nearly airborne, he was so excited. This was getting so cool—midnight phone calls, disguised voices, the stuff of big-screen movies.

He was sure it was Cantella. Leaving him a business card with his cell number had been a smart move. Going on the air tonight and being cryptic about his source—*Maybe it is, and maybe it isn't Michael Cantella*—had been a stroke of genius. The clear implication to all of Wall Street was that it *was* Cantella, and Cantella had too much of an ego not to control a story that had his fingerprints on it.

Bell spotted a cab, pushed aside a couple of Japanese tourists who were trying to get both a picture and a video of themselves climbing into a real New York taxi, and jumped into the backseat.

"Jersey," he said, and he gave the driver the studio address.

On the ride across town to the tunnel he checked his smart phone for e-mail. One that immediately caught his eye was from the Legal Department at FNN.

Heads up, it read. *I just received word that the U.S. Attorney's Office plans to hit you with a grand jury subpoena tomorrow morning to force you to disclose*

the identity of your confidential source. Not sure what
the basis for this is. But don't be alarmed when a fed-
eral marshal shows up at the studio.

Bell sat back, closed his eyes, and smiled. Tomorrow
was already playing out in his head. First, he would
bump Money Honey again at nine A.M. to announce
his refusal to comply with the subpoena. Maybe his
publicist could book him on *The View,* where he could
take the journalistic high road and proclaim his deter-
mination to do whatever it takes to protect his source
and the First Amendment. Then, to cap it off, on
tomorrow evening's edition of *Bell Ringer* he would
put on his boxing gloves, literally wrap himself in the
American flag like Sylvester Stalone in *Rocky,* and
pulverize two bears dressed in lawyerly pinstripes.
No, not bears. Kangaroos—as in a kangaroo court.
And he'd name them "Legal" and "Evil." With any
luck, a federal judge would hold him in contempt of
court for failure to comply with the subpoena, maybe
even throw him in jail overnight. Only then—"under
relentless government pressure"—would he capitulate
and reveal his source on *Larry King Live.* If he played
this right, he'd be on all the top morning shows and
every nightly news broadcast, speeding down the fast
track toward the mainstream media and life beyond
FNN.

And that didn't even account for what Cantella was about to tell him.

Looking good, baby.

"Fifty-two-fifty," the cabdriver said. They were already at the studio. Bell typed out a quick response to the lawyer's e-mail. "Got it," he wrote. "At studio now to meet higher source."

"Now it's fifty-three-fifty, buddy."

Bell hit Send, gave the driver sixty bucks, and watched the taxi pull away. He was behind the studio in the empty parking lot. The lighting wasn't what it should have been. He'd complained to maintenance many times, mainly because he had to park his Maserati at the far end of the lot to avoid door dings from losers in ten-year-old junks.

He didn't see anyone, and it was too cold and too damn dark to wait outside. He started across the lot and headed toward the light at the rear entrance of the building.

"Hey, Bell," a voice called out from the shadows.

As he turned he heard a muffled crack that—even though the parking lot was empty—sounded like a car door slamming. A hammerlike jolt to his forehead sent his head snapping back, and his body collapsed to the pavement.

His limbs were frozen, and he couldn't move. The right side of his face was flat on the asphalt, and it was impossible even to turn his mouth and nose away from the expanding pool of hot blood that encircled his head. He heard approaching footsteps, but his vision was gone, and he couldn't force himself to speak.

"Yup," he heard a man say, "that's a Bell Ringer."

Then he heard that sound again—like a car door slamming—and his world fell silent.

25

It was one A.M., and it occurred to me that I hadn't slept since I was thirty-four years old. Papa had warned me about the insomnia. Getting old sucks.

Getting screwed double-sucks.

Convincing the night manager of Hotel Mildew to return my last two hundred bucks wasn't going to happen. Nor would he budge on the $500 room rate. We cut a deal that allowed me to stay the night for the cost of my deposit—as long as I was out of the room by six A.M. instead of the usual checkout time of eleven A.M.

I wasted my first precious hour on the telephone with my credit card company, the first thirty minutes of which was spent trying to get through the phone menu to talk to an actual human being. Finally Anoop

Gupta from New Delhi assured me that by morning I would have a working card. I could only hope that he meant *my* morning, not his. I desperately needed rest, but at 2:35 A.M. I was still wide awake, staring at the ceiling in the dark.

I can't believe she's divorcing me.

According to Mallory, I should have seen it coming, but I could recall only one major blowup in the last year. We had our favorite charities, but when Papa told me about the volunteer work he was doing for a south Florida organization called "Charlee," I immediately wrote a ten-thousand-dollar check. Mallory went ballistic—not because of the amount of the donation, and definitely not because she questioned the merits of an organization that helped abused children. She just wished I had made the donation *anonymously.* She didn't explain why, and she shut me down the moment I even hinted at anything personal in her past. But it was as if she didn't want anyone asking questions about her own childhood.

I was beginning to wonder how well I had really known Mallory in high school—if there was a reason our friendship had never evolved to the next level, if something far more oppressive than twenty-plus hours a week in a dance studio had prevented such a pretty girl from seriously dating anyone, as far as I could remember.

My mind refused to shut off, but I had major problems to solve, and I needed to focus. The fact that the draining of my portfolio was part of a bigger setup to bring down Saxton Silvers made no difference to Mallory, but Papa's question was racing through my brain: Who were my enemies? Kent Frost was no fan of mine, but I had battled dozens of guys like him over the years. I was more worried about the enemy I had no memory of ever having met. The more I focused on guys like Frost, the more likely it would turn out to be Colonel Mustard waiting for me in the library with the dagger *and* the pistol because I had somehow killed his leveraged buyout of a candlestick-holder factory.

I had officially moved from paranoid to punchy.

Go to sleep!

A banging noise emerged from somewhere in the hall, and I bolted upright in the bed. I waited, then heard it again. Someone was knocking on the door.

"Housekeeping," a woman announced.

"Go away," I said.

She knocked again, and I looked at the clock: six A.M. exactly.

Damn!

My last two hundred bucks had been enough to get me a room for only half a night, but I couldn't believe the manager was holding me to such a ridiculously early checkout. I hadn't slept at all. Or maybe I had and just didn't realize it. That's how tired I was. I rolled out of bed, opened the door as far as the chain lock would allow, and begged for another five minutes.

"I'll be back at six fifteen," said the housekeeper.

A fifteen-minute bonus. Maybe my luck was turning.

I jumped in the shower, which was literally a scream—alternating blasts of ice-cold and scalding-hot water. The poor guy in the next room must have thought it was Friday the thirteenth and that he was sharing a wall with Freddy and Jason. I pulled on my clothes—the same clothes I had worn yesterday—and used the remaining five minutes of my reprieve to check my e-mail.

The first one was from Mallory. True to her promise, she'd e-mailed me the contact information for her lawyer. I scrolled past it, didn't even catch his name.

Probably Anoop Gupta.

It was the third e-mail from the bottom that caught my attention. I didn't recognize the sender—the address appeared to be a random combination of letters and numbers—but the subject line chilled me. It wasn't "random" at all.

Orene52, it read.

I opened it eagerly and retrieved the short message: *I can help. Let's meet. Time and place TBD. Check your e-mail at 10:30.*

The message was signed *JBU.*

I froze. Obviously it was from someone who knew my stolen passwords, which was a very small universe. Mallory. Saxton Silvers' general counsel and security director. The lawyer from Cool Cash and the FBI agents on the case. None of those people would have any conceivable reason to set up a secret meeting with such a cryptic message. But one other possibility came to mind: someone who definitely knew my passwords and who definitely would operate in such secretive fashion. The identity thief who stole my money.

JBU.

I strained my brain but could think of no one with those initials. I scrolled through my address book, but the only thing under "U" was Union Square Café.

Another knock at the door. It was firmer than the last one, meaning this time the housekeeper meant business. I thanked her on my way out the door as she handed me my free morning newspaper.

The headline grabbed me: *FNN's CHUCK BELL SLAIN.*

I stopped in my tracks. It was as if someone had just hit me again with that hot-and-cold shower. I stepped to the side of the hallway and read quickly for the gist: shot outside the studio sometime after midnight, body discovered by a security guard around 12:45 A.M., no leads on the shooter.

I reopened my e-mail from *JBU* to check the time it was received: 3:35 A.M. It obviously wasn't Bell who'd sent it. Then another thought came to mind.

I wondered if it had come from the guy who'd shot him.

My cell rang, and my home number came up on the display.

"Mallory?"

"You need to get over here right now," she said.

From her tone, I knew it wasn't about a change of heart.

"Is something wrong?" I asked.

"You tell me, Michael. There's a homicide detective here who wants to talk to you."

26

I called my brother from the vintage 1970s lobby of Hotel Mildew. It was the first time we'd spoken since Ivy's memorial service. Against my wishes, Papa had already told him that I would probably call, so it wasn't out of the blue.

"Don't speak to the cops," said Kevin.

"I didn't kill Chuck Bell."

"That's not the point. I don't care if your hair is on fire and Detective Joe Friday is holding the last bucket of water in New York City. Don't talk to the cops. Period."

I hated when he talked to me like that. I was three years older than Kevin, but ever since his law school graduation he'd copped a big-brother attitude toward me. In some ways, he did seem older: He was taller, started going gray in his late twenties, and married a woman nine years his senior. I guess what really irked me was that Kevin had stopped acting like Kevin.

"What do you suggest I do?" I asked.

"Call Mallory and ask her to give the detective my phone number."

"You know Mallory asked for a divorce, right?"

"Yeah, I read it in the *Post* this morning."

"What?"

"Kidding, just kidding."

Okay, so sometimes he *did* still act like Kevin.

"Papa told me," he said.

"Did he also tell you about the text message? About the guy who's apparently had me in his sights since tracking me down at Sal's Place last fall? And about the bug the FBI found in our general counsel's car?"

"Yeah, and you and I need to meet ASAP. Where are you now?"

I was embarrassed to tell him, so I didn't get specific. "Midtown."

"My office is down toward Foley Square, but do you want to come uptown first and say hi to Janice?"

Janice was his wife of two years. I'd missed their wedding, and I had yet to visit their Upper East Side apartment, so this shot at me was probably deserved. But I had to wonder if Kevin would have invited me to his apartment, much less to his wedding, without Papa pushing it. Sometimes I thought Kevin embraced me only out of guilt—his own need to rectify the perceived injustice of two boys having come from the same womb, one raised by his biological father in the land of plenty, the other sent away by his stepfather to live with the maternal grandparents and grow up thinking that frozen fish sticks every Friday were a treat.

"Let's meet in your office," I said.

"I can be there by nine." He gave me the address, then said, "I'm glad you called, dude. I'm happy to help. Really."

I thanked him and hung up, wondering how long this was going to last.

Really.

I called Mallory, and she promised to pass along Kevin's message to the nice detective. She also agreed to let me stop by and get some clean clothes and personal items. I found a small suitcase in the hallway. A pressed suit, shirt, and tie were hanging from the doorknob.

She might as well have taped a Do Not Enter sign on the door.

My gym was on the way to Kevin's office, and my prepaid MetroCard got me there to take a real shower and put on the fresh suit and clean shirt. The suitcase was technically too big for my locker, but I made it fit. My credit card still wasn't working—Anoop Gupta had failed me—so I put a strawberry smoothie and a granola bar on my tab. From a stuffed chair in the lobby, I took a few proactive measures to make sure my personal crisis didn't drag my career down with it.

Most major corporations lumped their green efforts under a vice president of social responsibility. I had meetings with five of them in two different cities scheduled over the next two days, so I did the socially responsible thing and let them know there was no way in hell that I was going to be there. That was the easy task. The next series of phone calls was much more difficult. I was trying to put my key people at ease, but they all watched the news, and I could hear the fear in their questions.

"What's going to happen?"

"Is it true we're up for sale?"

"I'm pregnant, Michael. If we go belly up—no pun intended—do I lose my health care coverage?"

I hung up, exhausted. I hadn't even come close to dealing with every managerial responsibility I had as head of the Green Division, but refusing to drink the Kool-Aid came with a price: Committing only one hand to management meant that my clients and contacts in

208 • JAMES GRIPPANDO

the world of production also had to be reassured. There were no small fish in my pond, and before I could dial his number, Moby Dick was calling me.

"Kyle McVee here," he said, his voice crackling on my cell phone. "I'm on my way downtown. I'll pick you up and we can talk."

He knew I hadn't worked downtown since 9/11, but this was McVee's style—you went where he was going, you didn't ask what or why, you talked when he wanted to talk. He was the president and CEO of one of the world's most successful hedge funds, Ploutus Investments, LLP. The firm's namesake was the Greek god Ploutus, the personification of wealth, not the Roman god Pluto, ruler of the underworld—though in recent years people were saying that the latter was more fitting. I couldn't say that I actually *liked* McVee, but bringing him to Saxton Silvers had definitely worked to my benefit. The big Wall Street brokerage houses hungered for hedge funds, which traded much more furiously than typical investors. Ploutus meant millions to Saxton Silvers in brokerage commission dollars.

"I'm at the gym, but I actually have a meeting at nine o'clock near the federal courthouse," I said.

"Perfect," he said. "We'll drop you off."

I gave him the gym's cross streets in lower Midtown and waited. And waited. It was sort of what

Wall Street as a whole had been doing for hedge funds since the late 1990s—waiting on them, picking up the tab for lavish "capital introduction parties" in places like St. Moritz or Palm Beach, publicly denying that we steered our clients their way in exchange for all that brokerage business they did with us. When I started B-school, there were about six hundred domestic hedge funds. Ten years later there were more than 6,300, about a third of which couldn't have told you the date of their last audit. Some were charlatans, boobs, or worse. But hedge funds like Ploutus were hiring some of the sharpest minds on Wall Street—including Ivy Layton, who had been with McVee only a few months before she'd died. Successful managers worked like dogs but were paid like hogs, taking a 20 percent cut of profits (the carry) on top of annual management and administrative fees—compared with mutual fund fees of, on average, 1 percent of assets.

A long black limo pulled up. The door opened, and out climbed McVee's twenty-five-year-old nephew, Jason Wald. He was talking loudly on his cell, seeming to make it a point that I overheard.

"Look, I'm not trying to be an asshole," Wald said into the phone, emphasis on the word *trying*. "We're selling the company, and you're out. It's over, T.J."

Wald was having too much fun with this call, and it was obvious that the timing was choreographed for my benefit. I knew he was talking to T. J. Barnes, CEO of one of the top one hundred companies in Dallas. T.J. was a middle-aged cowboy who had never worked for anyone a day in his life until—on a tip from me—McVee's hedge fund purchased a controlling interest in his company.

Papa's voice was echoing in my head again: *Who are your enemies, Michael?*

I climbed into the limo and sat on the black leather bench seat facing McVee and his nephew, my back to the driver.

In recent years, the face of the relationship between Ploutus and Saxton Silvers had been less and less about me and Kyle McVee. Jason Wald wasn't about to grab the helm from his uncle, but his influence was enough to steer Ploutus deep into the subprime waters of Kent Frost and his structured products factory. Since I was the one who started the relationship between the two firms, McVee must have felt compelled to drop the bomb on me, rather than on my CDO-making, market-shaking, bonus-taking colleague.

"There's no way to soft-pedal this, Michael. Ploutus and its affiliates have no choice but to withdraw all of our capital from our prime brokerage accounts at Saxton Silvers."

It was as if he'd just punched me in the chest. Prime brokerage was a highly profitable bundle of services we provided to hedge funds and other professional investors who favored short-selling and other leveraged megadeals.

"That's two and a half billion dollars," I said.

"As of this morning, yes."

"That money is the collateral for the deals we finance and the trading strategies we execute for you."

"I hate to state the obvious, but what I'm telling you is that Ploutus won't be doing any more deals or executing any further strategies through Saxton Silvers."

"This is the kind of move from a major hedge fund that others will follow."

I was sure he'd heard me, but he was suddenly gazing out the window. We were near the NYU campus, slowly rounding the corner. McVee's attention had shifted to the nearly completed building facing Washington Square.

"Coming along nicely," he said with a wan smile.

The university was getting a new arts center named for McVee's son Marcus. I had attended the groundbreaking ceremony as one of McVee's guests two years earlier. Marcus had been dead for several years now,

212 · JAMES GRIPPANDO

and still it wasn't easy to get McVee to focus on much of anything when his son was in his thoughts. But I had to try.

"Kyle, I hope you aren't making this decision based on the ridiculous things Chuck Bell has been saying."

"Nothing to do with Chuck, God rest his soul."

"No disrespect for the dead, but the man you're commending to the hand of God almost single-handedly ruined my reputation on the Street."

"Chuck called it like he saw it. And he made me a ton of money."

"Are you saying you're short-selling Saxton Silvers?"

"Everyone with a lick of sense is short on Saxton Silvers. Wake up and smell the coffee."

His nephew inhaled deeply, as if literally showing me how to do it.

Such a punk.

I could have tried to convince McVee to wait and see how the market performed before making his decision, but he was finished with me. Except for one more thing.

McVee leaned forward, looked me in the eye, and said, "It's nothing personal. I mean that."

The car stopped within walking distance of the federal courthouse. My brother's office was in the building on the corner. The driver came around and opened the door for me. McVee slapped me on the arm as I climbed out of the limo.

"Like I said: nothing personal."

"Ditto," said his nephew.

I watched from the sidewalk as the limo pulled away. A single "nothing personal" would probably have done it. Saying it twice was one time too many.

Ditto had almost made me puke.

I checked my watch: 8:40 A.M. The market would open in fifty minutes. I had to give Eric the news about Ploutus before disappearing into a meeting with my "big brother" the lawyer. My cell rang as I was dialing. It was the tech leader from my investment team. I had every computer-savvy genius I knew trying to figure out how the identity thief had accessed my password-protected accounts, and Elliot Katz was among the brightest.

"Breakthrough," he said. "I think I know how they got your passwords."

I spoke while zigzagging my way down the crowded sidewalk, weaving in and out among hurried commuters, joggers, and dog walkers. "Tell me," I said.

"Spyware. It infected your laptop and monitored your keystrokes."

"How did it get there?"

"I've seen it countless times," said Elliot. "Even police stations fall for this stuff and get their databases hacked into. Usually somebody opens an attachment to an e-mail offering 'free porn' or some other goodie from an unknown source."

"I don't open attachments from people I don't know."

"I know. That's a given. Which leads me to the jaw dropper: The e-mail attachment that launched the spyware on your computer didn't come from an unknown source."

"Who sent it?"

"I've traced it to an e-mail you received eleven days ago," he said. Then he paused, as if reluctant to deliver the news. "It was from your wife."

A noisy bus was pulling away from the curb, making it hard to hear. I stopped walking and plugged my finger into my other ear.

"Did you say *Mallory* planted spyware on my computer?"

"That would be correct," he said.

Eleven days ago—nine days before she had gone through that charade she called my surprise thirty-fifth birthday party. I was starting to feel beyond abused. Manipulated was more like it.

"Thanks for getting to the bottom of this." I had to get off the phone and figure this out.

"You're welcome. And, Michael, don't worry. I won't breathe a word to anyone about this."

I thanked him again, hung up, and was about to make another call when I nearly walked straight into a wooden barricade. The street was blocked off for the filming of some music video or commercial, and the crew was still packing up after an all-night shoot. The detour diverted the crowd to the other side of the street, and as I crossed, one of the crew leaned over the barricade and stopped me.

"Hey, buddy," he said in a heavy "New Yawk" accent. He was pointing an accusatory finger at me, a giant Styrofoam cup of coffee in his other hand.

"Me?" I said.

"Yeah, you. Ain't you the guy who was on FNN talking to Chuck Bell yesterday?"

I assumed he didn't mean the giant bear who'd gone down on a left hook from Bell in the first round. "Yeah, that was me."

His next move was like lightning, and suddenly his cup was empty and my shirt and suit coat were soaked with lukewarm coffee.

"That's for making me lose my ass on Saxton Silvers, you short-selling son of a bitch."

Online amateurs. *Gotta love 'em.*

I could have kicked his ass for ruining what was for all practical purposes the only clean business clothes to my name, but in a way I understood his anger. As far as he knew, I was a Wall Street jerk who had bet against my own company. It made me wonder how many more—*thousands* more—just like him were out there.

I shook it off and speed-dialed Eric Volke with the important news from Kyle McVee. The Mallory question had to wait. It would surely make Eric's day to hear that our biggest hedge fund had slit our throat—and that the run on the bank had begun.

27

The coffee assault forced me to backtrack to the gym for another change of clothes. I knew there were clean socks and underwear in the suitcase Mallory had packed for me, but only upon my return did I discover that it contained *only* socks and underwear. It was as if Mallory had yanked a drawer from the dresser, dumped it into a suitcase, and called it quits.

Man, she's pissed.

I arrived at my brother's office a few minutes late, dressed in the same slacks and sport coat that I'd worn to dinner with Papa. The only clean shirt in my locker had been a work-out T so faded that it was powder blue. I'd convinced myself that the jacket made it look stylish. In truth, it was like a bad pastel fashion statement from the days of *Miami Vice*, which of course Kevin jumped on.

"Are you supposed to be Crockett or Tubbs?" he asked when he came out to greet me in the lobby. We stood facing each other for a moment, neither of us sure if we should shake hands or embrace. Then Kevin came forward and gave me a hug. It felt a little awkward, and we both seemed relieved to have that part over with.

"Come on back," he said.

I followed him down the hall, and he pointed out the autographed sports memorabilia on the walls, as if we were a couple of kids on the way to his playroom. His office at the end of the hall was not exactly Eric Volke's spread, but it was nicer than I'd expected. Silk rugs, custom draperies, tasteful antiques. I would have guessed a decorator's hand, except there were too many family photos around. I canned the decorator Mallory had hired for me: "Family" photos were allowed *only* if the people in them died before the Great Depression and were part of someone else's family.

"How are Nana and Papa?" Kevin asked as he closed the door.

"Fine," I told him, and suddenly I realized that my brother and I were alone in the same room for the first time in I couldn't remember how long. He gestured toward the armchair, offering it to me, but I wasn't ready to sit.

"How's Janice?" I asked.

His answer was way too long, and as he rambled on, my gaze was drawn to those framed family photos that Mallory's decorator would have deep-sixed on day one. Kevin and Janice. Kevin and his golden retriever. Janice in her wedding dress. The older photos were on the credenza, and I walked behind his desk and picked up the one in a silver frame. It had to be at least twenty years old. Kevin, our younger sister, my stepfather, and their stepmother. The four of them together, smiling widely and standing in front of the Eiffel Tower. I had a similar photo of me with Nana and Papa buried somewhere in a box of mementos—except that the Eiffel Tower we saw was at Epcot Center, and we spent the night at the Howard Johnson's in Kissimmee.

Kevin walked toward me and said, "That was my middle-school graduation trip."

"Nice."

I placed it back on the credenza, and silence came upon us.

"Michael, let me just say—"

"I don't want to go there," I said.

"Please, listen to what I have to say."

I looked away from the eight-by-ten of Daddy Warbucks on vacation with his chosen family and pretended not to know where this was going. I knew.

"Doing divorce work has given me some valuable insights," he said. "Every family has problems. Ours is no different. We just have to get past the silly old jealousies."

My anger shot up. "You think I'm jealous of you?"

"I think my growing up rich and your growing up poor is one of the reasons you went to work on Wall Street. Maybe you don't call it jealousy, but it's something."

"I call that complete nonsense."

"So do I. Right up there with the stupid jealousy I had for you when we were growing up."

That took me aback. He smiled a little, clearly hoping to draw one out of me. I didn't exactly light up, not sure where he was going.

"Did you ever stop and count how many houses I had lived in by the time I graduated from high school?" he asked.

"Not really."

"Six," he said. "And you know why? Because Dad was always trading up. Every house we lived in was a stepping-stone to more land, more bedrooms, a better neighborhood. It was never home."

"Nana and Papa bought their place in 1957. They only moved to Florida when I went away to college."

"Exactly. Never once was the house you lived in up for sale. When I was thirteen, about to change houses for I think the fifth time, I remember Papa telling me the story about the developer who came knocking on your front door."

Now I did smile. "All the farmland around us and all the old houses in the neighborhood were being bought up to build new family homes on three-acre lots. Papa was the only guy in the subdivision who wouldn't sell. The developer finally came by with his checkbook and said, 'Okay, old man. You win. You're the last holdout. What's your price?"

"And when Papa told him there was no price," said Kevin, clearly having heard every detail, "the developer said, 'You don't understand: Money is no object.' "

We were sharing a smile now, as I finished the story. "And Papa looked at him and said: 'You don't understand: *This* is not an object.' "

For the first time in years, my brother and I laughed together, and I felt good about that.

"Now, can we move forward?" said Kevin.

In his mind, clearly it was "problem solved." He didn't seem to understand that while laughter was good medicine, medicine wasn't always a cure—especially when the diagnosis was completely off.

"Sure," I said, happy to shift gears. He offered me a seat again, and we each took a matching armchair, facing each other.

"Let's start with this sequence of threatening messages," he said, a yellow legal pad in his lap.

I gave him the longer version of the money-burning ceremony at Sal's Place, the flaming package, the most recent text—and finally the FBI's discovery of the listening device in Sonya's car.

"Looks like Chuck Bell may have been right," said Kevin.

"How so?"

"If someone is bugging the general counsel's Mercedes, maybe your identity theft *is* linked to a larger attack against Saxton and Silvers. I'll follow up with the FBI."

"You want me to be part of that?"

"Negative. I don't want you talking to law enforcement."

"Did you hook up with the detective who came by my apartment?"

"I did."

"Does he think I killed Chuck Bell?"

"I'm not sure. It may have been just a pretense, but he said the reason he went to your apartment was to follow up on the incendiary package you received yesterday morning. They have an interesting lead. It was white phosphorous, which is pyrophoric."

"What does that mean?"

"It ignites simply when exposed to the air. The police presume it was inside some kind of vacuum-sealed plastic liner, and when you tore open the package—poof. Flames. Once it combusts, it's hard to extinguish."

"I'll vouch for that."

"Highly toxic, too. You're lucky you got out of that elevator so quickly."

"So what leads are the police chasing?"

"White phosphorous is very hard to get your hands on, unless you have something to do with the munitions business. Russian or Israeli, most likely."

"Munitions business? Doesn't sound like anybody I know."

Kevin pulled his trusty Mont Blanc from his breast pocket, ready to take notes. "We're getting ahead of ourselves," he said. "Let's start at the beginning."

I talked, and my brother occasionally jotted down a word or two. At nine forty-five he let me switch on the television for a quick market check. FNN was broadcasting in split-screen format, an aerial view of the Chuck Bell homicide scene on one side, the NYSE trading floor on the other, as if to pose the question, Can you name the real crime scene? We had the sound muted, but the news was clearly bad on both sides.

SAXTON SILVERS DOWNWARD SPIRAL CONTINUES IN HEAVY TRADING, read the banner at the bottom of the screen.

FNN FAMILY IN SHOCK OVER DEATH OF BELOVED COLLEAGUE, the next banner read.

Kevin said, "Tell me more about the e-mail from Mallory."

I looked away from the flat screen. "Mallory studied drama at Juilliard," I said.

"I think I knew that," said Kevin.

"She has a flair for performing. Every now and then, she would send me an e-mail that was kind of sexy, kind of funny. This one was an early 'happy birthday' video. It was a parody of Marilyn Monroe singing 'Happy birthday, Mr. President' to JFK."

"You have political aspirations?"

"No. But the joke was that she always thought I would someday have Eric Volke's job—president of Saxton Silvers."

"So you opened the attachment to her e-mail?"

"It was from her regular e-mail address, so I had no reason to question it. But Elliot—that's my tech guy— tells me that's where the spyware came from."

Kevin scribbled a thought on his legal pad, then looked up. "I've seen lots of spying in divorce cases."

"But why would Mallory plant spyware in a way that could be so easily traced back to her e-mail address?"

"Not too technically savvy, maybe?"

"Granted, she's not a computer genius, but she's not stupid. We live together in the same apartment. She could have just crawled out of bed one night and loaded the spyware on my laptop."

"Maybe she didn't think she had the technical expertise to load the spyware correctly, so she hooked up with some fifteen-year-old geek to plant it by e-mail."

"Or the guy who sent me the text message."

"Let's not focus too much on *how* it was planted. The key point here is that if the spyware can in fact be traced back to your wife, then your identity theft claims don't add up."

"Why not?"

"Think about it. You want people to believe that someone planted spyware on your computer, stole your passwords, wiped out your bank accounts, and masterminded a complicated short-selling scheme against Saxton Silvers in a financial scandal that has rocked Wall Street—setting you up as the bad guy. Do you actually expect me to walk over to Federal Plaza and tell the FBI that the person behind all that is Mallory?"

"She could have had help." I didn't know why I was pushing this angle; I guess I had nothing else.

"It seems much more likely to me that Mallory planted the spyware for the same reason most married people plant spyware: to find out if she was married to a cheater."

He was making too much sense to argue.

Kevin said, "Did Mallory worry about another woman?"

"No," I said, then caught myself. "At least not a living one."

Kevin did a double take.

"No, I don't mean *that*," I said, then I paused. "She always harbored jealousy over Ivy."

"Did you two talk about that?"

"Not very often. At least not until recently."

"How did it come up?"

I told him about the passwords being tied to Ivy's birthday and how that had set Mallory off. "She said I haven't given up hope that Ivy's alive," I added.

There was silence. This was dangerous territory between my brother and me. As Kevin knew, even after the shark had been dissected, I continued to have doubts about what really had happened to Ivy. Kevin had stepped in and pushed the assumed role of "big brother" way too far, doing whatever was necessary to deliver the tough-love message: "Ivy is dead, and you need to move on." I could have handled that, but what drove the wedge between us came later, after the police had asked me to take the lie detector test. "I'm talking to you as a lawyer now," he'd told me. "If something happened—if you did something you regret—you can tell me. You *need* to tell me."

It wasn't so much what he'd said as the way he'd said it. It was clear to me that—at least at that moment—my brother was more than entertaining the thought that I had killed Ivy. And that was okay in his mind because he was being a lawyer. He had absolutely no clue how that changed his being my brother.

He still thought I was jealous of his family trip to Paris twenty years ago.

"By the way," I said, reminded of something from yesterday. "The FBI asked if I would take a polygraph exam about the identity theft."

"I'll tell them to forget it," he said. "If you pass, the government will say it's not reliable; if you fail, you're their prime suspect."

It was another awkward moment. Kevin had made his skepticism about polygraphs clear four years ago, when I'd passed the one during the Ivy investigation.

Kevin rose and moved to the leather chair behind his desk, suddenly more comfortable with a big antique oak barrier between us.

"Let's shift gears," he said. "Kyle McVee."

"What about him?"

He flipped back a few pages in his notes. "You said that when McVee dropped you off this morning, his parting words to you were 'Nothing personal.'"

"Twice he told me that."

"Do you believe him?"

I thought about it. "I don't think Kyle has had a 'personal' feeling toward anyone since his son died."

"What's the story there?"

"Marcus McVee was the heir apparent at Ploutus, about my age. Not a bad guy, actually. Completely unlike Kyle's nephew—Jason Wald—who now seems to be next in line."

"What happened to Marcus?"

I paused for no apparent reason, except that it was a subject that seemed to give everyone pause. "He killed himself."

"Over what?"

"I don't know. Is it ever just one thing?"

Kevin stroked his chin, thinking. We'd been at this for almost an hour, and I had the feeling that my brother was about to get all lawyerly on me.

"Here's what I'm going to do," he said. "First, I'll call the FBI to see what's going on with the identity-theft investigation, and also to find out if you're a target for illegal trading of Saxton Silver stock. Second, I'll follow up with this detective to see if you're being linked in any way to Chuck Bell's shooting. And then I'm going to call Mallory's lawyer and see if we can avoid the divorce-court version of mutually assured destruction."

"That's one hell of a list of problems," I said. "Hard to believe that we're actually talking about me."

"I hear that a lot from people sitting in that very same chair."

I was suddenly thinking about Anoop Gupta from New Delhi and the status of my credit cards. "This is going to eat up a lot of your time," I said. "How much do you charge?"

"I don't want your money."

"I insist."

"I refuse."

"But I want to pay you."

"All right," he said, "we'll barter. I'll be your lawyer, and you come for dinner with Janice and me at our place. You can even bring an expensive bottle of wine if you want."

My little brother had boxed me in. Papa would have been ecstatic.

"Okay," I said, managing a bit of a smile. "It's a deal."

I hurried out of my brother's office in plenty of time to be long gone when the next e-mail arrived from

JBU—the mysterious someone who supposedly wanted to help me.

That was the one thing I hadn't told Kevin about. I didn't need him thinking I was crazy all over again. I figured I'd deal with that if and when the follow up e-mail came. And it came right on schedule, at exactly ten-thirty A.M.

Orene 52, the subject line read.

I was emerging from the subway station on Seventh Avenue, about half a block away from Saxton Silvers' shiny glass office tower, closer than any cab could have gotten me to the building. Double-parked media vans and news trucks blocked several lanes of traffic on the street. The sidewalk outside the building's main entrance was jammed with reporters and camera crews jockeying for the perfect TV shot—right in front of the distinctive gold letters on the black granite wall that spelled SAXTON SILVERS. They pounced on anyone who came through the revolving doors, hoping for thirty seconds of breaking news. Through the windows on the third floor, I saw men and women dressed in business suits peering down on the frenzy. That was the Saxton Silvers foreign-exchange trading floor, normally a place of intense activity where traders were glued to their computer terminals, not standing at the window and pressing their worried faces to the glass.

Hopefully, none of them had it in mind to find a higher floor and jump.

Word was out that Kyle McVee had pulled the plug on Ploutus Investments' $2.5 billion prime brokerage account. According to the latest FNN online update, two more major hedge funds were about to follow suit. The media smelled blood, and I sensed that at least a few drops were my own. It made me want to stay clear of anyone with a microphone. I stepped onto the sidewalk, found a lamppost to hide behind, and opened the latest e-mail message—the one that was supposed to tell me when and where to meet.

Today at 4 p.m. Table for two in front of the statue of Prometheus. That was the entire message. Again it was signed *"JBU."*

"Michael?"

I turned at the sound of the distinctive voice and saw Papa standing next to a hot-dog cart. He was wearing a bright blue University of Florida Gators tracksuit, running shoes, and a pair of wraparound Oakley sunglasses so new that the tag was still hanging from the frame. All he needed was a garbage bag filled with knock-off Gucci purses and a selection of Rolex watches up to his elbow and he would have looked just like the sidewalk entrepreneur who'd sold him the glasses.

"What are you doing here?" I didn't mean to sound accusatory. I was just surprised to see him.

"I was trying to get up to see you, but I couldn't get near the building."

"Is something wrong?"

He came closer and lowered his voice. On the busy streets of New York, Papa really sounded like a mobster when he whispered. "The FBI came to see me."

"FBI? Why?"

"At first I thought it was about tracking down your lost money, so I was happy to talk to them. But then they started asking me all kinds of questions about the Bahamas, about Ivy, about—"

"About Ivy?"

"Well, not directly. It was more about that sailing trip you were on, and that guy who was your captain."

"Rumsey?"

"Yeah, that's the name. Did you know he was dead? Killed a few days ago in Harbor Island."

The news took me aback, and not just because Rumsey was one of the nicest guys I'd ever met. That made two people who knew me and who'd been murdered in the same week.

Papa said, "The FBI apparently knows that you travel down to Florida pretty often to see Nana and me. The agent was really pushing hard to find out if you ever hooked up with Rumsey on any of your trips to Miami."

"What did you tell him?"

"I said I don't know anything about that. But that's when I started to get a bad feeling about this whole thing. So I says to him, 'If this ain't about finding my grandson's money, I'm not interested in talking to you.'"

I glanced toward the growing crowd outside Saxton Silvers' headquarters. Suddenly it was hard for me to breathe. I knew who "JBU" was.

"Thanks, Papa. You done good."

28

Ten minutes later, I was headed for Long Island. The Ivy factor was growing stronger, and I needed answers.

A phone call from Andrea had pushed me over the edge. It came just five minutes after my conversation with Papa. I still didn't trust her, but the fact that my grandfather had also been approached by the FBI lent credence to her story.

"Heads up from a friend," she'd told me. "The FBI just interviewed me. They seem to be questioning all the wives and significant others, anyone who might have known your first wife or anything about her disappearance."

I didn't drive often, but I loved my car. My first set of wheels in high school had been a nine-year-old Monte Carlo two-door coupe with a smashed-in fender, a broken heater, and a headlight that pointed at the moon. I bought it with my summer earnings and a five-hundred-dollar loan from Papa. When I finally unloaded it after B-school, the two-hundred-dollar CD player mounted under the dash was worth more than the entire car. The joke was that the dirt was holding it together, and it got to the point where I was actually afraid to wash it—what if it wasn't a joke? Now I was head of the green team and drove a Mini Cooper Convertible, although it broke Papa's heart when I took him to see *The Italian Job* and had to tell him that the "scoopers," as he called them, weren't actually Italian.

"Hello, Olivia," I said when Mrs. Hernandez opened the door.

I didn't know Ivy's mother well. She was a widow who had never taken her husband's surname, the proud Latina half of Ivy Layton's heritage. I had spoken to her only once before Ivy's death, and our only face-to-face meeting was at Ivy's memorial service. I phoned her a couple of times after that, but it was clear that Olivia did not care to make me part of her life. At first I surmised that I was simply an unpleasant reminder of her daughter's tragic death. As time wore on, however, I sensed that she actually *blamed* me, as if I should have been more careful with Ivy on the boat, should have noticed she was missing sooner and radioed for help, or could have done something to prevent it altogether.

"You should have called first," she said from behind the screen door.

"I really need to speak to you," I said.

"I've seen your name in the news," she said. "Not too flattering."

"That stuff's not important. This is. It's about Ivy."

She stood there for a moment, saying nothing. Then she finally opened the door, and I was thankful to be inside. She led me to the parlor, and I glanced around the room as I settled into the armchair. I expected to see framed photographs of Ivy and of Olivia's late husband on the bookshelves and end tables. There were none, at least not in this room.

"Is this about Ivy's account?" she asked. Olivia bore a strong resemblance to her daughter—the perfect posture of a ballerina, the heart-shaped face of a classic beauty, a strong and healthy glow that must have truly shined in her youth. I couldn't look at her without feeling my loss all over again.

"I have some bad news," I said, and my voice suddenly felt weak. "It's gone."

"Gone?"

I nodded, and as concisely as possible, I explained the identity theft—the liquidation of my accounts, the transfer of my cash into Ivy's account, and the disappearance of both into the world of bank secrecy. She'd heard all of that on FNN—except the part about Ivy's account.

"Have you notified the police?"

"The FBI is working on it."

"Are they going to get it back?"

"I hope so."

"Well, they'd better."

Her tone was harsher than I'd expected. "That's why I wanted to talk this out with you," I said. "After Ivy's memorial service—when I offered you the money in her account—you said you didn't want it."

"I said to leave it right where it was."

"And that's what I did. Until it was stolen."

She made a face, obviously skeptical. "Stolen, you say?"

"Yes. Along with my entire personal portfolio."

"You should know how that makes me feel," she said, her voice quaking.

"I do."

"No, I really don't think you do," she said. "Nobody does."

"I understand how you never gave up hope on Ivy," I said. "Even if it was just a one-in-a-million shot that Ivy was still alive, you were the one who insisted that it would be bad luck to touch the money."

238 · JAMES GRIPPANDO

"That is what I told you," she said. "And it was a lie."

"Excuse me?"

The ballerina's posture was suddenly more like a pit bull's. "Refusing the money had nothing to do with the hope that Ivy might someday return. I have long been convinced that my daughter is dead."

"I don't understand."

"I left the money on the table, so to speak, because I knew the truth."

"I'm sorry, I'm not following you at all."

"Ivy's money gave you motive to kill her. That was one of the reasons the Bahamian police focused on you from the beginning. I knew that was the reason you offered me the money. You wanted to eliminate your motive."

"That's not it at all," I said. I was too tired to get angry. It was too ridiculous to get angry.

"Deep down, I have always known that if I left that money on the table long enough, someday you would take it. You would be content to let the money sit in the account and collect interest for years and then, when enough time had passed, you would grab it. And now you finally did."

"That's not what happened. Her money disappeared with mine. It's all gone."

"I'm not buying that identity-theft hogwash for a minute. I saw the way Chuck Bell picked you apart on his show. And the FBI told me about your marital problems. I don't know what you're trying to hide from your second wife, but I don't want any part of it."

"The FBI has come to see you?"

She rose and said, "You should leave now."

I couldn't believe how badly this was going, but if she was siding with Chuck Bell, talking with the FBI, and taking shots at my marriage, I didn't stand a chance.

"We can't leave it like this," I said.

"Go. Please."

"I loved Ivy, and I would never—"

"Stop!" she said, her voice sharp enough to silence a soccer riot.

She went quickly to the door and opened it angrily. I had no choice but to go, and the screen door slammed behind me as I stepped onto the porch.

"There's one other thing you should know," said Olivia.

I stopped at the foot of the stairs and glanced back.

"When the FBI came to see me, I told them exactly what I just told you—and I promised to help them in any way I can."

The door closed with a thud. I followed the winding slate walkway to the street, careful not to step on the daffodils—Ivy's favorite—as I climbed into my car. I pulled away from the curb slowly, still in shock, the engine little more than idling as I passed the house. The draperies were open, and through the big bay window, I could see into the parlor.

Ivy's mother was alone on the couch, her face in her hands, crying.

29

I was back in Manhattan in time for a late lunch, but there was barely time to eat. I had dozens of calls and e-mails from my team at Saxton Silvers, and a half dozen more from reporters who were casting their nets for quotes from anyone in management about the impending demise of the firm. One in particular was spearfishing for something far more specific.

"Michael, it's Rosario Reynolds at FNN," she said in her voice-mail message. "Calling to invite you onto my show. I know you were as shocked as we were by Chuck's shooting, but it's starting to look like he was probably on to something when he suggested a possible link between your identity theft and a bigger attack against Saxton Silvers. Love to get your views on the air. Call me."

I wasn't sure what to think. But there wasn't a minute to respond, even if I'd wanted to. At one-thirty P.M., my brother and I were in family court.

"All rise!"

Mallory had filed for divorce that morning, and if there had been any question as to whether it was "full speed ahead," the answer was now clear. The bailiff called the case, and the lawyers announced their appearances and introduced their clients to the judge. The knot in my stomach was beyond description. I was living a scene I had never dreamed I'd see—Mallory on the other side of the courtroom, refusing even to look at me in the case of *Cantella vs. Cantella*.

"Mr. Highsmith," said the judge, "your motion had better be the emergency you claimed it was when my secretary squeezed this onto my docket."

"It is, indeed," he said, rising.

Elgin Highsmith was the go-to divorce lawyer for Saxton Silvers wives, a Brooklyn-born former cop who walked into a courtroom with a set of brass balls. Literally. It was a bizarre intimidation tactic. He held them both in one hand as he approached the lectern, and I heard those balls of brass clacking together as he worked them through his fingers before eventually tucking them into his pants pocket. It seemed comical, but there was nothing funny about this guy.

Plenty of Wall Street hotshots could still hear those balls rattling around in their brain as the tow trucks hauled away their Bentleys and Aston Martins. This was the same master strategist who had told Mallory to clear out our bank account before I even knew what was coming.

"May it please the court," he said, stepping away from the lectern. He had no notes—more of the brass balls approach. "Your Honor, my client seeks to freeze all of Mr. Cantella's assets, and she demands a full accounting of all investments that were liquidated in the last forty-eight hours and moved to an offshore account in the Cayman Islands."

I nearly jumped from my seat, but my brother beat me to it.

"*What?*" said Kevin.

"One at a time!" said the judge, banging his gavel.

"But, Your Honor, this is—"

The judge cut him off with two bangs of the gavel, the second one so hard that it knocked his nameplate—THE HONORABLE SIDNEY STAPLETON—to the floor. Kevin started toward the bench to pick it up, but the judge again admonished him.

"Sit *down*, Mr. Warfield!"

I was beginning to wonder if Judge Stapleton had ever lost money with Saxton Silvers.

Who are your enemies, Michael?

The bailiff retrieved the judge's nameplate.

"Mr. Highsmith," said the judge, "you may continue."

Highsmith's hand went in his pocket, and I heard that rattling again. "Judge, in my thirty years as a divorce lawyer, I have never seen a more despicable and transparent attempt by a man to hide his assets from his wife."

On cue, his paralegal brought out demonstrative charts to help him explain the transfer of funds from Saxton Silvers to the Cayman Islands.

Highsmith continued, "You will note that—with the exception of Mr. Cantella's holdings in Saxton Silvers— many of these equities were sold at a substantial loss. Which raises the question: Why would such a knowledgeable man have such an indiscriminate investment strategy? Why was *everything* liquidated and sent off to a numbered account?"

"Because it was *stolen*," said Kevin.

The judge scowled, this time pointing with his gavel. "Not another peep out of you until I tell you it's your turn to talk. Mr. Highsmith, continue."

"This is a scam, Judge. Mr. Cantella knew that his wife had uncovered his secret and was about to file for divorce. That is when Mr. Cantella cooked up this identity-theft scheme and conspired with his lover to hide his assets from his wife."

"*What?*" I said, sounding like my brother.

"Mr. Warfield, I warned you—"

"I didn't say anything!"

It was just like old times, my kid brother blaming me.

"Sorry, Your Honor," I said, but I was looking at Mallory as I spoke. "It's just that my wife knows this isn't true."

Her eyes were cast downward, not even a glance in my direction.

"Mr. Warfield, please control your client. Mr. Highsmith, I'm warning you as well. I am not going to turn this hearing into a mini-trial on Mr. Cantella's alleged infidelity."

"Understood. For purposes of this motion, I have just three e-mails for the court to consider." Highsmith brought out three poster boards, one for each blowup. "Mr. Cantella received the first e-mail on the night of the birthday celebration his wife Mallory had planned for him—the same night that his equities were liquidated and moved into the secret account. The message simply reads: "Just as planned. xo xo.""

I whispered to my brother, "I showed that one to Mallory and gave it to the FBI."

Highsmith said, "Clearly the 'xo xo' suggests that this plan was from someone who had an intimate relationship with Mr. Cantella. The second and third e-mails are more recent, coming after my client asked her husband for a divorce. Read together, these two recent e-mails propose a secret meeting at the Rink Bar at four o'clock today. These messages are signed JBU."

Kevin looked at me, but I was dumbfounded. My tech guy had already removed the spyware. "I have no idea how she got those," I whispered.

"Objection," said Kevin, rising.

"This isn't a trial," said the judge.

Highsmith jumped on it. "Exactly, Your Honor. And at this preliminary stage of the proceedings, I believe we have made a sufficient showing to warrant the relief requested—a temporary freeze on Mr. Cantella's assets and a full accounting of every penny that was transferred offshore."

Kevin said, "Mr. Highsmith should at least be required to establish the authenticity of those e-mails. We have no idea where he got those last two about this supposed secret meeting."

The judge looked at Highsmith and said, "How did you get those e-mails?"

Highsmith smiled, and the hand went back into the pocket, reaching for the brass balls. "As the court knows, I'm a very resourceful trial lawyer."

"So resourceful," said Kevin, "that Mr. Cantella's wife planted spyware on her husband's computer."

I cringed. Kevin had pushed the wrong button, as was evident from the judge's sour expression.

"Stop the sniping," the judge said. "Let me just get to the bottom of this question of whether the e-mails are authentic or not. Mr. Cantella: Did you receive these e-mails or did you not?"

I hesitated. This was going to be news to my brother—and he wasn't going to be happy. "I did, Your Honor. But they're not from a lover."

"Who are they from?

"Well . . . I don't know."

"You don't *know*?" said the judge.

Highsmith chortled.

Kevin said, "What my client means to say is—"

The judge gaveled him down. "I told you that this is not going to be a mini-trial. The time will come for you to rebut these allegations, but for now I will grant the motion and prohibit Mr. Cantella from making any further sales or transfers of assets valued at more than five hundred dollars. Mr. Cantella has five days to submit to the court a full accounting of all assets transferred from his accounts within the last forty-eight hours."

"That's impossible," I whispered to Kevin.

"Judge," Kevin said, "that's—"

"*That's* my ruling. We're adjourned."

With one final bang of the gavel, it was over—or, as the expression on Highsmith's face suggested, we were just getting started.

"All rise!" called the bailiff.

As the judge stepped down from the bench, I heard a muffled noise from the rear of the courtroom— someone else rising from the wooden bench seats in the gallery. I turned and looked. It was Ivy's mother.

A sickening feeling came over me. Olivia wasn't just helping the FBI.

Could she be helping Mallory?

Kevin pulled me out of Judge Stapleton's courtroom and into the men's room across the hall. He checked the stalls to make sure we were alone, and then he tore into me.

"I want the truth: Were you having an affair?"

"No."

"Are you working with someone to hide your assets from Mallory?"

"Absolutely not."

"Then who is JBU, and why does he or she want to meet with you in secret?"

"I don't know for sure. It's hard to explain."

"Why didn't you tell me about those other two e-mails?"

I breathed in and out, wary of his reaction. "Because I knew that you and I would not see eye to eye on them."

He folded his arms and leaned against the paper-towel dispenser, as if he had more than enough time for the whole story. "I have no idea what you're talking about, but I'm all ears."

"On the first e-mail—the one that says 'I can help'—I had no idea who JBU was. But it hit me immediately when the second one came in. It was hard to ignore the fact that the meeting place was the Rink Bar at Rockefeller Center, the table right in front of the gold statute of Prometheus."

Kevin shrugged. "What about it?"

"That was where Ivy and I had our first date."

"Oh, no," he said, groaning.

I could see that I was losing him. I continued, "Ivy and I had a business relationship before I asked her out. If things between us didn't work out, she didn't want the hedge fund she was working for to exclude her from deals involving Saxton Silvers. That's why she chose the Rink Bar for our first date, a tourist attraction where we were less likely to see anyone we knew. But we hit it off, partly because we discovered that we were both fans of Norman Brown."

"Who?"

"He's a jazz guitarist, and he happened to be playing at the Blue Note the following week. We agreed to make his show on our second date, but we also agreed to keep the fact that we were dating 'Just Between Us,' which was the title to Brown's debut album."

"JBU," said Kevin.

"Right. It wasn't someone's initials."

He was with me—sort of. A look of concern came over his face. "But you don't think that—"

"That the e-mails came from Ivy?" I said, finishing his thought. I could almost see his head throbbing.

"*Please*, Michael. Don't tell me we're going down this Ivy-is-alive path again."

I said nothing, knowing he would resist.

Kevin suddenly dug into his briefcase, as if an idea had come to him. He pulled out a hard copy of another e-mail—the one from Mallory that had transmitted the happy birthday video and planted the spyware on my computer.

"Just as I thought," said Kevin. "This e-mail from Mallory has that song title in the subject line. It says 'Just Between Us.' *Mallory* is JBU."

"I told you we wouldn't see eye to eye on this."

Kevin scoffed. "Don't you get it? The e-mails came from Mallory, who is scheming—probably with

Highsmith's help—to create a bogus paper trail that makes it look like you have a mistress."

"I don't think Mallory would do that."

"Oh, get a grip, will you?"

"I'm serious. Mallory has a lot of resentment toward me—enough to put spyware on my computer. But make up evidence? That isn't even close to the woman I married."

Kevin came toward me, laying his hand on my shoulder. "Michael, Ivy is dead. She is not JBU."

"There's one way to find out."

He knew what I meant. "If you go to the Rink Bar at four o'clock, you will be playing right into Highsmith's hands. He will cite it as proof that you have a lover, and that the two of you are plotting to hide your assets from Mallory. As your lawyer, I absolutely forbid you to go."

"I don't care," I said, looking him in the eye. "I'm going."

30

A few minutes before four P.M., Tony Girelli was seated alone at a café table at the Rink Bar outside Rockefeller Center.

Every spring when the ice melted and the Zamboni went into storage, the famous skating rink in front of the gold statue of Prometheus became a popular lunch and happy-hour destination. A scattering of brightly colored umbrellas shaded tables for about six hundred margarita-loving patrons. Above them at street level, the year-round swarm of tourists stood at the rail, people watching. Girelli took it all in. His boss had extensive commercial real estate holdings, and Girelli wondered if he owned a piece of this place.

Real estate, however, was a sore subject for Girelli.

"Sparkling water," he told the waiter. "With lemon."

Girelli still carried a copy of a certain blast e-mail in his wallet, one that he—and hundreds of guys like him—had received last fall from a trader at the residential mortgage desk at Saxton Silvers. *As per Michael Cantella*, it read, *we will no longer be purchasing NINA loans. Please do not call. No exceptions will be granted.* At the time of that announcement, Girelli had been pulling down $125,000 in commissions—*a month*. He and his buddies would go into Miami Beach clubs almost every night, order four or five bottles of Cristal champagne at $1,500 a pop, and think nothing of it. Not bad for a guy who had once been flat broke but who was determined never to return to the world of a leg-breaking, brass-knuckled debt collector for the mob. He'd been shooting pool at a bar one night when a buddy had asked, "Wanna be a mortgage broker?" and he'd jumped on it.

Girelli's specialty had been NINA loans—"no income, no assets"—for, as he put it, "people who didn't have a pot to piss in." He'd load up an eight-dollar-an-hour housekeeper with a million dollars in mortgages on six houses, one for everyone in her family, including two sisters who were still trying to get here from Mexico. And what self-respecting taxi driver should be without three or four pre-construction-priced condos on Miami Beach? The loans were destined to go into default, of course, but that wasn't Girelli's problem. He teamed up with a buddy at Sunpath Bank, and they borrowed at a 30 to 1 ratio—$100 million against $3 million in capital—to fund all the subprime loans they wrote. Then Sunpath bundled all the subprimes together and sold them up the daisy chain to Wall Street, paying back Sunpath's lenders with Wall Street's money and keeping the profit. What a hoot. What a party. Until the e-mail:

As per Michael Cantella . . .

Never mind that Sunpath had already funded yet another $100 million in subprime loans in "business as usual." Never mind that there was no way to pay back Sunpath's lenders unless Wall Street bought the bundles. Girelli and his partner tried other investment banks, but Wall Street firms were like sheep: The minute a leader like Saxton Silvers decided to stop buying NINA loans, they all followed suit. Funny thing was, no one in the subprime pipeline had ever heard of this asshole Michael Cantella. The guy didn't even have direct supervision over the residential mortgage desk at Saxton Silvers. Some even said that the e-mail's attribution, "As per Michael Cantella," was just Kent Frost and his subprime factory taking a swipe at Cantella for sticking his nose where it didn't belong. Whatever the case, the plug was pulled. Sunpath closed its doors in a week.

Three hundred employees lost their jobs. The people at the top lost everything. Michael Cantella didn't even know their names.

Girelli intended to keep it that way.

"Here you are, sir," said the waiter.

Girelli squeezed the lemon and discreetly surveyed the crowd. Michael Cantella was nowhere to be seen, and in light of the disclosure of the e-mails at this afternoon's court hearing, Girelli doubted that Cantella's divorce lawyer would let him go to a secret meeting that was no longer a secret.

Wasting my damn time here.

The thought had barely registered when Girelli spotted a woman approaching the table referenced in the e-mail, the one right in front of the gold statue of Prometheus.

A tight smiled creased his lips.

Pay dirt.

31

I was at street level, standing at the rail that surrounded the concrete hole in the ground at Rockefeller Center, looking down on the Rink Bar. Had it
been December, I would have been crushed beneath a
ninety-foot-tall Norway spruce and five miles of twin-
kling lights.

On reflection, I'd decided that Kevin might be right:
The e-mails from "JBU" might all be a setup to help
Mallory prove that I was having an affair. *Might* be
right. It wasn't enough to keep me from going to the
Rink Bar at the designated time. It was enough, how-
ever, to make me take precautions.

Two reporters had hounded me all the way out of
the courthouse, a constant peppering of questions
about Saxton Silvers. I figured it was only going to get

worse as the media buzz honed the link between me and the firm's downfall. If I was going to the Rink Bar, I needed to be unrecognizable, but my suitcase full of socks and underwear didn't offer much in the way of a disguise. I stopped by the Days Inn and borrowed Papa's trench coat. The hem was frayed, the elbow was patched, and part of the lining was torn and hanging out of the sleeve. My guess was that he'd purchased it before I was born. He also loaned me a white golf cap with the red, white, and green Italian flag sewn onto it, his latest acquisition from Mulberry Street. It hadn't been my intention, but I could have passed for a homeless guy.

The last two days had been nuts on every level—too crazy for me to give serious consideration to Mallory's accusations. She was wrong: I did love her. But she was also right: I had not stopped loving Ivy. Maybe that kept me from loving Mallory enough. Love was Nothing if it wasn't the truth, and in my case the truth was painful: nothing compared to what I had felt for Ivy. If that made me a bad person, I hoped Mallory would forgive me. But if Ivy was still alive, I hoped she would forgive me, too—and tell me who or what had made her vanish four years ago.

And why was she coming back now?

"Excuse me, but would you take our picture?"

A young woman wearing a University of Wisconsin sweatshirt was shoving a camera in my face. Her girlfriends were already posed at the rail.

"Sure," I said.

I took a few steps back and aimed the zoom lens. I was facing east, toward the Fifth Avenue entrance, looking out over the top of the Rink Bar below us. Flags of the United Nations' 192 member states encircled the rink area and flapped in the breeze. I zoomed in, then out—then in again.

"Tell us when," the woman said.

I wasn't focused on them. I zoomed in over their heads, peering between the flags of Japan and Jamaica. On the other side of the plaza, a man was standing in the second-story window above Dean & DeLuca. It was the perfect vantage point from which to look down into the Rink Bar. He was almost entirely concealed by the curtains he was standing behind, but I noticed him because of the camera with the long telephoto lens in his hands. This afternoon's hearing had apparently expanded the media interest beyond me and Saxton Silvers to me and Mallory.

"Ready when you are," the girls from Wisconsin said, but I was still focused on that photographer in the window. I saw him adjust his lens, and although I couldn't be certain, he seemed to be shooting rapid-fire frames of the Rink Bar. I did a little triangulation in my head, and my gaze followed the aim of his lens. It was pointed in the direction of the statue of Prometheus— and then I froze.

A woman had taken a seat at the same table that I had shared with Ivy on our first date. She was alone.

And it was precisely four P.M.

Tony Girelli stared over the top of his menu.

He couldn't be sure it was her. The stylish wide hat shaded her face, and her sunglasses were huge. At this hour and in the shadows of tall buildings, there was really no need for that much protection from the sun. And she had shown up at the right place at precisely the right time. He decided to give it a test.

"Vanessa!" he called out.

It was almost imperceptible, but Girelli definitely saw her flinch. He laid his menu aside and kept watching.

Finally she glanced in his direction. Girelli tightened his stare, and although her eyes were hidden behind the sunglasses, he sensed her fear. Girelli knew all the signs—the tightening of the expression, a leg gone restless, the posture suddenly rigid.

Without warning, she bolted from her chair and ran for the exit.

Girelli launched himself after her, pushing aside a waiter, two women at the bar, and everyone else in his way.

On impulse, I ran.

"Hey, give me back my camera!" the college girl shouted.

I was already at full speed, thinking only of getting to the bar's exit at the top of the stairs on the other side of the plaza.

"Stop that guy!"

I could have tossed the stupid camera back at her, but I kept running, passing one flagpole after another, watching the commotion in the Rink Bar below as that man—whoever he was—bowled over tables, chairs, and people alike in pursuit of . . .

The thought that it might be Ivy had me flying on pure adrenaline. There was no denying that I had seen a woman take a seat at our table at four o'clock, watched her jump up and run, and saw another man chase after her.

My God, could it be?

She was halfway up the stairs, the man a few steps behind her, and I was approaching the top of the stairway from the opposite direction when someone screamed:

"A bomb! That man in the trench coat has a bomb!"

It was bedlam throughout the plaza.

Hundreds of tourists screamed and scattered, and the stairway was suddenly jammed with the surge of utter panic. I lost sight of the woman and the man in the ensuing stampede, and suddenly I was broadsided by what felt like a charging rhinoceros. My chest hit the sidewalk, and the air raced from my lungs. The moment was a blur, until I realized that I was pinned beneath two of New York's finest.

"Don't move!" a cop shouted.

"You got the wrong man!" I yelled back.

"You're under arrest!"

My heart sank as the cold metal cuffs closed around my wrists.

32

Mallory was alone in the backseat of a taxi, peering through the window as she drank from her go cup—a double vodka tonic she'd mixed before leaving her apartment. It wasn't even dinnertime, but she would have liked nothing better than to crawl into bed and sleep till morning.

"You're quite the piece of work," she said quietly to her reflection in the glass.

Storefront after storefront raced by her, the driver catching every green light as they sped south on Fifth Avenue. She downed the rest of her drink, laid her head back on the headrest, and stared at the taxi's tattered felt ceiling.

Today's court hearing had gone exactly as planned. Her reaction to it was nothing like she'd expected.

Accusing Michael of conspiring with a secret lover to hide assets left her with the uneasy feeling that "what goes around comes around," and Mallory knew she wasn't exactly standing on solid ground.

She'd met Nathaniel three months ago at the fitness studio. Mallory was serious about her workouts and didn't make small talk with guys who grabbed an eyeful of her body. But one day her Pilates instructor had failed to show up, and Nathaniel was kind enough to share his and turn a private lesson into a semi-private. Nathaniel was good—pairing with him was almost like having two instructors. So she kept up the semi-privates for a couple of weeks, and by week three they were going for coffee afterward. By week four they were sleeping together. The man was fun in bed, but it wasn't just that. He filled a need.

You don't love me, Michael. You like me, but you don't love me.

The cab stopped between Eighth and Ninth avenues, and Mallory stepped out. It was their usual meeting spot, one of the few places where she felt comfortable meeting her lover in public.

Therapy was a spacious lounge with killer decor, a friendly atmosphere, and cozy sitting areas. The food was good enough to get it a spot on *Hell's Kitchen*, and its tasty drinks bore memorable names like Freudian

Sip. Most important—and in keeping with Mallory's low profile—Therapy was one of the best gay bars in the city. Of course, meeting in a gay bar didn't take all the risk out of a heterosexual affair. While Therapy wasn't known as one of those places where investment bankers went looking for boy toys, it drew its share of Wall Street types, and Mallory was all too aware that one of them might have some connection to Saxton Silvers. Her little joke was that at least she would hear them coming. They'd be the ones humming Fagin's refrain from the Broadway hit *Oliver. In this life one thing counts, in the bank large amounts*—or something like that.

Mallory found Nathaniel waiting upstairs, where the lighting was low and the tables were arranged cabaret style. Stage shows here ranged from the whacky to the sublime, but the night was too young for live entertainment, so the booths in the back gave them relative privacy. Nathaniel had insisted on seeing her tonight, his text message saying, *Urgent.* She tried to smile as she approached, but her mind was busy searching for a way to tell him that she was in no mood for sex.

He rose and gave her a hug. No kiss. His smile was awkward. Right away, Mallory knew something was up.

"Are you okay?" she asked as she slid into the booth.

"Yeah, fine," he said.

He cast his gaze downward at his hands.

"Are you sure?" she asked.

Now he was looking toward the bar. "Yeah. I'm good."

Mallory's throat tightened. This was starting to feel like a page out of her first marriage. All of the bad signs were there.

"Look at me," she said.

Slowly his gaze drifted back toward her. Their eyes met, and Mallory's heart sank.

"Something's wrong," she said.

He grimaced, as if in pain. "I can't do this."

"Can't do what?"

"Us," he said. "It's over."

Mallory had to catch her breath. "You're the one who gave me the strength to divorce Michael."

"Don't put that on me."

She reached across the table and took his hand. "No, I'm not blaming you. Michael and I were headed for divorce, I'm sure of it. You gave me the strength to accept it."

He withdrew his hand and wrapped it around his beer bottle.

"I'm grateful to you," she said, trying to smile. "Let's face it: If it had been any other man but you, I would have been caught cheating long ago."

"What the hell are you talking about?"

"I don't have what it takes to pull off something like this. You knew all the tricks to keep Michael from suspecting." She squeezed his hand, but he pulled back.

"This isn't going to work anymore, Mallory. Get it? I'm outta here."

Her body stiffened. She'd never heard this tone from him before, and she was beginning to wonder if she had ever seen the real Nathaniel. After a day like today, it was making her downright angry, and she suddenly found a new kind of courage.

"An interesting thing happened in court today. Michael's lawyer informed the judge that there was spyware attached to that 'happy birthday' e-mail we sent to Michael." Her eyes narrowed, and she said, "Do you know anything about that?"

He shot her a look that cut to the bone. "This is exactly the kind of shit I'm talking about. I have no interest in getting caught in the cross fire of nasty accusations flying back between you and Michael."

"I just asked a simple question."

"Go to hell, Mallory. If you want to ask questions, go ask your husband why he flipped his lid and shot Chuck Bell in the head."

"You don't know that."

"It's what everybody is saying. Do you think I want my picture on the front page of the *Post* when this shit unravels?"

Mallory collected herself, then said, "You're married, aren't you."

"No," he said, scoffing. "I'm too smart for that."

She took that as a direct shot at her *second* failed marriage. "What's that supposed to mean?"

"Nothing," he said, and then he rose from the booth. "Look, we all have to make our own choices. I choose not to be part of your mess. So let's agree to do you, me, and your divorce lawyer a big favor: Keep me out of it."

He left a ten-dollar bill on the table for his beer and walked away. Mallory didn't watch him go. She stared at the money on the table and half laughed, half cried.

It was the first time Nathaniel had ever paid for anything.

33

I was in jail. I couldn't believe it. I was actually behind bars.

Before leaving Rockefeller Center, the arresting officers had patted me down, run a background check through their databases, and satisfied themselves that I wasn't actually carrying a bomb. But that didn't stop these men of the Midtown North Precinct from hauling me downtown. Technically speaking, it wasn't jail. I was in a holding pen in the Manhattan Detention Complex, where prisoners were held for relatively short periods of time pending arraignment or some other court appearance. Not that this was a step up from jail. I was locked in the very same cell in which a seventeen-year-old boy had used his shirt to hang himself the summer before.

"Got two more bodies," the guard announced.

The guards had a habit of calling us "bodies" when talking among themselves. It seemed kind of ghoulish, especially since the Manhattan Detention Complex was known as "the Tombs" to police, lawyers, criminals, judges, and anyone who had ever watched an episode of *Law & Order.* The nickname fit. Over the past two hours, I had climbed up and down several flights of stairs and in and out of three different holding pens. I had lost track of what floor I was on. I had been shackled, unshackled, and shackled again. The body search had been especially memorable, not so much for what actually had happened, but for fear of what might. On a sign on the wall, some joker had scribbled in the word "anal" between "Male" and "Search." Fingerprinting took another hour. The state-of-the-art machine kept delivering error messages: rolling too fast, too slow, not a clear image, multiple fingers detected (odd, since my other fingers weren't even on the screen), partial finger detected. At that point, I was willing to forgive the inaccuracy of one of my all-time favorite films, *American Gangster,* in which Denzel Washington's character is shown leaving the Tombs—a temporary holding facility—after a *fifteen-year* stay.

This could actually take fifteen years.

The mug shot was the final indignity—a real beaut that I was sure would end up all over the Internet, if not in the tabloids. Finally, the guards brought me back to my cell and gave me dinner, though I passed on the soggy bologna-and-cheese sandwich. It smelled so awful that I was going to flush it down the toilet, which was in open view in the corner of the cell. Instead, my cell mate tore the sandwich into pieces, rolled them into balls, and one by one pitched them into the toilet from various positions behind the imaginary three-point line.

Around seven o'clock, the guard returned.

"It's your lucky day, partner. You can go."

He opened the cell door and led me down the hall. We passed a window that was open just a crack, and I was certain that I could smell spring rolls. We were *that* close to Chinatown—and I was *that* hungry.

At the end of the corridor the guard pushed a button, a buzzer sounded, and the iron door slid open. Kevin was on the other side of the chute waiting for me, a look of complete disbelief all over his face.

"What the hell is wrong with you, Michael?"

"Good to see you, too," I said.

"You're lucky I have friends in the D.A.'s office," he said. "They're not charging you."

"They shouldn't. I didn't have a bomb."

Kevin clearly had much more to say, but the guard was standing just a few feet away. We went downstairs to collect my belongings—including Papa's old trench coat and Italy golf cap. When he saw what I'd been wearing, Kevin just shook his head and said, "We need to talk."

The lobby of the station house was far from private. Uniformed police officers coming and going, two prostitutes in a territorial dispute, a drunk with a bloody nose, and a homeless guy with vomit all over his shoes sitting on the end of a long wooden bench. It was like something out of that show *Hill Street Blues* that Papa used to watch when I was a kid.

Kevin led me down the hall to a small room. I could see the stenciled words ATTORNEY CONFERENCE backward on the glass as he closed the door. It was a stark room with yellow walls of painted cinder block, a small wooden table, and two oak chairs. Kevin asked me to sit, but after two hours on the hard benches of the holding cell, I didn't want to. We just stood on opposite sides of the table.

"You could have been in a heap of trouble," he said. "Two witnesses said it was the homeless guy—*you*—who ran off with a college girl's camera and started the whole panic by threatening to set off a bomb."

"That's not what happened. A woman shouted that I had a bomb. And then it was chaos."

272 · JAMES GRIPPANDO

"Did you steal the camera?"

"No. I was taking a group picture for these girls and then I . . . I saw something, and I had to run."

"What did you see?"

"I'm pretty sure I saw Ivy," I said.

Kevin groaned, and then his expression turned serious. "I'm worried about you."

"Why?"

He took a breath, as if to calm himself. "I'm worried that it's more than you—more than *anyone*—could handle. The divorce, the identity theft, the attack on Saxton Silvers, the pillaging of your financial accounts, the lack of sleep. You aren't thinking clearly—dressing up like a homeless guy, setting off a panic attack in one of the most popular urban tourist areas in America, all this talk about seeing Ivy."

"I know what I saw."

"You didn't see Ivy."

"Could have been someone pretending to be Ivy."

"Why would someone pretend to be Ivy?"

"I can't think of a reason. That's why I say it was her."

He groaned even louder. I was undeterred.

"And I think she was literally running for her life when she took off and ran from that man who was chasing her."

"Michael, you're my brother, and I want to help you. But I've had just about enough."

I could see he wasn't kidding. It was time to change the subject. "Can we get something to eat?"

"Yeah. Good idea."

I gathered up Papa's trench coat and hat. Kevin yanked open the heavy entrance door and together we walked outside. We were at the base of the steps, and I was pulling on Papa's old coat, when two men approached from behind a construction barrier on White Street.

"Mr. Cantella?"

Kevin and I stopped. I recognized one of the men as he flashed his shield.

"Malcolm Spear," he said, "FBI."

It was the same agent I'd met in Eric's office with our general counsel. Spear had another agent with him, not the computer fraud specialist I'd met before. It was Agent Coleman, the one who had come to my building to investigate the elevator fire. I noticed a spot of duck sauce on his jacket, and I could almost smell it. We were *still* that close to Chinatown, and I was *still* that hungry.

"Let me guess," I said, "you found my money."

Spear showed no reaction. "Heard you had a temporary change of address," he said. "Wanted to come by and ask you a question."

Kevin stepped between us. "He's not talking to the FBI."

"Who are you?" asked Spear.

"His lawyer."

"No tricks here," said Spear. "I just want to ask him about Chuck Bell."

"Since when does the FBI investigate homicide?" said Kevin.

"We're talking about a pattern of criminal activity that includes a number of federal offenses. It's all our business."

"Sorry, he's not talking," Kevin said.

"I simply want to know if your client can tell me where he was between twelve and one A.M. night before last, when Chuck Bell was shot."

Instinct told me not to answer, but a flash of excitement came over me. "As a matter of fact, I can," I said, reaching for my wallet.

"Hold it," said Kevin as he grabbed me by the wrist. "For the last time: He's not talking to the FBI."

"But I want to answer," I said.

"*Don't*," Kevin told me.

He was probably right, but as always, something about his tone made it impossible for me to heed his advice.

I showed Spear the ATM receipt—the one that read "nonsufficient funds"—and said, "I was at an ATM on Third Avenue trying to get money to pay my hotel bill."

He checked the receipt, stroking his chin. "So, if we went to the bank and reviewed the tape from the security camera, we'd see that it was indeed you who conducted this transaction?"

"You sure would," I said smugly.

"Interesting," he said.

"Why is that interesting?"

Kevin was about to explode. "That's enough," he said. "You've got your answer, Agent Spear."

"I just want to know why that's interesting," I said.

Spear narrowed his eyes. "About a year ago I investigated a racketeering case. Mob guy took great pains to make sure he was on camera at an ATM in Manhattan at the exact moment the trigger was pulled in Jersey. He wanted to be able to prove up an alibi." He paused for effect. "We nailed him on murder for hire."

My expression fell.

"May I keep this?" he asked.

"No," I said, taking the receipt back. I gave it to Kevin. "I think my lawyer will want that."

"Fine," said Spear. "We'll see you around, gentlemen."

I watched as the two agents walked away. Then Kevin looked at me, glowering.

"Don't *ever* do that to me again."

There was that tone again. "I have an alibi," I said.

"Not anymore you don't. Now he knows the correct charge against you is not murder. It's a murder-for-hire case. That's why you *never* talk to law enforcement."

My stomach was suddenly in knots. Maybe Kevin was right: This was more than anyone could handle. Too much had happened in too short a time, and if I didn't get some food and sleep, I was well on my way to becoming my own worst enemy.

"Let's go eat," I said.

"No," he said. "You go."

"Don't be like that."

He took a breath, then paused to measure his words. He spoke in an even tone, but I could hear the anger behind it.

"I'm really trying, Michael. But you're making this way too hard. So please, get something to eat, and get a good night's sleep. Because if you're still talking crazy in the morning, you're going to need a new lawyer."

He walked away. I started after him, then stopped.

Better to let him go, but as he rounded the corner, it suddenly occurred to me:

I had no idea *where* I was going to sleep.

34

From the detention center I went to my car, then drove to Long Island, when a thought popped into my mind. I didn't call first; I knew Olivia would tell me not to come. By the time I pulled into her driveway my thoughts had gelled, and I was so pumped with adrenaline that I nearly flew up the sidewalk to ring the doorbell. It was getting dark, and in the shadows I must have looked like some lunatic on a home invasion. But that wasn't the reason Olivia left the screen door closed between us.

"I thought I made myself clear earlier," she said.

"You definitely put on a nice show," I said.

"A show?"

"You know exactly what I'm saying."

She leaned closer to the screen and glanced at my feet. "Are you sure you're allowed all the way out here with an ankle bracelet?"

278 · JAMES GRIPPANDO

"Very funny. I'm not wearing one. But I *am* curious to know who told you I was arrested. Was it . . . Ivy?"

Had I been wrong, the question would have been cruel, and I wasn't sure where the courage—or audacity—to take that risk had come from. My need to know was overwhelming, but the gradual realization that Ivy could still be alive had moved from the analytical to the emotional, and I had reached the breaking point.

Olivia took a half step back, as if offended, but she must have seen something in my eyes or demeanor that cut through Act II of her performance. I didn't know exactly what was in her head, but I sensed an opening.

"You pushed too hard, Olivia."

Her silence said it all.

"It was so out of the blue," I said, my voice shaking, "the way you suddenly turned against me and accused me of murdering Ivy. It was as if you were trying too hard to convince me, the FBI, and the rest of the world that Ivy really was dead. My gut told me that you were hiding something—or protecting someone. And now that I've pieced things together, I know that the 'someone' is Ivy."

More silence. I kept talking.

"When I saw you in the back of the courtroom today, I thought you were helping Mallory. I don't think that anymore."

"It's a public proceeding," she said. "Anyone's allowed to watch."

"That's true. And after those e-mails were made public, it must have been pretty frightening for you to realize that *anyone* could know about my four o'clock meeting with JBU."

"Why would that frighten me?"

I gave her an assessing look. "Your performance is getting much weaker."

She averted her eyes, so I kept talking—faster and faster—giving her no chance to deny any of it. "You knew that Ivy wasn't keeping a minute-by-minute tab on my divorce. She had no way of knowing that those e-mails had come out in open court. And it was entirely possible that the people who had forced Ivy to disappear four years ago *did* have those e-mails and knew all about the four o'clock meeting. That was a risk you couldn't take. You went to the Rink Bar. When Ivy got up and ran, and when that man ran after her, you did the only thing you could think of to protect your daughter: You created chaos by screaming 'That man has a bomb!'"

Finally she answered: "Actually, it was 'That man in the trench coat has a bomb.'"

Her words chilled me. "Where is she, Olivia?"

She shook her head. "There are things you are better off not knowing."

I stepped closer to the screen door. "Olivia, please. *Where is she?*"

"She's dead, Michael. That's all you need to know. Ivy is dead."

I suddenly couldn't speak.

Her expression turned deadly serious. "Don't come back here again, or I will call the police."

The door closed, and I heard the chain lock rattle. Olivia switched off the porch light from inside the house, leaving me alone in the dark.

35

Tony Girelli went for a ride. He was seated in the passenger seat of a new Lamborghini Gallardo Spyder, and Jason Wald was driving 80 mph—cruising speed for 520 horsepower—across the Triborough Bridge. It seemed that every time Girelli saw Wald, the kid had a new set of extremely fast wheels. Business was obviously good at Ploutus Investments, and it never hurt to be Kyle McVee's favorite nephew—even if you were a sorry replacement for his dead son.

"Where we going?" asked Girelli. He had to shout over the rumble of the engine.

"Queens," said Wald.

No shit, thought Girelli, but he didn't press for specifics. Self-esteem for punks like Wald came from holding all details close to the vest—even the details they were too stupid to recognize as meaningless. Girelli figured they were headed to a debriefing about what had gone down at the Rink Bar. If information was power, Girelli held it for now. Only he knew that the chaos had all started when he'd used the name "Vanessa."

"Nice car," said Girelli.

"You want to drive it?"

"Sure."

"Blow me."

It was a familiar banter from better days between the two men, back when they used to hang out in Miami Beach and party with the skinny models on Ocean Drive who would give it up to any guy with money after two Red Bulls and vodka. That was during the subprime heyday, when Girelli was pulling down $125,000 per month and Wald was raking in ten times that much on thousands of mortgages he purchased from guys like Girelli and sold to Kent Frost and others on Wall Street. When the infamous e-mail from Saxton Silvers—As per Michael Cantella—had ended all that, Wald and Girelli vowed to nail that son of a bitch.

They got off the bridge. Wald steered the Lamborghini around the sharp corner and into an alley, pulling up to the rear entrance of a body shop. It was well after business hours, and all of the paint and body shops on the block were closed. The garage doors were shut, iron burglar bars covered the remaining doors and windows, and coils of razor wire ran like a giant, deadly Slinky along the top of a ten-foot chain-link fence. It wasn't exactly the ideal neighborhood in which to park a $250,000 Italian sports car at night.

Wald tapped the horn, the garage door opened, and they pulled inside. He killed the engine, and with the push of a button the doors on either side opened at an upward angle like the wings of a butterfly. The two men climbed out of the car as the garage door closed behind them.

Girelli's radar was at full alert. He'd gone on rides like this before—to warehouses and body shops in Queens—but never as the guest of honor. But he wasn't worried. Girelli was packing a fully loaded Beretta 9 mm pistol, and Jason Wald was a dolt. That was two strikes against the home team, and the game wasn't even under way.

"Glad you could make it, Tony."

Girelli turned, unable to see the man standing off to the side in the shadows, but the distinctive accent was enough to give him pause. Two against one was no problem, unless one of the two was who he thought it was.

The silhouette took a half step forward, and then, with the flick of his lighter, he removed himself from the dark. Girelli's pulse raced, his fears confirmed by the instantly recognizable face—or more specifically, by that deformed right ear.

The last person Girelli wanted to see tonight was Ian Burn.

36

I wasted the ride back from Long Island. I should have put the top down on the Mini Cooper, cranked up just enough heat to take off the chill, and felt the wind on my face as the lights of Manhattan and the world's most recognizable skyline swallowed me up. When I bought my convertible, I had signed a contract stating that I would drive it 90 percent of the time with the roof open. It was a marketing joke, but the way things were going, I wondered if they might actually sue me.

Yes, I was sweating the small stuff—like where the hell I was going to sleep tonight.

The Saxton Silvers parking garage was my destination, mainly because it was free and I still hadn't straightened out my cash flow. To get there, I had to pass the firm's main entrance on Seventh Avenue. Television crews, photographers, and a phalanx of other people crowded the sidewalk outside the revolving doors, and a line of double-parked media vans hugged the curb. A small but vocal group of demonstrators marched in a circle in the middle of all this. Anger was all over their faces, even angrier words on their handmade signs:

CROOKS!

SCREW YOUR BONUS. WHERE'S MY PENSION?

I was suddenly thinking of Ivy again and that day we'd stumbled into the FTAA riots in Miami. I rounded the block and pulled into the garage.

My Mini made a funny noise when I shut off the engine. To me, it definitely sounded like the carburetor, except that I hadn't owned a car with a carburetor since I dumped the 1975 Monte Carlo after B-school. That was how much I knew about auto mechanics.

Apparently, about as much as I knew about Ivy.

Mallory had been right: Over the last four years I'd fooled myself into thinking that I had moved on, but I hadn't. Perhaps my reaction now should have been one of sheer joy: *Ivy is alive!* There was some of that, to be sure. But it was much more complicated.

Why did you run, Ivy?

The funny noise in my engine stopped, but I remained in my car, thinking. I still hadn't resolved the small things, but now it was the big stuff that consumed me. My personal portfolio had vanished into cyberspace. Saxton Silvers stock had dropped 90 percent in value. The FBI seemed to think that I was the traitor who'd used Chuck Bell and the power of FNN to bring down my own firm. Bell was now dead, and I was apparently being blamed for that, too. To top it all off, my wife was divorcing me over a dead woman who—suddenly—was no longer dead.

The timing of it all made me consider a dark possibility: What if Ivy didn't share the joy I felt over a potential reunion? What if she had come back from the dead, so to speak, only to visit on Michael Cantella a fate worse than death?

Couldn't be. Or could it?

My thoughts drifted back four years to our sailing trip and the dream I had told her about—the one about riding my bicycle on a dark highway, getting run off the road, and rushing my injured dog Tippy to the DQ. The gist of that strange dream had actually happened: A week before our trip, a black SUV had knocked me into a ravine and left me for dead. Afterward—and this was the reason for the nightmares—I wondered if the driver had been a Wall Street loser with a score to settle.

It's only gonna get worse. That had been the warning from the anti-FTAA demonstrator who pulled me from the taxi in Miami. I had always wondered if he was really just talking about corporate greed. Was it possible that the same maniac had followed us to the Bahamas and played some role in Ivy's disappearance? Again, I had to ask:

Why did you come back, Ivy?

Were the last few days payback for ruining her life? Did she finally emerge from hiding only to move my money into an offshore account and make me out as the villain behind the destruction of Saxton Silvers? Did she also destroy my marriage? Was she done with me yet? Those were terrible thoughts about a woman I loved. But with four years to plan it, Ivy was definitely smart enough to implement such a scheme, and with her birthday—orene52/25enero—at the root of my passwords, I had to consider the possibility. And after all, I couldn't shake the memory that, in my dream, the hit-and-run driver of the SUV had been Ivy.

Stop it. Ivy would never—

My phone rang. It was Eric Volke. He and our CEO had spent the last twelve hours at the New York Federal Reserve in downtown Manhattan, in a room once used to cash coupons on Treasury bills. On the other side of the table had been the masters of the world's biggest economy—the Federal Reserve chairman, the secretary of the treasury, the New York Fed chief, and the Securities and Exchange Commission chief.

Eric was calling from his limo. "Meet me at my house in thirty minutes," he told me. "It's important."

He hung up before I could ask what it was about.

But I already knew.

37

I an Burn stared out over the flame of his butane lighter.

His fascination with fire was logical enough, given his surname. It was bogus, of course. So was the name Ian, an acronym for "Islamic Armed Nation," a terrorist organization that Burn supplied with the tools of the trade—detonators, explosives, and munitions of all sorts. He had an especially reliable source of white phosphorous. He was paid with Saudi oil profits that poured into a certain American hedge fund run by Jason Wald's uncle. "Burn" was a nickname he'd earned by torching anyone who got in his way. Only once had a job blown up in his face—literally. Working with napalm was dangerous stuff. Burn had a grotesque scar on his neck and a melted right ear to prove it, but even that mishap had unfolded true to the old playground adage: "You should have seen the other guy." It amazed Burn how so many people had never even heard of fifth- and sixth-degree burns, as if the always-fatal flame that caused complete destruction of muscle and bone didn't belong in a class by itself.

"I'm not the enemy," said Girelli, but his voice betrayed him, cracking with fear.

Burn capped his lighter, extinguishing the flame. Another thug jumped out from behind a tall stack of tires, and two more emerged from behind a canvas tarp. Before Girelli could react, there was a gun at this head. They forced him into a wooden chair and tied him to it with a heavy-duty extension cord that wrapped around his body several times.

Burn stepped closer and dropped a handful of eight-by-ten photographs on the concrete floor in front of Girelli. Wald switched on a snake light and aimed the beam at the photos.

"Jason shot these from his uncle's building," said Burn.

Immediately upon seeing the close-ups of the woman seated at the table in front of Prometheus—Vanessa—he knew he was in trouble.

"You lied," said Burn. "And some very important people are extremely angry."

Girelli stood firm. "That's not who you think it is."

"Really?" said Burn. He took a hundred-dollar bill from his pocket and dropped it on the photo at Girelli's feet. "A hundred bucks says you're lying."

Girelli knew the routine, and he forced a nervous smile. "Come on. Let's not play this game."

"You're right. You aren't worth a hundred bucks." But he wasn't smiling. He never smiled.

Burn tucked the bill back into his pocket, then grabbed a paint can from beneath the work bench. The can had no lid on it, and beside it were the remnants of several Styrofoam coolers that had been chopped to pieces—a ready source of polystyrene. Burn pulled on a pair of thermal gloves, then grabbed a paint stick and stirred the sticky mixture inside the can as he approached Girelli. The consistency was near perfect, but for Girelli's benefit he dropped another chunk of Styrofoam into the can and let it dissolve. He stirred slowly, making sure that Girelli could smell the gasoline. And the benzene. Most of the amateur pyromaniacs on the Internet simply dissolved Styrofoam in gasoline, which basically created a sticky gel that burned. Add benzene—available from chemical companies if you had phony credentials—and voilà: You had essentially the same "super napalm" used by the U.S. military in Vietnam.

"This burns at about a thousand degrees centigrade," said Burn.

He lifted the stick from the can. A big glob of gel clung to it. Burn held it over Girelli's head and let the gel slowly drizzle down onto Girelli's hair.

"Ever seen the pictures of the napalm girl from 'Nam, Tony?"

The goo ran down Girelli's forehead, swallowed the bridge of his nose, moving at a lavalike pace until it covered his right eye.

"That shit stings!" Girelli shouted. "Get it off!"

Burn scooped a second glob from the can and again held the stick over Girelli's head. This one oozed over his left ear and down his neck.

"Not a pretty sight, that napalm girl," said Burn. "Clothes burned off, running down the street naked, her burned flesh ready to fall from her body."

Girelli's hair was soaked with gel, the right side of his face completely covered.

"This gel sticks to your skin," said Burn, "and you can't get it off. It just keeps burning and burning, hotter and hotter."

"Okay, okay!" Girelli shouted. "It was her!"

Burn dropped the stick onto the concrete floor and set the can aside. "That's a problem, Tony. Because you were supposed to get rid of her four years ago."

Wald said, "He told us he *did* get rid of her."

Burn pulled a stick match from his pocket.

"Don't burn me!" Girelli shouted.

Burn struck the match, but he held it away from the gel. "Why'd you lie to us, Tony?"

Girelli's voice raced with fear. "I thought she was dead! I really did!"

Wald said, "You told us you shot her. You said you took her from the sailboat, did the job, and fed her to the sharks."

"She was dead!" Girelli shouted. "That's all that mattered. You wanted her dead so—"

"So you told us what we wanted to hear," said Wald.

Burn dropped the match. It fell onto the glob on the floor, igniting it instantly. The fire produced a black, noxious smoke. Above them was a huge overhead fan that normally sucked out car exhaust. One of Wald's thugs switched it on to keep them all from suffocating.

"Why did you lie?" asked Burn.

"I thought she was dead, I really did."

"Did you work with her? Did you help fake her death and let her run?"

"No, no! I swear, I thought the bitch was dead. I just needed the money, and the only way to collect my fee was to say I shot her before the shark got her."

The homemade napalm continued to burn near Girelli's feet. It was close enough to make him sweat, and he was peering out nervously with the eye that wasn't covered in goo.

"Tony, Tony," said Burn, shaking his head. "What are we gonna do with you?"

"Get this shit out of my eyes. It's killing me! Please, just give me another chance!"

"Hey, now there's an idea," said Burn.

"Yeah," Wald joined in. "We let Tony live if he does the job right this time."

"I'll do it for free," said Girelli. "Just don't burn me, dude."

"Brilliant," said Burn, and then he glanced at Wald. "Why don't you and your buddies beat it so Tony and I can work out the details."

Wald smiled as he reached for his car keys and climbed into his Lamborghini. The garage door opened, and he pulled out. Three other men walked out after the car, and the door closed automatically again.

Burn watched the fire at Girelli's feet, which had grown hotter with the shot of fresh air.

"I can do this right," said Girelli. "No bullshit this time."

"I'm thinking about it," said Burn.

"Just let me live, and I will get the job done. I swear I will. She'll wish I had done her four years ago."

"Unfortunately, the decision is not up to me. But I can get an answer pretty quickly."

Burn pulled a sealed envelope from inside his coat pocket. It was a delivery package that opened with a zip tab—just like the one he'd sent to Michael Cantella.

"Open your mouth," said Burn.

Girelli hesitated, then complied.

"Bite down," said Burn as he placed the envelope between Girelli's teeth.

His mouth closed with obvious reluctance, but he had no choice. The envelope was firmly in place. The thick gel continued to run down Girelli's face and gathered on the flat side of the envelope.

"Now," said Burn as he reached for the tab, "let's see what the boss man thinks of your smart idea."

38

"It's over," said Eric.

It was after nine P.M., just the two of us in the first-floor study of his Tudor-style mansion in Rye, New York. I say Rye, but the *Haute Living* feature story said that the ten-acre estate actually spanned three towns and had five addresses, putting his annual property tax bill somewhere north of $300,000—all worth it, no doubt, if you and your wife needed nine bedrooms, twelve bathrooms, two swimming pools, a clay tennis court, a putting green modeled after the famous twelfth hole at Augusta, a collection of beehives, and three large paddocks. Throw in a river running through the wooded backyard and a trout-stocked private lake, and life had to be good. Most of the time.

Eric was standing at the credenza between a pair of Tiffany lamps, pouring himself a scotch on the rocks. I was seated on the camelback couch.

"Over?" I said.

I'd driven there thinking I had some explaining to do about my arrest at Rockefeller Center, never thinking that it would be "over" before I even started talking. I almost didn't care; it seemed almost certain that Ivy was alive—and nothing mattered more. "It was all a misunderstanding," I said. "You can't fire me for that."

He turned and shook his head. "I meant *us*—the whole firm."

His voice shook, and as he laid his hand atop his favorite Remington bronze, I caught a glimpse of his face in the unflattering light of a halogen spot that was intended to illuminate the sculpture. In the past three days, he had aged ten years. He took a long drink, then went to the framed memento on the cherry-paneled wall: his very first paycheck from his days as a broker with Saxton Silvers, which he pointed out every time I came over. It was flanked on one side by the first bottle of wine produced by the vineyard he owned in Napa Valley and on the other side by a *Forbes* article about WhiteSands, the investment management firm he'd founded and taken public to the tune of a nine-figure personal profit.

The check was for two weeks' pay: six hundred dollars.

"This firm survived the Civil War," he said, "two world wars, the Great Depression, a currency crisis, and the destruction of our headquarters on nine/ eleven. Two members of the Silvers family even survived Auschwitz. And now it's over."

"What do you mean over?"

"There will be no bailout from the Fed," he said. "The short sellers won: Saxton Silvers is filing for bankruptcy tomorrow morning."

"But you said the deadline was Sunday."

"That was when we had merger talks going with the Bank of New World. Those broke down this morning. I've been speed-dialing Louis Kendahl all day. That prick wouldn't even take my calls."

Kendahl was the CEO of New World, the largest commercial bank in the country.

"I even tried him at home," said Eric. "The machine picked up three times, and on the fourth his wife answered. I stressed how important it was. Do you know what she told me? She said: 'If Louis wanted to speak with you, he would have called you back.'"

Ouch, I thought.

Eric walked across his study, leaned on the edge of his desk, and looked around. "Damn," he said, the exquisite furnishings of home apparently having triggered a work-related thought. "I can't believe I just spent a million one renovating the executive suite."

My sentiment exactly—even before the subprime shit had hit the fan.

"A lot of good memories," he said, his gaze drifting back toward the Saxton Silvers paycheck on the wall. "All of them good, really. Except one."

He was looking at me now, and of course he meant the outing in the Bahamas, where Ivy disappeared.

"All but one," I agreed.

"I should never have let—"

"Don't go there," I said. There was no need for anyone to start taking the blame now. "You didn't *let* Ivy and me go off on our own. We just went."

He poured himself another scotch. "Do you ever wonder if she . . ."

I waited, hanging on his open thought. I wondered if he had intuited—or heard—something.

"If she's alive?" I said, finishing for him.

He nearly dropped his glass. "No, not if she's *alive.* I was going to say . . . she came into your life so all of a sudden. Then vanished. Did you ever wonder if that's all she was ever meant to be?"

He was starting to sound like Kevin, and it didn't seem like the time to start the conversation that Ivy was indeed alive.

The phone on his desk rang. He went to it, seemingly glad for the interruption, as if he had never intended the conversation to get this personal.

"This is the call I've been waiting for," he said as he put on his headset.

I started toward the door, but he stopped me.

"Have a seat," he said. "This is why I invited you over. I want you to hear this."

I was confused, but I obliged by taking a chair by the fireplace as Eric answered the phone.

"Agent Spear," Eric said into his headset, "what can I do for you?"

I did a double take. Spear was the lead FBI agent who had interrogated me in Eric's office.

Eric pushed a button on the phone that allowed him to use the headset without Spear knowing that the call was on speaker—or that I was in the room.

"Thanks for making time to talk with me tonight," said Spear. "I know you have a million things going on."

"A million and one now," said Eric.

"I'll make this quick. I just have some follow-up on Michael Cantella. We subpoenaed his cell phone records for the night Chuck Bell was shot."

My chest tightened. It was intimidating to feel the power of the federal government in action.

Eric was unfazed. "And?"

"Interestingly enough," said Spear, "Michael and you had a phone conversation just after midnight, not too long before the shooting."

The last few days had become a blur, and I had to think a moment before recalling that I'd spoken to Eric on my way back to the Hotel Mildew from the ATM.

Eric said, "Michael and I have been in very close contact lately."

"Did you talk about Chuck Bell in that conversation?"

"Could have."

"Did Michael say anything about Bell?"

"Not that I recall."

"Do you remember anything at all about the conversation?"

"Not really."

"All right," said Spear. "Just wanted to plant the seed. When the dust settles with Saxton Silvers, we can talk more."

"You got it. Good night," said Eric. He pushed the red button to end the call, then tossed his headset aside.

I had a lump in my throat the size of a golf ball. "You lied," I said.

He stepped away from the desk and sat on the edge of the chair, facing me. "Like a rug," he said.

"Why?"

"Because I have a very specific memory of what you said that night. And it bothered me very much."

"What did I say?"

"You were furious at Bell for suggesting on the air that you were his source. And you told me, 'One way or another, I'm going to get a retraction out of that son of a bitch.' "

"I didn't mean *violence*. And I definitely didn't mean I was going to kill him."

"Did you know that Bell had been subpoenaed before he was shot?"

"Subpoenaed for what?"

"To reveal the identity of his source."

"I wasn't his source, Eric."

"I'm simply telling you what I've gathered from my conversations with the FBI. That's what this latest follow-up was all about—and that's why I wanted you to hear it with your own ears. Spear is convinced that you knew Bell had been subpoenaed. He thinks you wanted to stop him from revealing his source. One way or another."

It was a less-than-subtle underscoring of how well my own words fit with the FBI's theory. "What are you really telling me, Eric?"

He walked over from his desk and put his hand on my shoulder. "Two things," he said. "One: That phone conversation you and I had is between us. No one—especially not the FBI—is going to know about it."

"You don't have to protect me from anything," I said.

"Two," he said, letting his promise stand. "Make no mistake: There is one thing far worse than being accused of killing Chuck Bell."

"What?"

"Being the accused killer of Saxton Silvers. A few people will make money when this firm goes down. A lot more will lose money. A *lot* of money. Shareholders, creditors, employees—they all get wiped out in bankruptcy. One thing you can be sure of. Somewhere in that long line of losers is someone mad and crazy enough to blow you away—if they get the opportunity. You understand what I'm telling you?"

I nodded, but he said it anyway, his expression deadly serious.

"Don't give them the opportunity."

39

Ivy Layton was on the run. That was nothing new. Running from one hiding place to another had become a way of life. What made tonight so different was the level of fear—a fear she hadn't experienced since those terrifying days and nights in the Bahamas following the happiest day of her life. They had found her.

Again.

A bit of dust fell from the twilled linen cloth as Ivy climbed out from under it. The marble floor felt cold on her hands and knees.

Ivy had spent two of the last four years in Italy, where there seemed to be a Catholic church on every corner. Confessionals had become her go-to hiding spots. Tonight, it was just her luck that she'd darted into an Episcopal church—no confessionals in the Anglican tradition. A beautiful damask that covered the altar inside the chantry chapel had served her needs in a pinch.

St. Thomas Church is at Fifty-third Street and Fifth Avenue, a few blocks north of its more famous Catholic neighbor, St. Patrick's Cathedral. Ivy recognized the French High Gothic style, and everything but the length appeared to be of cathedral proportions. Her first thought had been to conceal herself behind the high altar, which was front and center in the traditional design. Halfway down the nave she found the chantry chapel in its own alcove. It would have been perfect for a small wedding—and the hollow space beneath the small altar was an excellent hiding spot.

Ivy stepped cautiously from the chapel, her gaze sweeping across fifty rows of empty wooden pews in the church nave. Two hours earlier, when she'd rushed inside in a panic, the entrance doors had been unlocked and the chandeliers had been on. The vast interior was now dark, save for the indirect lighting on the sculptured stone wall behind the high altar. Hopefully lights off didn't mean doors locked—as in Ivy spending the night.

She turned away from the lighted altar and walked slowly toward the narthex, trying not to let her heels click on the inlaid marble floors as she passed by the World War II memorial. Just thinking about the close call at the Rink Bar made her pulse quicken. If not for the bomb scare, it would have been the end of the line. She probably could have been in Canada by now if she had just kept running, but she had taken enough risks for one night. Her next move, she decided, would be just a few blocks to the west. Her friend Phillip would give her something to eat and a place to sleep. He'd helped her more than any man since Michael, but the relationship was completely platonic. Phillip was gay, a bartender at Therapy. Michael's new wife wasn't the only one who thought a gay bar was a good place for a woman to hide.

Lucky for Ivy that she had recognized Mallory before Mallory had recognized her.

Or maybe not.

Ivy pushed against the carved Archangel Gabriel on the heavy church door—the same door through which she'd run earlier. It was locked. She tried the one next to it, carved with the Archangel Michael—hoping that the name alone would bring good fortune. Locked, too. She put her shoulder into it, more out of frustration than an actual attempt at escape, only to discover the hard way that these old doors were made to last a millennium.

Wonderful.

The back of her neck tingled with goose bumps. That gut-wrenching fear was returning—not for herself, but for Michael. Now that she'd tipped her hand and they knew for certain that she was alive, she was not the only one in danger.

Ivy returned to the cavernous nave of the church, her gaze drifting toward the dimly lit high altar. There had to be a way out, and she knew she would find it. Somehow she'd always managed to stay one step ahead of them.

Her only worries were for Michael.

She drew a deep breath, and since she was in a church, she figured a quick prayer couldn't hurt. Then she reached for her cell and dialed Michael's number.

40

"Michael, it's me."

I thought I was emotionally up to speed with the fact that Ivy was alive, but hearing her voice on the phone blew me away. People sometimes describe these moments in their lives as "time standing still," but that must have happened only in movies from Papa's generation. The feeling was the complete opposite for me. It was hard to fathom how so much of our past could be resurrected in a split second. Just those few words—*Michael, it's me*—triggered a flood of memories, instantly bringing back all the things I had feared I was forgetting. Her laugh. Her touch. Her kiss. Even the smallest details of our first phone conversation, our first date, our first naked adventure were compressed into that nanosecond of joy, scores of emotional threads unraveling at warp speed and on parallel tracks that led straight to my heart.

But the sense of urgency in her voice was unlike any I had ever heard.

"Where are you?" I asked. I didn't know what else to say.

"I can't tell you."

I was in my car driving back to Manhattan and was ready to go wherever she was.

"Just listen, please," she said. "We are in so much danger now that they know I'm alive. They might torture or even kill you to lure me out."

"Who are *they*?"

"Just *run!*"

"Wait! I need to see you."

"Michael, *please!*"

An eighteen-wheeler flew past me in the next lane and nearly took the ragtop of my Mini Cooper with it. Tiny cars and the Cross Bronx Expressway were not a happy marriage.

"If you won't see me, then why did you come back?"

"You know why. I *told* you."

Her response caught me by surprise. "When? How?"

"My first warning."

"I never got any warning."

She hesitated, and I sensed her fear.

"Michael, the first text message. Two weeks ago, right after I saw Mallory in that gay bar with another man."

"What?"

"Are you saying you didn't get the message that said 'beware the naked bears'?"

Naked bears? "I didn't get anything like that."

"Shit!" she said, her tone even more urgent. "Then they must be intercepting your messages. They might even be listening right now! Michael, you have to run."

"I have to see you!"

"It's too dangerous."

"Ivy, don't do this to me!"

"Don't let yourself end up like Chuck Bell. *Run!*"

"Ivy, please—"

A loud crack on the line stopped me cold. It sounded like a gunshot.

"Ivy?"

The line was dead. My heart was in my throat.

My God, Ivy!

41

Mallory poured herself another glass of wine, emptying the bottle. She needed a shoulder to lean on—even cry on a little—and she found it in her friend Andrea.

"Let's open another," said Andrea.

Mallory grabbed a key from a hook on the wall. "Here," she said, sliding it down the bartop to Andrea. "Michael's personal stash is locked up in the cellar."

"No offense, but do you really want to drink the good stuff in your condition?"

"Yesh," Mallory said, slurring. "And the bottles we don't drink we can pour down the drain. Bottom's up, Michael."

Andrea walked inside the climate-controlled cellar behind the bar, came out much too soon to have made an intelligent choice, and placed her selection on the bar.

Mallory made a face. "Damn, girl. You picked the twenty-dollar bottle of Italian toilet water that Michael's grandfather gave us for our first anniversary."

Mallory started to get up, but the effects of too much wine rushed to her head. She lowered herself back onto the bar stool, suddenly guilt-ridden. "Sorry, Papa. I shouldn't take this out on you."

"You're sloshed," said Andrea.

"I had a few glasses before you got here."

Andrea smiled as she came around the bar and cozied up. "Good. Now I get to hear all the secrets."

"You want to know a big one?"

Andrea leaned in closer, her eyes eager. "How big?"

"Huge," said Mallory. "Get this: I think Michael's first wife is still alive."

"Ivy what's her name? I thought you said she was eaten by a shark."

"I don't think so. Not anymore."

"Have you lost your marbles?"

"I'm totally serious," said Mallory.

"Okay, I'll bite, no pun intended. What makes you think Ivy has literally risen from the depths?"

Mallory attempted to cross her legs, and Andrea grabbed her just in time to keep her from falling off the stool. Mallory gathered herself, speaking with the forced precision of a drunk trying to sound sober.

"Do you have any idea what it feels like when your husband sleeps around?"

"I've never been married, but it can't be good."

"It's horrible. When I caught Don—asshole number one—with his second girlfriend, I said, 'Never again. I am never going to let a man make me feel like this again.'"

"But you said Michael wasn't cheating on you."

"He wasn't. But I was getting that same horrible feeling. Like I wasn't his one and only. That was when I started sleeping with Nathaniel."

"What does that have to do with Ivy being alive?"

Mallory blinked hard, fighting through the alcohol to get back on track. "Ah, excellent question. I was paranoid that someone would find out about Nathaniel and tell Michael. So every night when Michael went to sleep, I crawled out of bed and checked his voice mails, his text messages, his e-mails—just to see if anyone snitched on me. Sure enough, he got one two weeks ago. A text."

"He got a message you were cheating?"

"Yeah, but I deleted it. He never saw it."

"What did it say?"

"Something like 'Mallory is cheating on you,' and then 'beware the naked bears.'" She drank more wine, then continued. "I've never heard anyone call someone's lover a 'naked bear,' have you?"

"No," said Andrea. "Definitely not."

"I Googled it, and all I found were old gay men with hairy bodies. *Gross.*"

Andrea's glass was empty, so she took a sip from Mallory's. "Focus, Mal: How does any of that make you think Ivy is alive?"

Mallory walked around the bar, hanging on to the rail as she came to Andrea's side.

"Because it was signed 'Just Between Us.' And I happen to know that the song 'Just Between Us' had special meaning to Michael and Ivy."

"You know what their song was?"

The way Andrea had said it made Mallory feel pathetic. People just didn't understand. "You think I'm sick, don't you?"

"No, not at all," said Andrea.

"You've never seen Ivy's picture. She was beautiful. Smart, too."

"So are you, Mallory."

"But I didn't use my brain to build a successful career in Michael's world. I quit teaching dance and spent all my energy on something much more difficult: trying to make him want me." She shook her head. "What a mistake."

"Don't go there," said Andrea. "You sound jealous of Ivy."

"I wasn't jealous. I just needed to understand. So I snooped through Michael's stuff. I read every card and every letter Ivy ever sent him. That's how I discovered the special meaning of 'Just Between Us.'"

"So the message was signed 'Just Between Us,' and you knew it was from Ivy."

"Mmm . . . no. At the time, I figured it was someone Michael was friends with when he and Ivy were together. Someone who didn't want to get involved but who was trying to tell him that his new wife was no Ivy Layton. It just set me off."

"What did you do?"

"I could have kept it to myself, bottled it up like I always do. But this time I was so pissed that I used it in a special birthday e-mail I sent him."

"Used it how?"

Mallory did her best in her state to effect the posture of a vintage-1960s sex symbol. "Nathaniel filmed me singing like Marilyn Monroe."

"How funny."

"It wasn't just a joke. In the subject line of the e-mail I wrote 'Just Between Us.'"

The doorbell rang.

"I'll get it," said Mallory, but she had trouble rising from her bar stool. Andrea told her to stay put and answered it.

"Hey, Mallory?" Andrea called out from the foyer.

"Yeah?"

"It's the police," said Andrea, sounding worried. "They have a search warrant."

42

Jason Wald was dipping into Ploutus Investments' petty cash. The thick envelope atop the small, round cocktail table contained ten thousand dollars in hundred-dollar bills.

Boy toys like Nathaniel didn't take credit cards.

The two men were in the lobby of the Plaza Hotel, seated at a table near the plate-glass window overlooking Grand Army Plaza, away from the marble stairway that led to a noisy nightclub on the second floor. For Wald's money, the Plaza just wasn't the same since the condo conversion, and he had agreed to meet there only because Nathaniel had "other business" upstairs: cheering up a new resident who had a slightly less-than-perfect view of Central Park from the multimillion-dollar suite that her Russian husband had foolishly bought for her, sight unseen.

Such punks Wald had to deal with—important work, to be sure, all of it totally underappreciated by his uncle Kyle. No nephew could fill the void of a lost son, especially when the old man had elevated him to sainthood in death. His uncle seemed to forget that he'd never even set foot in Marcus' lower schools when the boy lived at home, never visited him at Andover when he went away in ninth grade, never took his son on a family vacation that wasn't for all practical purposes a summer office for Ploutus in the Hamptons or the south of France.

"Does this payday come with a Wall Street bonus?" asked Nathaniel.

Wald knew he wasn't joking. Nathaniel was cockier than a porn star with a foot-long tool—his previous job description—and more trouble than he was worth. Wald could have hired any number of handsome men to fool a rich, lonely Wall Street wife into thinking that her pleasure was this young stud's reason for living. But there was no denying that Nathaniel had delivered the goods. He filmed Mallory's "happy birthday" video, and it was Nathaniel who—without Mallory's knowledge—embedded the spyware in the video before Mallory e-mailed it to her husband. The spyware monitored Michael's keystrokes and yielded the passwords to his investment accounts. There were other ways to plant spyware, of course, but the beauty of this plan was that it hid the identity of the true spy and made the whole thing look like just another symptom of a failing marriage.

"No bonus," said Jason. "Especially for soldiers who hold out on me."

"What do you mean? I haven't held anything back."

Jason glanced around the lobby to make sure no one was within earshot. He waited for two rich Kuwaitis with their six blond girlfriends to cruise upstairs to the nightclub, then continued.

"I just found out that Michael Cantella got a message two weeks ago telling him that his wife was cheating on him. And that he should beware the naked bears."

"Right, the text message," said Nathaniel.

"You knew about that?"

"Sure. Mallory intercepted it. She was paranoid about him finding out about me. She started checking Michael's text messages, e-mails, and voice mail for about three weeks to see if anyone ratted her out."

"Did she show the text to you?"

"No, but she told me about it. It was like you just said—a warning to Michael that his wife was cheating and that he should 'beware naked bears.'"

"Why didn't you tell me about it?"

"Didn't think it was important. Mallory and I even laughed about it."

"Laughed?"

Nathaniel smiled and said, "I've never been called a naked bear before."

Wald smiled back. It was understandable that a guy like Nathaniel wouldn't know that a "naked bear" was a special kind of short seller. What amazed him, however, was the number of women he knew like Mallory: a graduate of an elite school like Juilliard who was married to a high roller on Wall Street—and who knew absolutely nothing about industry terms. Neither she nor pretty boy had any idea that the warning was about a bear raid on Saxton Silvers—a short-selling scheme that was orchestrated in such a clever way that the world thought Michael Cantella was behind it.

Wald pushed the envelope toward Nathaniel, who peeked inside. He knew better than to count money in a public place, but he didn't have to do any math to see that it wasn't enough.

"How much is this?" said Nathaniel.

"Ten grand," said Wald.

Nathaniel frowned. "You're five thousand short."

Wald wrote a name and a phone number on a cocktail napkin and passed it to Nathaniel. "Call him for the balance."

"Ian Burn?" said Nathaniel, reading it. "Who's he?"

"Someone I can count on to get the job done. He'll take real good care of you."

Nathaniel shrugged, then rose and tucked the envelope into his coat pocket. The men shook hands. "Pleasure doing business with you."

"Likewise," said Wald.

Wald sank back into his chair, watching Nathaniel walk to the exit. He smiled thinly, confident that Burn wouldn't simply make Nathaniel forget about the five grand he was owed.

Soon enough, Nathaniel would *beg* Wald to take back the ten thousand he'd already been paid.

43

My hands were shaking as I rode up in the elevator to Papa's hotel room.

The phone call from Ivy had left me somewhere between total confusion and panic. Could I possibly call the police and say that my first wife—for whom we'd held a memorial service four years ago—may have just been shot? They'd think I was nuts.

And what was that about Mallory and a man two weeks ago—in a gay bar?

Probably just having a drink with one of her old dance pals from Juilliard.

The elevator opened. I went to Papa's room and delivered a firm knock on the door. He answered, dressed in pajamas—or at least as much of the pajamas that he ever wore. When I was little, it seemed odd the way

Papa would never wear pajama bottoms to bed—just the top and some boxer shorts. The mystery was finally solved when my great uncle once spent the night at our house and came to the breakfast table wearing an undershirt and—what else?—pajama *bottoms.* It was then that I learned that Papa had grown up in a family that could afford only one pair of pajamas for the boys. Big brother got the bottoms; little brother, the top. Old habits die hard.

"Hey, Michael," he said with a smile, even though I'd clearly woken him.

I entered quickly and locked the door as Papa pulled on a robe.

"Papa, I don't want you to worry, but it's important for you and Nana to leave New York."

"When?"

"Now."

"Go back to Florida tonight?"

"No, don't go back home. I want you to go on vacation."

"Michael, you're talking crazy. This *is* our vacation."

"I've already bought the plane tickets," I said, which was sort of true. I was still having credit card trouble, so I'd redeemed some of my many frequent-flier miles. "There's a twelve-thirty A.M. flight to Los Angeles."

"Los Angeles? Don't they have earthquakes out there?"

It wasn't his fault, but I had no time for this. "Papa, listen to me carefully. There's a limo and a driver waiting downstairs. His name is Nick. A good guy—Italian—you'll like him. I've used him many times. You and Nana are going to get in Nick's limo, go to the airport, and fly to Los Angeles. I wrote out your flight information," I said, handing him the paper, "and your hotel reservation. It's all paid for."

His eyes clouded with concern. "Does this have to do with that man named Rumsey that the FBI was asking about—the guy who got killed in the Bahamas?"

Rumsey. I'd almost forgotten about that part of the puzzle. "I don't know."

I could have elaborated, but it wouldn't have helped. Papa seemed to understand.

"You be careful," he said as he gave me a hug. Then he gave me another look of concern. "Where are you sleeping tonight?"

I hesitated, reluctant to tell him that I hadn't figured that out yet.

"You might as well use this room," he said. "It's paid for." He got the key for me, then gave me a kiss on the cheek. "I love you."

"I love you, too."

I left as quickly as I'd come and hurried to the elevator. Papa knew something was wrong, but he couldn't have comprehended the magnitude of it even if I'd tried to explain. My personal net worth: gone. My wife: divorcing me. My firm: worth $75 billion a week ago, now hours away from bankruptcy. Chuck Bell, the man who had cast me as the scumbag who'd short-sold his own firm down the river: dead. Ivy had returned for a moment, and now she might be dead. Again. Or not.

Run! That had been her only advice to me. Run, or end up like Chuck Bell. But where was I supposed to go? My cell rang as I crossed the hotel lobby. It was my brother—my lawyer. Ex-lawyer. Soon-to-be-ex-law—Whatever.

I didn't answer, mindful of Ivy's warning that "they"—whoever *they* might be—were eavesdropping on my cell. We had security seminars on that kind of thing at Saxton Silvers—how anyone with ninety-nine bucks and no fear of jail could purchase spyware on the Internet, target even the most sophisticated wireless devices, and listen to your phone conversations from across the city. I stepped outside the hotel but couldn't find a pay phone anywhere on the sidewalk. A college-aged tourist with a backpack was texting on his phone.

"Twenty bucks if I can use your cell for two minutes," I said.

He seemed skeptical, but Andrew Jackson's face was staring straight at him. "Sure," he said, handing it over.

I dialed Kevin, who immediately launched into the bad news.

"I just got a courtesy call from the D.A.," he said. "She's giving you the option of surrendering to authorities rather than having the police come out to arrest you in the morning."

"Arrest?"

"I'm sorry to have to tell you this. You're being charged with conspiracy to commit murder in connection with Chuck Bell's shooting."

"That's crazy."

"The D.A. won't tip her hand as to the entire case, but I did find out that Bell sent an e-mail to the FNN in-house counsel just before he was shot. Said he was on his way to the studio in New Jersey to meet a 'higher source' from Saxton Silvers. The D.A. is linking that message to the meeting you had earlier with Bell in the lobby of his building to say that the 'higher source' was you."

"I wasn't anywhere near the studio when he was shot. I showed you and Agent Spear the receipt that proves I was at an ATM on Third Avenue."

"That's why it's murder for hire. I'm sure the FBI gave the D.A. a heads-up to bring a conspiracy charge instead of indictment for first-degree murder."

328 • JAMES GRIPPANDO

"But if it's conspiracy, they still have to connect me to the shooter, right?"

"Apparently the police executed a search warrant at your apartment tonight and found some way to make that connection."

"What is it?"

"I don't know."

"Who's the shooter?"

"Some guy named Tony Girelli."

"Never heard of him. Who is he?"

"Small-time thug with mob connections. That's all I know."

The tourist wearing the backpack was suddenly hovering over me. "It's been more than two minutes," he said.

I waved him off, focusing on Kevin. "It's clear somebody is trying to frame me for Bell's murder the same way they framed me for the 'murder' of Saxton Silvers. You have to find this Girelli," I said, "and make sure he tells the police that it wasn't me who hired him."

"Where are you now?" asked Kevin.

"I'm . . . unavailable."

"Don't play games with me, Michael. You need a lawyer, and—well, I can't leave you hanging now. I guess I'm it."

"I thank you," I said.

"And as your lawyer, my first piece of advice is to surrender peacefully tomorrow. Don't make the police cuff you and haul you in. But if I call the D.A. tonight and tell her that we've got a deal, you can't go back on it. I want you in my office at nine A.M. and we'll go from there. You good with that?"

I paused, then said, "I think so."

"No," he said sharply. "No 'I think so.' A deal is a deal. Tell me now if you're turning yourself in. Because if you're not, they're coming for you in squad cars."

"If I do turn myself in, will I get bail?"

"I'd say yes. But it won't be cheap."

"How much?"

"You're a rich Wall Street player. Could be a million."

"What?"

"Easy, Michael. If we bond it out with collateral, you have to come up with only ten percent."

"My life savings are gone, my wife's divorcing me, and I can't even get my credit cards to work. How am I going to bond out a million dollars?"

"It might take a few days, but we'll work it out."

It was unfathomable—me sitting in jail while Ivy was on the run in New York. But this way I could at least keep the cops at bay for the next twelve hours.

"All right," I said. "Call the D.A. and tell her I'll turn myself in."

"Good decision. I'll see you in my office at nine."

"See you," I said.

The kid snatched his cell from my hand as soon as I hung up, and he was gone before I could thank him. Several lanes of light traffic cruised north on Eighth Avenue. I honestly had no idea where to go. I had the key to Papa's hotel room, but going there wasn't exactly in keeping with Ivy's advice—*Run!* Ivy was at the top of my list of concerns, but convincing anyone that she was in trouble wasn't going to be easy, especially after a murder arrest. I had to make someone believe that I wasn't crazy, and Kevin was my only choice—I had to get some face time with him while I still could.

I crossed Forty-ninth Street on my way to the subway station. I had the green light, but a delivery van came flying out of the twenty-four-hour parking garage on the corner. It barreled down on me like a heat-seeking missile, as if determined to T-bone me in the crosswalk. The van cut me off, then screeched to a halt, stopping half in and half out of the crosswalk. I was about to cuss out the maniac driver when the rear doors flew open. Two men jumped out and grabbed me. I tried to resist, but these thugs were amazingly strong, and they had me. They threw me in the back of the van and slammed the doors shut.

"Don't move," the man with the gun said.

I tried not to panic as the van sped away.

44

I had no clue where we were headed. Or who had me.

Or what they intended to do with me.

I was alone in the back of a commercial van, seated on the metal floor with my knees drawn up to my chest and my back to the side panel. There were no windows, and the only source of light in the cargo area was a dim sliver glowing at the edges of the closed door that led to the cockpit. It was so dark that my abductors hadn't bothered to blindfold me. They hadn't even bound my hands; the rear doors were padlocked, making escape impossible. My head was near a wheel well, and the tires whined on the pavement below me.

I knew that Forty-ninth Street was one-way, east to west, so I deduced that the first left turn we'd made was onto Ninth Avenue, headed south. I was trying to track our travels in my mental map of Manhattan, but a series of turns confused me, until the sound of the tires changed dramatically. Noise came not just from the wheel well but from all directions. I surmised that we were inside the Lincoln Tunnel headed for New Jersey, but I wouldn't have bet my life on it. Then again, maybe I already had.

Is that bag what I think it is?

My eyes were adjusting to the darkness, but it was the odor that I had noticed first. It was coming from a green plastic bag—much larger than a garbage bag—on the other side of the van. Other than me, it was the only thing in the cargo area. I squinted, trying to focus, but my sense of smell dominated. It was like burned meat. Two thoughts ran through my mind.

Don't look inside.

Look inside.

I moved closer to the bag, trying not to inhale. The odor made me think of that guy who'd burned a hundred-dollar bill at Sal's Place, and of the incendiary package that had nearly set me ablaze in the elevator. Most of all, however, I was thinking how much the bag resembled a body bag, and how the burned meat smelled not quite like any other meat I'd smelled before.

Open it.

It wasn't perverse curiosity that drove me; it was the need to defend myself. I was certain that there was a body inside and that it was not going to be pretty. I needed to know what I was up against with these guys—maybe I'd even find a knife or a tool of some sort that would make these thugs sorry they hadn't bound my hands.

I tugged at the zipper on the bag, but it was open only six inches when the odor overwhelmed me. I was suddenly nauseous.

The van stopped. I heard men talking in the cockpit, and their voices traveled with the sound of their footfalls around the outside of the van to the rear doors. The engine cut off, but I heard another one running—a motor of some kind, but it was hard to tell if it was another vehicle or something else. I heard more voices, then the rattling of the padlock. The rear doors swung open. The lighting was only slightly better now than it had been, but to my dilated pupils, it was blinding. I heard laughter.

"I see you met our friend Tony," one of the men said.

More laughter, and I couldn't help shutting them up with what I'd learned.

"Tony Girelli?" I said.

"Whoa, Mr. Wall Street has been doing his homework."

The men climbed into the van and came toward me. Two guys restrained me and pulled my arms behind my back. Another bound my wrists and blindfolded me.

"Yeah," he said, knotting the blindfold behind my head, "poor Tony Girelli got some bad sushi at the Rink Bar today."

That cracked up the rest of the crew, and the smell of bourbon breath now mixed with that of burned meat.

"Let's walk," the man said, but the goons practically lifted me out of the back of the van and onto a concrete floor. We walked about ten steps, and from the echoes I could tell we were in a spacious place. We stopped, and a noisy roll-down gate closed behind me. I was inside a big garage, or a warehouse.

This can't be good.

Someone tugged at my blindfold, and it dropped to the floor. No one said a word during the short time it took for my eyes to adjust to the dim lighting and focus on the two men in front of me. The sight startled me. A young, handsome man was hanging by his wrists from a chain. He'd been hoisted up by a pulley system that was used to lift car engines. He was naked from the waist up, the expression on his face one of utter terror. The other man—a guy with burns on the right side of his neck and a deformed right ear—looked at me with a familiar stare—the stare I'd seen last fall, sitting across the table from him at Sal's Place.

"Who are you?" I asked.

The two thugs standing behind me snickered. The man's cold stare was more than enough to silence me.

"The name's Burn," he said. Finally, he looked away and picked up a soup can from the floor, flicking something toward the hostage. A small glob of goo about the size of a silver dollar stuck to his bare chest. Then he struck a match and looked at me.

"Call Vanessa," he said in an even tone.

"Who?" I asked.

Without expression, he brought the lit match to the glob on the prisoner's chest. It burst into flame, and the screaming was unbearable. He kicked and writhed, crying out in pain for a long time—an eternity for him, no doubt. Finally it burned out. The man hung limp from his wrists, his chest and stomach heaving with exhaustion from the excruciating pain.

Burn flung another glob of goo at him. This one stuck to his stomach.

The prisoner groaned and sobbed at the mere thought of round two. "Please, no! Stop!"

Burn lit another match. "Call her," he told me.

"I don't know who you're talking about!" I shouted.

"Vanessa," he said, "your way-too-clever first wife. The one who ended your phone conversation by firing off her own gun just to make us think she'd been shot."

Ivy hadn't been shot. *Thank God.* But they were monitoring my cell, just as Ivy had feared.

"Why do you call her Vanessa?"

He flicked the flaming match at the glob on the prisoner's stomach. It was the same horrific result—the screaming, the kicking, the smell of burning flesh. I looked away, unable to watch, and had my hands not been bound I would have covered my ears. The unbearable sounds and smell nearly brought me to my knees.

When the flame had finally burned out, the sadist walked toward me, the soup can in hand. He grabbed my T-shirt by the collar and ripped it down to my third rib. Then he flung the rest of the goo at my chest. It smelled of gasoline as it oozed down my sternum.

"Call her, and tell her to come and get you."

"I don't know how to reach her. I swear."

His expression was like ice. He lit a match.

"I'm not lying!"

"Call her."

"I don't know how to reach her. I don't. I really *don't.*"

Burn stared into my eyes. It could have been the smell of the other man's charred flesh in the air. Or the remains of Tony Girelli in the body bag. Or perhaps it was the burning match about to ignite the flammable goo all over my chest. Whatever it was, he seemed to believe me.

He blew out the match. Then he jutted his face just inches from mine. There was no bourbon on his breath. The leader of this group was stone-cold sober.

"If you go to the police," he said, "we will find you. Talk to anyone, we will find you. The only exception is Vanessa. I want you to tell her exactly what you saw here tonight. Tell her you met Ian Burn, and that he has granted the two of you your final pass. Do you understand?"

I wasn't sure why he kept using the name Vanessa, or what he meant by giving Ivy and me a pass, but I wasn't going to push my luck by pressing for information. "I understand."

Burn stepped away from me and gave a nod to one of his men. Before I could react, I felt the jab of a needle in my thigh and the cold pressure of an injection. The garage was starting to blur as the men walked me back to the van. The rear doors opened. Someone said something—he seemed to be talking to me—but my mind couldn't process the words. I felt my feet leave the floor, but it was someone else's doing. They shoved me into the back of the van like a dead animal. I lay there, motionless. I heard the engine start, and there was one more scream—far worse than the earlier ones. The doors closed, the van lurched forward, and then I heard nothing.

45

It was still nighttime when I woke on the sidewalk. My T-shirt was ripped, but someone had cleaned the goo from my chest. Instinctively, I reached for my cell, but it was gone. I started to get up, then stopped.

Whoa, my head.

I moved slowly. Whatever Burn's men had injected into my leg was still in my system, but I fought through it. I rose up on one knee, let my head adjust to going vertical, then climbed all the way to my feet. Slowly, things came into focus.

A quiet dead-end street. Red-brick apartment buildings rising up ten or twelve stories on either side. Tree roots pushing up slabs of the concrete sidewalk. Still in a fog, I walked toward the intersection, which was completely without traffic. I had no idea what time it was, but it had to be late. I looked up the street, and the familiar cantilever truss structure of the Fifty-ninth Street Bridge told me where I was. A glance back at the green-and-white street sign at the intersection confirmed it: SUTTON PL. I was just a block from my apartment. Mallory's apartment.

Then I heard that scream again—but only in my mind—and it hit me hard. The body count was now up to four: Rumsey, Bell, Girelli, and now this latest victim in the garage who had undoubtedly died a horrible death tonight. I had to call the police. There was a pay phone on the corner, and I could have just dialed 911 from there.

If you go to the police, we will find you.

The man who called himself Burn could not have made his warning any clearer. Even with the pending divorce, Mallory was still my wife, and I felt a sudden need to know that she was safe. And, admittedly, I was curious about Ivy's warning—that she'd seen Mallory in a gay bar with another man—the operative word being *gay*.

Or were the operative words "another man"?

I ran up the street toward our apartment and breezed right past our night doorman in the lobby. He came after me. Mallory had obviously told him about the divorce.

"Where you headed, Mr. Cantella?"

I kept walking toward the elevator. "Personal emergency."

"I'm going to have to call Mrs. Cantella."

"You do that," I said.

One of the elevator doors opened—the other one was still out of service from the flaming package—and I rode up to our apartment. I rang the bell, and the door opened about a foot, stopped by the chain.

"Go away, Michael."

The voice startled me, and then I realized it was Mallory's friend, Andrea.

"This is important," I said.

"It's one o'clock in the morning. Go away, or I will call the police."

I realized how bad this looked—the husband on the receiving end of divorce papers showing up at the wife's door in the middle of the night, just hours after the first court hearing. The ripped T-shirt probably didn't help my case—powder blue at that, making me look like a cracked Easter egg.

"I got mugged," I said. "They took my phone, my wallet, everything. I need to come in, call the police, and get some clothes—probably my passport, too, just so I have photo ID."

The door closed, and I heard them talking inside, but I couldn't make out what they were saying. The chain rattled, and the door opened all the way this time. As I entered, Andrea stepped in front of me, cutting me off. Had the expression on her face been any tougher, she probably would have qualified for Secret Service detail.

She held her cell in hand and said, "If you make one false move toward Mallory, I'm dialing nine-one-one."

"I'm not here to hurt anyone," I said. "I actually want to make sure she's safe."

"She's fine. We're watching a movie. Safe from what?"

"Give me your phone, and you'll find out."

She pulled back, clutching her phone, as if I'd just asked for her spleen.

Mallory emerged from the TV room with our cordless landline. "Use this one."

It was the first time she'd made eye contact with me since filing for divorce. Maybe I was kidding myself, but I didn't see contempt. I could tell she'd been drinking, however.

Andrea took the phone and handed it to me. I punched 9–1–1.

Mallory and her friend stood and listened as I told the dispatcher how the men had thrown me into a van, taken me to a garage that I believed was somewhere in

New Jersey, and tortured another man before my eyes. I told her Tony Girelli was dead. I described Burn as best I could, and when I described the victim and what Burn had done to him, Mallory gasped and ran to the other room.

"I'm routing this to a detective," said the operator. "Is this the best number to reach you at?"

I wasn't sure how to answer. "Give me a number to call, and I'll let you know."

She gave it to me along with an incident reference number. I hung up and gave the phone back to Andrea. She didn't seem shocked by anything she'd just heard— definitely nowhere near as upset as Mallory.

"I need to talk with my wife," I told her.

Andrea no longer had her finger on the domestic disturbance panic button, but she followed me into the TV room just in case. Mallory looked scared to death, seated on the couch, and part of me wanted to go to her and tell her that it would all be okay. Andrea sat beside her and squeezed her hand.

"Mallory, can I talk to you alone for a minute?" I asked.

She shook her head firmly. "No."

We were back to no-eye-contact mode. "Do you mind if I get a few things to take with me?"

"Go ahead."

I desperately wanted a shower, but I had to settle for a quick stop in the bathroom to sponge away the lingering smell of gasoline from my chest. In the adjoining master bedroom I changed clothes in record time, losing the Wall Street look entirely, just blue jeans and light sweater. I grabbed my passport and a few other essentials, then returned to the TV room.

"Mallory, there is something I have to say."

She didn't answer. Andrea was still at her side on the couch, and she shot me a look that said, Say it and go.

"I don't blame you for wanting to leave me," I said, trying my best to pretend that it was just me and Mallory in the room. "You deserve a man who loves you with all his heart. But your lawyer's spin in the courtroom about those e-mails was completely wrong. I don't have a lover, and I haven't been plotting to hide any money from you."

I wanted to ask her about the man Ivy had seen her with, but putting her on the defensive and sounding like the jealous husband wasn't going to help my immediate cause.

"You came here to tell me that?" she said, her eyes cast downward.

"No," I said. "I wanted to share some things that will probably make you think I'm crazy. But I'm going to tell you anyway, because I want you to be safe."

"Stop scaring her," said Andrea.

"I'm not saying this to frighten you. Mallory, I'm going to be arrested for supposedly hiring a guy named Tony Girelli to shoot Chuck Bell. That's probably going to happen tomorrow. It's a frame-up, but that's not even close to being the crazy part. Ivy is alive."

Mallory looked up, and I could read the expression on her face. She was screaming without words: *I knew it!*

"She and I are both in a lot of danger," I said. "I don't know what it's all about, but these are very bad people. They killed Chuck Bell. They've killed other people, including that guy I just called nine-one-one about. I'm afraid everyone I know might also be in danger. Possibly even you. I want you to get protection for yourself. Hire a bodyguard, go to the police. Promise me you'll do that."

Her gaze was fixed on me now, her expression a blend of confusion and amazement.

"Promise me, and I'll go," I said.

"Go where?"

I sighed at the size of the question. "Not sure," I said. "They warned me not to call the police, so I guess I need to go someplace they can't find me."

"You need to turn yourself in," said Andrea. "If you're being charged with the murder of Chuck Bell, that's the only thing you can do."

"That's the one thing I *can't* do," I said, "and not just because I'm innocent. I'll be a sitting duck in a jail cell. After what I saw tonight, I have no doubt that these men will kill me just as soon as they realize I can't help them find Ivy. I have to run."

I started toward the hallway, then stopped. "Mallory, I borrowed your cell, all right?"

"You what?"

I had taken it from the master bedroom. "They took my cell. They'd been monitoring my line anyway. I need yours."

"No!"

"Mallory, I just watched a man get burned alive tonight, and I have to go back out onto the street after doing exactly what they warned me not to do—call the police. I need a cell. Help me that much."

"I said *no.*"

Her anger was hard to comprehend, but suddenly I realized that in the past couple of days I had grossly overanalyzed everything—from Mallory's high-school dating history to her anonymous support for abused children—in search of some past trauma that might explain our divorce. My wife was just *done* with me. I wasn't saying it was her fault or mine, but it was time to stop soothing my Wall Street ego by holding everyone else accountable—her parents, an old lover, her first husband, her new friend Andrea—for *my* life.

"It's okay," said Andrea. "Let him have it."

Mallory exchanged glances with her friend, then handed me the phone.

"Thank you," I said, but Mallory didn't acknowledge it. I wanted a better understanding of what was going through her mind, but there wasn't time. And I didn't want her to do an about-face on loaning me her cell. I said good night and let myself out quickly.

Three minutes later I was back on Fifty-seventh Street. Never before had I felt so unsafe in my neighborhood. In the first sixty seconds, I must have checked over my shoulder a half dozen times. A car approached, and my heart raced. It went right past me. Nothing.

How did Ivy do this for four years?

Her warning—*run!*—reverberated in my mind. Burn's men had emptied my pockets, so I no longer had the key to Papa's hotel room. But the booking was under the name Cantella, and I had to sleep somewhere. I wondered if the night manager would recognize me and let me in if I just showed up. I walked toward the subway, but the cumulative effects of the night's events finally coalesced into a sense of urgency, and I started jogging and then running down the sidewalk. A car screeched around the corner and stopped at the curb, and I froze. The passenger's-side door flew open, and then I knew I wasn't merely paranoid. I was about to run in the other direction when I caught a glimpse of the driver.

It was Ivy's mother.

"Get in!" she shouted.

I hurried toward the car but stayed on the sidewalk. "You need to keep away from me," I said, the dome light glaring between us.

"I'm here to help you."

"Don't. I don't have time to explain, but anyone who helps me is in serious danger."

"Do you think I'm any different from you?" she said.

I looked at her for a moment, and from the expression on her face I could see that Olivia, too, was running from them—whoever *they* were.

"Get your Wall Street ass in the damn car!"

I jumped in the passenger seat, and the car squealed away.

46

"How did you find me?" I asked as I buckled my seat belt.

"Your brother called me."

"Kevin called *you*?"

We were driving toward the East River. "He's been trying to reach you for hours. Thinks you lost your mind and went looking for Ivy, so he called me."

"How did you know where to find me?"

She hesitated, then glanced over at me. "Ivy told me."

I started to speak, but she silenced me. "Don't ask, Michael."

I had to push. "For a while, I thought they shot her tonight. I heard the gun go off when she called me."

"She shot the lock off a church door."

"What was she doing in—"

She stopped me again with her expression.

A quick turn, and we were soon flying down the FDR Drive, with virtually no traffic. Olivia grabbed a granola bar from the glove and gave it to me. "You must be starving."

"Thanks," I said. It was gone in three bites. She gave me another.

"Where are we going?"

"Downtown, to meet your brother. He has a contact at the DTCC."

"At two o'clock in the morning?"

The Depository Trust Clearing Corporation was on Water Street, just a couple blocks away from the stock exchange. Most people had never heard of the DTCC, but if Wall Street was the stage, the DTCC was backstage. Before the DTCC was formed, brokers physically exchanged certificates to effect a trade. Electronics changed all that, and the DTCC settled the vast majority of securities transactions in the United States, more than $1.86 quadrillion annually—or roughly twenty times the economic output of the entire planet.

How the hell my brother knew that, I had no idea. Sure enough, though, he was right outside the building, waiting for us.

"Tony Girelli's dead," I said, and before he could even react I told him everything I had reported to 911.

To say that he was overwhelmed by my words was to say that Napoleon was uncomfortable at Waterloo. I stopped short of telling him about Ivy, knowing that would push him over the edge.

"Let's sort this out after we get what we need here," he said.

Kevin took us to the back entrance. An extremely nervous DTCC employee was there to let us in. The thought of bringing *three* people inside after hours made him even more nervous. Olivia agreed to wait in the car.

Kevin introduced the skinny young man with a goatee as Tim Darwood. He skipped right past hello.

"I could lose my job over this," he said.

"And if not for me," said Kevin, "your current job would be making license plates. So let's call it even."

Darwood led us down the hall toward the security desk. The building was quiet, as to be expected at this hour, and for someone who worked there, Darwood sure did seem to check over his shoulder a lot. This was not his normal work hour, and the jeans and black T-shirt were clearly not his normal work clothes. It was at this point that I noticed the silk-screened image on the back of his cotton tee—Alan Greenspan in flapper drag singing "Tonight I'm Gonna Party Like It's 1929."

We passed the elevators and stopped. Two men and two women were checking in with security, and just the sight of them nearly sent Darwood into cardiac arrest.

"In here," he said, quickly pulling us into the men's room.

My brother and I stood with our backs to the stalls as Darwood paced furiously before us.

"You are going to get me *so* fired," he said, anxiously running a hand through his hair.

"Who were those people at the security desk?" I asked.

"Our lawyers," he said.

"At two o'clock in the morning?" It was the second time I'd asked that question in the past ten minutes, and this time Olivia wasn't there to say, "Don't ask."

"They're gearing up for battle," said Darwood. "With rumors flying that Saxton Silvers is filing for bankruptcy in the morning, everyone's banging on the door—figuratively, except for you guys—to get whatever information they can about the short sellers."

"Then I guess we're not asking for anything out of the ordinary," said Kevin.

"Give me a break," said Darwood. "DTC fights to keep that information secret even when we get hit with a subpoena. Why do you think our lawyers are here? If they see me with you, I *will* lose my job."

"We're not on a fishing expedition," said Kevin. "We want very specific information. Just help us confirm the identity of the offshore corporation that used Michael's money to go short on Saxton Silvers' stock."

Darwood paused, then said, "I can't do it."

Kevin's voice took on an edge. "We agreed that you would."

"I said I would help, if I could. I can't."

Kevin looked at me, as if it were somehow my fault that the guy had changed his mind. I wasn't sure if he was upset because I wasn't getting the help I needed or because Darwood had blown Kevin's opportunity to be the one who gave me that help—a fine distinction that only brothers could understand.

I looked at Darwood and said, "Would it help if I told you that it was a matter of life or death?"

"Cut the bullshit," said Darwood. The expression on his face was truly pained. I had no way of knowing what attorney-client pressure point Kevin had pushed to get us in the door, but it was obviously tormenting this poor guy.

What would Darwood do if Mr. Burn came calling?

"You guys are looking in the wrong place anyway," said Darwood.

"What do you mean?" I said.

"People are always blaming the DTC for every problem in the marketplace that could conceivably be caused by short sellers. Wake up, guys. When Saxton Silvers goes down, the *really* big profit isn't going to be from short sales."

"I still don't know what he's talking about," Kevin said to me.

I gave Darwood a careful look. He was sweating, but I sensed he wasn't lying. In fact, he seemed to be doing his best to help—the faster to get us out of there.

"He's saying that if we want to know who's really behind the attack on Saxton Silvers, we need information he doesn't have access to."

"Exactly," said Darwood.

"Who does have it?" asked Kevin.

"Honestly," said Darwood, "I'm not sure there's anyone at DTC who can provide it. But if we can, it's in the Deriv/SERV Warehouse."

"Deriv what?" my brother said.

"Let's go, Kevin," I said.

"Wait. You got an address for that warehouse?"

"It's a database, not a building. I got all I need. Let's *go.*"

Darwood leaned over the sink and splashed cold water on his face. "Please. Go. Before I—"

"I know, I know. Lose your job," Kevin said.

Darwood made sure the coast was clear, then led us out of the men's room, down the hall, and to the exit. The glass doors locked automatically behind us.

"Why did you let him off the hook?" Kevin asked me as we headed down the sidewalk.

"Like I said: I have what I need."

Oliva's car pulled up at the curb, and again the passenger's-side door flew open.

"Get in," she said.

"He's going home with me," said Kevin.

"No, he isn't," said Olivia.

"He needs to be in my office by nine, and then we have arraignment at eleven."

"Can't do that," said Olivia.

Kevin chuckled. "Thanks for tracking him down. But unless he wants the cops to haul him in wearing handcuffs, he's leaving with me."

"Then he'll never see Ivy."

Her words chilled me.

"That's not a threat," she said. "That's just a fact."

Kevin grabbed my arm. "Michael, do not let her push your buttons about Ivy, and do not get in that car."

"Ivy's alive," I said.

"Stop it!"

"I talked to her on the phone tonight!"

Kevin froze.

Olivia said, "Do you want to see Ivy or don't you?"

"Michael, I don't know what kind of crazy shit's going on here, but we have a deal with the D.A. If you don't show up, you will be a fugitive."

"If you do show up, you're dead," said Olivia. "Don't you understand, Michael? They only let you live because they think you can lead them to Ivy. If you're in jail, you are of no use. *They will kill you,*" she said.

My mind was humming.

"Who are *they?*" asked Kevin.

I looked at him and said, "I think I know. And I have to go."

I climbed in the car and slammed the door, my head snapping back against the headrest as Olivia burned rubber.

47

At six A.M. Andrea and her fiancé were seated at the dining room table for an emergency meeting with their operations supervisor.

Overlooking the old sheep meadow in Central Park, Andrea's Upper West Side apartment was by far the nicest place she had ever lived. In February, when she'd moved in, she could watch the ice skaters in Wollman Rink from her window, and every night the Midtown skyline was a spectacle of lights. Of course, this ten-million-dollar dream apartment was way beyond Andrea's personal budget. Formerly owned by a Colombian drug lord who'd fled the country and forfeited his U.S. assets in lieu of standing trial on racketeering charges, it was currently on loan from the Drug Enforcement Agency to the FBI for special assignment.

"We need to arrange protection for Mallory Cantella," said Andie.

Special Agent Andie—"Andrea"—Henning was in the fourth month of her Saxton Silvers undercover assignment, and her tenth year as an FBI agent. Hardly a lifelong dream of hers, the bureau had been more of a safe landing for a self-assured thrill seeker. At the training academy, she became only the twentieth woman in bureau history to make the Possible Club, a 98-percent-male honorary fraternity for agents who shoot perfect scores on one of the toughest firearms courses in law enforcement. Her first major undercover operation had been the infiltration of a cult in central Washington. Her supervisors saw her potential, but she'd resisted doing more undercover work until the Wall Street assignment came up.

Since autumn, law enforcement had suspected that Saxton Silvers was being targeted by a particularly ruthless band of short sellers who would apply any means—legal or not—to bring the firm crashing down. Andie thought she'd be immersed in the high-stakes business world, trying to find out who was working on the inside. Instead, her undercover "fiancé" enjoyed the daily stimulation of sleuthing around Saxton Silvers' risk-management division while Andie played the sometimes mind-numbing role of a Saxton Silvers significant other. "Wives talk" was the underlying rationale, and Andie had proved to be an effective plant.

So effective, in fact, that within a month, she'd managed to completely shift the chief focus of the investigation away from short selling and toward something far more evil.

Her supervisor, Malcolm Spear, drummed his fingers atop the mahogany table as he considered her request for protection.

"Our operations budget is not unlimited," he said, his expression deadpan. "I can't even get headquarters to approve full-time surveillance on Michael Cantella, and you want round-the-clock protection for his wife?"

"Have you listened to the tape of Michael's nine-one-one call? He doesn't know it, but the victim he's describing is clearly Mallory's lover."

"Agreed," said Spear. "Nathaniel Locke's apartment was searched this morning. It would appear that he has gone missing."

"Which only reinforces Michael's conclusion," said Andie. "Mallory could be in danger, too."

"Sounds like you are taking everything Mr. Cantella said at face value."

"I was standing right beside him when he called nine-one-one. I was sitting at his wife's side when he literally pleaded with her afterward. In my judgment, yes, he was sincere."

"You were also in the apartment when a search warrant turned up an envelope with Tony Girelli's phone number written on it. Local homicide detectives are beyond confident that the five grand inside was Girelli's fee for shooting Chuck Bell."

"To me, it smells suspiciously like a plant, especially if it's true that Girelli is now dead."

Spear shook his head. "Your undercover role has brought you too close to the Cantellas."

"My judgment has not been compromised."

"Really?" said Spear. "Just yesterday you called Cantella to tell him that the FBI was turning up the heat on his first wife. What was that about?"

"I wasn't telling him anything he hadn't already heard from his grandfather. That was a no-lose way for me to earn his trust, which I need to do if I'm going to play my role effectively."

Spear seemed somewhat persuaded on that point, but he held his ground. "Look, we're in agreement that Nathaniel Locke is the victim of foul play. But we have a fundamental disagreement as to the perp's identity."

"I don't know who killed him."

"Consider this possibility: Michael Cantella."

"Why?"

"Two motives. One, the man was sleeping with his wife. Two, Nathaniel Locke was the anonymous source for Chuck Bell at FNN who brought down Saxton Silvers."

The second point was news to Andie, and it took her aback. It was Andie who had picked up the telephone after Bell's "Maybe it is, maybe it isn't Michael Cantella" remark, dialed Malcolm Spear, and pushed to subpoena Bell—First Amendment issues be damned. But Bell's death had derailed that plan.

"I thought the name of Bell's source died right along with Chuck Bell," she said.

"Turns out that Chuck Bell kept a file on his source," said Spear. "FNN shared it with us after his death, thinking it might help find his killer. In it we found e-mails and photographs that Locke had given to him, which made it abundantly clear that Mallory was sleeping with him."

"I don't follow the logic. Bell's story had nothing to do with infidelity."

"Apparently Bell had enough integrity not to broadcast rumors about Saxton Silvers unless he had a credible source. Locke's credibility was tied to his status as Mallory's lover. Michael trusted his wife enough to confide in her, and Mallory shared those confidences with Locke, who in turn shared those golden nuggets with Bell."

"Why would he do that?"

"Bell may have paid him. We haven't confirmed that yet."

Andie considered it, but before she could speak, Spear closed the loop on the FBI's analysis.

"It's a fairly simple equation," said Spear. "Sleeping with Michael Cantella's wife gave Locke all the information he needed to be Bell's source on Saxton Silvers. Bell was murdered after sending his lawyer an e-mail that said he was on his way to meet an even 'higher source' from Saxton Silvers. Now Locke—the original source—is also dead. Girelli, the triggerman, is dead, too. The only logical step for the FBI at this point is to work with local law enforcement to bring Michael Cantella into custody immediately."

"Your whole theory crumbles unless Michael made up the story about being abducted and taken to a garage in New Jersey where he saw Girelli's body and witnessed a man being tortured."

"Michael Cantella is a Wall Street liar," said Spear. "That's the worst kind."

Andie shook her head. "I believe he was being truthful about what he saw. The same goes for his first wife's being alive."

"Whom he was suspected of killing," said Spear.

"He passed a polygraph."

"Many sociopaths do. Many of them also claim that their wives are still alive, even though they've been missing for years."

"It's not just Michael who's saying it. I've gotten to know Mallory well. She believes it, too."

"Like I said: You've let yourself get too close to the Cantellas."

"With all due respect, sir, I think something is going on that the FBI doesn't fully understand. And I'm requesting permission to continue my undercover role until I get to the bottom of this."

"Permission granted, on one condition."

"Name it."

"As far as the FBI is concerned, it's full speed ahead in bringing Michael Cantella into custody. You are to take no action that is at odds with that objective."

Andie hated those broad edicts. She'd worked for too many bosses whose idea of supervision was to tell his subordinates to "do everything that needs to be done."

"You have my word," said Andie.

48

I fell asleep in the car and woke in a bed. The sight of a woman seated at the foot of the mattress scared me into the jackknife position.

"Who are you?"

"It's okay," she said as she turned to look at me.

I quickly realized it was Olivia—and that last night had not merely been a bad dream.

"Where am I?"

"North Bergen."

"New Jersey?"

"On Tonnelle Avenue, to be exact."

The street noise was so loud that I wondered if we weren't literally *on* Tonnelle Avenue. I sat up in bed, still wearing last night's jeans and sweater. Only my shoes had been removed. A sliver of morning sunlight was streaming in through an opening between drapery panels, and I noticed Olivia's car parked right outside our motel room. One of the local morning shows was playing on the television atop the bureau, but the volume was too low to hear it.

"What time is it?"

"Not yet seven. When we got here last night, you woke up just enough for me to help you in from the car, but you were out like a drunk the minute your head hit the pillow."

I'd needed the rest, to be sure, but the lingering effect of whatever Burn and his men had injected into my body undoubtedly had more to do with it.

"You want coffee?"

"Black, thanks."

She poured some from an in-room machine. There was so much I wanted to ask her, but I figured I'd go right for the home run.

"Why does Kyle McVee want Ivy dead?"

I expected a show of surprise, maybe even shock—at least a reaction of some sort. Olivia simply handed me the plastic coffee cup and sat on the other bed, facing me.

"How did you know it was McVee?"

"He was the last person Ivy worked for before she disappeared."

"You were the last person Ivy married before she disappeared."

Clearly she was playing devil's advocate.

"McVee has the kind of capital it would take to short-sell Saxton Silvers into the ground and make it look like I did it."

"So do dozens of other hedge-fund gurus."

"McVee is into credit-default swaps in a big way. That's the point my brother's friend at the DTC was making tonight: Credit-default swaps are where the huge money is going to be made when Saxton Silvers files for bankruptcy today."

"Credit-default what?" she asked.

In another six months, even Papa would have a working knowledge of the esoteric derivative products that investment geniuses like Warren Buffett had labeled "financial weapons of mass destruction." But at this point, not even Wall Street fully understood the dangers.

"Credit default swaps," I said. "They're not technically insurance, so there's no government regulation to speak of. But in essence they are a form of insurance that investors cash in if Saxton Silvers can't pay its debts."

"So if you borrow money from me, I would buy a credit default swap that would pay me off in case you defaulted?"

"Correct, assuming you and I are major financial players. And what's really interesting is that if you loan me money, Tommy Ho in Hong Kong or Crocodile Dundee in Australia or Hansel and Gretel in Germany can also buy a credit default swap that pays them off in case I default on your loan."

She did a double take, as if not quite comprehending. "So total strangers basically place a bet that you're going to default on my loan to you?"

"You got it. On six billion dollars of debt, it wouldn't be unheard of for there to be sixty billion dollars in credit default swaps. Of course, no single person really knows how much is tied up in the swaps, because they're not sold through the stock exchange. It's an over-the-counter market."

"Isn't that a problem?"

"Hell yes, especially when you tie in other strategies. Think of it this way: Buying credit-default swaps on Saxton Silvers' debt obligations and then going short on Saxton Silvers stock is kind of like buying a life insurance policy on your neighbor and then running him over with your car."

"So when Saxton Silvers goes bankrupt, McVee cashes in."

"Big-time. On an investment bank like Saxton Silvers, he could conceivably be sitting on a billion dollars' worth of credit default swaps."

"That's incredible," she said.

"It is. But it's also a little beside the point."

"How do you mean?"

"Let me ask you again: Why did McVee want Ivy dead?"

She tasted her coffee, then rose and went to the Formica counter beside the closet. "I don't know exactly," she said, adding more sweetener to her cup. Then she turned and looked at me. "But this much I am certain about: It's not what you think. McVee's reasons for wanting Ivy dead have nothing to do with credit-default swaps or short selling—it has nothing to do with business at all. This is personal."

"It's about me, isn't it?"

My words seemed to confuse her. "Why would you say that?"

I told her about the black SUV that had run me off the road before the trip to the Bahamas. "I think it was a warning," I said. "I ignored it at the time. And I think Ivy paid the price."

Olivia came back and sat on the edge of the other bed, looking me in the eye. "None of this was your fault. That SUV wasn't a warning to you. It was a warning to Ivy. As long as Ivy was alive, they were going to take it out on you and everyone else Ivy loved—including me."

Again I was thinking about that anti-FTAA protestor who'd pulled me from the cab in Miami. "Is that what that man who sprayed me with pepper spray meant when he said, 'It's only gonna get worse'?"

She nodded. "You and Ivy were followed all the way from the Miami airport. Ivy knew that. And she knew that the man was talking to her, not to you. Things would only get worse . . . so long as she was alive. So Ivy made them think she was dead. That's why she disappeared."

I was having trouble comprehending how a normal person with a normal life could pull off something like this, but from what Olivia was telling me, I was beginning to wonder if Ivy ever had been "normal."

"That man last night—every time he mentioned Ivy, he called her Vanessa. What's that about?"

The mere mention of "Vanessa" made Olivia flinch. "That's the name Ivy used after faking her death."

It was a plausible explanation—but it didn't really explain the way Olivia reacted when I mentioned the name.

My phone chirped. Actually, it was Mallory's phone. I was reluctant to use it. If Ivy was right and the calls on my cell had been monitored, it was possible they were monitoring Mallory's, too. I got up and checked it. The message was from me, which took me aback.

Those goons had taken my cell last night, so it had to be from them.

Want to see your lover? the message read.

I was confused at first, not sure what they were trying to tell me. Then I realized that they weren't telling *me* anything. They had no way of knowing that I had Mallory's phone, and the message was for her. It was like a roundhouse kick to the solar plexus, even if she was divorcing me.

Of course that guy she was meeting in the gay bar wasn't gay, you moron.

I had been in denial, but it was time to take my final lumps and officially crown myself "the last to know." I scrolled through the text messages stored in Mallory's phone, found a recent one from "Nathaniel," and read it. It made me cringe. There were many messages just like it, dating back more than a month. It was clear now why Mallory had been so reluctant to give me her cell.

"What's wrong?" asked Olivia.

"Nothing," I said. "Just a little high-tech confirmation that I'm a blind fool and that my wife was seeing another man."

She leaned over and laid a hand on my forearm. It was the first sign of any affection she'd shown toward me—and strangely, I felt some of Ivy's warmth in her touch.

"We'll get through this," she said. "It *will* get better."

"You think?"

She smiled a little. "Can't get worse, can it?"

The television suddenly caught my eye. "Today's Big Story" was at the top of the *Today* show, and right behind Ann Curry was an image of me. The mug shot taken at the Tombs after my bomb-scare arrest had, as I'd predicted, come back to haunt me. I actually looked like a criminal.

I jumped up and raised the volume, catching the report somewhere in the middle:

"—arrest warrant for Wall Street power broker Michael Cantella, who is facing charges in a murder-for-hire conspiracy that resulted in the fatal shooting of Financial News Network's Chuck Bell."

I listened in stunned silence as the national coverage recapped my nightmare for the entire country, before shifting to the mud slides in California.

My phone—Mallory's—chirped again. Another message, a follow-up to *Wanna see your lover?*

It read: *He's hot.*

I knew what these guys were capable of, and I got the double meaning. But that didn't lessen the shock when I clicked on the attached file and saw the photograph. The image was gruesome—several pyromaniacal steps

beyond what I had witnessed last night. But it was definitely the same man. Burn had killed my wife's lover.

And he'd sent these taunting messages to Mallory—
proof of a grisly homicide—with *my* cell.

"What's wrong?" asked Olivia.

"So much for your promise that things *will* get
better."

"What do you mean?"

I glanced at her, then back at the image on Mallory's
cell. "They just got worse."

I laid Mallory's cell on the nightstand and started
dialing on the room's landline.

"Who are you calling?" asked Olivia.

"My brother."

"What for?"

I paused after punching out half of Kevin's number.
"He can't guarantee that I'll be released on bail, so I
need to tell him that he won't be seeing me in his office
or in court this morning."

"Smart move."

"And to make him understand that I can't be a sitting duck in a prison cell waiting to have my throat slit
by another thug hired by Kyle McVee."

"You can't mention McVee's name."

"I'm going way beyond that. I'm going to instruct
Kevin to write down everything I've learned, wrap it
up in McVee's name, and take it to the FBI."

A look of horror came over her. "Have you lost your mind?"

"Sorry, but if you can't tell me why McVee wanted Ivy dead, maybe Kevin and I can help the FBI figure it out."

I finished dialing, and Kevin's line was ringing. Olivia continued pleading.

"Don't you understand? The FBI couldn't protect Ivy from Kyle McVee. They can't protect you, me, or anyone else from a man like him. That's why she ran."

The call went to Kevin's voice mail. I hung up, immediately hit redial, and as the line starting ringing again, I tightened my stare on Olivia.

"Why did McVee want Ivy dead?" I asked her.

"I told you, I don't know."

"You told me there were things about Ivy that I was better off not knowing. That's not the same thing."

"That's exactly what Ivy told *me*. Can't you see she's protecting us?"

"Can't you see the game has changed? I'm not willing to live the rest of my life the way she's been living hers."

"If McVee finds out you're helping the FBI, you won't have to worry about *living*, period.

The ringing continued, but not even her desperate tone could make me hang up and hide out in a motel room while Kyle McVee framed yours truly for crimes that would bring down me, my firm, and maybe all of Wall Street with us.

Olivia lowered her head into her hands.

On the fifth ring, Kevin answered his cell.

"Kevin, it's me," I said.

"Please, don't," said Olivia.

I looked away and told my brother everything I wanted the FBI to know.

49

Kyle McVee arrived early to the office for an eight A.M. meeting. The Midtown headquarters of Ploutus Investments occupied the top four floors of a Third Avenue skyscraper, the highest floor being off limits to anyone but McVee and his closest confidantes.

The penthouse level had just two private offices. One was McVee's. The other had belonged to his son Marcus, untouched since his death, a de facto vault for thirty million dollars' worth of original artwork by Jasper Johns, Andy Warhol, and other masters whom Marcus had collected over the years. Art had been his final passion in life. Before that, wine had been his thing, and before that, a collection of classic cars. Marcus never went into anything half baked, and that passion was his trademark. In the hallway between the two offices was a photograph of him at base camp on Mount Everest. In his first attempt he'd managed to scale the hard blue ice of Lhotse Face and climb to Camp III at 23,500 feet, where weather forced his team back. Few people doubted that he would someday get beyond Camp IV and on up to the top at 29,028 feet. Even fewer doubted that he would soon be at the top of Ploutus Investments.

Marcus' involvement in the business went against a certain logic. McVee had essentially worked through Marcus' childhood, so busy in the world of Wall Street that he barely noticed his son. As an adult, Marcus would have had every right to disown his old man. But the opposite had occurred.

Three months after Marcus' graduation from college, McVee and his wife had traveled to Bermuda for their twenty-fourth wedding anniversary. A business commitment forced McVee to fly back to New York for a day, which turned into two. When he returned to Bermuda, he found his wife in the hotel room beneath a cool white sheet, an empty bottle of Valium beside her in the bed. Her death made him recall the special things he had loved about the young bride he had married—and regret how little he knew about the seriously depressed empty nester she had become. After the funeral, he started to see the best of Evelyn in their son Marcus. Not just the dazzling intelligence but the bursts of awe-inspiring creativity, the way he devoured things that interested him. McVee reached out to his son, and his son reached back. For nearly ten years they were an inseparable team that not only grew the business but sat right behind home plate in Yankee Stadium together. By his thirtieth birthday, Marcus McVee had become everything a father could want in a son—and more. The "more" part was the problem.

At various times in his life, Marcus—like his mother—had been treated for anxiety and depression.

"I have good news," said McVee, shaking off the constant thought of his son. "Saxton Silvers will file for bankruptcy just as soon as the courthouse doors open today."

McVee was standing at the window, the morning sun throwing a zebralike pattern across the room as it shone through the venetian blinds. An English solicitor named Graves was seated on the silk-covered couch, listening. He represented a Kuwaiti multibillionaire whom McVee had never met in person. It was a rare occasion that a client was allowed in the penthouse. This was one of them.

"The sheikh will be very pleased, I'm sure," said Graves. "What will the final numbers look like?"

McVee stood at the window, casting his gaze across Third Avenue toward the Lipstick Building, a thirty-four-story office tower that, to some, resembled a tube of lipstick. The seventeenth floor there was the center of operations for the king of hedge-fund managers.

"A hell of a lot more impressive than the twelve percent Madoff gets you."

"Bernie's been very good to us."

"Unfortunately, Ponzi schemes are illegal."

"You don't know he's running a scheme."

McVee scoffed. "Ever seen the man's golf scores? My Palm Beach caddy told me Madoff didn't play for a year, then he came out and claimed to shoot an eighty-four—one shot worse than the last time he picked up a club, and dead-on his handicap since 1998: twelve. That's an interesting number, considering his clients have been earning twelve percent returns through two decades of booms, busts, bubbles, bears, and bulls. Even the SEC knows it's a Ponzi scheme. He's one of many."

"Are you telling me *this* is a Ponzi scheme?"

McVee smiled thinly. "No. That's the beauty of it. There's nothing illegal about credit-default swaps."

"And you're sure no one will know how much we make?"

"No chance. We made your purchases through a web of derivative instruments that no one can unravel."

"And the sellers can pay?"

"We're talking about the biggest insurance companies in the world. All A-plus-plus ratings. Nothing to worry about."

McVee handed him a summary of the instruments, the cost basis for each, the expected ten-figure payoff—and, most important, the hefty fee payable to Ploutus Investments. Graves inspected it, obviously pleased.

"You're brilliant," said Graves.

"I know."

True, McVee was never modest, but in this case he was really in no position to share the credit for a scheme that had been conceived aboard a sailboat on Lake Como six months earlier. The essence of the plan—bringing down an overleveraged Wall Street investment bank through short selling and rumors on FNN, then cashing in on credit default swaps—had been the brainchild of McVee and one very smart lawyer. A mob lawyer. To be a Ploutus client, all it took was money. Lots of it. From any source. And the deep desire to make more of it.

"Who's next?" asked Graves. "Lehman? Merrill?"

Another strike was not out of the question. It had indeed been McVee's decision to target Saxton Silvers, but in the subprime insanity, other firms had made themselves equally vulnerable, borrowing as much as thirty or forty dollars for every dollar of capital they held in reserve, and then using it to purchase toxic NINA mortgages.

"We'll see," said McVee. "They can all come down."

"If that's the case, I'm curious: Why did you start with Saxton Silvers?"

"I had my reasons."

"Cantella?"

"Nothing to do with Cantella."

"I don't believe you."

The solicitor's tone was not merely one of idle conversation, and McVee knew where it was coming from. Just this morning, a story in the *Post* raised the possibility that Cantella was a fall guy for bigger players in the market. Graves, it seemed, was barking up that same tree, and flat denial would only have made him more curious.

"Okay, I admit," said McVee. "It was a little personal. For two years I'd been wondering when Wall Street would realize that subprime lenders all over America were ignoring a fundamental rule that's been around since the Stone Age: You make loans based on the borrower's ability to repay, not on Wall Street's ability to repackage them and pass the risk of default up the daisy chain to someone else. But it really hurt that it was Michael Cantella—a guy who didn't even have direct responsibility for mortgage-backed securities—who sounded the alarm last October and told his firm to wake up and smell the poison. My nephew and his mortgage-lending associates had over nine hundred million in NINA mortgages already funded and in the pipeline, and suddenly there was no Wall Street buyer. It was as if Cantella had finally stopped the music, and I was left without a chair."

"So this is especially sweet for you."

"You have no idea."

Graves seemed satisfied. He rose from the couch, and the men shook hands. Together, they walked down the hall and boarded the elevator. On the ride down, Graves reiterated that the sheikh would be "more than happy" to be the financial muscle behind the next go-round. McVee made no promises. He certainly didn't bother to disclose that he didn't really need outside money, that the sheikh was along for the ride only because the mob wanted an oil-rich Kuwaiti to blame on the off chance that Congress would finally drop its obsession with steroids in baseball and maybe even hold a hearing or two on what the hell was going on with Wall Street.

McVee walked them out to the street, where Graves climbed into a limo.

"We'll be in touch," said Graves.

McVee watched from the sidewalk as the limo pulled away. His explanation for targeting Saxton Silvers had placated the sheikh's solicitor, but destroying Michael Cantella was about so much more than money. The obsession had begun last fall, when he received a phone call from Florence.

"She's *alive*," Ian Burn had told him. "She's changed her look, but we locked eyes just before she ran, and I would bet my life it was her."

If true, the tip meant Tony Girelli was a liar—he hadn't turned Ivy Layton into fish food. McVee was skeptical at first, but Burn was adamant that his eyes had not failed him. The way to lure Ivy out of hiding, he said, was to put the people she loved in danger— the very people she had protected by disappearing in the first place. McVee began cautiously, but last November's sit-down between Burn and Cantella at Sal's Place had been far too subtle, drawing no reaction from Ivy. Burn pushed for more convincing measures, and it was the anniversary of Marcus' suicide that had put McVee over the edge. The thought of Ivy living a new life while his thirty-year-old son rotted in the ground was too much. It was then that McVee decided to turn the attack on Saxton Silvers into an all-out assault against Michael Cantella—destroying his marriage, wiping out his personal fortune, making him a traitor to his own firm. Then Ivy blinked. She warned her precious Michael and, in so doing, revealed herself. Tony Girelli—liar that he was—became the first wave of collateral damage. There would be more. But eventually McVee would get Ivy. And make himself richer in the process.

Another limo with dark-tinted windows stopped at the curb. The driver got out and came around to open the rear passenger's-side door. McVee climbed in, and the door closed.

"Hello, Ian," he said.

Ian Burn was seated on the bench seat with his back to the soundproof partition. McVee sat opposite him, facing forward, and the limo pulled into traffic.

"My nephew told me about last night," McVee said.

"Went well," said Burn.

He was wearing a hooded jacket and dark sunglasses that reminded McVee of the old FBI sketches of the Unabomber.

McVee said, "I'm concerned about the number of bodies."

"I agree: The Bahamian was a long shot. He didn't know anything about Ivy. That was a needless one."

"I don't care about him. It's this flurry in my own backyard that worries me. It's a dangerous cycle.

Girelli put a bullet in Bell's head because Chuck didn't
have the balls to buck a subpoena and refuse to name
Mallory's boyfriend as his source. The boyfriend had to
go because sooner or later he would name my nephew.
Girelli had to go—well, just because Girelli had to go."

"Is there someone in that group you wish was still
alive?"

"I just want to make sure we're efficient. You kill
these fringe players, yet you let Michael Cantella go."

Burn removed his sunglasses. The lighting was dim,
most of the sun's rays blocked by the tinted windows.
But with the glasses off, the scars on the right side of
Burn's face were evident.

"This is my life's work," he said.

"I understand."

"No, you don't. Have you ever wondered how I got
these scars?"

Of course he had. "Not really," said McVee.

"It has to do with money."

"Doesn't everything?"

"This was a very special kind of money," Burn said,
his Indian accent suddenly more noticeable. "Dowry.
It still exists in some parts of my country. If a bride's
family doesn't deliver as promised, that can be very
dangerous for a new wife. The husband might even
take her into the kitchen or garage, douse her with

kerosene, and burn her alive. Happens about every ninety minutes in India. It happened to my sister."

"I'm very sorry."

"So was her husband after I caught up with him. That was my first experience with homemade napalm. I got the job done," he said as he pulled back the hood, exposing his melted ear. "But it didn't go perfectly."

McVee sat in silence.

Burn tightened his stare. "Everything since then *has* gone perfectly. *Everything.*"

"I'm sure."

Burn pulled up the hood and put on his sunglasses. "Michael Cantella's freedom is only temporary. He's holed up with Ivy's mother in a motel over in Jersey. Your nephew is watching him as we speak. The minute Cantella makes a move, I'm on him. There is no doubt in my mind that he will lead me to Ivy Layton. Then they'll both be toast. Literally."

"You should have just put a gun to Cantella's head and threatened to blow his brains out if Ivy didn't show up in thirty minutes."

"Wouldn't have worked. Even if we could get a message to her, it's not like a normal kidnapping. We can't say, 'We have your husband, give us a million bucks.' Ivy knows that what we're saying is, 'We have Cantella, now come here and get him so we can burn you both alive.' She's not going to walk into that. We need Cantella to lead us to her."

"There's logic to that," said McVee.

"Of course there is. Trust me. This is going to go perfectly."

The limo stopped. McVee pulled an envelope from his breast pocket. It was filled with cash.

"Money to Burn," he said, handing over the envelope. "If you don't wrap this up soon, I may have to create a special expense category on my balance sheet."

Without a word, Burn opened the door, climbed out, and left McVee alone in the back of the limo.

50

I dialed Papa's cell from the motel landline. I got his voice-mail greeting:

"I'm sorry I can't take your call right now, but I'm either away from my phone or still trying to figure out how to use this damn thing. Please leave a message."

I waited for the beep. "Papa, I called the airline, and they tell me your plane landed in L.A. an hour ago. The hotel says you haven't checked in yet. I want to make sure you're okay. I'll keep trying, but if you see an incoming call from my old number, don't answer. Someone stole my cell." I paused, realizing that my message was sounding a little scary. "Anyway, I'm hard to reach, so just call Kevin and let him know you're okay. Bye, love you."

I hung up and looked at Olivia.

"Still can't reach your grandfather?' she said.

"No. And the airline won't even tell me if they were on the flight. It's some sort of security policy."

"He probably forgot to turn his cell back on after landing."

That was more than likely. But with all that had happened, there were less benign possibilities. "I feel like I'm in an information dead zone in this motel. I need to get out of here."

"We can't go anywhere. We're being watched."

"How do you know?

"McVee's men let you go last night only because they're betting that you'll lead them to Ivy." She walked to the window and crooked her finger to part the draperies an inch. As best I could tell, we had a view of a graffiti-splattered concrete wall with Tonnelle Avenue beyond.

"They must be out there watching," she said.

"So you don't *know*," I said. "You're assuming."

"It's why we're safe—at least for a little while. The cops can't find us if we stay put, and McVee won't touch us so long as they think Ivy might show up here, or that we might lead them to her."

"That means I didn't hurt anything by telling Kevin to give McVee's name to the FBI."

"In the short run, no. In the long run, you pretty much cinched it that they'll kill all of us. I just hope it's not at the hands of Ian Burn."

Burn had told me his name last night, but I hadn't shared it with Olivia. "How do you know Ian Burn?"

"How do you think?"

"I'm through guessing."

She put her foot up on the bed and rolled up her pant leg to the knee. The scar on her shin bone wasn't that big—about the size of a half dollar—but the crater was deep and grotesque, as if the flames had burned into the bone.

"I've met him," she said.

I was speechless. I'd heard that women had a higher pain threshold than men, but napalm burning a hole into your shin had to be even beyond childbirth.

"I'm sorry, Olivia. When did that happen?"

"After Ivy's memorial service."

"Burn paid you a visit?"

She nodded. "My decision to cremate Ivy's remains and scatter them in the ocean made McVee suspicious. He seemed to think that I was trying to close the book on any further DNA testing. He was right, of course. But when Burn couldn't get anything out of me, that served as confirmation enough that Ivy was really dead."

"Back up a sec," I said. "How did you get the first DNA test to come back with a match for Ivy?"

"We're talking about a crime lab in the west Caribbean, Michael. Think of the Natalie Holloway case—that young girl from Alabama who went to

Aruba on a high school graduation trip and vanished from the beach one night. Never found a body, no charges ever stuck. The incompetence on some of those islands is surpassed only by the corruption. Money talks."

"So . . . whose body was inside the shark?"

"There never was a body," she said. "It was two pelicans and a half-eaten dolphin."

"So the ashes that we scattered were what?"

"Flipper and his flying friends. I know that sounds crazy, but the shark was an afterthought. The plan we originally came up with was for Ivy to disappear, lost at sea. But we were afraid that McVee would never stop looking if there was no body."

"So the shark with the phony human remains was a way to have a body without having a body."

"Right. Kind of an interesting story how the shark idea came to her. Ivy attended an art exhibit with Marcus McVee before his suicide."

"With Marcus?"

"She worked for him, Michael. Anyway, the exhibit included that Damien Hirst piece, a dead shark suspended in formaldehyde in a vitrine. A fourteen-foot tiger shark, to be exact—'something big enough to eat you,' was what Hirst was after. I think Steven Cohen eventually paid eight million for it."

Cohen was a hedge-fund superpower who had amassed a collection valued in the hundreds of millions of dollars. Marcus McVee was kind of a mini-Cohen. For some of these hedge-fund guys, art was a passion. For others, art was simply the new precious metal: a material object that was valuable, available only in limited quantities, and sellable in a recognized market.

I was still processing all that—including the fact that Ivy had gone to an art exhibit with Marcus McVee—when Mallory's cell rang, displaying Kevin's number. I let it ring through to voice mail and dialed Kevin on the landline.

"What's up?" I said.

"Nana and Papa are missing."

That was a jolt I didn't need. "What do you mean, missing?"

"I wasted an hour trying to unravel this, and finally it took a friend in law enforcement to get through the red tape. They never got on the plane."

"What happened?"

"I have no idea," said Kevin. "Did you tell anyone they were on that flight?"

"Just my regular driver who took them to the airport. I told him to call you if anything went wrong."

"Who bought the tickets?"

"I cashed in miles by phone."

Ivy's warning was suddenly burning in my ear: *They must be intercepting your messages! They might even be listening right now!*

"McVee could have gotten the information," I said, "if his men were eavesdropping on my cell."

"Paranoid conspiracy theories are not likely to fly with the police. Especially ones that come from a fugitive and his brother, even if I am your lawyer."

"Then you should be the one to deal with the cops. I can't go to them anyway, unless I want to be locked up. That's a good division of labor."

"What *division*? What are you going to do?"

"Find our grandparents. Any way I can."

51

Eric Volke entered the glass skyscraper via the bowels of the parking garage through a door marked DELIVERIES. Saxton Silvers' main entrance on Seventh Avenue was still blocked by hordes of reporters, cameramen, photographers, confused employees, desperate clients, and the just plain curious. Volke wasn't sure why, but he was thinking of men—boys—like Michael Cantella's grandfather at the age of nineteen or twenty, storming the beach on D-Day, watching their friends die, carnage all around. Climbing out of his limo and sneaking up the rear service elevator, he felt like a complete coward.

The bankruptcy lawyers had filed a Chapter 11 petition—the largest in U.S. history—at nine A.M. The CEO was dealing with the firm's partners and major stockholders. It wasn't specifically in Volke's job description to address the employees, but they were owed at least that much. He went from floor to floor, meeting with large groups of dazed traders, managers, and others who slowly came to realize that they were wasting their time listening to management and should have been typing a résumé. A few were loyal to the end. One of the traders gave him a bronze plaque that had rested atop her desk for six years, a quote from Act II, Scene II of *Julius Caesar* that Eric had referenced in one of his many inspiring speeches: "Cowards die many times before their death; the valiant never taste of death but once."

"Hang in there," was the more common refrain, though many looked at Volke with dagger eyes, as if to say, I'd like to hang *you*.

Volke's last stop was the foreign-exchange traders on the third floor. The open work area was half-empty. Apparently his hollow message had already trickled down from the equity floor above, and many had decided that it wasn't worth waiting for. Scores of desks had been cleaned out, personal items boxed up and hauled away, row after row of darkened trading screens left behind. Empty coffee cups rested on tables. Suit jackets hung on the ends of cubicles. A platter of bagels and doughnuts was virtually untouched; few employees had the stomach to eat. An open bottle of tequila sat atop a file cabinet, some having found gallowslike solace there. Pairs of traders exchanged sad smiles of resignation and shook their heads in disbelief. One cluster perused a copy of the bankruptcy court papers, astounded by the sheer heft.

"Good morning," said Volke.

"What's so good about it?" someone fired back.

An uneasy silence came over the loose gathering, and it stretched all the way across the floor. Some moved closer to listen in. Others stayed where they were, refusing to give up their desk chair, defying the cold reality that it was no longer theirs.

Volke took a step back, glancing out the third-story window at the crowded street below, where double-parked news trucks and cameramen jockeyed for position outside the building's front entrance. Saxton Silvers employees, trying to escape with their belongings and at least some of their dignity, had to push through a media gauntlet where everyone from CNN to Internet bloggers begged for "just thirty seconds" of interview time. A young guy wearing a green Saxton Silvers T-shirt carried a sign that read WHARTON MBA, TWINS ON THE WAY: WILL WORK FOR ANYONE.

"It's a very tough day in our history," said Volke, beginning the way he'd begun each of the dreaded morning talks. But the words halted.

Scanning the room, he avoided making eye contact with any single individual, and his gaze came to rest on some Legos atop a trader's desk. Someone had decorated his workspace with a toy tower of colored plastic bricks—just like the ones that study teams built on the first day of classes at Harvard Business School. It was a Day One collaborative ritual that Volke knew well, and seeing that playful reminder of his alma mater brought back a flash of memories. The thrill of the acceptance letter. The horror of the first "cold call" in the lecture hall. The "up-yours" letter he could have mailed to the first-year accounting professor who'd told him he wasn't going to cut it. Volke didn't fancy himself a historian, but he had lived through "New Yorkonomics," having arrived on Wall Street when the city was suffering from the exodus of manufacturing to cheaper places. He witnessed a spectacular resurgence fueled by innovations in financial services—everything from junk bonds and leveraged buyouts to mortgage-backed securities and hedge funds. It was all a product of the remarkable concentration of smart people in New York City, each learning from the other how to get rich. Saxton Silvers was once a shining example of success, and it was painful to end up as the poster child of "how *not* to do it."

He ditched his prepared words and took an entirely different tack.

"There was a time when the kings of Wall Street were not the commercial banks," he said, "but entities far less regulated. They controlled ungodly sums of wealth, and the more they controlled, the more investors fed them. The average American still lived off the sweat of his brow, but the rich sure got richer. The Wall Street creed was to make money. Big money. Fast money. Rules were bent. Ethics were relative. Laws were swallowed by loopholes. It was all okay; Adam Smith told us so. It all came crashing down, of course. The stock market suddenly lost almost fifty percent of its value, and banks simply stopped making loans."

He paused, his gaze sweeping across a sea of perplexed faces.

"That was 1907," he said. "I guess we didn't learn much."

He drew a deep breath, then let it out. "The doors will lock at five o'clock. I'm sorry," he said, eyes lowered, "especially for you young people. I'm very, very sorry."

Suddenly a bagel flew across the room and nailed him squarely in the chest.

"Fly home in your helicopter and fuck yourself sideways," someone shouted. "You and Michael Cantella both."

A security guard went to the president's side, but no one else moved. No one said a word. The indignity of silence simply hung there.

Volke brushed the crumbs and traces of cream cheese from his Hermès tie, then turned and left the room.

Ivy Layton rose from the couch as Volke returned to his office on the executive floor.

"Thanks a ton for telling me to go with the 1907 mea culpa speech," he said as he tossed his stained necktie onto the chair. "Went over like a mink coat at a PETA convention."

"Maybe the apology didn't come across as genuine," said Ivy.

"Maybe I don't have anything to apologize for," he said.

Ivy didn't go there. All across Wall Street, it was someone else's fault.

Volpe went to his closet and found another tie. He spoke with his back to Ivy, using his reflection in the window as he knotted a perfect double Windsor.

"You can't hide here forever," he said. "The bankruptcy team will be inventorying my office in about four hours."

"I know. It's been a long time since I've spent more than one night in any one place anyway."

He turned to face her, straightening the knot. "Any longer than that and I'd have some explaining to do to Mrs. Volke."

"I understand. I'll go. But I need your help."

"What now?"

"I have nowhere else to turn," she said. "No one else has the power to bring down Kyle McVee."

"Don't you watch FNN? He's already kicked my ass."

"I want you to tell the FBI that it's him, not Michael, who's killing the firm."

"I already have. It's falling on deaf ears. I know you've been away, but now more than ever, Wall Street is like the Wild West, no sheriff in town. Players like McVee do as they please."

"Then you have to make the FBI understand what kind of man Kyle McVee is. Make them realize that he's capable of murder."

"How am I supposed to do that?"

Ivy paused, then forced out the words. "I want you to tell the FBI about me."

"Tell them you're alive?"

"Yes. And why I disappeared."

He stopped and looked at her. "Have you lost your mind? I can't do that."

"Why not?" she asked.

"For starters, I helped fake your death. That's a felony."

Helped was almost an understatement. Eric had arranged for payoffs to the Bahamian medical examiner and DNA expert who had linked Ivy's name to the decomposed "remains" found in the belly of the tiger shark.

"I was just watching television," she said. "A warrant has been issued to arrest Michael for the murder of Chuck Bell."

"That's not my fault. In fact, I protected Michael. The FBI was very interested in knowing what he said to me in our phone conversation before Bell was shot, and quite honestly, Michael's words could have been used against him."

"What did he say?"

"Something to the effect that he was going to put a stop to Bell 'one way or another.'"

"I'm sure Michael didn't mean kill him."

"I know he didn't. That's why I kept that conversation between us."

"One of us has to tell the FBI what's really going on."

He went to her, his expression deadly serious. "That was not our deal," he said. "I helped you disappear with the understanding that you would never come back, no matter what."

"Things have changed, Eric. I tried running, and I'm out of options. If you won't go to the FBI, I will."

He stepped away, running his hand through his hair. But he didn't push back the way she had expected.

"You're right," he said. "The only way to derail Kyle McVee is to make the FBI understand that, in his twisted mind, bringing down Saxton Silvers is secondary to finding you."

"Everything is secondary to finding me. I should have told the FBI that four years ago."

"The FBI couldn't protect you then. And they won't be able to protect you now."

"I'm not worried about me. I'm worried about Michael and my mother."

He took her hand and squeezed it. "They'll be fine. I promise."

"You got their backs?"

He nodded. "McVee will never find them. I don't care what it costs. I may have lost my shirt in Saxton Silvers, but thankfully, money will never be an issue for me. I've still got WhiteSands."

Eric was talking about the investment management firm he'd founded in the 1980s, before his rise to power within Saxton Silvers. Some said it was the proverbial tail wagging the dog, with over a trillion dollars in assets under management, yet 49 percent owned by Saxton Silvers. Eric, individually, was still a major shareholder.

"Thank you, Eric."

He nodded. "I don't regret the way I helped you four years ago. And, of course, we all want to help Michael. You just have to figure out a way to do it without throwing me under the bus."

She knew he was right. She gave him a quick hug, then stepped away.

"Good luck, Ivy. And for the last time: good-bye."

52

Ivy took the express elevator from the Saxton Silvers executive suite to the garage and left the building through the rear entrance. She walked toward Columbus Circle, weighing her options. Somewhere above the plywood tunnel that said POST NO BILLS, a demolition crew outshouted their jackhammers in a heated Mets vs. Yankees argument. A delivery truck blocked the cross street as fishmongers tossed tonight's sushi over their shoulders and hauled it down into a restaurant cellar. On the sidewalk alongside the newsstand, hip-hop dancers whirled on their heads like spinning tops, all for a few bucks that passersby tossed into a hat. A bus pulled up, hydraulic brakes hissing. Every square inch of it, including the windows and door, was a mobile advertisement for *Jersey Boys*, "winner of four Tony

Awards, including best musical and best actor . . ."
They'd missed out on best actress.

Should have gone to Ivy Layton.

She missed living in the city. Ironically, she never
would have returned, had it not been for Ian Burn.
Their chance encounter at a restaurant in Florence
last fall changed everything. She wasn't certain that
he had recognized her, but the exchange had been
too dangerous to ignore. Ivy knew how McVee oper-
ated. If Burn was able to convince him that Ivy was
alive, McVee would target Michael or her mother
to draw Ivy out of hiding. She had to warn them,
or at least keep her finger on the pulse of the situation, which meant returning to New York. She'd
arrived in February—right about the same time
Mallory's friend Andrea moved to the Upper West
Side. It had occurred to Ivy that the timing was no
coincidence.

Speaking of "best actress."

Ivy jumped in a taxi and rode up to Le Pain Quoti-
dien near Columbus Circle, where Mallory met Andrea
for coffee almost every morning after her Pilates class.
As long as Ivy had been watching them, Andrea always
arrived ten to fifteen minutes early and snagged a
table in the café away from the bakery, surrounded by
other skinny women who tried not to get too close to

warm loaves of pain au chocolat or—Andrea's morning favorite—the organic hazelnut flûte. Andrea usually scarfed one down before Mallory arrived. And there she was now, enjoying one with coffee at her usual table when Ivy approached.

"Wow, coffee *and* a pastry. How'd you get the bureau to approve *that* in your undercover operation budget?"

"Excuse me?" said Andrea.

She extended her hand, still standing. "Hi, I'm Ivy Layton."

Andrea showed surprise but stayed in role. "Michael Cantella's first wife?

"That would be me."

More surprise, but now it was coming across too thick. "But you're supposed to be dead."

"Careful, girl," said Ivy. "They don't give Tony Awards for overacting."

Andrea was suddenly speechless. Ivy smiled, then turned serious.

"Let's clear that up right now. I'll stop pretending to be dead, and you stop pretending that you're not an FBI agent. Deal?"

"I don't know what you're talking about," said Andrea.

"Oh, come on," said Ivy. "It takes one to know one, and I've known about you for quite some time."

Andrea paused, clearly coming to realize that the jig was up. "It's a crime to impersonate an FBI agent."

"I didn't mean it literally. I just recognize an undercover agent when I see one. It's the little things. The way you always show up early for your eleven o'clock meeting with Mallory, probably to run through the conversation in your head and figure out what information you're going to pry out of her. The body language that tells me that you're only pretending not to listen whenever Mallory takes a call on her cell—that you're trained to make Mallory think you're reading the menu or checking your BlackBerry when, in fact, you're all ears. The way you hang on every word that Mallory utters, always encouraging her to say more." She tugged at the chair. "May I?"

Andrea didn't say anything, so Ivy took a seat.

"I've been watching Michael for years," said Ivy, "keeping my distance, of course. That's how I found out his wife was cheating on him. And that's how I knew you were an FBI agent working undercover."

Andrea still said nothing.

"I understand," said Ivy. "You can't confirm or deny. But let me guess. The federal investigation into the manipulation of Saxton Silvers stock is now in its . . . fifth month? Sixth? The FBI was counting on Chuck Bell to crumble under subpoena and reveal the confidential source who fed him the false rumors about Saxton Silvers. Michael Cantella was one of the short sellers who profited from the rumors. Bell could have exposed a chain of players that led directly back to Michael—motive enough, perhaps, for Michael to have Bell silenced before he could testify before the grand jury."

The women locked eyes.

"Am I even close?" asked Ivy, but Andrea met her with more silence.

"I thought so," said Ivy. "So here's the truth. Eric Volke told me that he's already laid out these facts for you, but maybe you'll believe him if you also hear it from me: Michael is innocent. Kyle McVee is your man. He set up everything to make you think exactly what you're thinking about Michael."

Andrea considered it, and Ivy knew she finally had her engaged.

"Why would Kyle McVee single out Michael Cantella?"

"Because of me," said Ivy.

"That much I've figured out. I need specifics."

"That's the best I can do."

Andrea's stare tightened. "You don't seem to understand. Anyone who fakes her own death has defrauded the IRS, created a false Social Security number, used a phony passport, committed fraud and perjury in connection with identification documents—the list of federal crimes goes on and on. You have no choice: You *have* to do better."

Most of what Andrea described was Eric Volke's doing. Even if Ivy had wanted to tell the FBI everything, she couldn't sell out the man who'd put himself at risk to help her create a new identity and disappear— effectively saved her life.

"Compared to the financial crimes you're targeting in the undercover operation, that's all very petty stuff," Ivy tried.

"Petty? You're looking at one to ten years of imprisonment for each offense."

"Okay. But before you haul me in, hear me out. Like I said at the beginning: I've known about you for quite some time. Which should make you wonder: Why have I kept it to myself? Why didn't I just come right out and tell Eric Volke or Michael or my mother that Mallory Cantella's friend Andrea is an undercover FBI agent?"

Andrea was trying to show no interest—but was failing.

Ivy almost smiled. "I decided to keep my mouth shut until I needed a favor. And that time has come. It's a simple one, but without it, I can assure you of this: The world will know by sunrise that you are an

FBI undercover agent. Then you can watch months of undercover work go up in smoke with no payoff."

Ivy let her chew on that one for a while, and finally it drew a response.

"And if I agree to grant you that favor?"

"Then I'm willing to tell you more than Eric Volke has already told the FBI. I'll tell you exactly why Kyle McVee wants me dead."

Andrea gave her an assessing look. "All right," she said, extending her hand. "You good on a handshake?"

"I am if you are, Andrea."

"Call me Andie," she said as they shook.

"Okay," said Ivy. "You may want to call me Vanessa."

"So start talking, Vanessa."

Ivy leaned closer. And then she told her.

53

I was inside the closet, tapping on the back wall with my knuckles.

Our motel room was like every other I had ever seen. The front wall facing the parking lot was a prefabricated door and window with a built-in climate-control unit. The room had no other way in or out. In the back was a small bathroom on one side, a Formica counter with a mirror and vanity setup in the middle, and a step-in closet on the other side.

I tapped again on the back wall of the closet.

"What are you doing?" asked Olivia.

"One of my clients once bought a motel chain. I remember him telling me that the rooms don't back up to other rooms. There's usually a service corridor that runs the length of the building."

"So?"

"So if it's true that we're being watched, all we have to do is bust through this back wall, leave through the service corridor, and they'll never know we're gone."

Olivia came into the closet and knocked. "But it's *a wall*."

"Not a bearing wall," I said. "It's hollow. And these studs are twenty-four inches apart, not sixteen."

"It's still *a wall*."

I took a wire hanger from the rack and straightened it out. Holding it with both hands, I pressed the tip to the wall and pushed. It went right through, like a poker. This was going to be even easier than I'd thought; there was wallboard on only my side of the studs. The service corridor on the other side was obviously unfinished, the studs exposed. I pulled out the hanger, placed the tip an inch above the previous hole, and pushed again. Olivia caught on to what I was doing, straightened out another hanger, and started on the other side of the closet. In ten minutes we had the dotted outline of a punched rectangle on the wall.

"Stand back," I said.

Olivia stepped aside. I got a running start, jumped at the rectangle, hit it squarely with both feet, smashed right through it—and landed flat on my ass on the concrete floor of the dark service corridor, covered from head to toe with broken bits of wallboard.

"Owww—*shit*."

Olivia appeared in the opening, gazing through the dust. "Are you all right?"

My breath was gone. "This never happens to Jason Bourne."

Olivia climbed through the hole and helped me to my feet. I brushed the debris from my shirt as I looked around. One end of the corridor was blocked by laundry carts that were overflowing with towels and linens. The door at the other end was clear.

"This way," I said, leading her down the hall at a medium jog. The door was unlocked, and we stepped into a sunny courtyard. It took a moment to get my bearings. If the entrance to our room was being watched, we were out of view, no longer right on busy Tonnelle Avenue. I led Olivia around the building, away from our room, to the opposite side of the motel. A cab was parked beneath the carport. We hurried toward it and jumped in the backseat.

The driver put down his newspaper.

"Where to?"

"Nutley," I said. Nick, the driver who had taken my grandparents to the airport, lived in New Jersey, and I was hoping he would have some idea what had gone wrong last night.

"Where about in Nutley?"

I'd been to Nick's house for his daughter's First Communion, but I didn't remember the exact address.

"Walnut Street, I think. I'll recognize the house. Just hurry."

"You got it," he said.

The meter started running, and both Olivia and I ducked down to the floor as the taxi pulled onto Tonnelle Avenue.

"Hey, hey," said the driver. "None of that in my cab."

We stayed low until we were a good half mile from the motel, then climbed back into our seats. Olivia gazed out the window at oncoming traffic on the divided highway, a wan expression on her face, as if searching hopelessly for her daughter. I should have let her have time to herself, but something was weighing on my mind.

"Why did it bother you so much when I told you that Burn knew Ivy as 'Vanessa'?"

Olivia glanced back, seemingly puzzled. "I told you: That's the name Ivy used after she disappeared."

"What was her surname?"

Again, she bristled—the same way she had earlier, when I told her that Burn had used the name Vanessa."

"What?"

414 · JAMES GRIPPANDO

"When Ivy became Vanessa," I said, "what was her last name?"

Olivia continued to fumble—why, I wanted to find out.

"I don't know," she said.

She turned her attention back to the passing cars and road signs. I let it go. Her reaction was more telling than anything. Something wasn't adding up.

I checked Mallory's smart phone. Back at the motel, calls had come through, but it had been an Internet dead zone. Now I was getting the Web. On a hunch, I linked Vanessa with Olivia's surname—"Hernandez"— and ran it through the electronic white pages. The result wasn't promising: "Hernandez," the search summary told me, was the twenty-second most common surname in America. Slap "Vanessa" in front of it, and the full name was only slightly less popular than "Valerie Clark"—1,950,000 hits. In a last-ditch effort, I typed "Vanessa Hernandez and Ivy Layton" and pressed Search. Only a few hits came up, and I clicked on a link that took me to a photo gallery for "Ivy Layton." Most of the photos looked to be twenty years old or more. My specific link was to a photograph of two high school girls wearing soccer uniforms. I looked closer. One of them was named Ivy Layton. I didn't recognize her. The girl next to her was named Vanessa Hernandez, and I froze.

It was Ivy.

Her hair was longer and darker, her face more girlish, but eighteen-year-old Vanessa Hernandez from Gulliver Academy in Coral Gables, Florida, class of 1990, had grown into the woman I knew as "Ivy Layton."

My head was spinning. Admittedly, I had never known much about Ivy's childhood. She'd told me that she was homeschooled in Chile. That her mother—Olivia—was from Santiago. Her father, long since deceased, was an engineer in the mining business. Details were sparse; Ivy didn't like to talk about the past. "Life's about the future," she would tell me. She was so full of energy, and I was so in love with her, that her forward focus always seemed healthy to me. Now it seemed duplicitous, perhaps nefarious.

I clicked on the Home button on the menu bar, and I discovered that I wasn't in just any photo gallery. It was a *memorial* book—a tribute to Ivy Layton that her friends had created for the tragic no-show at their ten-year high school reunion. She'd died in a car crash. Ivy had not become Vanessa after she'd disappeared from our sailboat. Vanessa Hernandez had become Ivy Layton. For the short period of time I had known her, Ivy—Vanessa—had used the name of a deceased high school girlfriend so that she could become . . . what?

And why?

"Here you go, buddy," said the driver. "Walnut Street."

I looked up. Nutley's former residents included everyone from Martha Stewart to Little Sammy Corsaro, a Gambino crime family soldier. Nick's part of Nutley was more along the Little Sammy lines. To my left, a huge willow tree overpowered the small yard, hiding all but the screened-in porch of an old frame house.

I spotted Nick in his driveway.

"Stop!"

The cabbie hit the breaks. Nick looked over. The black suit and cap that he wore as a limo driver were instantly recognizable, but it was odd to see him dressed that way behind the wheel of his own modest Chevy. He was backing out to the street, on his way to work, giving me no time to confront Olivia about Ivy's real name.

"Go," she told me, "I'll cover the fare."

I jumped out of the cab, ran across the street, and practically threw myself in the path of Nick's car. He stopped at the end of the driveway and cranked down his window.

"Mr. C., what are you doing here?"

I was about to explain my paranoia about using a cell phone—Ivy's warning that McVee might be listening—but skipped it. "I wanted to talk to you about last night. Did you get my grandparents to the airport okay?"

My question put him on the defensive. "Yeah, almost two hours before the flight. Something wrong?"

"They didn't get on the plane. And no one has heard from them since."

He seemed genuinely shocked. "That's weird."

"Did you see anything strange? Anyone at the airport who looked out of the ordinary?"

"Nuttin' that worried me," said Nick. "They seemed in good hands when I left."

"Whose hands?"

"There was a woman who met them at the curb."

"You mean curbside check-in?"

"No, I dealt with that. She was . . . a friend, I thought. Good lookin', too. Anyways, they seemed to know her and were glad to see her—*really* glad. Like they ain't seen each other for a long time. I didn't think nothin' of it."

I froze, almost too perplexed to ask. "Did you catch her name?"

"Your grandpa called her Ivy."

Ivy.

"Mr. C.," said Nick, breaking my chain of thought. "I know you got a lot on your mind, but I heard about the bankruptcy on the news this morning. I was just wondering about my stock."

"You own shares of Saxton Silvers?"

"Well, yeah. The wife and me, we been saving for years, but it just wasn't keeping up with the way tuition was rising. You seemed like a successful guy. So we talked it over and put the kids' college fund in the market. That's not gone, is it?"

It felt like a knife in my belly. I wondered how many guys like Nick were out there. "We'll talk about that," I said.

My cell rang. Mallory's cell. I didn't recognize the number, so I ignored it, figuring that it was probably one of Mallory's girlfriends trying to reach her. Immediately it rang again—the same caller redialing rather than going to voice mail, as if the message were urgent. I was so out of sorts from what I'd just heard from Nick that I'd momentarily forgotten Ivy's warning about using the cell phone. I answered it.

"Michael, it's me." Her voice was racing.

"Ivy?"

"Shut up and answer this question yes or no: Are you still in New Jersey?"

Suddenly I remembered the eavesdropping, and I was afraid to say. "Why is that import—"

"Stop!" she said. "I don't care where you are. Get to North Bergen and go to the nearest DQ."

"What?"

"Focus, Michael. Listen to *exactly* what I'm saying. Meet me at the North Bergen DQ. How soon can you get there?"

"Well, we just got out of a cab so—"

"Stop it! Less than half an hour or more?"

"Less—I think."

"Good. Get there as fast as you can. You got that? Go to the *DQ*. Right now! And take the battery out of Mallory's phone before you go."

"What?"

"Just do it! Remove the battery and go!"

The call ended, and she was gone.

Olivia came up the driveway, clearly alarmed by the expression on my face. "Everything okay?"

I slid the battery off the back of the phone, then looked at Nick and said, "We need a ride."

54

"Just got out of a *cab*?" said Jason Wald.

Wald was in the back of a white van that was parked in the bus lot across the street from the Tonnelle Avenue motel. Seated in the captain's chair beside him, wearing headphones, was his tech expert. Between them was a laptop computer. Weeks earlier, Mallory Cantella's "boyfriend," Nathaniel, had given them everything they needed to program Mallory's cell with spy software. Ivy's conversation with Michael had come through the speakers on the laptop in real time, loud and clear.

"How did they get out of the motel without us seeing them?" asked Wald.

It was their job to let Burn know exactly when Michael and Olivia made a move. A wireless camera on the fence was aimed at the motel room door, with either Wald or his tech guy watching the image on their computer screen at all times.

"What does the GPS say?" Wald said.

"For some reason the spyware still isn't giving me a read from the cell phone."

"What about Olivia's car?" Wald had gone over in the middle of the night and planted a backup under the bumper.

The tech guy pulled up the satellite coordinates on the computer screen. "The car hasn't moved."

"Of course it hasn't," said Wald. "They took a cab. Try getting the GPS reading on the cell phone again."

"Definitely won't work now. She told him to take the battery out."

Wald yanked at his hair, as if trying to pull the answer out of his head. "I just don't understand how they could get out."

"I don't either," said his techie. "I gave the manager twenty bucks to let me look inside one of the rooms, just like you asked me to. There's only one way in and one way out—and that's the front door."

"This has to be a ruse. They must still be in there."

Wald flung open the passenger's-side door, jumped from the van, and ran across the street toward the motel, hurdling over the concrete barrier that separated the divided highway. He stopped at Olivia's car and laid his hand on the hood. It was cold; the car hadn't moved since they'd pulled up last night. He went to room 107 and put his ear to the door. Silence.

They can't be gone!

He wanted to bang down the door and find out for sure, but if it turned out that they were still inside, what would he say when Cantella answered the door? He needed another plan. A maid's cart was two doors down. He ran to it and found the housekeeper making the bed inside room 103.

"Come quick!" he said. "I think my friend in room 107 is sick!"

She paused.

"Come!" said Wald. "You have to open the door."

She followed him out to room 107. Wald retreated a few steps and waited in the doorway to room 103, behind the maid's cart, where he would be out of sight when the door opened. The maid knocked on the door to 107.

No answer.

"Open it!" Wald said, speaking in a hurried whisper.

She knocked again, harder this time. Still no answer.

"Open the damn door!" he said, his whisper even more urgent.

The housekeeper was getting nervous and more than a little suspicious. "I'll get the manager," she said.

Wald cursed under his breath as she walked away. Every fiber in his body was telling him Cantella had somehow escaped, but he had to see with his own eyes. He went to the window. The drapes were drawn, making it impossible to peer inside. He tried the knob, but it was locked. He put his shoulder into the door, but it didn't budge.

The maid's cart was still in front of room 103. He went to it, grabbed a large bath towel, and pulled the gun from his jacket. With the weapon in hand and his finger on the trigger, he wrapped the towel around it, aimed it at the lock, and fired once. The makeshift sound suppressor reduced the noise level to that of a cap gun, and the lock was destroyed. He pushed open the door and burst into the room. The gaping hole in the back of the closet immediately told the story.

"Son of a bitch!"

He tossed the powder-burned towel aside, tucked away the gun, and dialed Burn.

"Cantella's on the move," said Wald. "She called him and said to meet at the Dairy Queen."

"Which one?"

"The one in North Bergen."

"What street?"

Wald struggled, no more information. "Hell if I know."

Wald could hear Burn's keyboard clacking in the background. It took less than thirty seconds.

"It's on Kennedy Avenue," said Burn.

"You want me to meet you there?" asked Wald.

"No," said Burn, a certain finality in his voice. "I've got it."

55

Because of its location on the Hudson River—on River Road near the George Washington Bridge, Lincoln Tunnel, and major highways—Palisades Medical Center in New Bergen had one of the busiest emergency departments in New Jersey. Nearly thirty thousand patients came each year for lifesaving care.

No one came for ice cream—and neither did I.

Meet me at the DQ was a reference to the weird dream I'd shared with Ivy right before asking her to marry me—the one about the SUV running me off the road, forcing me to rush my dog to the DQ for emergency medical treatment. Ivy had conveyed her instructions to me in code, alert to the fact that Mallory's cell was probably being monitored. "Meet me at the DQ in North Bergen" meant "meet me at the ER," and the closest one to an actual DQ was at Palisades.

By my calculations, Ian Burn was having a hot fudge sundae as we spoke.

"You came to the right place," she said.

I was standing by the vending machine in the crowded waiting room when the voice had come from behind me. I recognized it right away, but when I turned in response, the face wasn't exactly the one I had remembered. She sensed my confusion.

"Rhinoplasty," she said, turning to show me her profile. "Pretty nice work, no?"

She'd cut her hair and darkened it, too, returning to the color I'd seen in the photograph online—but it was Ivy, and instinctively I grabbed her and nearly squeezed her to death.

It's hard for me to say how long we stayed in each other's arms. Long-term memories were powerful forces, and just the smell of her hair seemed to unleash an emotional rush that—for a moment, at least—let me forget the circumstances of our reunion. I was remembering things that I had yet to realize I'd forgotten. The ease of our embrace. The warmth of her face against mine. How good her hands felt on my shoulder blades. The first coherent thought to bring me back to earth was a tinge of guilt—a thought about Mallory, about our pending divorce. I pushed that aside as irrelevant, but the magic was slipping away. I was slowly coming back the to harsh reality of the huge problems at hand.

"Your grandparents are safe," she said, as we separated.

We were standing face-to-face, her fingers still loosely intertwined with mine, oblivious to the typical ER commotion around us—the boys playing soccer with a balled-up wad of white medical tape, the sneezing and coughing old man in the corner with the vomit bucket in his lap, the moaning construction worker with the bloody rag wrapped around his smashed finger.

"You met them at the airport?" I said.

"Intercepted, I guess, is a better word for it. McVee uses any pressure point he can. Family and loved ones are at the top of his list. I was afraid that if he got hold of your grandparents, you'd be at his mercy."

"Where are they?"

"The FBI is protecting them."

"According to your mother, you went into hiding because the FBI couldn't protect you. Why would you put my grandparents in their hands?"

"They're tertiary targets who don't know anything. McVee won't go to the same trouble to track them down as he would to find me—or you, for that matter."

"That makes sense, I guess."

"Plus, this time I have leverage," she said.

"What kind of leverage?"

"If the FBI screws up, I blow the lid on Mallory's friend Andrea—who, by the way, is an FBI agent."

It was clear from her tone that Ivy was expecting a serious show of surprise from me. But I wasn't so shocked. Little things had always made Andrea seem different from Mallory's other friends—the way she wolfed down pasta at Carmine's, the blond-in-a-bottle dye job, the way she'd pressed for names when I told her about short sellers. All along, something about her didn't meet the eye.

One thing still didn't make sense.

"How did you know my grandparents were going to the airport?"

She sighed and said, "There's something you should know about me."

"You think?" I said with a mirthless chuckle.

She smiled a little, then led me to a quiet corner of the room where her coat was hanging on the back of a chair. She sat me down, pulled her coat back on, and took a seat facing me.

"I've been monitoring your limo driver's wireless communications."

"What the hell?" I said, shaking my head. "Am I the last guy on earth who doesn't know how to listen to other people's cell conversations?"

"Cell conversations, text messages, e-mails—none of it's private. All it takes is simple spyware that you can buy on the Internet. The more sophisticated programs don't even require me to touch your phone for setup. I just plug in the number, program it, and I can see every message you send or receive, and listen to every conversation you have. I can even program my device to ring every time you use your phone, so I don't have to sit around monitoring you. The only way to break the connection is to remove the battery from the targeted phone."

"Which is why you told me to take the battery out of Mallory's phone."

"Exactly. Everyone in the business uses cell spyware now."

"And what business is that?"

"You must have some inkling," she said.

There was a semblance of a smile on her face, a gentle understanding in her voice. But it was my most disquieting moment with Ivy so far—the sense that she knew what I knew, that she knew what I didn't know, and that I had no idea how she knew any of it.

"Tell me about Vanessa Hernandez," I said.

She didn't hesitate in the least, didn't even try feigning ignorance.

"Vanessa Hernandez had no problems with her nose," she said, showing me her profile. "It was Ivy Layton who insisted on getting the work done."

"I'm serious," I said.

Her smile faded. "I was born in Miami. My parents were undercover agents for the DEA. My mom was born in Colombia, so she played the go-between for wealthy American dealers trying to hook up with Colombian suppliers."

"Not exactly the Chilean schoolteacher and ex-pat engineer you told me about."

"It was the same cover story they told our neighbors in Miami. They were always headed off to another copper-mining project in Chile, when in reality they were infiltrating the cocaine cartel in Colombia. Anyway, when I was five years old, a job went bad in Bogotá. Their target figured out that my father was DEA. My mother watched them drag him out of the car, shoot him in the back of the head, and dump his body on the side of the road."

"I'm sorry. Your mother obviously escaped?"

"Somehow she was able to convince them that she had no idea he was an undercover agent. They let her go."

"Did she stay with the DEA?"

"For a while. But she hasn't worked with them for years. She got into corporate security as a consultant."

"So . . . which way did Vanessa go?"

"No interest in law enforcement. But when I grew up and went to business school, the world of corporate espionage intrigued me. I joined a huge corporate security firm and when I was twenty-nine years old, my mother got a call from an old friend on Wall Street. He needed a brainy young woman with guts to infiltrate a billion-dollar hedge fund. That fund was Ploutus Investments. The friend on Wall Street was Eric Volke. Vanessa got the assignment, and that's when I became Ivy Layton."

I drew a deep breath, trying to get my arms around the whole thing. "Your mother knows Eric?"

"Yes. She's in a taxi right now, on her way to meet up with him. Eric promised me that he would keep the two of you safe while this plays out between me and McVee."

I paused again, still overwhelmed. "So when you and I met, you were doing corporate espionage for Saxton Silvers?"

"No. Eric hired me for WhiteSands."

I knew WhiteSands. Sometimes its services complemented those of Saxton Silvers, and sometimes Eric was criticized for holding such a large ownership stake in a publicly traded company that, at least on the investment-management level, competed with Saxton Silvers for business.

"But you were *spying*," I said.

"'Spying' has such a negative connotation. Eric knew that someone was manipulating the stock of

WhiteSands, and he was convinced that the man behind it was Kyle McVee at Ploutus. The basic MO was similar to what just happened to Saxton Silvers. McVee used FNN reporters to spread rumors about WhiteSands, and McVee's hedge fund bought low on the negative rumors and sold high on the favorable ones. Eric suspected that McVee was behind it, but he couldn't prove anything. My job was to expose his plot by going to work for Ploutus and reporting my findings back to Eric."

"Is that why McVee wanted you dead?"

"That was only the beginning," said Ivy.

She suddenly stopped, and the expression on her face alarmed me.

"Ivy?"

"Holy shit," she said.

"What?"

She was staring out the window into the parking lot. "Your driver."

"Nick?" I said as I turned and looked. His Chevy was about a hundred feet away, parked beneath a tree. The sun was setting and the streetlights had just flicked on; their glare at dusk made the weblike crack in the windshield all the more evident. Nick's head was facedown on the steering wheel.

"They got him," said Ivy.

56

Ian Burn entered the emergency room through the ambulance entrance. No one stopped him. He figured Cantella and Ivy were keeping an eye on the main entrance to the ER. By entering from the other side, where access was restricted, he would catch them off guard. He started down a maze of sterile corridors, guided by the signs marked WAITING ROOM. Ironic.

He couldn't wait to get there.

Cantella's limo driver had been a good source of information over the past few weeks. The tip about Cantella's true destination had been Nick's best yet. And his last. In an operation this big, Burn never kept people around after they were no longer needed. That held true even for the little guys—*especially* the little guys. It was always the housekeeper, the limo driver, or the bartender who ratted you out and sent you to prison. Nick had served his purpose and needed to go—though the cracked windshield and brain splatter were regrettable. His 9 mm Glock pistol had been too much firepower for such a close-range shot.

"Excuse me, sir. Can I help you?"

It was an elderly hospital volunteer. Nobody policed the halls of the "authorized personnel only" area like a seventy-year-old woman from Jersey who worked for free.

Burn ignored her, picking up his pace. He had no time for delays. Six months of tracking Ivy Layton had taught him plenty about the way her mind worked. She felt safe in public places, and probably the last thing she expected was for Ian Burn to walk into a crowded waiting room and start shooting. It was a risky maneuver, even for Burn, but acting contrary to a target's expectations was the key to success in his business. Reporting back to Kyle McVee that Ivy Layton had slipped away again was not an option.

The gray-haired hospital volunteer came after him.

"Sir, this area is restricted."

He knocked her to the floor and pushed through the double doors that led to the ER waiting room. The old woman's scream turned heads and robbed Burn of the element of surprise, sending Ivy and Cantella running across the waiting room at full speed. The automatic glass exit doors parted, and Ivy was flying through the opening with Cantella on her heels when Burn spotted them. He raised his semi-automatic pistol and took aim. The sick, the injured, and the healthy alike scattered in every direction, screaming and diving for cover beneath the chairs and behind gurneys as Burn squeezed off six quick rounds. The echo off the tile floor and walls of painted cinder block sounded like cannon fire, and the shots shattered the glass doors as they closed. There was hysteria all around, but Burn's focus was unshaken.

In the shower of shiny glass pellets just beyond the exit, Ivy Layton—Vanessa—fell to the sidewalk.

57

The sight of Ivy going down hit me like hot shrapnel. One moment we were running at full speed, and the next it was a war zone. The noise was like firecrackers in a campfire. We were beyond the glass doors, but the exploding pellets of shattered glass caught up with us. The rest happened in a split second, but the image and sounds unfolded like slow motion. Several bullets slammed into Ivy's back. Her body jerked forward, as if someone were knocking her to the ground with a hammer. I could actually hear the bullets pelting her—which struck me as odd. The jerking body was odd, too. Papa had told me that when people got shot, they dropped. Period. He'd seen it happen in World War II. Bodies weren't knocked back, held up, or slammed against the wall like in the movies.

Her Kevlar had changed everything.

Ivy's trench coat looked ordinary, but the lining was body armor. She'd worn it every spring for the past four years, and when the threat level went from orange to red, she practically lived in it. She'd removed it only for our embrace. Thank God she'd put it back on before Burn had burst into the waiting room and started shooting.

"Roll!" she shouted.

I dived to the ground and did exactly as told, landing on the grass at full speed and rolling like a log down a hill. I heard more shots from Burn and noticed two or three miniature explosions of dirt as we rolled toward a tree. We were safely behind the massive oak's trunk when Ivy pulled a gun from her jacket and fired two quick shots back toward the emergency room.

"There are people in there!" I said.

"I'm hitting the roof, but Burn doesn't know that. Now run!"

She pivoted and fired two more shots from the other side of the tree trunk. I'd never seen her with a handgun, but she had obviously gotten serious training.

"Run!" she told me.

"Where?"

"Get with Eric. He'll keep you safe."

"I'm not leaving you here."

I heard sirens in the distance. The police were on the way.

"If we're still here when the cops arrive," said Ivy, "they'll arrest both of us. We're sitting ducks in jail."

I didn't have an answer to that.

She grabbed the back of my neck and pulled my face toward hers. "I'll run to the left," she said. "You run right. I'll find you. I promise."

I was thinking of that trip in the Bahamas four years earlier, when she'd promised I would never regret our decision to ditch the Saxton Silvers crowd and charter a sailboat.

"I can't—"

She silenced me with a kiss—and I hoped it wasn't good-bye for good.

"Take my cell," she said, pressing it into my hand. "McVee's techies haven't compromised it yet with their spyware. Speed-dial number one is my mother. Call her, and hook up with her and Eric. Then keep it on. I *will* call you. I promise."

There was that word again—*promise.*

Then she turned, ran, and fired two more diversion shots toward the hospital as she disappeared into the dark shadows beneath the canopy of sprawling oaks. Burn returned fire in her direction. I ran the opposite way, clutching Ivy's cell.

I knew that Ivy wanted me to clear the area as quickly as possible, and the sirens told me that the police were getting close. But I needed to check on Nick. I zigzagged between parked cars until I came upon the Chevy. The driver's-side door was unlocked, and when I opened it, Nick's slumped body fell out of the front seat and onto the pavement.

I couldn't help but gasp at the sight of such a horrible, bloody mess at the base of his skull. There was another gaping hole in his forehead—a through-and-through bullet wound was what my years of watching *CSI* on television had taught me. No doubt about it, Nick was gone.

With blood splatter everywhere—the seat, the steering wheel, the dash, the cracked windshield—I couldn't have taken the car even if the thought had come to me. The truth is, it never even crossed my mind. Adrenaline took over, and I didn't even slam the door shut. I turned and ran like an Olympian, crossing the parking lot in seconds, determined not to be chased down by Burn, the police, or anyone else who might be in pursuit. Block after block, I just kept going, heading away from River Road and major thoroughfares. Dusk had turned to night by the time I found a pay phone—I didn't want the call traced to the cell Ivy had given me—and I stopped on the sidewalk outside a deli to dial 911.

"A man's been shot," I said, breathless, "in the parking lot at Palisades Medical Center. The shooter's name is Ian Burn. Six feet tall, dark complexion—maybe Indian decent—a bad scar on his right ear from a burn." I continued to rattle off every distinguishing characteristic I could recall, and then wondered if the scar was on his left ear and not his right. The more I spoke, the more my thoughts scattered, and I shuddered to think what the recording of this call would sound like. I finished with a flurry: "He is an extremely dangerous professional killer. You have to find him!"

I hung up and sprinted away. I was on Park Avenue, which bore as much resemblance to *the* Park Avenue as Rome, Georgia, did to its namesake. Just beyond Gunther's Bargain Corner and directly across the street from a used-furniture store called the Tickled Pink Petunia was a twenty-four-hour Laundromat. I ducked inside and grabbed a chair in the corner away from the noisy machines where I could catch my breath. I was still recovering when I hit speed-dial number one on the cell Ivy had given me.

"Hey, girlfriend," said Olivia.

She'd clearly assumed from the incoming number that the call was from her daughter.

"It's Michael," I said, and then I told her about the string of mishaps that had landed Ivy's cell with me.

I was still processing the whole shoot-out myself, and the full impact of Nick's death didn't even hit me until I spoke of it.

"Burn shot my driver dead," I said, my voice quaking. "Nick's got two little kids, for God's sake."

She sighed so loudly that her voice crackled on the line. "Where is Burn now?"

"I'm sure he ran. I guess someone dialed nine-one-one. Police were on their way. I called, too, just a minute ago."

"You *what?*"

"Don't worry. I used a pay phone. They now have Ian Burn's name and a pretty good description of him."

"Michael, don't take risks like that. I'm sure Ivy has already given all that information to her FBI contact."

"It doesn't hurt for them to hear it twice."

"There's an arrest warrant out for you," she said. "For the tenth time: If the police haul you in, you're dead. And now that you've called nine-one-one, patrol cars are probably in the neighborhood looking for you as we speak."

"I didn't leave my name."

"Good. Just don't make any more calls. We're coming to get you."

"You and Ivy?"

"No. Eric and me. Where are you?"

I told her.

"That's in Guttenberg," said Olivia. "Give us five minutes and we'll pick you up in Eric's car. Just stay right there."

Across the Laundromat was a young mother folding sheets while her two boys ran wild up and down the aisle. I thought of Nick's widow, her two kids, and their college fund filled with worthless Saxton Silvers stock.

"Don't worry," I said into the phone. "I'm not going anywhere."

58

Olivia and Eric picked me up in less than five minutes. In forty-five more, we were in central New Jersey—Somerset County, to be exact, one of the oldest and wealthiest in the United States. WhiteSands had moved there after its World Trade Center headquarters was destroyed on 9/11, one of many financial firms displaced by the sudden loss of the office-space equivalent of twenty-five Empire State Buildings. The firm had no plans to return to Manhattan, its current CEO rather liking the comfortable distance between himself and WhiteSands' founder and board chairman emeritus, Eric Volke.

"Make a left here," said Eric. It was his car, but I'd insisted on driving. Thirty years of chauffeured limousines had turned Eric into a terror on the highways.

It felt like the country, but most of Somerset's agricultural roots had been lost long ago to developers. We were actually on a dark private road owned by WhiteSands—still owned by them, despite the bankruptcy of its 49 percent shareholder, Saxton Silvers. In fact, no aspect of WhiteSands' business was affected by the recent filing. Not its 2.3 million square feet of office space in Franklin. Not the 275 acres it owned inside the Princeton Forrestal Center. Not the billions of dollars' worth of other real estate holdings throughout the United States and Europe. Not its seven hundred investment advisors with over $1.3 trillion in assets under management.

And most important of all—at least for my immediate purposes—not the company helicopter and on-site heliport.

"The pilot won't be here for another forty minutes," said Eric.

I checked the time on the dash—nine-forty P.M.—and tried to remember the last time I'd eaten. "Is there food at the hangar?"

There wasn't, so Eric navigated our way into the complex and into the corporate cafeteria for something quick. We ate cold sandwiches in the corporate dining room, the flat screen playing on the wall. Pundits on CNN were analyzing the financial fallout from the failure of Saxton Silvers. The cast of losers included everyone from guys like Nick and his kids' college fund to a group of Japanese banks that were out $1.5 billion. Somehow, I knew who would be all right, and who wouldn't be.

I switched to a local news station, where the breaking-news coverage was all about the emergency-room shooting in North Bergen. I was happy to hear that "miraculously, no one was injured," but I was suddenly wondering if I would ever see Ivy again. Was she gone for good this time, another disappearing act? The reporter's closing words jarred me loose from my thoughts.

"The suspect escaped before police arrived," she said into the camera, speaking from the parking lot outside the hospital, "and he remains at large. Anyone with information about this crime is encouraged to notify the police."

She signed off, and I nearly choked on my sandwich. "I told the nine-one-one operator who did it," I said. "Why the hell don't they have Ian Burn's name and photograph all over the airwaves?"

"Don't take this personally," said Olivia, "but maybe they're waiting for a credible source before they send everyone looking for a Mumbai hit man with a french-fried ear."

Olivia excused herself for a bathroom break, leaving Eric and me alone in the dining room. He switched the station to FNN, where experts were saying that the ripple effects from Saxton Silvers and the subprime crisis could push the Dow as low as 10,000—a prediction "as lunatic as gas going up to four dollars a gallon," shouted Chuck Bell's replacement.

I wrapped up the last few bites of my sandwich and opened a bottled water.

"So what's going to happen next?" I asked. "To Olivia and me, I mean."

Eric lowered the television volume. "We drive out to the hangar. The helicopter will get you into Martha's Vineyard before midnight. My yacht's ready to go as soon as you land. You should be on your way to Bermuda in a few hours. If it's still not safe by the time you dock there, we'll refuel and keep you moving."

"How long can that go on?"

"As long as it takes."

I drank my water. "Is that what you told Ivy four years ago?"

We exchanged glances. I hadn't intended it as a barb exactly, but he did seem to take my meaning. I grabbed the remote and clicked off the television, making it clear that I needed to get to the root of it.

"When we were in the emergency room," I said, "Ivy told me about the corporate espionage she was doing for WhiteSands. She started to tell me why McVee wanted her dead, but the shooting started before she could finish."

Eric showed little reaction, his tone matter-of-fact. "She did a good job. That's why McVee wants her dead."

"What does that mean?"

"Ivy didn't just figure out what Ploutus was doing to manipulate the market for WhiteSands' stock. She caught the mastermind himself red-handed. If we had gone to the D.A., the things she'd uncovered could have put Kyle McVee's son in jail for a very long time."

"Why *didn't* you go to the D.A.?"

"We would have. Except that . . ."

"He killed himself."

"Yes," said Eric. "No one saw it coming. But he took his own life."

"McVee blames Ivy for that?"

Eric gave me a sobering look. "He sure as hell doesn't blame himself."

I was well aware that Marcus McVee had committed suicide. I'd seen the newspaper photographs of his Maserati parked on the waterfront in the Hamptons. I'd read the story of his body slumped over in the front seat, an empty liter of tequila on the floor and a half-empty bottle of Vicodin on the seat beside him. The autopsy confirmed that he'd washed down at least two dozen 500 milligram pills with the tequila. I was also aware—firsthand—of how the loss of his only son had changed the old man, turning Kyle McVee from simply aggressive to outright ruthless on Wall Street. But I'd had no idea how ruthless.

"So long as Ivy was alive," said Eric, "no one she loved was safe. We spoke on the phone on your wedding day. She told me about the SUV that ran you off the road. And the hired thug who roughed you up at the FTAA riot in Miami."

"I don't understand. Usually when the mob or someone like that goes after your family, isn't it because they want you to pay them money, or because they want you to forget that you were a witness to a crime? They want you to do *something*. What is it that McVee wanted Ivy to do?"

"Suffer," said Eric. "McVee was in agony over the death of his son. He wanted Ivy to agonize with the fear of something terrible happening to someone she loved—namely, you or her mother. So his thugs played with you. Ran you off the road with an SUV. Roughed you up in Miami. She knew eventually McVee would get bored with the game and step things up."

"Or maybe not," I said. "The flaming envelope was more of the same, four years later."

"But he will tire of it—this we knew four years ago. Then he would kill Ivy. Or maybe he would kill you or her mother, let Ivy live with the sense of loss that she had forced him to live with. The SUV running you off the road could have killed you. That envelope could have killed you. The bottom line was clear: So long as Ivy was alive, someone was going to end up dead— either her, you, or her mother. Ivy knew it. And so did I. That was when I helped her disappear."

It was starting to make sense. But not entirely.

"You're the guy who hired Ivy," I said. "Why would McVee want her blood but not yours?"

"I guess he decided to wait for the right time and hit me where it really hurt. He brought down Saxton Silvers—assassinated it, in plain English, with his short selling."

"But he hasn't put you in the poorhouse. You still have WhiteSands. There has to be more to this."

Our eyes locked—but not in an adversarial way. It was more like two men coming to an understanding that something needed to be said—probably should have been said a long time ago—and that things would never be the same between them once it was out there.

Eric crossed the dining room to the doorway and checked the hallway, making sure that Olivia was not on her way back from the restroom. Then he closed the door, and the expression on his face was about as serious as I'd ever seen.

"I never wanted to be the one to tell you this, Michael. But it's time you knew the God's honest truth about that woman you married."

59

Ivy heard it all—everything Eric Volke told Michael in the seeming privacy of the WhiteSands' corporate dining room.

Ian Burn heard it, too.

He dimmed the LCD on Ivy's cell to conserve the battery. Her speakerphone function was still activated, however, relaying every word that was uttered within range of the cell that Ivy had given Michael outside the emergency room in North Bergen. Ivy hadn't morphed into one of those smartphone-aholics who carried both a BlackBerry and an iPhone in her purse. It was simply a matter of survival. When you spent every day of your life on the run, the thought of being trapped in a church or other hiding place with a cell that said *No service* was enough to make you carry two devices—each with a different provider.

"Very impressive," said Burn, admiring the technology. "A master smart phone programmed for remote activation of the speakerphone on a slave cell that goes everywhere Michael goes. And they have no idea that as long as the phone has a battery in it, we can hear every word they're saying, even though it's just sitting there. I have to confess," said Burn, "your spyware is every bit as good as mine."

The white commercial van was parked less than a mile from WhiteSands' headquarters, and Ivy was alone with Burn in the rear cargo compartment.

"It's really pretty basic," said Ivy.

And it wasn't just about eavesdropping. Ivy's spyware also had GPS tracking capability, enabling the master to follow the slave wherever the slave took his cell. Tracking Michael all the way from North Bergen to Somerset County had been a snap. It was so reliable that Burn had even felt comfortable stopping on the way for food. He was finishing off the last of the hand-stretched naan, a round flatbread that was a staple in northern India, but in the United States was mainly for rich folks who shopped in trendy grocery stores in places like Somerset County.

"What are you going to do with me?" asked Ivy.

She was seated on the metal floor of the van, her back to the side panel. Her jaw felt slightly out of alignment from the left cross that Burn had delivered, and her ribs were still sore from the takedown to the pavement in the hospital parking lot. She worked at the plastic handcuffs that fastened her wrists behind her back, but there was no slack whatsoever.

"What do you think I'm going to do?" said Burn.

She knew his reputation, but she didn't let her mind go there.

"Let's put it this way," he said in an icy tone. "You will wish you really had been lost at sea and eaten by sharks."

Ivy was silent. There was nothing she could say. She should never have gone back toward the hospital in search of Michael. She should have kept running, just as she'd run for the past four years. In hindsight, seeing Michael face-to-face had probably been a mistake. Emotion had taken over, and even though splitting up outside the ER and heading off in opposite directions had been the correct tactical move, she'd doubled back in hope of finding him and escaping together. A silly romantic notion—and a complete blunder that had allowed Burn to capture her. And now he had hijacked her spyware as well. She wished now that she hadn't given Michael her spare cell, though it had seemed like the right thing to do at the time.

Suddenly, her mother's voice was on the speaker. Olivia obviously had no idea that her words were being

454 · JAMES GRIPPANDO

picked up by Michael's cell and transmitted from the corporate dining room to Ivy's phone a mile away.

"We'd better get going," Ivy heard her mother say.

Burn also heard. "Let's do what Mamma says," he said to Ivy.

One last time, Burn checked the tension on the cuffs behind Ivy's back. Satisfied, he moved to the van's cockpit, placed Ivy's phone on the dash, and climbed behind the wheel.

"We'll see you all there," he said as he turned the ignition.

60

"We're all set," said Wald, as he tucked away his cell phone.

He was seated beside his uncle in the cabin of a Eurocopter EC225 Super Puma helicopter. They'd just touched down on a helipad in Somerset County after a short flight from Manhattan that had reduced the famous skyline to a blur of lights on the horizon. The whir of the rotors was almost down to nothing, making it unnecessary to use headsets or even raise their voices when talking.

"Very good," said McVee.

It was his nephew's second update of the night. The first had been within minutes of the shoot-out at the hospital: Ivy Layton wasn't dead, but her run had come to an end. Burn had her at his mercy and under his

control, and the death van was en route to an appropriate disposal site. McVee had been just fine with that—
until the surprise phone call from Michael Cantella's
brother: "Michael knows it's you," he'd told McVee,
"and if anything happens to him, me, or anyone in our
family, the FBI is going to be all over you."

Wald glanced out the window at the rising moon,
then back at his uncle.

"Are you sure about this?"

McVee's expression tightened. "There are two ways
to read that call from Cantella's brother. One, he's already gone to the FBI. Or two, it was a threat. A very
serious threat."

"I understand, but—"

"No 'buts,'" said McVee. "If he's already gone
to the FBI, there's nothing we can do about it. But
if it's a threat, and if we back away from it, extor-
tion is right around the corner. The first payment is
never enough to keep a blackmailer from telling the
police what he knows. They keep coming back, and
the price tag is always higher the next time. In this
case, it'll just keep going up and up until it's out of
sight—especially when Cantella and his brother get a
better understanding of exactly how much we stand to
profit from credit default swaps after Saxton Silvers'
bankruptcy."

Wald smiled. "A cool bonus that taking care of Ivy Layton is so profitable."

Remarks like that made it so clear to McVee that his nephew could never lead Ploutus. The kid always had everything backward. "Getting rid of Ivy Layton is the bonus on top of the business, genius."

"Huh?"

"Even before she was in the picture I had plans to short sell an investment bank into oblivion. Ivy's showing up just made it that much easier to decide Saxton Silvers should be first on the list."

"How much do we stand to make?"

"More than you can fathom," said McVee, "and it's none of your business. Your job is to deal with the threat."

"Well, we're all set. I spoke directly to Burn. There's been a temporary stay of execution for Ivy Layton. He is to use her as bait."

"There's no compromising on this point. My gut tells me that Cantella and his brother haven't gone to the FBI yet, and I'm not about to pay them hush money for the rest of my days. Burn has to be prepared to eliminate all of them."

"The mother, too?"

"She's no innocent. Ivy never would have gotten away without her help. And something tells me it was

458 • JAMES GRIPPANDO

the mother who taught Ivy all her tricks in the first place."

"Understood," said Wald. "All of them. I'll tell him it's 'as per Michael Cantella,'" he added, referring to the infamous e-mail.

McVee unbuckled his seat belt, then stopped before rising. "Did you work out a price?"

"He said you two already came to an understanding when you went for a ride in the limo."

"What understanding?"

"At first I thought he was making a joke," said Wald, "but he was serious. Something about the new line on our balance sheet: Money to Burn."

McVee almost smiled, recalling the conversation and his own play on words. He took Burn's meaning: this job would cost so much that McVee would have to pay it quarterly, maybe even in annual installments. But it would be worth it.

"Fine," said McVee. "Money to Burn it is."

61

We entered the hangar through the maintenance office, and Eric switched on the overhead lights.

At the end of a long private access road from the corporate training center, the WhiteSands heliport was one of two dozen heliports in Somerset County and one of about 365 statewide. Not all were equipped for nighttime landings and takeoffs, and some were little more than open space in a flat field of grass. As would be expected, the private facility at WhiteSands was equipped with far more amenities than it needed, including five separate hangars, each one large enough to accommodate a medium-size helicopter. We entered Hangar No. 3, which housed our ticket to escape—a pimped-out Sikorsky S76 that the head of WhiteSands'

Sovereign Fund Division "just had to have" after touring Malaysia in one with the sultan of Johor.

"Hello?" said Eric, his voice echoing as he called out.

The hangar was a gaping structure of corrugated steel, concrete block, and heavy, exposed metal beams. High-intensity lighting shone down from suspended luminaires, creating a ghostly pattern of perfectly round and evenly spaced pools of brightness across the polished concrete floor that surrounded the craft. Eric's query had drawn no response—the hangar was completely still, no sign of anyone.

"I guess our pilot's not here yet," said Eric.

I walked toward the Sikorsky. It was Matterhorn white with dark blue and red accent stripes, and it looked almost new. Someone had expended untold hours of elbow grease on the wax finish. It was a habit I'd inherited from Papa, seeing an impressive piece of machinery and wondering not how much it cost or who the stuffed shirt was who got to use it, but rather, who was the average Joe who so proudly took care of it.

"Do you have his number?" I asked.

"Yeah," said Eric, "let me give him a ring."

He went back toward the office and dialed from the landline on the wall. I watched and listened as Eric left a message on the pilot's voice mail.

"No answer?" I said as he returned.

"Uh-uh," said Eric.

I glanced at Olivia. She had pretty much been a rock up until this point, but signs of stress were starting to show.

"What's wrong?" I asked.

"I'm getting a bad feeling," she said.

"He's only five minutes late," said Eric. "I'm sure he'll be here."

"Try him again," said Olivia. "Michael already lost his driver tonight. For a guy like Burn, pilots are no less expendable."

Eric glanced at me, but I could hardly disagree.

"Wait a second," he said, as he fumbled for the pilot's business card in his wallet. "I dialed his office number. Let me try his cell."

He went to the wall phone again and dialed.

62

Burn was motionless, crouched behind the second row of passenger seats inside the helicopter. Ivy was belted into the seat in front of him, her hands still cuffed, afraid to move or make a sound. Burn's gun was pressed against the base of her skull.

Ivy's phone lay in the seat beside Burn, and Cantella's cell was still transmitting to it. The speaker was switched off, however, with Burn listening through earbuds. The attack on Ivy in the emergency room had filled Burn's risk-taking quota for the evening, and it was important to eavesdrop now more than ever. Ivy's mother seemed to be losing her nerve.

"I'm getting a bad feeling," she said, her voice playing into Burn's earbud.

"He's only five minutes late," said Volke. "I'm sure he'll be here."

Burn glanced toward the aisle to where the pilot lay on the floor—a dead heap, his neck broken.

Don't bet on it, folks.

Burn peered out the window. The glass was tinted so dark that no one outside the helicopter could have possibly seen him. Still, he was cautious, raising his head up just enough to see out, not an inch more. The five-gallon fuel cans he'd filled were still in the corner, ready for use. The Sikorsky's turbine engines used Jet A fuel, and Burn had filled two portable cans—more than enough to torch the entire building, let alone the helicopter and its passengers. His gaze drifted back toward the triangle of conversation near the maintenance office, and as he watched, a strange feeling came over him. Before tonight, he'd never set foot in this hangar, yet there was something eerily familiar about the situation, if not the setting. The cold concrete floor. The bright garage lights shining down. Two men. One woman. The situation growing increasingly tense, the woman on edge. And the smell of kerosene. It was on his hands—Jet A fuel was a derivative of kerosene—and the odor triggered memories. Kerosene was cheap and plentiful in Mumbai.

It was the preferred fuel for bride burning.

His sister's screams were suddenly in his head, along with the indelible image of her husband and brother-in-law dousing her with kerosene and setting her afire in the garage. He hadn't actually seen it happen, but her wounds had told the story. For five horrendous days in the hospital, Charu—her name meant "beautiful"—had managed to survive with burns covering 95 percent of her body. He never left her side, knowing what they had done to her. By the time she expired, he could see the men in that garage unleashing their unspeakable cruelty on a twenty-year-old woman from the Dhravi slum whose family was too poor to pay the expected dowry.

And all these years later, he could still see it.

"Wait a second," said Volke, his voice transmitting through Burn's earbud and drawing him back to his mission. "I dialed his office number. Let me try his cell."

The words struck panic: *The pilot's cell!*

Burn dived toward the body and snatched the phone from the pilot's pocket. It made a slight chirp— the ring was just beginning—before he managed to remove the battery and kill the noise. He quickly went to the window and checked to see if Cantella and the others had heard the ring from inside the helicopter. He wasn't sure. But it was time to make a move.

He removed the earbuds and switched off Ivy's cell. Then he pressed the gun firmly to the side of Ivy's head and, with the other hand, unfastened her seat belt.

"Stand up slowly," he said, "and if you do exactly as you're told, maybe the others will live."

63

The noise from inside the Sikorsky made me do a double take. It sounded like a half ring from a cell phone after Eric dialed the pilot's number. Eric and Olivia had heard it, too. The tinted glass was virtually opaque beneath the hangar lighting, making it impossible to see inside. Suddenly, the tinted glass door flew open. The sight of Ivy standing in the opening with a gun to her head—and Ian Burn behind her—sent chills down my spine.

"Nobody move," said Burn.

The three of us froze.

Burn looked almost exactly the way I remembered him from our very first meeting at Sal's Place. To hide the scar on his neck, he wore a black turtleneck beneath a black leather jacket with the collar turned up.

A knit beanie covered the deformed right ear. The expression on his face was all business, no sign of panic. He nudged Ivy forward, and they stepped down from the helicopter to the concrete floor. I noticed that Ivy's hands were fastened behind her back. More than that, I noticed the look in her eyes—a desperate need to tell me something.

I looked away, still wrestling with what Eric had told me back in the WhiteSands dining room—away from Olivia—about the woman I had married.

"You," said Burn, speaking to Eric. "Step away from the others."

As Eric moved closer to the hangar door, my phone rang—the cell that Ivy had given to me. It startled me, but I didn't move. It was that funny double ring—the kind that announced a new voice-mail message. Somewhere between North Bergen and Somerset County a call had come through while my phone was either roaming or completely out of signal.

"Reach into your pocket slowly," said Burn, "and take out the phone."

I did as he told me.

"Who's the voice mail from?"

I checked the display. The number was familiar, and it only took a moment for it to register in my mind. I'd seen it a dozen times just a few hours earlier at the

Tonnelle Avenue motel, when scrolling through the call history on Mallory's cell. The number was her friend Andrea.

And thanks to Ivy, I now knew that Andrea was FBI.

"I don't know," I said.

Apparently I was a lousy liar around loaded weapons; Burn clearly didn't believe me.

"Put it on speaker and play the message," he told me.

I retrieved the message and hit the speaker button. The message was almost ninety minutes old:

"Ivy, it's Agent Henning. I tried your other cell and couldn't reach you there either. I'm calling with a heads-up. After we talked, I checked all of my contacts to find out if Eric Volke had, in fact, told the FBI that Kyle McVee was behind the bear raid on Saxton Silvers and the murder of Chuck Bell. I know he claims to have informed everyone, but it turns out that he hasn't said anything of the sort to *anyone*. He lied to you. So just be careful, and call me when you get this message."

The message ended.

"That's not true!" said Eric. "I did tell the FBI!"

Something was starting to smell rotten, and I was nowhere near Denmark.

"Quiet!" Burn shouted. "Put the phone on the floor and slide it over here. Slowly."

Again, I obeyed.

"Now everybody hold still," Burn said as he reached for his cell. "We have some distinguished guests to invite."

64

Kyle McVee was behind the wheel of a black SUV, driving toward WhiteSands. His nephew had arranged for transportation to be waiting for them at the private heliport a few miles away when they landed. He was in the passenger seat, too busy fussing with his new toy.

"I'm liking it," said Wald.

He was inspecting his new weapon for the tenth time, an older but nicely refurbished Italian-made Beretta 92FS Compact. From a technical standpoint, it was everything he needed—thirteen rounds of 9 mm ammunition in a quick-release magazine, a smaller and more easily concealed version of its big bad-ass cousin, the M–9 pistol used by the U.S. military.

"I can see why Tony liked it so much," he said, weighing it in his shooting hand.

"You kept Girelli's gun?"

"My trophy."

McVee flung his fist at him, hitting his nephew square in the chest.

"Ow! What was that for?"

"Dump that damn gun the minute we're done here," McVee said. "Now put it away before you shoot yourself."

Wald double-checked the safety and tucked his trophy back into his shoulder holster. "Like I'm the only one taking unnecessary chances," he said.

"What is that supposed to mean?" said McVee.

"The way we've played this so far, it would be difficult for anyone to place you in the same zip code as Ian Burn, let alone in the same helicopter hangar."

"Fine. Your concern is noted."

"I understand that they all have to go," said Wald. "But there's no need for you to be there when it happens."

McVee gripped the steering wheel even tighter. "You know *nothing* about my needs," he snapped.

"I'm just saying, we can handle this."

They rode in silence for another minute, but McVee's emotions were beginning to roil.

"You don't know me," said McVee, "and you certainly didn't know your cousin."

"Marcus?" said Wald. "Of course I knew—"

"You *didn't*," said McVee.

He paused, struggling to get control of himself. There was nothing to be gained by unloading on Jason at this point, but the kid seemed to think that this was all part of Kyle McVee's business plan and personal vision, that he was proud of the way his nephew was comfortable in dealing with the darkest elements of organized crime. The boy couldn't have been more wrong.

"You think this is what I wanted Ploutus to become?" he said. "You think I like being the Wall Street thief who manipulates the market? The go-to hedge fund for mob money?"

He glanced at his nephew, and from the look at his face, the younger man had never really reduced it to such vile terms.

"You pay a price," said McVee, "when you reach a point in your life when everything you've worked for is bullshit. When it doesn't matter anymore. When you *need* a man like Ian Burn to make it right."

Wald was about to speak, then stopped, seeming to sense that silence was the wiser course.

"Do you have any idea what it feels like to see lightweights like Eric Volke rise to the top? To see a know-nothing like Michael Cantella named in *Forbes* magazine as Saxton Silvers' youngest-ever investment advisor of the year? It would be hard enough to stomach that shit in any case, but in a world with my son dead and buried, it's unbearable. Marcus was a dynamo," he said, his voice quaking, "and we had plans. Big plans. If he were alive today, he'd be the CEO of Ploutus—a thirty-six-year-old king of the world. I'd probably be president of the NASDAQ. All that ended when that bitch came along. I was happy when she was lost at sea and the sharks got her—and just *enraged* when I found out four years later that it was all a lie. That Girelli didn't really get the job done."

"He was a punk," said Wald.

"So are you," said McVee, disdain in his voice. "How my sister popped you into the world I'll never understand."

Jason looked out the passenger's-side window, toward the passing darkness. It wasn't the first time he'd heard the insult.

"But I can tell you this," said McVee. "Marcus was no punk. And for him, I'm going to spit in that woman's eye before she burns alive in a WhiteSands helicopter with her conniving mother and the biggest punk of all—Michael Cantella."

Wald's phone rang. He answered. It was Burn. The conversation lasted just five seconds. He ended the call and looked at his uncle.

"Show time," he said.

The engine revved as McVee accelerated down the last half mile of the WhiteSands access road.

65

The main hangar door was closed, and I heard a car pull up outside. The narrow row of polycarbonate windows that stretched across the big sliding door from end to end was above eye level, but Burn was standing on the boarding step to the helicopter, high enough to see out. He did not seem alarmed. A moment later, the smaller entrance door opened to the darkness of night. Jason Wald entered first, followed by his uncle.

Kyle McVee was dressed casually in a navy blue sailing jacket, linen slacks, and deck shoes, as if he were on his way to a weekend getaway at his waterfront estate in the Hamptons. His demeanor, however, was anything but relaxed. He walked toward Ivy and stopped in front of her, his glare like lasers.

"I've waited for this day," he said.

"So have I," she said.

McVee wasn't the only one confused by her response.

Ivy said, "I've always wanted to know why you held me—and me alone—responsible for Marcus' suicide."

"You can't seriously mean that," he said.

"It was Eric who hired me for the assignment. But you never blamed him."

She was clearly pushing buttons, taking her cue from the voice-mail message I'd played from Agent Henning. But McVee seemed to find something humorous about the exchange, and he was looking at me while talking to Ivy.

"Still playing the good wife to Michael Cantella, I see."

"The only role I ever played was the one Eric hired me to play. But in the end, he wasn't the one you came after."

Eric spoke up for himself. "A little corporate espionage is what any reasonable businessman would do to protect his own company."

"I'll handle this," said McVee, silencing him. "But Eric is right: He was doing something that anyone would do. You, on the other hand—you were different." He stepped closer, his stare tightening. "There was no need for you to do the things you did to Marcus."

"What things?"

"I'm sure you researched matters before starting your undercover role. You knew the family history was there—that his mother had taken her own life. You saw Marcus' highs, and you knew how low his lows could be. And still you did whatever it took to get the information you needed out of him. You flirted. You slept with him. And you even pretended to be in love with him."

"That's not true!" she said.

"When you had the information you needed to report back to Eric, you crushed Marcus—told him to his face that he'd been played for a fool. My son didn't kill himself because of anything Eric did. He killed himself because of *you*—the way you destroyed him."

"You've got it all wrong," said Ivy.

"You used my son the same way you used Michael Cantella. Hell, you were even willing to marry Michael, if that was what it took to pull off your disappearing act."

I exchanged glances with Eric—McVee had just repeated the story that Eric had told me in the White-Sands dining room—and then I looked at Ivy.

Her eyes pleaded with me. "Don't believe any of this, Michael. I married you because I loved you. I never slept with Marcus. Okay, I may have flirted—that's part of the game—but it was never intimate. Never. And definitely not while I was with you."

I didn't know what to think, but an idea came to me on how to get to the bottom of it. I looked at McVee and asked, "How do you know Ivy was sleeping with your son?"

"Eric told me," he said.

"Just like Eric told *you* in the dining room!" said Ivy. "It's a lie, Michael."

I wasn't sure how she knew about that conversation, but it didn't matter.

"That's not *exactly* what Eric told me," I said. "He said it was Kyle who told *him* that Ivy was sleeping with Marcus."

McVee glanced at Eric, and I could see from the expression on his face that I'd raised his suspicions. "That's not true," said McVee. "Eric was the one who told *me*."

Again, Eric was under the microscope. He wasn't holding up well.

"Look," he said, his voice shaking. It was as if he had finally realized that he was in way over his head. "I'm not trying to get anyone hurt or . . . killed. I'm just—"

"Shut up!" said McVee.

His words startled Eric—and everyone else as well. The tension in the air may have made it the worst conceivable moment for me to speak up, but it felt like now or never. I spoke straight to McVee, as if it were just the two of us in the hangar.

"Eric is lying," I said. "And the reason he's lying is because your son didn't commit suicide."

Thankfully McVee wasn't holding a gun, because he would have shot me dead right then and there.

"No, I don't mean he disappeared like Ivy," I said, clarifying. "I mean his death wasn't suicide."

Slowly McVee's need to hear me out prevailed. And even though I was speculating to a large extent, it wasn't just something that had popped into my head on the spot. My suspicions had begun when Ivy told me that Andrea was FBI, and my focus had turned to Eric during our conversation in the WhiteSands' dining room. I had to believe that everything Ivy and I had shared four years ago was real, and that Eric's claims were false. There was no way she would have prostituted herself on a corporate espionage mission for WhiteSands. I knew she wasn't just pretending to love me. I knew she didn't marry me just to facilitate a plan to escape. Eric was lying. And people usually lie to protect themselves.

I had to go with my instincts on this one. It was life or death—literally.

"I knew Marcus," I said. "Your son was a savvy businessman who did his homework. So savvy that I think he knew Ivy was a mole. He used *her*; she didn't use him."

"What are you talking about?" said Eric.

I continued my focus on McVee, ignoring Eric and everyone else. "Eric hired Ivy to work undercover and prove that Ploutus was spreading false rumors about WhiteSands to manipulate the stock price. The reality was, Marcus wasn't spreading false rumors. The dirt he uncovered was absolutely true."

"That's preposterous," said Eric.

"Maybe that information wasn't just damaging to White Sands," I said. "Maybe it was embarrassing to Eric, personally."

"Michael, that's enough."

I was on to something. I could hear it in Eric's voice. "Are you going to make me keep guessing, Eric? Or are you going to tell me what laws you broke?"

"Michael, stop right now, or you are going to take us both down."

"Is that what you told Marcus," I said, "when he confronted you with his discovery?"

Eric was silent, and I knew him well enough to realize what his silence meant. I almost couldn't believe what I was saying, but everything was suddenly making sense to me.

"That's why you killed him, isn't it, Eric. Or maybe you had him killed. Made it look like he took his own life. Then you went to his father to tell him how sorry you were for the loss of his son. To tell him that it was all Ivy's fault, that you never dreamed she would push him to suicide in playing her role. I'm guessing that you didn't anticipate what Kyle McVee's reaction would be—that he'd want Ivy dead."

Ivy filled in the rest, with me every step. "So you helped me disappear, which worked out very nicely for you. That left no one to dispute your version of what happened between Marcus and me."

"Once Ivy was gone," said McVee, his train of thought lining up right behind ours, "I stopped looking for the person who was really responsible for Marcus' death."

His glare came to rest on Eric.

There was chilling silence in the hangar as the truth settled in. Ivy, her mother, McVee, and on down the line—everyone was waiting for Eric to say something in his defense. But even Eric knew that there was no convincing anyone any longer. McVee stepped away from the helicopter. He stopped just a few feet away from me, his gaze still fixed singularly on Eric.

"Jason," he said to his nephew, "spill the fuel."

66

"Whoa, *whoa*," said Burn.

I was so spent, I'd almost forgotten that he was still standing on the boarding step at the open door to the Sikorsky, a head taller than Ivy.

Wald was approaching the helicopter and stopped suddenly, a fuel can in each hand. "What's wrong?"

"Are you nuts?" said Burn. "You can't just dump that much fuel inside a helicopter hangar."

Wald lowered the cans to the floor, practically dropping them. Five gallons of jet fuel were much heavier than he had expected. "Who's going to stop me, the EPA?"

Burn grabbed Ivy by the hair, as if reining her in. "This one's itching to try another disappearing act. What do you think will happen if this building is filled with fumes when I have to shoot her? Each one of those cans is like eight hundred sticks of dynamite. We could all be toast."

McVee and his nephew exchanged glances. It seemed they had finally seen eye to eye on something: the wisdom of having a guy like Burn in charge.

"What's your plan?" asked McVee.

"I'm thinking a fuel leak from the helicopter, maybe from a bad filter seal or ruptured fuel line. An untimely spark. Tragic results. Help me get these guys aboard, then beat it. I'll take care of the spilled fuel."

"Good luck with that," I said. "I count four of us, three of you, and only one gun."

"Two guns," said Wald as he pulled a pistol from his coat.

Burn pushed his gun against Ivy's head with so much force that her chin hit her chest. "And there can easily be one less of you."

Ivy said, "Don't try anything stupid, Michael. Just do what they say. The FBI is on the way."

"Yeah, sure," Burn said with a chuckle. "The FBI, the cavalry—they're all rushing right over here."

"I'm not lying," said Ivy.

"There's not a person here that you haven't lied to," said Burn.

"What if she's telling the truth?" Wald asked nervously. "What if the FBI *is* coming?"

"No chance," said Burn. "Michael played a voice mail from Agent Henning right before you arrived. It was on speaker. Henning would have said they were on the way, if, in fact, they were."

McVee smiled at me. "I knew you didn't go to the FBI." He turned to his nephew and said, "Give me your gun."

"Why?"

"Because it wasn't your son who was killed."

Wald didn't like it, but he removed the safety and, with a push-pull of the slide, loaded a round into the chamber.

"You're ready to go," he said, handing it over.

McVee pointed the gun at Eric. "All right, Volke. You first. Get on the helicopter."

"Me? Why me? You don't believe all that bullshit, do you?"

"Get on the helicopter," said McVee, his eyes narrowing.

Eric stared right back. There was no way to win this argument, but he dug in his heels anyway. "Kiss my ass, Kyle. I'm not getting in that helicopter."

"Then I'll shoot you right now, damn it."

"That beats burning alive."

"You son of a bitch," he said, aiming at Eric's groin. "I'll shoot you right in the—"

A loud *pop* suddenly filled the hangar as a window in the sliding door exploded. My focus had been on McVee's showdown with Eric, but the strange sensation of a bullet whizzing past my ear shifted my attention right away.

Those next few moments were a blur, and even though many different things transpired simultaneously, they registered in my mind sequentially. A series of sounds and snapshots nearly overloading my ability to comprehend anything. Tiny bits of the shattered window glistening beneath the lights and falling to the floor. Burn's head jerking to one side, his black beanie flying through the air. The sound of Ivy's scream as the hot crimson spray showered her neck and shoulders.

Both Ivy and Burn tumbled away from the helicopter, and it was all too confusing to know if I had heard a second shot. Ivy hit the concrete first, and Burn landed on top of her. Somewhere in that moment—before or after Ivy's fall, it was impossible to know which—I heard the clack of Burn's weapon on the floor. The top of Burn's skull was missing, a ghastly wound marking his certain death. His body was still moving, but not on its own power. Ivy was pushing out from under his dead weight.

As if on a sheet of ice, she pivoted on her hip bone, spun her legs around clockwise, and kicked Burn's weapon in my direction.

"Michael!" she shouted, as it slid across the concrete.

I dived to the floor and grasped it.

And then the lights went out.

67

The emergency-exit light glowed over the door, casting a surreal orange-red pall over the chaos. It was hard to know exactly what was going on, if the shooting was over, or if more rounds were coming. Obviously, whoever had fired the sniper shot from outside the building had also cut the power. I had no idea if Ivy had been bluffing about the FBI's being on its way, but if she wasn't, a SWAT team should have been busting down the door right about now.

No one came.

"Run!" said Ivy.

I looked up and saw Ivy and her mother racing toward the door beneath the exit light, Ivy's hands still clasped behind her back. Out of the corner of my eye I saw Eric running in the other direction, toward the office. Wald was in pursuit. And I saw McVee raising his weapon and taking aim at Ivy.

The last time I'd fired a gun I was a fourteen-year-old hell-raiser trying to shoot the NO out of a NO HUNTING sign posted along our dirt-road neighborhood in Loon Lake. My best friend had dared me and loaned me his shotgun. I couldn't even hit the damn sign. I prayed for better aim with a pistol, squeezing off two quick shots in McVee's direction. I missed, but it sent McVee diving for cover. Ivy and her mother also dived to the floor at the sound of gunfire.

"Keep running!" I shouted as I sprinted after them.

I turned and, just for cover, fired another quick shot back at McVee. Ivy and her mother were at least ten steps ahead of me. Olivia hit the door first and pushed it open. She made it out, and Ivy was right behind her. Through the open doorway, I could actually see stars in the night sky. Then I heard one more crack of gunfire.

I dropped like a stone. The pain in the back of my thigh was somewhere between getting whacked with a hammer and stabbed with a red-hot screwdriver.

"Michael!" screamed Ivy.

She was halfway out the door when she stopped. I could see that she was about to turn and come back to get me, though what good she could have done with her hands bound behind her back wasn't clear. Another shot rang out, and I heard the bullet slam into the wall of painted cinder block behind me.

"Go!" I shouted, rolling toward the door.

Two more shots followed, the second skimming off the metal door, missing Ivy by inches. My leg was getting hotter and wetter, and then I saw the blood. Less than I would have expected—clearly no major artery involved. This was a survivable wound, I was sure of it. But I was equally certain that another bullet would finish the job if I didn't keep moving. The pain and loss of blood was making me light-headed, but I drew on my reserves and kept rolling across the floor in Ivy's direction.

Ivy was outside the hangar now, crouched low, hiding behind the door and holding it partly open for me. Bullets continued to skid across the floor, ricocheting off the concrete. I lost track of the number of rounds McVee had fired so far. At most seven, and even with my limited knowledge about firearms, I knew there were plenty of pistols with magazines bigger than that.

I continued moving toward the door, but my momentum was slowing. My leg was starting to feel numb, and my head clouded up with congestion in places I had never felt congested, as if my entire brain were turning into cotton. Losing consciousness was an immediate possibility.

Another bullet whizzed past my ear. McVee continued to fire in my direction, but I couldn't see him. I, on the other hand, was a sitting duck, and as my thoughts became less and less coherent, I had a memory flash of Papa telling me the story of the LST—"large stationary target"—that had transported him and some other very unlucky souls onto the beach at Normandy. I fought off the mind fog, giving it my all, but it felt as though I were moving at a turtle's pace. Had McVee been a better shot, I would have been dead already. But I couldn't remain out in the open, an easy target— LST—just waiting for him to finally hit the bull's-eye. I suddenly recalled Burn's warning about the fuel. I reached inside for one last burst of energy and sprang toward the open doorway. In midair I reached back and aimed in the direction of the fuel cans Wald had dropped to the floor. I squeezed off a shot as I rolled out the doorway.

68

"What the hell is going on?" shouted Agent Andie Henning.

Andie was three hundred yards from the heliport, inside an FBI mobile command unit that was parked on the entrance road. A full hostage negotiation team was with her.

Minutes earlier, FBI tech agents had just completed an infrared-camera scan of the hangar, which picked up a fourth hostage inside the helicopter. A recent corpse could give off enough body heat to be picked up by a scan, but the possibility of a fourth hostage tipped the already shaky balance away from an all-out SWAT assault. A peaceful resolution also seemed highly achievable once Kyle McVee had entered the building, a powerful businessman whose entire life was about cutting deals. The negotiators were just thirty seconds away from initiating contact by loudspeaker when the shooting started. Andie raced out of the command unit and couldn't believe what she was hearing in her headset. WhiteSands Hangar No. 3 sounded like a war zone.

Andie was immediately on the bone microphone with the FBI sniper, who was on the rooftop of White-Sands Hangar No. 2, directly across the heliport from Hangar No. 3.

"The order was to hold your fire!" she shouted.

"Roger that," came the reply. "No shot from here."

She switched over to the SWAT unit commander. Agent Kowalski and his team had taken various strategic positions, completely surrounding Hangar No. 3, invisible even to Andie, ready to move in the event that the planned negotiations broke down.

"Are you green on breach?" asked Andie.

The breach was forced entry—showtime in SWAT-speak. Green was the assault—the moment of life and death, literally—after yellow, the final position of cover and concealment.

"Negative," said Kowalski, his voice crackling with radio squelch. "Hot environment, no element of surprise. Holding at yellow."

From the sound of things in Andie's headset, Kowalksi was positioned right outside the building.

"Who went green?"

"Local SWAT."

"Repeat that, please."

"Local SWAT sniper did not copy the order to hold fire."

Andie had been in a similar situation before. It seemed that everyone right down to neighborhood crime-watch volunteers had a SWAT unit these days. Usually the SWAT leaders were able to agree and coordinate efforts. Usually.

An unmarked car squealed around the corner, and it screeched to a halt so quickly that its front bumper nearly kissed the pavement. Supervisory Agent Malcolm Spear jumped out and hurried toward Andie at the mobile command center.

"What the hell happened?" he shouted.

Andie looked toward the flaming building just as it exploded.

69

It may have been a direct hit, or perhaps my shot ricocheted off the floor, skipped up, and punctured the fuel can. Regardless, the explosion threw me out the door and at least another ten yards toward the helipad, which was a good thing. The hangar was engulfed in flames.

And then I blacked out—but only for a moment. When my eyes blinked open, I was looking up at Ivy. Olivia was beside her.

"Michael, can you hear me?" Ivy asked.

It was a feeling I'd never had before—knowing my name only because she was calling me "Michael."

"Yeah, I can hear you," I said. I tried to sit up, but Olivia gently pushed me back onto the pavement.

"Be still," said Ivy. The expression on her face was somewhere between fright and concern; her tone was beyond urgent. "Do you have pain anywhere besides your leg?"

Olivia's coat was tied around my thigh to stop the bleeding, and before the question, the pain had oddly gone away. But suddenly my leg was throbbing again.

"Just in the hamstrings," I said.

There was another explosion from inside the hangar, and I felt the blast of heat on my face. Fortunately, we were far enough away to be out of danger. Sirens sounded from somewhere down the road. Olivia jumped up and darted off into the darkness. I could no longer see her, but I heard her shouting for help.

"Over here!"

"You're going to be okay," said Ivy.

"This way!" someone else shouted.

A moment later I was looking up at another woman. It gave me a moment of confusion—*What the hell is Mallory's friend doing here?*—but then my thoughts cleared, and I remembered that she was an FBI agent. She had paramedics with her, and right behind them was the FBI SWAT unit dressed in full tactical armor. A fire truck rumbled right past us and the firefighters jumped off and went immediately into action. The SWAT guy cut Ivy's hands free from the plastic cuffs with a serrated knife. As the paramedics checked me out and lifted me up onto the gurney, I heard Andie screaming at two men, one from FBI SWAT and the other wearing a black flak jacket that said SHERIFF in white letters. Both men were shouting back at her. As best I could tell, the plan had been for SWAT to hold its fire until negotiations failed, but there had been a miscommunication. It was hard for me to comprehend a blunder like that, but it would soon mesh perfectly with everything I would read about law enforcement activities directed toward Wall Street.

The paramedics lifted me into the ambulance, and Ivy started to climb inside with me.

"Sorry, miss," said the paramedic. "You can't ride in here."

"You can't stop me," she said.

He grabbed her arm. "Who are you?"

"I'm his wife," she said.

"And I'm her husband," I said, just feeling a need to say it.

The paramedic was too rushed to argue.

"Hurry up then," he said.

Ivy climbed inside, and it felt good as she took my hand and laced her fingers with mine. Through the open ambulance doors, we glanced back at the firefighters battling the inferno, knowing that there was no way McVee had survived. Ivy's reason to run was no more.

The ambulance doors closed, and I looked up at her face. She leaned forward and kissed me on the forehead.

"You feeling okay?" she asked.

"Yeah."

"You sure?"

"Yup," I said, feeling a little foggy again, another one of those memory flashes to Papa coming on. "Just another beautiful day in paradise."

Epilogue

I spent a couple days in bed after the explosion. Nana was a retired nurse, so my grandparents stayed in New York to drive me crazy—I mean care for me. I couldn't stand watching the television, so Papa brought me a book from the library. An old book—ancient, you might say.

When I was a young boy, Nana worked nights at the hospital, so it was my grandfather who used to bathe me before bed, put me in my Spiderman pajamas, and read to me from Aesop's Fables as he rocked me to sleep. His personal favorite was "The Ant and the Grasshopper." As the fable goes, the ant was the disciplined one, storing up food for hard times. The grasshopper was the singing and chirping party animal—er, insect—who blew through summer as if life were one red-hot streak at a blackjack table. And then winter came.

Papa was an ant, a Depression-era immigrant raised on an honest wage for an honest day's work. We never talked about stocks. The first I'd heard of the Dow Jones Industrials was in fifth-grade social studies class, and I still find it unbelievable that when I was ten the Dow was at 802. That was just fine for ants, but the grasshoppers of the 1980s dreamed of riding in limousines. In the 1990s, it was stretch limousines. Then, in the insanity of the twenty-first century, it had to be a stretch Hummer limousine with a hot tub, a posse, and at least one B-list celebrity with no panties. But ants had no use for any of this. They knew winter would come.

Never had I dreamed that I would be a grasshopper. That all my friends would be grasshoppers. That the entire *world* would be one big swarming, borrowing, and spending orgy of grasshoppers—a world in which anything worth doing was naturally worth *overdoing*.

Like I said before: There was a time when people all but worshipped guys like me. Now, of course, they've come to hate us. It was understandable; the man I'd worshipped deserved no forgiveness.

Eric Volke was one of Bernard Madoff's feeders.

I'd had no way of knowing that on the night everything blew up—literally—in WhiteSands' Hangar No. 3. It came out much later, after Madoff pleaded guilty to the largest investment fraud in Wall Street history and became federal prison inmate No. 61727–054 for the rest of his life.

Only then did I learn the chief purpose of Agent Andie Henning's undercover investigation at Saxton Silvers. After 9/11, the FBI's focus shifted to homeland security, and the number of agents investigating financial crimes was cut by more than 75 percent. But Agent Henning presented a simple mathematical formula to her supervisors, showing that Madoff's track record—10 percent returns or better for almost two decades—was the statistical equivalent of a major-league baseball player batting .960 for the season. She got approval to investigate. Her mission was to expose one of the biggest players to steer investors in Madoff's direction, and hopefully get him to cut a deal with prosecutors and testify against Madoff.

Virtually none of Madoff's feeders had conducted any due diligence before dropping to their knees and kissing the ground he walked on. The ones who had were even worse; they knew or at least suspected that he was a fraud and still fed him clients. But a very select few—Eric Volke among them—had known the truth from the very beginning. Over the years, Eric's "fund of funds" at WhiteSands channeled billions of dollars from charities, pension funds, universities, and others into Madoff's hands. The payoff for these feeders was enormous, and the warm turquoise waters surrounding a 160-foot yacht at the private island of Mustique could wash away a lot of sins. But the fact remained, Volke and people like him made Madoff's scam into a colossal catastrophe, a giant Ponzi scheme.

Marcus McVee had figured out that Volke was dirty long before anyone else did. All it took was a call to the Chicago Board of Options Exchange to confirm that the total S&P 100 options that Eric's WhiteSands option fund claimed to have acquired through Madoff exceeded the total open interest in S&P 100 contracts at that strike price. In Papa's terms, that meant Eric claimed he was buying veal parmigiana when the only thing on the menu was spaghetti and meatballs. But Marcus' decision to confront Eric rather than go to the FBI had cost him his life. Eric rode with him to the waterfront in the Hamptons, where he forced him to drink a bottle of tequila at gunpoint. I doubt that Marcus knew that Eric had dissolved a lethal dose of Vicodin into the tequila.

Eric Volke died in the hangar explosion at White-Sands. So did Kyle McVee. Ironically, Ian Burn was dead before the fire even started. Ivy would never have to worry about them coming after her.

McVee's nephew, Jason Wald, had beat Eric to the exit through the hangar's maintenance office. He suffered burns on his back, but recovered well enough to talk through his lawyers. He would save some jail time by pointing the finger at his dead uncle for the contract killings of Chuck Bell, Tony Girelli, Nathaniel Locke, my driver Nick, and Rumsey the charter sailboat captain down in the Bahamas.

From one Monday to the next, Saxton Silvers went from a Wall Street landmark to bankruptcy. It was the beginning of the end for investment banks on Wall Street. The nation was one step closer to hearing words like *bailout* and *stimulus* about as often as *hello* and *good-bye*.

A week after the explosion at WhiteSands, I was getting around pretty well, weaning myself from crutches. The leg wound was healing, no signs of infection, no serious vascular damage, no broken bones. Doctors presumed that I'd caught a ricocheted projectile rather than a direct hit. On the following Friday morning the bankruptcy trustee allowed me back into the building to pack my belongings into a cardboard box. My brother helped. Papa came to supervise.

"No offense," Papa said, shaking his head, "but I still say it's all one big Fonzie scheme."

Kevin looked up from the half-packed box in front of him. "Don't you mean Ponzi?"

"No," I said, "he really doesn't."

My box was full, and I lifted it from my desk. About a dozen clear Lucite cubes pushed right through the cardboard bottom and fell to the floor. Deal toys, they were called. Little desktop mementos that, depending on the nature and size of the transaction, could be anything from a simple rectangle encasing a miniature pineapple to a light-up sculpture of knights in shining armor jousting over the engraved sum of $125 million.

I raised the box higher, letting the rest of the toys drop to the floor.

The bottom falling out.

I almost had to laugh: how quickly things could crumble. In the late 1980s, junk bonds and federal indictments brought down Wall Street's fifth largest investment bank over a period of years. Twenty years later, Moody's downgrades the creditworthiness of the world's largest insurance company on a Thursday, and on Monday it's on life support. Were we headed for a

world in which the destruction of major financial institutions and the people who run them could happen in a
matter of hours? Minutes? The click of a mouse?

I didn't want to hang around to find out.

"I'll get them," said Kevin, reaching for the fallen
deal toys.

"Leave them," I said.

"You sure?"

"Yeah," I said, tossing a Lucite-encased replica of a
waterless urinal onto the pile. Green investments came
in all shapes and sizes, too. "I'm sure."

Kevin loaded the last box onto the cart. We wheeled
it down the hall and got on the elevator.

"Going down," the mechanical voice said.

"You have no idea," I replied.

Papa looked at me strangely, not really catching my
drift. The door closed, and the elevator started its de-
scent.

"So," said Papa, "what's going to happen with all
that money you lost in your account?"

"Still working it out," I said.

Kevin said, "We're bringing suit against McVee's
estate. Might take a while, but we'll get it back."

"Less Mallory's share," I said. I had no idea what
that would be. Her lawyer had advised her not to attend
her dead lover's memorial service, so they were clearly

still posturing. Little did I know that in the coming months it would be the market, not Mallory, to take half of my remaining net worth.

The elevator doors opened and we exited through the main lobby. We had to step around the scaffolding on the sidewalk. Two workers above us were removing the signature gold letters that had once spelled SAXTON SILVERS on the building's black granite facing. It was now down to SAXTON.

"I remember when they did that to Mr. Roebuck," said Papa.

A couple of photographers were snapping away at the change in signage on the former Saxton Silvers' headquarters, but the bulk of financial media had moved down the street, waiting for the next institution to crater beneath the weight of its own mistakes. It wouldn't be long.

A taxi pulled up to the curb and stopped. Ivy was in the backseat, but she didn't get out. She lowered the window and smiled.

"Hey, handsome. Need a ride?"

I hobbled over. "So, are we still hitched?"

Ivy had been meeting with a family-law specialist to sort through our marriage, her disappearance, my marriage to Mallory, Ivy's return, and my pending divorce.

"Here's the way I see it. We can pay a lawyer thousands of dollars to research the hell out of this. Or we can pay fifty bucks to the city of New York and get married again."

There was silence. Of the two choices, the answer was obvious.

Papa stepped in and offered a third option. "Or . . . you could just have fun and get to know each other again."

We looked at each other.

Ivy said, "It couldn't hurt to talk it over."

"Talk is good."

"Yeah, let's definitely talk about it," she said.

"We could get a coffee."

"I was thinking more along the lines of the Hôtel de Crillon."

"In Paris?"

She held up two airline tickets. "We leave from JFK at five-twenty."

I smiled. "That doesn't give me much time to pack."

"You could just run inside and buy a few things from Sax," she said, pointing.

I turned. The workers had removed three more gold letters—T-O-N, leaving only the phonetic equivalent of the Fifth Avenue department store.

"Hop in," she said. "I packed for you."

Papa helped me into the taxi. I was about to close the door, but he stopped me, stuck his head inside and said, "Have fun. And remember: Love each other. That's the main thing."

I will never understand how he did it. That was his gift—the ability to say such cornball things and make them sound genuine.

"We will, Papa," said Ivy, smiling.

I smiled, too—all the way to the airport.

Acknowledgments

oney to Burn is a first novel of sorts—my first
with Sally Kim, my new editor at HarperCollins.
If you enjoyed it, give her the credit. If not, blame my
agent, Richard Pine. It was Richard who shot me an
e-mail way back in 2007 and started me down the road
of a "Wall Street thriller"—long before anyone saw the
real-world crisis coming. The guy is *that* good.

My thanks also to editorial assistant Maya Ziv; to
my assistant, Marie McGrath; and to my early readers,
Janis Koch, Jeff Roberts, and Gloria Villa. I also had
plenty of help along the way from New *Yawkers* like
Julie Fisher, and from a few financial good guys (David
McWilliams, Jeff Roberts, Jim Jiao, Mike Moran, and
others) who were of more help than they realize. Of
course, the mistakes are all mine.

My deepest appreciation goes to Gloria and James V. Grippando, my parents, part of the greatest generation—two "ants" who could teach "grasshoppers" plenty. I wrote most of the outline for *Money to Burn* while at my father's bedside, then banged out the book after his passing. To the end, he smiled about what he had, never griping about what he'd lost. His strength of character found its way into *Money to Burn* in ways I may never fully understand. He certainly gave me a unique perspective as, in the name of "research," I watched Wall Street implode in real time. I loved him dearly and miss him terribly, and through Michael Cantella's "Papa," I feel his spirit on the pages of this book.

Finally, I thank my wife, Tiffany. Finding the creative juices to write a novel in "My *Least* Favorite Year" was no easy feat. I daresay it would have been impossible without her love and support.

JMG, MAY 2009